Catey –
They say "readers live a
thousand lives." I hope
walking around in Salem

Dream Big!
Amy Leigh S-

IF

the girl next door

SPRING

book three

COMES

AMY LEIGH SIMPSON

If Spring Comes
By Amy Leigh Simpson

Copyright 2018 Amy Leigh Simpson

Cover, Jeremy Stehlick
Editor, Andrea Ferak

ISBN-13:9781981085064

For more information on this book and the author visit: www.amyleighsimpson.com

What others are saying about
The Girl Next Door Series

"Amy Leigh Simpson is a brilliant wordsmith. Wow. This author knows how to write fresh and feverish! This book has edge and wit and lots and lots of lyrical goodness that made my little writer's heart pitter patter to a happy beat."

-**Nicole Deese**
Carol award-winning Author of *The Promise of Rayne*

"One word persistently leaps to my mind as I read and reflect on this delightful story... HOT! ... There is nothing dull, cool, or mediocre about this story! It is a blazing FIRE of brilliance!!!

-**Faithfully Bookish Blog**

"I highly recommend this series from Amy Leigh Simpson. I'm grateful to have discovered her series and lovely writing and look forward to discovering more of her stories. From Winter's Ashes is a timeless romantic, suspense love story encompassing forever friendships, complex relationships, deep manipulations, engaging mystery, and sweet charm."

-**TeriLyn**
Amazon Reviewer

"Yet again, Simpson weaves an incredible tale ripe with thrilling suspense, witty dialogue, and dazzling romance."

-**Pepper Basham**
Author of *A Twist of Faith* and
Charming the Troublemaker

"Sparks sizzle in Simpson's sophomore novel. Ripe with tension, danger, and the pain of the past, you'll be ripping through pages to see what happens next. Grab your oven mitts before you pick this one up, you're going to need them."

-**Jill Lynn**
Author of *Her Texas Family*

"If you're looking for a sit on the edge of your seat, don't turn out the lights and don't go to sleep until the last page is turned read this summer, From Winter's Ashes is it! Wonderful characters with real hurts to overcome, romantic tension, intrigue, yikes moments and everything in between, Simpson has created another delicious novel that will sweep you away and hold you captive until the very end. Don't miss this one!"

-**Catherine West**
Author of *The Things We Knew* and
The Memory of You

"Simpson's books are fast-paced romantic suspense that keep the reader reeled in from beginning to end. The author has a lyrical voice that is fresh and quirky."

-**Julia R.**
Professional Reviewer

"This is one hot book--and not just because the hero is a firefighter! Sizzle crackles off the pages as the two well-drawn main characters try to elude a pursuer with murderous intent. Turn up the AC and enjoy!"

-**Irene Hannon**
Multi-award winning author of
Dangerous Illusions and *Tangled Webs*

To my daddy, for singing grace over me
from the very start.
I'm so blessed to be yours.

Zephaniah 3:17

February 11
St. Louis City Morgue
8:38 a.m.

Prologue

Another perfect crime. The familiar rush blazed like fine scotch through his veins. There was no greater high than eviscerating lives, scraping away each painful layer of humanity, witnessing a last breath, and invoking pure, unequivocal terror.

The fevered bloodlust stirred anew, heating his skin despite the crisp temperature in the morgue.

Mmm. There was something delicious about it all. Their fear, their respect. He was craving more, and this was already his second score of the season.

It was no longer enough, but he couldn't afford to get sloppy. His palate for their suffering ... *her* suffering had refined to a thing of beauty—a symphony of pain and pleasure that helped her song live on and on. For him alone. Forever and always. The aching need licked across his nerve endings.

Spring couldn't come soon enough.

Watching from the side corridor, he remained hidden while the harsh lighting exposed every detail of his handy work for his viewing pleasure—from his victim's bones stripped of their lovely covering to the fluttery vein pulsating in the new medical examiner's elegant bronze throat.

She spoke quietly into her tape recorder, collecting the few remaining scraps of flesh clinging to the charred remains of his latest masterpiece.

This one didn't rattle easily, but right now he could almost feel the fear raking over her small body like a rosined bow rasping taut strings. He could smell it too and almost moaned in response. Cold sweat and heated adrenaline mingling with hints of a sweet floral musk.

She had smelled like flowers too. Her fear as tangy and fresh as the beautiful crimson ribbon he ceremoniously sampled from his first slice—before the injections would taint her essence. "*Sarah*." Her name breathed out on a tasty little whisper, the slight intrusion of his voice jarring against the reverent hush.

The screaming was long over for Sarah. She'd had such a lively timbre to her voice, and her cries had blended quite nicely with Vivaldi's "The Four Seasons—Winter." Though she'd lasted longer than most, the pleasure of the duet died with her screams.

Her silence was monotonous. The static hum of the lights, the occasional clink of the coroner's tools on the metal tray, and the ME's quiet dictation provided her soundtrack now.

How he loved watching the whole pathetic lot of investigators, coroners, and scientists try to scrounge up a single scrap of useable evidence against him. It was almost as enjoyable as taking every last thing he wanted from each victim.

A grin tugged at his mouth. How fitting for the police to find her today—on the anniversary of his first.

Forty-one pretty little blondes. Forty-two really. That opening act had been an appetizer, awakening his lust for killing before he could acquire the right taste and trademark his style. He'd collected so many exquisite screams since then.

He licked his lips, remembering the taste and feel of Sarah as the ME—what was her name again? Stevens, yeah, Dr. Candice Stevens—started examining the victim's mouth. Dentals would confirm Sarah Hoyt's identity as there was little else identifiable.

Dr. Stevens leaned forward, obstructing his view with her

undeniable curves. Though she might try to hide them under those shapeless blue scrubs and apron, she was a rare and eclectic brand of beautiful. Petite yet voluptuous, with eyes like a slip of whiskey and golden threaded mocha hair. Not his type.

Lucky for her.

Though there was something about her that—

What was she doing? He couldn't see with her back to him. The motion of her arms looked like she was winding string.

She straightened with a start. Her gloved hand snatched the handle for the lighted magnifying scope, dragging it closer to examine whatever had snagged her attention.

When she pivoted to grab a specimen container, he caught a glance of the forceps in her grasp. They didn't appear to be holding anything.

He couldn't see her eyes, but her sudden stillness and the hitch in her breathing suggested they were riveted on something significant.

Surely, she was reaching. He was flawless and meticulous.

Unstoppable.

And right under their noses.

February 11
St. Louis, Missouri
8:59 a.m.

Chapter 1

Candice Stevens

This could be it. The break they needed. The Vivaldi Killer, as the media had dubbed him, had upped the ante this winter, claiming an extra victim in addition to his usual seasonal kill. And while Candice had only gotten the job as the lead medical examiner for St. Louis City a little over four months ago, the gruesome deaths and eerily staged victims had made national news and garnered the attention of lawmakers, medical examiners, forensic anthropologists, and concerned citizens across the country for nearly a decade.

Now it was up to her to stop him.

Sweat slicked beneath her gloves, and her normally steady pulse ignored her fancy new job title and quivered in her fingertips.

The sterile cast of the florescent bulbs overhead made a dark place harsh and bright. Despite the efficiency of her new workspace, the dandelion yellow of the outdated cabinetry and speckled terrazzo flooring made the morgue feel jaundiced and sickly.

Focus, Candice.

With a shake of her head, she re-examined the scant little scrap she'd technically flossed from between the victim's back teeth, praying it would be what she thought it was.

DNA evidence.

Praying this victim had fought to get a piece of that monster before he carved and roasted her alive. And that maybe this impossibly small piece had found the only place it could manage to survive Vivaldi's thorough incineration.

Candice looked down at the remains, flinching at the thought of the woman's slow and torturous last hours. The shudder rippled over her skin, sinking in until her unease became a soul-deep fear she knew only Vivaldi's conviction and death sentence could exorcize.

Professional reasons aside, she wanted this guy. Wanted to be the one to lock the sick, twisted, serial killer up for the rest of his miserable life. He'd infected her. Corrupting her with a poisonous obsession for the evidence. Or lack thereof.

It all hit just a little too close to home. And this time … this time she wouldn't miss a thing.

Alone in the still aftermath of tragedy, there was no direct way to cope with the blackened bones of a woman in the prime of her life. No one to share in Candice's unexpected sorrow over the death of a stranger. Tears threatened.

Don't you dare cry. This is not about you.

Cracking her neck and pumping her shoulders, Candice shrugged away the guilt that always seemed to smother her in the presence of one of Vivaldi's victims.

From the measurements of the ectocranial suture closures on the skull and the set of her pelvic bones, Candice knew the woman was in her mid-twenties and had never given birth. As she stared at the mutilated cartilage of the nose, the large gaping sockets of her eyes, the soft arch of her cheekbones, and the delicate curve of her jaw, Candice could visualize the tissue markers, imagining the pigment and beauty of the Caucasian woman's face as if she hadn't been reduced to scorched bones.

"God, help me stop this," she breathed the words, both an oath and a plea to use her smarts to help avenge the deaths of these victims. She couldn't bring them back, but she could fight to break the vicious cycle by putting monsters like Vivaldi in the nearest place to hell before they faced the ultimate judgment.

She curled her fingers over the edge of the autopsy table and let the bones speak.

What was her name? Her story? *How had the music taunted her?* It was all part of the puzzle.

Dental impressions had already been sent off to be scanned through the FBI database, courtesy of the director of the FBI himself. This case was a top priority, so she should know the woman's name soon. But in the meantime, Candice would do her best to forget the mutilated pile of bones before her were a life that mattered to someone.

And someone had failed to keep her safe.

She pressed a gloved hand to the clear plastic apron she wore over her scrubs to quell the sudden ache.

Carefully preparing the scrap evidence she'd plucked from the victim's teeth, she eased the slide under the microscope, held her breath, and flipped the switch to illuminate the sample. Except when she pressed her eyes to the scope, nothing but darkness reflected back.

Huh.

Leaning to the side, she checked the power cord, then flipped the switch at the base of the stand again. Nothing.

Must need a new light bulb. Their other microscope had been broken just last week when her linebacker-sized coworker failed to notice a rogue stream of blood leaking onto the floor from the autopsy table. When his foot found the slick spot his hefty body rode it like a banana peel across the room and shattered thousands of dollars' worth of equipment. And since the equipment was old and budget cuts were a reality, as evidenced by her solo shift, their meager funds were set aside to replace the current setup, not repair it.

She just needed a few seconds of illumination under the powerful scope to see if the flossed scrap had sebaceous glands, or even a single hair follicle. As it was now, she'd have to order a new bulb and wait, or submit a request to take the sample to a different lab.

So frustrating. This was her turf now, and she needed to

meet and exceed the high expectations her reputation as the "bones whisperer" had promised in securing this position. But once again, things were beyond her control. Story of her life.

The sudden stall in her momentum peeled a layer back on her insulated awareness of time and place. The morgue was so quiet her breathing was like a lone voice in an auditorium, spilling over the cavernous silence with an empty echo. Weaving with the sound of her breath, the clock at the far end provided a metronome, measuring and exposing the eerie stillness.

Death was like that in the end. Silent. And most often, being alone with her thoughts was a welcome relief from the pollution of sound that made the world outside both boisterous and lonely.

But right now, the silence was ominous. The fine hairs prickled on her neck and shoulders. Wisps of chilled air squeezed past her collapsing windpipe.

She could feel more than hear something shift behind her. The sustained silence cemented the threat.

Candice gulped down a breath of formaldehyde and stretched her hand calmly toward a scalpel.

Promising herself she wouldn't scream, she steeled her nerves and spun around, scalpel ready to stab, or perhaps fling like a ninja star. Skills a scrawny kid picked up on the streets of Jersey.

"Hey Dr. Stevens." Her assistant medical examiner's eyes flashed to the poised weapon; shock replacing the ruddy, rosacea red of his cheeks with the pasty shade of lifeless the morgue was known for. "Whoa." Splaying raised hands, he backed away a step, then two.

"*Blaine*? Man alive! I oughta let this thing fly to teach you a lesson about sneaking up on people." She already had problems with her lazy coworker. Pinning him to the wall probably wouldn't help matters.

When she lowered her arm, Dr. Blaine Attwood exhaled a

loaded breath. "Jumpy much?"

Candice swallowed a growl. "I've been here alone most of the night after I left the scene. I think I'm starting to get delirious."

"I can relate. I had a doozie of a date this weekend."

Ugh. She forced her lips in a tight smile. "What are you doing here? You're not due for..." She glanced up at the clock to reorient herself. "Another three hours."

Well before then she would've had the preliminary results back on the tissue sample if he hadn't nearly brought down the lab last week. Of course, his careless mistake couldn't possibly be his responsibility. *No sir.* Wouldn't want to put a nick in that bloated trust fund just to replace what he'd damaged, rendering them crippled for the mammoth task of hunting down their city's infamous serial killer. And doing it before Vivaldi stole another woman's future with his deadly song.

Biting her lip, she canned the rising snark of her inner Jersey-girl, striving to keep the notion of professionalism a few steps ahead of her ingrained mouthy-ness.

She had to keep a level head. The sample was her priority. Not playing nice with her sloth of a coworker.

Once she confirmed the scrap was legitimate tissue she could test for DNA—which would take much longer. And unfortunately, the piece was so miniscule it would likely be all used up during the process. Consumed evidence didn't tend to hold up well in court. Which was why she needed to know what it was before the process of discovery destroyed it.

If it was just some leftover prime rib from dinner her hopes of catching this guy were gonna crash harder than her mother used to after a late-night bender.

"Trust me. I'd rather be at home sleeping off this headache. Anyway ... Vivaldi struck again, huh?" Blaine's observation jerked her out of her ruminations. She watched him wander to the autopsy table and glance casually over the remains.

Instinctively she backed against the counter containing the precious sample, blocking the potential find with her abundant backside. "Yeah, fits his MO. Carved, charred, and found with a looped digital recording of Vivaldi's 'Four Seasons—Winter.' Untraceable, as usual."

Vivaldi always coordinated each kill with the appropriate song of the season. The twisted logic of a serial killer. Though there was *nothing* logical about carving a woman's body and then wielding a blow torch to melt off what remained. Not even in February, and especially not to a Baroque classic.

Also particularly disturbing to know how long his victims suffered, as evidenced by the artificial adrenaline injections she'd discovered in the tiny nicks in the bones. As well as the careful yet grotesque wielding of his knives managing to skillfully avoid severing the major arteries to prolong each woman's survival.

Closing her eyes, she drew a bracing breath.

Working in a place like this required an iron stomach and a whole lot of fully functioning detachment mechanisms. It wasn't usually this hard to look past the gruesome fragments of existence if it meant helping to avenge what had been so maliciously stolen.

But not with Vivaldi. Bile clawed up her esophagus, making her want to retch out what little remained of the jumbo Italian-sub and full can of Pringles she'd had for lunch yesterday.

She'd hated missing dinner. Hated missing any meal because she needed the energy and the calories to stay strong. But having spent the evening at another one of Vivaldi's repulsive drop sites, and then all night working on the autopsy, her appetite had vanished.

"I was summoned to come in early so you could take a break. I know we're understaffed, but since I'm not a nationally acclaimed *double threat* like you I'm not sure I'm going to be all that useful."

Not that Blaine was very useful on an ordinary autopsy either. He didn't have an additional PhD in Forensic Anthropology like Candice, so he wasn't particularly insightful with bones. Wasn't particularly insightful with anything, in truth. A pending endowment from the all-powerful Attwoods ensured her hands were tied in terms of disciplinary action. His family name had likely been his *in* since he didn't appear to possess much in terms of ambition, or upholding justice. And he'd yet to prove he cared about anything but punching a time card and having the prefix Dr. before his name—one that didn't require a bedside manner.

But the worst of it was he was careless with the details. Didn't he realize the littlest nick could have been the entry point of a lethal drug, even faint subdural hematomas could catalogue the victim's struggle and create a virtual blueprint of the crime? Each scratch, each tiny hair could be a clue to the location, the weapon, the motive—a signature left behind by the killer himself, daring to be caught.

Sure, Candice's credentials and IQ proved her to be uncommonly smart, but patience and painstaking attention to those details had been the key to carving out a name for herself among the elite echelon of forensic science. So her years of old fashioned hard work and determination were why she'd been entrusted with such a high-profile case. Bad luck and nepotism are what had saddled her with an inadequate assistant to solve it.

Seems about right.

"I'll take a stab at it and surmise we've got nothing to work with, as usual. So I guess my job's pretty easy today since I see you already removed and weighed what was left of the organs, and I'm assuming you took samples of the little remaining tissue?" He expelled a noisy sigh and turned to scope out the clock, as if he were tired of working after being here all of five minutes and not lifting a finger. "At least I can call my auto shop. Got a scratch on some *very* important paint."

Tuning Blaine out, Candice stole a peek at the tiny sample still trapped in the useless microscope. It was too important. A miraculous find. She couldn't let Blaine anywhere near it. The bumbling oaf would probably lose it on a sneeze.

She did her best to tamp down the panic cramping in her gut. "Uh, yeah, I took samples. They're in those containers on the tray."

Blaine ambled over toward the scraps peeled from the bones, several of which were already flagged for their bugs, dirt, and slime guy, Soren Michaels. The forensic entomologist slash mineralogist slash resident hunk would check for insect matter, particulates, and debris in the remaining tissue. Then they would need to clean the bones and let them tell their story.

But more urgently she needed to protect the hope contained in the tissue behind her.

Utilizing Blaine's distraction, Candice swiftly pulled the sample from the scope, capped it in the small sealed container, and slid the cylinder into the v-neck of her scrub top.

Great, now she was hiding evidence in her cleavage.

It's just until you get back.

She turned and found a very formidable Blaine only a few feet behind her. His eyes were a cool gray-blue. His sparse reddish-hued goatee at odds with his thick, immovably gelled Ken-doll brown hair.

Despite his pedigree and his laissez-faire professionalism, there was this barely caged aggression lurking beneath the facade. Somehow she didn't think it'd take much for Blaine to snap. And that, more than all the other annoyances, was the reason she didn't trust him.

She swallowed down whatever moisture remained in her throat, and tried to read the intent of his stare. "You have a question, Blaine?"

A divot pinched the skin between his brows. His towering

height—reducing her to mere munchkin status—meant he could peek over her shoulder at the microscope with little maneuvering.

The chilly steel edge of the lab table fingered through the thin weave of the scrub top as it dug against her low back. She suppressed another shiver and safely tucked away facial evidence of guilt. At least she hoped she did. It would be a lot easier is she could slip that in her bra too.

"I guess not."

"All right then." Candice clasped her hands, meshing her clenched fingers against her chest in a nervous sort of prayer pose. The flat, quarter-sized evidence container pressed into her skin beneath the pressure of her hands, assuring her it was still stowed, but not secure enough for something so critically important.

She had no reason to feel guilty.

Okay, fine, the guilt was already eating a hole in her stomach.

But evidence in a Vivaldi case was so rare she'd do anything to protect it. The scrap smuggled between her breasts could be the first DNA sample discovered in the ten long years of his sick killing spree. And hopefully the first piece of material evidence that wouldn't mysteriously go missing after twelve hours. If she left it in the hands of someone like Blaine, they might as well kiss this opportunity goodbye and Vivaldi would kill again.

Not if she could help it.

But if she stayed any longer, the dip of her blood sugar might tempt a fainting spell. She had no desire to be unconscious in Blaine's presence. Heaven help the man if he took it upon himself to revive her. "I'm gonna run home and recharge. Be back in a little bit." Walking a wide path around him, she snatched up the pictures she'd printed from the crime scene and slid them into the front pocket of her briefcase, refusing to look up to confirm Blaine's suspicions.

Her bold red Pumas squealed on the glassy floor as she

pivoted to swing open the morgue door for her escape. "Oh, there's a Jane Doe in drawer three you could start on. When I get back I can show you the serrations I found on Robert Miller's ribs that lead to the murder weapon and height and weight of our killer, if you're interested?"

A peace offering. If he could learn something beyond a standard Y-slice, he might not be quite as useless. Because in a city like St. Louis, there was more than enough work to keep them busy around the clock. She could use another set of competent hands.

He crossed his arms over his burly chest and shrugged. "All right, Double Threat." His eyes took a lazy journey down past her lips and kept on going.

"A souvenir?"

It took her a second to realize where his gaze had landed. Either he was like every other man on the planet and couldn't keep his eyes up top, or he could see the container straining against her bra. She felt the heat of guilt burn in her cheeks. Or maybe it was the heat of rage from being reduced to a set of boobs in her place of work. Whatever it was, it took the edge of her unexplainable desperation and nudged her over to righteous indignation.

"Excuse me?" Feeling her nostrils flare, she fired off a warning in her tone. One that said, yes, she was as tough as she looked. These were the sorts of delusions *Jersey* planted in her head.

"You never leave without changing out of your scrubs and those crazy red kicks." He spared a glance at her shoes before going ocular on her chest again. "So that's weird. But you've still got your lab smock on, and there's some dried blood smeared across the front. Since there's no Zombie Run this month, it might not be a great idea walking around downtown like that."

Candice was surprised she'd gotten out of there without bursting into flames. The anxiety was spreading like a rash, prickling so deep her bones itched. Even just the lying itself should be grounds for some kind of karmic smackdown. Any moment now lightning would strike the elevator, or perhaps the cable would snap and she'd plummet all of one remaining floor to her, eh, minor injury.

Alone behind the closed doors of the elevator, she let the stress heave from her lungs—compensating for the forced calm facade that had left her nearly asphyxiated for the last twenty minutes of gambling with her livelihood on a hunch.

What if someone found out? She could lose her job. Then she'd never wash her hands of the guilt that made her take this position in the first place.

She squeezed her eyes shut, desperate to keep blinded eyes to each of the unpleasant scenarios her impulsivity could bring. Had it been the right thing to do? Was she really protecting the evidence or was it more about validating herself?

Talk about a mission impossible. The damage she was so desperate to redeem was irrevocable, and the effort ... sixteen years too late.

Candice kept her eyes closed, embracing the darkness for fear of what the light might expose about what she'd done. And why she'd done it today.

But then, something worse than the fear of her mistakes flooded through her mind. Like a parade of death, she saw each of Vivaldi's un-avenged victims. Saw their families suffering; driven mad by all the raw, loose ends of their unsolved injustice.

Then she saw the pile of bones that haunted her the most.

Her eyes shot open, but the darkness still lingered in the shadows of her heart, thicker than the power of the light. And so much stronger than she, little "Candi," could ever be.

With a quivering hand she slipped her fingers down her sternum to check the sample. What was she doing? Running off with evidence? Whether she had acted on a divine warning or some twisted need to sabotage her career, all she knew was she needed out of here.

As soon as the elevator doors parted she fled like Vivaldi himself was on her tail ready to silence her with a knife, a blow torch, and a song.

Shoving open the entrance, she tumbled out into the noisy city beyond the morgue doors, and meant to keep running but—

Her momentum slammed like the first crash of a domino.

Impact. Her feet stuttered forward in correction, catching a seam in the sidewalk. Then gravity went sideways and she was falling slowly on a strange hitch of time. It was as if her panicked brain, her frantic body, and her surging adrenaline all hit a brick wall in a single instant.

Oddly enough, the landing wasn't really all that painful.

It took a second to realize someone had caught her. Or rather, she'd plowed down some poor guy.

Whoever he was, he was tall—Candice's head was against his chest, her ear serenaded by the thrumming of his heart. No more than a handful of heartbeats passed, but the crash had set her world in slow motion.

Had she hit her head? Was she even conscious? The soundtrack of the city was muted to a cottony fog.

The heady scent of coriander, cedar, and some kind of sweet, smooth musk like a warm breath of vanilla smoke curled through her tangled senses.

"Are you okay?" The voice rumbled from his chest.

Oh, right. A chest she was currently *laying* on. Before she could move, strong hands shifted to prop her up a few inches.

Lifting her head, she brushed away the curtain of hair plastered to her cheek and braced her other hand against a firm chest that boasted such lean definition it was practically an anatomy lesson.

Definitely conscious now.

Nonsense. Food. What she needed was food.

With a final flick of her hair out of her eyes, she looked down, one breath away from a familiar pair of dark chocolate eyes, and the world's widest and stupidest grin.

Chapter 2

Dorian Salivas

"Dorian?" Only Candice Stevens could deliver his name like an insult.

Her eyes shone bright with embarrassment, like a splash of sunrise through splintered glass. They were wide set, exotic, and as usual, completely disarming.

Of course, her being on top of him might add something to that effect.

"Listen, if you don't like the taste of it, you could always go with *Sal* like everyone else." By the time he'd finished the thought he was grinning again. She did that to him.

"Sal makes you sound like some tough, cranky mob boss. It just doesn't fit." Her smile was so patronizing she might as well have pinched his cheeks and called him "Buddy."

"Whatever makes you happy, Candi."

Her infuriating big sister look was instantly replaced by lines of tension tightening down her neck and flaring though the body still wonderfully atop his.

"How about we cool it with the nicknames. We're coworkers. Sort of. I'll be Dr. Stevens, or Candice since we have a shared group of friends. And you can just be Dorian."

Just be Dorian. He answered the exhausting woman with a sigh.

"What?" She shrugged, her hands resting on his chest, her body once again soft and perfectly mind-numbing. Lush tendrils of hair stirred on the wind, torturing him with the wild, sweet scent of her. "It *is* your name."

Oh, he hated how this woman looked at him like a five-year-old. Two could play that game. "You're a brat."

"Takes one to know one." The gleam in her gaze turned a little bit naughty, though he was sure she didn't mean it that way.

Candice wasn't the easiest person to read, but his abridged version said she wielded humor in an effort to stay detached. She was also completely ignorant of her appeal on the opposite sex, and incredibly sharp and driven, but under heavy guard from some sort of phantom pain hidden behind her smile.

Unfortunately for Sal, the heavy guard was more like a full suit of armor equipped with a bulletproof vest, chastity belt, and an iron will.

It was as if she denied herself any emotions or advances that might remind her she was a woman. Restaurant closed. Female on lockdown, reinforced with barbed wire and an electric current.

A current that was, at this very moment, live and zapping him with conductive skitters of testosterone.

Candice didn't seem to realize she was still lying on top of him. On the sidewalk. On Clark Avenue.

Loosing his hands from her arms he let them slip around to the small of her back. "Does this mean you might actually take me up on my offer to dinner?" He lifted an eyebrow in challenge.

"Oh, for—!" She squirmed. His body reacted and she froze. He saw the second she reacquainted with reality—and their horizontal status on the sidewalk. "Oh, geeze. Sorry." Shoving to her knees, she brushed off her hands as if contact with his coat had left her gritty.

He watched her as she stood. Twinges of pink blotted onto her café au lait-colored skin. Her breathing had quickened, her pupils dilating before her eyes averted.

Despite her brusque demeanor—and the way she'd just

less than delicately tackled him—she held a certain grace about her when caught off guard. Her neck long and controlled, her shoulders pressed, the drift of her spine and her arms fluid like wind stroking sheer curtains.

She didn't offer her hand. And it would seem he did a poor job hiding his wince when he braced against his good knee and straightened because she gasped.

Her petite hand touched her lips before she stretched it out to touch his chest in consolation. "Did I hurt you? I'd forgotten about your surgery. Knee replacement, right?"

Even with the straggling pains darting through his nervous system he chuckled. "Is that a no for dinner then?"

She retracted her hand as if scalded. Some small realization blooming another spray of roses on her cheeks before she snapped back into character. *This* Candice smirked, crossed her arms, and jutted her hip like his asking, again, had been a complete waste of air.

"I feel so used." He smoothed a hand down his chest, making light of the ache this woman kept pounding into him with her persistent refusal.

This was only a hat-trick effort. It's not like he'd been pelting her windows with stones or spouting sonnets below her balcony at midnight. Though if she'd give him a date he'd agree to just about anything.

Something about her drove him a little bit crazy. Perhaps that's why he was so enthralled by her. She was part fascination, part mystery. And very seldom did Sal encounter a puzzle he couldn't crack.

Her secrets ran deeper than Sal's radar could reach. But his cold read said right now Candice had him quarantined, refusing to really see him lest he throw some color on her tidy, stark white life.

Lucky for him he could sense things she couldn't hide nor control. It'd only been a couple months. He'd get to her. Eventually.

With one blink, her sassy attitude dissolved faster than he

could say *"adios."* Her eyes sprang wide, her pulse pounded double-time at her neck. And then she did something odd. With a frantic jerk of her arm she stuffed her hand down her shirt.

"Digging for gold?"

She ignored him and continued to re-arrange herself, which he had to admit, he'd never seen a woman do with quite so much gusto.

"Aww, lighten up, that was funny."

She didn't laugh, and any element of grace she'd had was lost in the panic. When she finished frisking herself, she whipped her head around, scanning the sidewalk. Her silk-spun chestnut hair flipped and writhed with each agitated turn.

Before he'd inquired further, she'd dropped to the pavement, feeling around like a blind squirrel on a nut hunt.

Twisting to assist her search for whatever she'd lost, he saw nothing but city stained concrete until a strand of sunlight glinted from beyond the curb. Glass or plastic, and it looked like a—

"Move!" She barreled past, shoving him aside to fling herself into oncoming traffic.

She bent over her prize, unfazed by the SUV speeding toward her. With a driver who didn't seem to notice the excessively short woman crouching down in his lane.

"Candice." He warned. "Candice, look out!" Pain ripped through him as he lunged into the street, hooked an arm around her waist and dove back to the curb. They met the sidewalk hard and fast. The vibration of the tire brushed the sole of his shoe. He tucked his legs up and around Candice. A rush of air surrounded them, warning how close they'd come to being roadkill.

He kept his arms around her, not wanting to let go until he was sure she was safe. And maybe not even then.

The adrenaline started to recede, and the strain in his lungs shot fragments of painful awareness to his collection of injuries still in the process of healing.

Candice's back was against his chest, their breaths heaving in sync. The shock of the moment leaving them once again lying on the sidewalk. Only this time they were spooning.

He shifted her in his arms, turning her back to the ground so he could assess her for injury. Once he'd confirmed she was just as fine and perfect as ever, he pressed his forehead to her temple, closed his eyes, and willed his heart and lungs to reboot. "We have to stop meeting like this."

He didn't need to see her lips to know she was smiling. And for a solitary moment in time, she wilted, completely at rest in his arms. His touch, or perhaps just shock, short-circuiting her defenses.

"Yes, we do." Pulling up to a seated position, she lifted his arm that had tucked her against him and shrugged it off like a shackle of rope. Again she stood, this time offering her hand.

Sal took it and managed to get his feet beneath him. His knee throbbed. His left lung was stiff and aching. His head a bit swimmy. He was definitely gonna pay for all this later.

"So what's in the evidence jar?" He nodded toward her hand, her fist wrapped around the small vial she'd risked her life to protect.

Her eyes shifted, cheeks pulling taut like she'd clenched her teeth together. "Nothing."

"Liar, liar, pants on fire." He took a step closer. "You're not stealing evidence, are you, Doc?"

There was a moment's pause, the faintest gulp. Barely a hitch of hesitation, but it told him all he needed to know.

She shook her head, her eyes repelling from his. "No, I—"

"Save it." It was from last night's Vivaldi victim. He held out his hand, watching the guilt scan across her features like his own personal wire-tap into her psyche. "If you hand it over right now, I'll get it back before anyone notices it's gone. And I won't have the bureau press charges."

Sliding the contraband into her front coat pocket, her smile faltered. "I told you it's nothing."

More convincing, but still miles from the truth.

"Besides, you're not even active with the FBI right now. What makes you thing you have the authority to confiscate my personal property?"

Burn. She had him there.

She wanted to play dirty? Fine. She had no idea who she was messing with.

Her hand resurfaced empty, and she patted her pocket. Her confidence was back in full swing as the chilled wind tossed that smooth, silky hair over her shoulder. "I've gotta run."

He wasn't sure she realized what she was doing. Maybe she thought she was using her wiles to distract him for a clean escape—which was a very good plan—but he managed to remain on task when she leaned in and placed her cool palm against his shirt between the open front of his coat.

He tried not to let the press of her hand and the implied intimacy of her body language affect him. Did a pretty good job too because if ever a touch could be patronizing, Candice had it down to a science.

"Thanks for catching me, Dorian."

She'd set herself up perfectly. It was almost too easy. Using his index and middle finger he lifted the vial from her coat pocket, leaving behind the quarter from his, and casually shoved his hands back into his pockets.

As she walked past him he caught the faint tip of her lips, confirming she remained unaware of the shift of power.

"Hey, Brat." He waited until she glanced back, and then he winked. "You can land on me anytime."

Despite the tightness gripping his lungs, Sal cut through the water with the ease of a dolphin. Dim lighting stretched from the rafters of the natatorium and distorted to smeared asterisks behind his goggles. He felt both depleted and replenished. Each effortless stroke a small, though unchallenged, victory.

At least that's what it felt like.

An escape. A way to forget about the pain nagging his body day in and day out. Too bad the water couldn't mute out the pain that ran so much deeper.

Sal turned his head and gulped in a breath. The left lung was repaired, but it still seemed to inflate like a withered balloon.

A knee replacement, a dislocated hip, a collapsed lung, a concussion, and the least exciting—compartment syndrome, where the EMTs had sliced open the front of his non-mangled leg knee to ankle to relieve the internal pressure from the blunt force trauma of a vehicular assault.

He could still smell the exhaust choking from the gunned engine when he lay in bed at night. Could hear the sickening sound of his bones crunching when the car struck him. The sound of his friend Joselyn's helpless screams to escape a killer while her guard lay pinned to the asphalt unable to even writhe in agony.

Even now, months later, every movement elicited a scream of protest from somewhere.

Except when he was here. The world and his body were quiet. Guilt drowned under the pure, forgiving waters. There was no analyzing, no clever jokes. Nothing mattered but the steady rhythm of his arms, the power of his stroke dragging his damaged body through the calming swish of weightless relief.

But this wasn't how it was supposed to be. He wasn't supposed to be swimming laps and drowning in thought. He was supposed to use his gift to make up for all the lives he'd ruined. He was supposed to make his brother proud.

He owed it to Gabe. Not only because they were brothers. Not only because Sal had destroyed their family. And not only because Gabe was in a wheelchair, paralyzed from the waist down.

But because Sal was the reason why.

He executed his final flip turn, free-style sprinted the last fifty meters to the shallow end wall, and burst through the surface.

"You pruney yet?" Reverb disguised the voice, but he knew who it was.

Jerking off his goggles, Sal turned to the bleachers and spotted the only other occupant.

Archer.

"It's all right if you miss me, Arch. Honestly, I'm flattered." Pushing up, Sal retreated from the cool oasis, felt the captured water pour from the fabric of his taut Fastskin swim trunks and puddle around his feet.

His partner gave a good-natured chuckle. "Your mind-reading skills must be slipping with old age."

Ha ha. Sal was almost twenty-eight, but everyone treated him like the baby. "Is that some gray I see at your temples there, big guy? Don't be jealous when you're all shriveled up like a leather handbag, and I'm still young and ridiculously good lookin'."

"You ever heard of George Lopez?"

Sal walked toward the bench without even the slightest twinge in his knee. "You ever heard of Antonio Banderas?" He countered. "I am pretty handy with a blade. We could change my nickname to Zorro." Threading a towel around his neck, he used one end to sponge the water from his face, then scrubbed it through his hair.

Tipping his head back, Archer mumbled to himself. "And to think, this is what I've been missing for weeks."

Pulling the towel free Sal wound it up and whipped the tail. The soaked end would have snapped at Archer's knees, but the ever impressive *Karate Kid* caught the edge of the towel in his fist and ripped the whole thing from Sal's grasp.

Biting back a growl, Sal fought to ward off a shiver as goose bumps puckered his skin. He refused to give Archer the satisfaction of groveling for the towel he'd lost fair and square, so he crossed his arms and held his ground.

There wasn't anyone Sal respected more than Archer Hayes—decorated Army sniper, big wig at the bureau, and made of more metal than anyone he'd ever known. But just once, Sal wanted to clench a victory in his own fist, and silence those jabs about his inexperience and age for good.

"I didn't pass, did I?" He didn't need to hear the words to know the results of his third attempt to re-up on his training drill. Archer might be his partner and his best friend, but he was also the Special Agent in Charge of the FBI. He was here to deny Sal's reinstatement to the bureau. For now. And it was nothing short of infuriating.

Sure, Sal was still a newbie with the FBI, and yes, maybe he was eager to earn his stripes and prove his worth. But he'd hit every target—not even shaving the bull's-eye by an eighth of an inch, he was sure of it.

Well, maybe not that last one when he'd fired blind, predicting exactly where the target had been. He would have gotten it too, had his knee not buckled in the same moment he fired off that last shot.

One near miss, with a gun no less, and they didn't think he could hack it? Give him knives and he'd stun 'em all into silence. Besides, his aim wasn't even close to being his most valuable asset to the bureau.

"Sorry, pal." Archer's tone said the admission was as unpleasant as the sudden resurgence of pain in Sal's leg.

Yeah, he got it. If he wasn't back at his A-game he could be a liability out in the field, but he was going crazy bumming around the house with his brother. Sure, it might sound like a nice hiatus, but instead of going to college Gabe was embarking on a new profession in audio engineering. Mostly church recordings. Some of the music itself was kinda catchy, but all day and even into the night it was a blast of some kind of happy noise. Nauseating. Another few weeks of that and he might need to seek another kind of therapy.

But he didn't need a shrink to tell him how to get back on track. He needed to secure his job at the bureau, prove to Gabe he was staying on the straight and narrow. And maybe convince Dr. Candice Stevens to give him a chance. That sure wouldn't hurt matters.

He thought of the evidence he'd tucked in his bag. Wondered what kind of trouble she was in. And he sure as heck wanted to know if he'd just dragged himself into the fray.

He'd been trying to protect her, but at what cost? If the bureau found out …

No. Couldn't happen. His job was the only thing keeping him from becoming his father. He would just run one last play, break in to the morgue and return the evidence before anyone noticed it was missing.

Even the thought of dabbling with the wrong side of the law made his skin itch. Maybe it was the chlorine?

Nope, he knew better. It was a warning. There was no way to pretty up a lie. Or a con. Both were the Salivas specialty. A legacy he hoped had died with their father.

"Gabe told me you were here. And since I saw the Challenger still parked at your place, I'm assuming you walked. How about I give you a lift?"

"Uhh, sure." Still lost in thought, Sal snatched his duffle from the bench and made quick work of getting dressed in the locker room.

His mind churned with risks and outcomes, his unease about the contents of his duffel unraveling his hard-fought integrity strand by strand.

"Ready?" Archer called, and Sal walked through the long dark corridor. A light flickered overhead, the casts of shadows beckoning him like Darth Vader to the dark side.

He hadn't lost anything when he'd played by his own rules. Each scam had been a perfect game. He'd held all the cards and knew how to play each opponent.

The power had been intoxicating. Clueless Dorian existed

below everyone's radar, it had been brilliant.

Until that fateful day when everything shifted on its axis, the cosmos, maybe even God himself, laughing as one bullet blasted a ripple effect so devastating it destroyed Sal's entire world.

"Yep. Ready."

No, there was no going back.

He strode out into the light, tossed his bag over his shoulder, and made small talk about grabbing some Mexican food for dinner.

"Sal, you're Hispanic, I get it. You can eat something besides *Hacienda* once in a while." Archer clapped him on the shoulder and jostled him like a big brother might do. Had Sal ever done that to Gabe? When was the last time they'd even had a real conversation?

He exhaled the tension brewing in his chest and stabbed his fingers through his wet, spiky hair. Would he ever get it right? He couldn't atone for all the damage he'd caused, but he could do right by Gabe. Or die trying.

The answer seemed simple, but the path unclear. He'd either have to turn Candice in, force her to confess, or put the evidence back himself. The last involved dabbling into his old ways. A gamble he knew would cost him too much, windfall or fail.

Candice was smart. Probably already knew the evidence was missing and would be coming at him with all the ferocity of a mama bear with a bone to pick.

To Candice, Sal was nothing more than an interfering cub.

A cub that couldn't be her ally as long as she was testing the other side of the law. He was a federal agent, desperate to make the title stick down to his very core. He had no choice but to take her down.

Climbing into Archer's blacked out Suburban, Sal slammed the door on the cold seeping through his coat, trying with equal force to slam the door on his unrequited feelings for the woman who was about to slide head first into a whole lotta trouble.

Maybe a few more weeks away from the bureau would help to clear the Candice fog. The seemingly straight-laced medical examiner of his dreams had gone rogue. It was a game he couldn't play again. Not even if the prize was the most hypnotizing beauty he'd ever laid eyes on.

From now on, no more Candice Stevens.

Pulling out onto the street, Archer nudged Sal with his elbow. "Oh, I almost forgot. Your new neighbor was moving in." A foreboding grin spread on his face. "Something tells me you're gonna like her."

Chapter 3

Candice Stevens

"Sadie, you really didn't have to come by. I can handle the last of the boxes."

Lord knew why a single woman should have so much junk. If it was up to Candice, she would stay in this perfectly charming Victorian until the day she died. Then she would never have to unload anymore baggage ever again.

Wouldn't it be nice if that was how life worked?

Candice swiped at her forehead, then loosened the tie at her waist and let the bitter February wind chase through her coat.

Her new house was nestled in the elegant, understated suburb of St. Louis called Webster Groves. A canopy of mature trees and deep, tidy yards lined the grid of historic streets boasting enough class and character to make each property uniquely suited for a *Better Homes and Gardens* spread.

The second she'd spotted the narrow two-story with its dove gray shingled siding, creamy white filigreed trim, and wide welcoming porch with a swing she'd known it was home. It was everything she'd dreamed of having when she'd been a child. Better yet, it was the furthest thing from life on the docks of New Jersey.

Safe, stable, and surrounded by families living the American dream. She could almost picture little neighborhood kids riding their trikes down the sidewalk in the spring, young boys scooping up a stray baseball from her garden, crushing the sprouted greens from the bulbs she'd have to figure out how to plant. She wasn't naturally domestic—with her childhood, it'd be about as natural as a cheerful daisy sprouting up in Hades. But she'd get there. She'd figure this suburban thing out, squashed tulips and all.

Exhaling a dreamy sigh, she chewed the cuticle of her thumbnail and gazed lovingly at her fresh start. Yes, there were signs of weariness and wear, but the little scars only bonded them more.

The surrounding houses matched hers in charm. The craftsman next door had a newer muscle car parked in the driveway. A spicy reddish-orange hot rod with dual black stripes flexing over the door from fender to taillight boasting its machoness. Even sitting there it nearly growled. It was actually pretty hot. The kind of car, and probably the kind of guy, that would have had the old Candi exercising her art in poor choices.

It seemed out of place for such a quiet street. Hopefully it wouldn't steal away the tranquility she was hoping to find here.

"I'm happy to help." Sadie chimed in, hauled another box labeled "shoes" into her arms, and had to stagger to keep the impressive weight in balance. "Good grief, Candice, this has gotta be one heck of a shoe collection. You don't happen to wear a size six, do you?"

Candice circled around to assist lugging the jumbo-sized box.

"Because I could see pretty little peep-toed perks in my future," Sadie grunted.

Chuckling in response, they shuffled up the porch steps and wormed through the front door. "I do, actually. One of the repercussions of being so vertically challenged. I barely wear any but the red ones, so feel free to shop in my closet later."

"Sweet. Real shopping is torture. Between your closet and

Joselyn's boutique, I'm set."

Was this what it was like to have girlfriends? The foreign concept settled into place like the surroundings, daring her to let go and give in to its charm. She'd tried in the past to connect with the girls she'd grown up with, but the Gardallo boys liked Candi isolated. And no one messed with the Gardallo boys.

Or anything that was theirs.

Sadie, who might as easily be named "Tomboy Barbie," was married to Agent Archer Hayes of the FBI, one of Candice's main contacts at the bureau. The spunky blonde had helped with a case involving the murder of her neighbor last year. She'd strong-armed Candice into accepting an invitation to girls' night and then continued her assault with a dozen other non-negotiable invitations designed to shatter all of Candice's walls. Three outings in, and Candice had her first friend.

Relationships were time consuming. Disillusioning. Painful. But Sadie's persistence and uncommon welcome offered up something so uncomplicated and honest, it made Candice feel like she'd grown up in the bowels of the earth, where everything, and everyone, was polluted and conniving and ruthless.

Moving to St. Louis exposed a world unlike the seedy underbelly she'd known all her life. Sure, there were bad parts of the city. And most days her job was a major buzzkill. But on this street, tucked in this quiet little pocket of the world, it was like discovering her own Mayberry.

Easing down near the staircase Candice released her end of the box, shed her coat, and then stretched to relieve the nagging in her back. After five years of hunching over dead bodies, her muscles should know the drill but somehow her back was inclined to revert to the old habit of spinelessness. Something she was desperate to remedy, but feared no number of added pounds or good intentions could change. And the constant ache at her spine didn't make the past any easier to forget.

"I was thinking we should wait until Archer gets back. He can be our pack mule and haul all this heavy stuff upstairs."

Candice wanted to bristle against needing a man's help. But torturous fingers gripped her low back in a vice. If she wasn't careful she'd throw her back out. Again. With her case load, now was not a good time to be out of commission.

"Yep. As much as I hate to admit it, I'm gonna need some help." Kneading her fingers against the ache, she waddled over to the couch sitting askew in the front room.

Crisp white daylight streamed through the naked windows, draping over the muted colors and soft textures of her furnishings to make the room nearly glow with a calming energy.

Ahh. *Home.*

"Your back acting up again?" Sadie grabbed the bag of York Peppermint Pattie bites peeking out from Candice's purse and slumped down beside her on the couch.

"Ehh, yes. The bane of womanhood." Candice snatched a pattie, tore open the silver foil, and speared a bite of creamy dark chocolate bliss between her teeth. "I swear, if I'm laid up one more time with this junk I'm getting a reduction."

Smirking, Sadie bit into her own confection. "No way." She shook her head. "Not a chance you give those up."

Candice rolled her eyes. Not only were her breasts cumbersome, and devastating to her spine's stability, but they made her much too noticeably female. Something that had gotten her into trouble in the past.

"Hey, you're the one who started taking me to church. Isn't there a scripture somewhere that says if a man's hand causes him to sin he should cut it off? I see no difference here."

Sadie nearly spewed melted chocolate from her lips. Clearing her throat, she issued several exaggerated blinks. "That's quite a literal interpretation, sweetie. Besides, we're going on five months of friendship here and to my knowledge you haven't been on a single date. Pretty sure your girls haven't been getting you into any trouble."

Swallowing, Candice pressed her thumbnail between her front teeth and nibbled. There was a whole other Candice no one knew about. But as much as she wanted to be the kind of person to bond over old scars, form deeper connections than the shiny veneer she put forth, what she wanted most was to forget all about who she'd been.

And what she'd done.

Candice shrugged to make light of a complicated matter. "No one's caught my eye. Though I might pluck one of those out too because they haven't been all that reliable in the past. Better yet, I'll just retire to my rocking chair with some bifocals and call it a day."

Banter. It was the best she could do.

"Well, girl, sometimes our eyes don't see what they should. But keep looking. He's out there. Maybe even closer than you think." Sadie elbowed her and then dove back in for another indulgence. "And don't go hating on all your womanly assets," she whistled, "because, girlfriend, you've got some serious talent."

Candice gave in to a much needed laugh. It was always exactly the right cure after a long night in the morgue. She had such a somber profession for someone who loved to laugh.

But very few people could do what Candice could with a set of remains. Or rather, see what she could see. And there had been more than enough indicators that this was the way she could make her mark on the world.

Maybe then, she could finally forgive herself.

There was a firm knock on the door before the hinges squealed. "Anybody home?"

Sadie perked up, turning her head toward the sound of her husband's voice. "Hey, hon." She hopped up from the couch and sashayed over to Candice's very tall, uber-handsome coworker.

Candice had zero interest in men after the last one. But even she could admit Archer Hayes was exceptionally easy on the eyes. And the newlyweds made a stunning pair. Petite Sadie with her wild blonde locks and gemstone eyes, and Archer, a tall dark drink of rugged masculinity poured into a well-cut suit. Yeah, they made quite the picture.

As much as Candice wanted to say their unabashed affection for each other was nauseating, when Archer's thumb tipped Sadie's chin, and his lips lingered over hers, a palpable sort of longing diffused into the air. It swirled an envious little potion that poked at her deepest loneliness.

A grinding throat drew her attention from the newlyweds. "Well, color me crazy." The grin spreading on his tanned face was a little less goofy looking than she last remembered it.

Dorian strolled to where he could tower over her, angled his dark eyes downward, and quirked his lips. "Hey ya, Brat."

Candice knew why the look he gave her made her squirm. Well, she was fairly certain. "Dorian," she gritted out.

"If it isn't our city's finest and most *dedicated*," he emphasized the word, his eyes flashing when he continued, "medical examiner."

The evidence.

Sadie had been here when Candice pulled up. With the delivery of the moving truck and the rare splurge of girl talk over the past two hours, she'd somehow managed to unfasten her brain from the events of the day. Most often, she clicked off the second her foot crossed the threshold from the morgue. It was the only way to survive working in such a depressing place. But today?

How could it have slipped her mind?

She'd be heading back to work soon. It'd be a hive of renewed activity by now. After a few hours, she'd relieve Blaine and then she could get everything back on track. This was just a precaution. So then why did it suddenly feel like she'd been careless?

Shooting a look at the coat hanging from the banister, she then parted half a glance at Archer who had finished properly greeting his wife and stood watching her and Dorian's exchange with unveiled interest.

Candice opened her mouth to say … something, but froze, unsure how to run with this. Had Dorian told Archer of his suspicions? Should Candice just preempt and explain herself before it looked worse than it was?

"What are you yammering about?" Archer's wry smile unbound her petrified lungs. *Whew.* So he hadn't flapped his gums all over the bureau. She'd only have to contend with Dorian. That was a relief.

A slow twitchy grin pulled at Dorian's mouth. He kept his eyes fixed on her to be sure she'd witnessed it. "Well, you see, Candice and I already bumped into each other today."

Crap, nevermind. Candice felt the blood leach from her cheeks.

"She agreed to go out with me tomorrow night." Dorian licked his lips like L.L. Cool J, then turned a smug grin at his partner.

Why that blackmailing little —

"How lucky for me that my date is my new next-door neighbor."

In that moment, a trace of creamy mint slithered down Candice's throat and caught. "Neighbor?" She croaked out a cough, not sure why *neighbor* was the thing inciting the most protest at the moment. The date was just as offensive, if not more so.

Looking to Sadie, Candice communicated what she hoped would invoke some sort of emergency-out clause.

Sadie bit down on her lip to smother her amusement, ignoring her cue.

So much for friendship!

Everyone seemed amused at the fluster "Sal" had caused. Everyone but Candice.

He was such a clown. No wonder she'd never seen him with a date. He had to resort to blackmail to even get one!

Hardball, huh?

Unleashing her sweetest smile, she batted her eyes at the idiot before her. "Oh, right. The ballet is in town at the Fox Theatre. Dorian has such a soft side for the arts. Not many guys have the confidence to go to something like that alone. I was happy to help a pal out." Candice shrugged, tore open another York bite and shoved the whole thing in her mouth before giving him a smug, closed-lipped grin.

She'd been trying to trip him up, but Dorian didn't miss a beat. Bending down, his lips feathered atop hers. The faintest whispered suggestion of a kiss.

It was like watching a train wreck—so quick, so unexpected, everything went off the rails before it could be stopped.

Then again, there'd barely been even a hint of contact. She suspected he wanted to make it look like more than it was.

And if it'd been any more, or even a second longer, she would've had the opportunity to react and beat him senseless. Which wouldn't have taken long considering the source.

A flush of tingles prickled her freed lips. Her chewing had ceased, and a congealing lump of candy now stuck to the roof of her mouth, clogging any sort of protest.

"*Mmm.* Minty." With a wink, he pivoted to walk out. "Pick you up tomorrow at six. Dress nice." He tossed those final words over his shoulder just before the door closed behind him.

Candice blinked.

"I, uh …" Archer filled the silence with more awkwardness. Candice knew the feeling. Sadie was still biting back a grin.

"I need to catch up with Sal." Arch concluded by nodding to Candice and then kissing his wife once again. "I just need a few minutes, and I'll meet you out front."

"'Kay," Sadie replied, perfectly dazed until her husband made his exit. Then she turned back to Candice, and if her face said anything, she was fighting hard not to laugh. "Sal sprung that one on you, didn't he?"

Whether she meant the date or the kiss Candice couldn't say. But she knew Sadie was enjoying this way too much.

Candice gulped down the dissolving mass of chocolate, smearing the back of her hand across her mouth to eradicate any remnant of his kiss. "I've made my feelings for Dorian painfully obvious. I don't know why he bothers." Picking a speck of lint from the couch cushion, she pondered how she could make her feelings plainer.

Sadie shrugged. "He knows what he wants. I wouldn't be too quick to write him off if I were you."

"You've got to be kidding me." Candice sank back into the sofa and crossed her arms in a huff. "He's so ... immature. And ... and goofy, and insincere. He's only chasing because I turned him down. He's a puppy, Sadie."

The puckish grin was gone. Sadie's gaze catalogued Candice's features as if inspecting a rare species. "If that's what you think, you don't know Sal at all." With a pitying look, and a pitifully indulgent pat on the hand, Sadie stood, gathered her purse, and headed toward the door. "Gotta run. Meeting with the board this afternoon, and I've got some more hospital beds shipping out. Call me later."

Sadie ran a multi-million-dollar non-profit organization that provided health and home care for the underprivileged elderly. Everything she did was genuine, which was why her rebuttal of Candice's comment gave her pause.

"Uh, okay. Thanks for the help today." The room felt brittle, something Candice learned to detect early from a lifetime of walking on eggshells.

Had she been cruel to say those things? She hadn't meant to be dismissive but weren't the statements true? And would the truth cost her first friendship?

Sadie reached the front door and turned back with her

usual glittery smile. "Let me or Joss know if you need something to wear tomorrow."

Wear?

The puzzlement must have shown on her face because mirth deepened Sadie's grin. "You can bet your booty one ultra-fine Jay Hernandez look-alike will have those tickets and will be knocking on your door at six o'clock on the dot. Don't say I didn't warn ya."

Chapter 4

Dorian Salivas

"What do you mean, like some sort of *Mentalist*-type consultant?" Sal paced the length of the living room, suddenly needing a few throwing knives and an hour of target practice. That he could control. This?

Fine. In truth, he was a bit like a mentalist; reading non-verbal cues and involuntary responses, forming connections that might otherwise escape notice.

"It's only temporary." Archer looked calm and composed leaning forward on Sal's couch with his elbows on his knees, fingers laced and relaxed, making Sal's anger-march seem all the more absurd.

Swinging open the closet door rigged with a dart board, Sal swiped a handful of darts from the shelf and paced back out into the room, then aimed and threaded the first spear through the bull's-eye.

How much longer could it be, really? A week? Two at the most? Sal wouldn't settle for less than being a full-time agent. No injury would set him back to some sort of desk jockey or weak, gunless mind-reader performing party tricks for the FBI. He tossed two more darts back-to-back, shaving the first by a millimeter and re-piercing the center.

He deserved his badge. He'd done his time in the trenches, worked his way up the ranks, and now what? He was being demoted? With a frustrated grunt, he lasered the last dart at the board, nudging the other three to share the pinpoint target.

"How temporary? I mean, if I re-up on my drill and pass next week, I'm back right?"

Though it was so slight most wouldn't have noticed, Archer's cheeks tightened and the fine lines fanning his eyes strained.

Tension gripped Sal's spine. "What aren't you telling me, Archer?"

Archer held his gaze as a sign of respect, though Sal could see he was fighting the compulsion to look away in discomfort. A small consolation for whatever was coming.

"Jensen is bringing in a new agent from Quantico to help with the Vivaldi cases."

"*What*? You and I are on those. Vivaldi is *mine*. I bust up my leg on duty, need a few weeks to recover, and Jensen has the gall to replace me?" Sal's blood burned hot. He kept a tight rein on his temper. In fact, he couldn't remember the last time he'd raised his voice in anger. He was *Rain-X*; everything beaded up and rolled off.

But not this. Stripping him of his livelihood and pacifying him with some bogus consultant gig while a new agent got to traipse all over his turf, take credit for all his hard work? No. Not a chance in—

"Sal." Archer held up a hand, severing Sal's thoughts, "Like I said, it's only temporary. Agent Chrissick is new to the field. Graduated from MIT before heading off to Quantico but is apparently a whiz with encryptions and tracking. Jensen thought it would bring us up to another playing field. There was that one voicemail recording from Stephanie Mueller's phone back in June no one could track. Any other evidence we had has always gone missing in the first twenty-four hours. Our guys have hit a dead-end where Vivaldi is concerned. We need fresh eyes. And if it'll keep DC from storming in and taking over ..." He shrugged.

"But—"

"*But*, if you take the consulting position you won't be out of the loop and you can remind Director Jensen what an asset you are to this team. I might even let you tag along on a call." Archer's smirk unloaded a challenge.

But it felt like defeat. Surrender of the worst kind. He couldn't undo what had happened to him, and he couldn't simply will his body to be fully healed. It was yet another cruel and unrelenting stalemate to add to his collection. Such was his luck.

"Fine." He snapped. "But once I pass my test, I get my old job back, right?"

"Of course," Archer ground his throat. A sick little gleam lit in his eye. "As long as you play by my rules and don't give me any reason to doubt you."

"Yeah, yeah, Ace. Have I ever given you reason to doubt my mad skills?" He dusted his shoulder with a feigned lightness he'd perfected but seldom felt.

Blurting a laugh, Archer pushed up from the couch and started for the door. "Almost daily."

"Hey now. Isn't lying against your religion?"

"My days *have* been awfully boring in your absence."

They were good with quips, made for easy conversation. But this time his signature smirk melted away, and his carefree attitude slipped from his grasp. "Arch ... why does it feel like I'm being punished?"

Archer's hand stalled on the doorknob. "I knew this would be tough to swallow." He turned and slouched back against the door. "I wouldn't be any happier about it than you, believe me. But you're doing good work for the bureau, Sal. Hang in there. You'll be back on your feet in no time. Oh, and you need to run back to the office and talk to Jensen about all this. Preferably today."

He straightened but made no move to leave. The resolve in his posture made Sal's acute senses sharpen. "I know you hate feeling helpless as much as you hate relying on anyone else but me to back you up—even that took time. But not all roadblocks are meant to be bulldozed right away. Sometimes they're exactly where you need to be to stop and stand still long enough to take in a new perspective. Food for thought."

And with that, he left.

"Sweet. Apparently I need to be run over by a car to be taught a lesson." Sal murmured, and crumpled onto the sofa.

What lesson was the question. How could anything good come out of this? He'd nearly died. Lost the ability to do his job. Lost a hefty dose of his self-worth in the process. And yet every day he was fighting a fruitless and tedious battle to reclaim himself. Like he had to earn the right to be Agent Dorian Salivas again after risking his life to protect another.

It was hardly fair. But even when Sal did everything in his power to play by the rules, life and even death, seldom did the same.

It hadn't even been two full months, and yet each time he walked through the doors to the bullpen at the FBI he felt a profound sense of loss. He stuffed his hands into his pockets and nodded as he passed Sandy the receptionist.

This place had become Sal's home. It had reset his moral compass and given him a purpose for something bigger than himself. But right now, passing the tidy, barren space of his desk, he was a little lost puppy, sniffing around in the dark, waiting for someone to take pity and return him where he belonged.

Ignoring the twitch in his thigh muscle and the prickly nerve at his knee, he strode as lithe and confident as he could muster past the agents who shared his workspace, tossing casual greetings to those who met his eye.

The light wasn't on in Archer's office and the door was closed, so he'd likely taken a long lunch with his sassy little wife.

Yes, they were a little bit annoying with all their love-glazed exchanges, their quick banter, and their inability to keep their hands to themselves.

But didn't it just rankle a guy down on his luck to see his best friend get promoted to his boss—well, supervisor. Watch him sail through every darn case crossing his desk—though Sal was a big part of that. Not that anyone appeared to care about his stats now.

And to top it all off, then a *perfect ten* practically falls into Archer's lap. They'd probably start having their two-point-five kids soon, and Archer's life would be storybook perfect.

The irritation spread like poison ivy. One minute you're happy-go-lucky and then next you got the itch all over you. Sal shook his head and re-invigorated his stride toward Director Jensen's office.

He'd never been the jealous type. In truth, he was genuinely happy for his best pal and the babe. Today was just one of those days when it was almost impossible to see the sunrise through the fog.

Okay, so maybe it was more than just today. Though most days it wasn't this hard to wield his carefree attitude like a shield, acting as if he was impervious to another avalanche of disappointments.

He'd crawl out of this hole eventually. He had to. Gabe needed him, and Sal wouldn't let his brother down. Not again.

Because as much as Sal was what he seemed—a lawman, a protector, and yes, very often a screwball for the enjoyment and benefit of the masses—he was also a man with scars buried so deep they festered like a slow-acting poison. This was no subdermal rash or flesh wound.

Hidden behind the hapless front was an admittedly not-too-serious man with a desire to start fresh, run like hell from the flames that nipped his heels and taunted his failures.

He wanted to know what it felt like to fall crazy, what's-that-guy-smokin' in love. Start a family of his own. Earn a do-over. And if by some miracle of fate he could be granted any of those things, maybe it would mean his curse had finally been lifted.

So far fate hadn't dealt those cards. And even the most skilled con couldn't rig that deck.

Stopping outside Jensen's office, Sal hesitated before his knuckle struck the door.

What, exactly, would a restitution of his soul look like?

The past was engraved in stone, irrevocable. But if he could make his life count for something now—line up his ducks, as Archer called it—he'd figure out how to be the father and mother he'd stolen from Gabe. He'd get back the job that kept him on the straight and narrow. Then he'd use his gift to absolve himself of the curses it had brought.

And if he was lucky enough to have it all, he wanted …

Candice.

Ridiculous but true.

Confounding, stubborn, and gorgeous nuisance that she was. When he'd first laid eyes on her five months ago, she'd become the only woman who'd ever stilled his relentless mind and rendered him speechless. One look, one word from her lips and his restless world came to a dead stop.

In that brief hiccup of time, he caught a glimpse of the man he wanted to be. The kind of man who could catch the bad guy, coach little league, say grace at dinner, and write his own sappy love song about the woman who smelled like sugared flowers and slept every night curled up in his arms.

The kind of woman who could make him a better man.

Only today he'd realized the ever-perceptive insights of his nearly psychic brain had missed the mark and picked out the wrong girl.

Sal shook his head and exhaled slowly. He'd stalled long enough.

This wasn't a meeting he was looking forward to but then again, speaking with Jensen was kind of like talking to a pompous cue ball. Sal liked the guy okay, he was exceptionally efficient and a good leader. He didn't fluster or rile for any reason, which Sal respected. But it was also annoying to not have an advantage over him. There was no reading Director Carl Jensen.

He raised his fist to knock when the door swung open. Without warning, the woman hastening from Jensen's office barreled into him. Sal flung one hand to the door frame to brace himself and the other around the woman's back so they didn't both wind up on the floor. She jerked away from his touch, overcorrected, and fell against him once more. This time in no apparent hurry to release him.

"Oops." Straightening the starchy navy blazer and slacks to line up over a white-collared shirt, the woman gained her composure, shuffled the russet brown waves of her hair over her shoulder and produced her hand.

"Pardon." A rosy flush tinted her pale, angular cheeks when his hand engulfed hers. "Didn't see you there." She wobbled some more.

Once he was sure the tall, no-longer skittish woman was firmly grounded, he released her hand and shrugged. "That's okay. I've been a virtual landing pad all day. Agent Dorian Salivas, at your service."

A tiny squeak of laughter escaped the dame with clear blue eyes and a wide smile. "Nice to meet you Agent Salivas, I'm—"

"Sal. You're here. Come in, we need to talk." Jensen stood just beyond the woman, his expression blank. With pale blue eyes like chunks of arctic ice, a deeply lined, subtly scarred face punctuated by a sharp divot in his chin, and a wispy cul-de-sac of hair, Jensen stood about six feet and lean, same as Sal. And yes, uncanny how much the man resembled the actor Ed Harris. He could stunt double, easy.

"Uh, yes, sir." Without a word, the woman bustled around Sal and clipped down the hall.

In true Jensen fashion he ordered Sal to sit and then lorded his standing height over his audience by propping against the lip of his desk, crossing his arms and ankles in a ritualistic move he executed hourly.

"I take it Archer talked to you about your new consulting role?"

Sal swallowed the bitterness burning in his throat and nodded. "He told me I could *temporarily* help out while I finish convalescing."

"Yes, well, I don't want you to get your hopes up, Sal. You sustained several traumatic injuries. No one would blame you if you couldn't get back one hundred percent."

Sometimes it worked to one's advantage when no one expected anything from you. Growing up it had been Sal's chips and salsa. This was not one of those times.

"I'm happy to help out in the meantime, but with all due respect, nothing will keep me from earning my job back, sir." They would not simply write him off because of an injury. And just because he wasn't big and bulky like a lot of the other agents who snacked on small children and lived in the weight room, didn't mean he wasn't tough.

He could still remember each time his father had taken a baseball bat to his legs and back.

As well as little Dorian's greatest feat of magic when he escaped four of the most sadistic and heavily muscled members of the EL6 gang after they took turns padding their resume with attempted manslaughter-by-assault.

Sal was as much of a survivor as he was a fighter. His strength came from steadiness and perseverance. And an incredibly high pain tolerance. He could take anything they threw at him.

This certainly wouldn't be the thing that broke him.

Jensen simply nodded, but for once Sal could see a gleam of respect in the man's eyes.

"There's something else I want you to keep an eye on for me." Wonder of wonders, Jensen relinquished his high throne and moved to the chair adjacent to Sal's. "This is confidential, even within the bureau. You understand what that means?"

A chance to prove himself. Maybe nail down one of those

ducks. "Look at me, sir, I'm the picture of discretion."

With a little smirk that dug smiling, never-before-seen brackets into his boss's cheeks, Jensen leaned forward. "I need someone with your unique skill set, and I also need you to fly under the radar. Something tells me you're the man for the job."

Chapter 5

Candice Stevens

After inhaling a large bacon cheeseburger and fries from Five Guys, Candice kept one hand on the wheel of her Jetta TDI and used the other to smear away the ketchup and mustard residue stamping her with the indiscretion.

Her stomach revolted, the mass of junk food not the least bit cathartic for her nerves like some would think. It wasn't stress eating. It was all about illusion and survival.

Crumpling the smudged napkin and grease-lined foil in her fist, she chucked the wad into the empty carryout bag on the passenger seat, wishing she could purge the disgusting meal and exist like a normal diet-restricted female instead of what she was.

Weak.

Candice spied the boxing gloves and knuckle tape on the floorboard beyond the trash, reminding herself she had a date with a punching bag as soon as she sorted out this tissue sample business.

She smoothed her faintly sticky hand over the wool pocket of her coat, tracing the flat round cylinder still safe and sound. She didn't dare lift it out and risk dropping it again. Apparently she was as clumsy and careless as Blaine today. And this was much too important for a fumble of any kind.

Blowing out a breath, she snatched her phone from the cup holder, wiped the condensation her Pepsi had misted on the screen against her thigh and scrolled to the right contact.

He answered on the third ring.

"Yellow."

"Soren, hey, it's Candice Stevens. Have you come by the morgue yet today?"

She prayed she hadn't missed him. Considered a hard slap to the cheek for how stupid it'd been to tarry at home and accept Sadie's help when there was a much bigger fish to fry.

"Nope. Got a call from the FBI forensics team saying they didn't need me."

He sounded miffed. She knew he hated how a lot of the suits at the FBI talked *at* him like he was some first-place science geek who spent his days sifting through excrement, pureeing and analyzing maggots, and counting the ants in his homemade ant farm.

Except, he did do those things. Well, maybe not counting the ants part, but he was a scientist—one of the best entomologists/mineralogists she'd ever worked with. It was true he hadn't been particularly useful for the Vivaldi cases. But there'd never been any particulate evidence for him to analyze other than ashes. All of which had yielded a big, fat nada.

And though what he did was kind of disgusting—and honestly, who was she to talk about disgusting professions—the man himself was anything but.

Candice shook her head to scatter his image. "Why would they say that? I have tissue flagged and waiting for you. Just because we haven't had any luck with the Vivaldi victims so far, doesn't mean that couldn't change."

And if the scrap in her pocket was what she thought it was, they wouldn't need to rely on luck at all.

She heard him exhale a gruff sigh, knew he was probably running a hand through his gold, shoulder-length hippie hair

"I don't care what the FBI guys told you. I need you."

"Be still my putrefied heart." The words were as decayed as his painfully dry sense of humor. One might actually call him crusty.

Candice trapped the phone between her shoulder and ear, peeked at her blind spot, and crossed two lanes on I-44 to prepare to exit downtown.

"I'm almost back to the morgue. Just come, okay. And do me a solid, bring your microscope."

Some of her finest hint-dropping had gone down for the past thirty minutes, but Blaine Attwood had yet to vamoose. Then she'd not so subtly urged him to go get dinner, go home, go browse the behemoth racks at Brooks Brothers. Nada. And the man loved himself some finery. Pressed designer suits, polished loafers, a watch that most definitely cost more than her gently used car ...

Not that she didn't like to present herself a certain way, but Blaine truly lived to excess. Born and bred to privilege and always quick to name-drop his important inner circle of connectivity. Yet another one of his annoying traits.

All was quiet in the morgue once again. Sitting anxiously behind her desk, Candice scrolled through the X-rays of Vivaldi's latest blonde, Sarah Hoyt, whose identity had just been confirmed from the dental impressions.

Countless nicks and lacerations were etched into her bones on the films, none broken except for a few stress fractures in the lunate and capitate of the wrist.

Sarah Hoyt hadn't been content to wait on death. She'd fought back. And that meant the little quarter-sized container in Candice's coat might very well crack this case wide open.

Candice minimized the digital films and found herself staring into the sparkling brown eyes of the pretty blonde victim. Eyes that spoke of enthusiasm and innocence.

The picture from her driver's license might as well have been a Glamour Shot. Silky blonde hair with blunt ends skimming her collarbones, large doll-like eyes and dimpled cheeks. She was Miss America down to the details, except one. She was dead.

Queasiness and bacon grease didn't mix well in her overstuffed stomach. Something about the Vivaldi cases made Candice feel victimized, like *she* was the one laid out on the autopsy table.

Blaine grumbled something Candice hadn't caught.

"Hmm?" She peeled her gaze away from the beautiful tragedy, and saw the other ME slipping out of his lab coat, tweaking his platinum cufflinks so his initials were displayed upright and even.

"I *said*, since you're apparently too busy to show me your little trick with the bones right now, I'm gonna run out for a bite. Maybe track down a foxy redhead. Put my idle hands to good use." His tone said he was annoyed.

Yeah, well, join the club.

Soren Michaels would be arriving any minute, and she wanted the freedom Blaine's absence would allow in viewing and protecting the sample.

His swanky loafers clicked against the tile as he walked to the hooks by the door and slipped into his rich, camel-colored trench. Candice tried to remain calm, forcing the trapped oxygen in her lungs to release. Today had been a nightmare. Too many questionables. From her impulsive snatch to the deferred hope of finding useable evidence.

But if Blaine left, and Soren showed up in the next few minutes as promised, she could press restart on the whole day and get back to what she was good at.

She was lousy at sneaking around. Hated the suspicion she saw in Dorian's usually guileless, adoring eyes. Well, she hated the adoration too. Most women would probably bask in it. But Candice knew where it could lead.

Which was why she much preferred someone like …

Speak of the devil.

Blaine reached for the knob, but the door swung open. A cone of light spilled over Soren Michaels' honey blonde mane, broad shoulders, and tense facial snarl as he pushed past Blaine without a word.

It was legitimately cold outside, and yet Soren wore only a snug army-green T-shirt with a biohazard symbol stretched across his most impressive pecs, a ratty pair of painfully attractive Levi's, and some splattered hiking boots.

She tried not to think about what the splatter might be. Which was easy because Soren Michaels was plenty distracting. He was golden and tanned for a white guy in winter, though not even slightly sunny. His perpetual frown made him appear hard and fierce, but it was more than that that left the impression.

Six two, solid as a tank, with hawkish gray-green eyes, the man looked like he belonged in a gladiator ring in ancient Rome. No, better yet, he looked like the guy from Thor. Effortlessly barbaric and brooding. And yes, utterly devastating. She fought the urge to fan herself.

Blaine turned from the door and tipped his slightly crooked nose in the air. "What are *you* doing here? Shouldn't you be mating beetles or disimpacting a frog, bug boy?"

For one second Candice silently mused about the origins of the crook in that pompous nose. Thinking fanatical thoughts about it not being congenital but about someone having planted a fist between Blaine's eyes to knock him off his very high thoroughbred.

Sure, like Blaine, Soren was also kind of rude. But Blaine made it an artful anomaly, polluting any room with a toxic mixture of disdain and pretention that could make even the most easy-going person bristle. And easy-going, Soren was not.

The entomologist shifted the backpack off the bunched trapezoid of his burly shoulder and set the bag she hoped contained the microscope on the counter without a glance.

A muscle worked in his jaw; the twitch narrowly concealed by about five days' worth of sandy-colored scruff. "You have exactly ten seconds to disappear. Starting now."

"Or what?" Blaine scoffed.

"Or you'll be welcomed home tonight by a hellstorm of fire ants finding new residence in your Tempurpedic mattress." Every muscle in Soren's extensive collection seemed to stand at attention, and yet hands hung loose at his sides like he was Wyatt Erp waiting to draw his six-shooter for a showdown.

"Pff. You think you scare me, *maggot?*"

Blaine had recently switched over from the county coroner's office to the city. Candice had never seen these two together, but she was guessing there was more to the rivalry than professional differences. The band of tension in the room was maxed out. One more snip from either of them and the rest of the lab would probably end up in the dumpster with both of the useless microscopes.

"What is this, a pissing contest?" Candice winced at her word choice, snapped the rubber band she wore around her wrist, and stepped between the two men. It seemed like a good idea at the time. Inserting a buffer before flaring tempers touched the wrong fuse.

But the men weren't deterred, and things got cramped. The imposing presence on each side threatened to squash her like one of Soren's pet bugs. The sound of someone's knuckles cracking registered faintly over the roar of blood in her ears.

Anxiety squeezed her chest so tight she could scarcely wheeze in a breath. Nearing hyperventilation, she gulped down the knot of fear crowding her throat and forced steel behind her quivering larynx. "Blaine, go get dinner."

One of his large hands curled around her bicep to jerk her away, the pressure of his meaty fingers pumped heated panic through her veins. "And if you don't take your hand off me, we'll continue the discussion we had earlier today with my scalpel. Accidents happen in the morgue every day, and I'll be sure to make it look like one."

A surprising amount of conviction managed to interlace

her threat. It would seem her chutzpah had rallied at the thought of being manhandled again. Then again, she might have a bit more pluck at the moment since there was another witness in the room. Either way it was a stride in the right direction.

With the bite of Blaine's big mitt bruising her arm, visions of rearranging his grill were no longer enough. Her knee itched to make him sing like a soprano. She was about to add that little tidbit to the bluff, but he released her arm and fired one last searing glare at them before stomping off.

Once the door clicked behind Blaine, Candice whipped around and came face-to-stony-face with Soren.

"What was that all about?"

The menace in his eyes was chilling, but honest.

Other than some uncanny genetics, it was precisely what was attractive about him. He didn't want her. She'd never once seen his eyes wander. Never once felt any kind of inclination in his stare.

There wasn't enough disdain there to lump her in with Blaine, whom he obviously despised. But there was indifference. And it was wonderful and safe. It made it easy for her to indulge in her own private attraction for the surly man she could never fall in love with.

"You need to mind your own business." Soren growled, his expression unchanging even as his words switched gears. "Did he hurt you?" Did the man snack on rusty nails? The irritation scraping from his throat was almost alarming.

Crossing her arms, she rubbed away the sting of Blaine's touch and the memories tagging along unbidden.

"Next time you want to dance, Tarzan, take it outside." Great, now *she* was using nicknames. *How very professional.*

One corner of his lips tipped up, though he didn't look very amused. Funny how painful it seemed smiling was for this man. And yet, by contrast, how excessively Dorian Salivas had his signature grin slathered on his face.

But why was she thinking about Dorian?

Candice turned away from Soren and went straight to her coat.

Excitement bubbled up from her stomach. Actually, it felt a little like indigestion, but excitement sounded better.

Slipping her hand between the stiff folds of wool, her fingers closed around the evidence vial and resurrected the hope of catching one of the most prolific serial killers of all time.

Except when her palm unfurled the small disc, there was no escaping the curse that exploded from her lips. She slammed the decoy down onto her desk and plucked the rubber band against her wrist as hard as she could—sure to leave a well-earned welt for the expletive that felt too necessary to deny.

Dorian.

"I'm gonna kill him."

Chapter 6

Dorian Salivas

"So how'd it go at the office?" Sal's little brother twirled his spaghetti and shoveled down another bite mid-speech.

"Uh, well ..." It was complicated. Complicated and confidential. Boiled down, Jensen suspected they had a mole within the FBI. Leads seemed to keep disappearing. Paper trails lost. Even the scant amount of physical evidence in the dozens of Vivaldi cases were always instantly unaccounted for. Sal was now his own sort of mole. A mole to find a mole.

In the scatter of a second, Sal was examining Candice. Not in a way he was used to.

She wasn't with the FBI, but her position with the city gave her some pull and more access than Sal could shrug off.

Jensen hadn't mentioned her when he'd run down the list of weak links, save when he alluded to appeasing the brass by bringing in the best specialists in the field. Which, meant Candice and this Chrissick guy. Sal gritted his teeth and forced his mind back to the meeting. Thankfully, Jensen's suspicions centered around the uber-creepy voodoo-obsessed analyst Garrett Veer who worked on the second floor. The few words they'd exchanged in passing over the years had been odd enough to give Sal a serious case of the willies.

Gulping down a mass of noodles and meat sauce, he let the flare of the habaneros he'd added to their dinner simmer in his throat a moment longer before answering. "I'm not back in an official capacity as of now. Won't be much longer though."

If he could dig into the mind of a serial killer, surely he could brave the wickedness he sensed behind Voodoo Veer's dark eyes. Besides, his job was on the line. And without his badge there was always the possibility the old Dorian could wander off his leash.

"You've always been more than capable of handling whatever life threw at us. I have no doubts you'll land on your feet." Gabe spoke while polishing off his third helping, then belched in finale. "That was tasty." He arched back against his recently upgraded wheelchair, stretching rangy arms above his head. "I've got a few more tracks I need to mix tonight, so I'll probably be in the studio late."

Sal nodded, hating the chasm between them but never knowing how to bridge the gap. Despite both of their efforts to be casual, their relationship was as stiff as the frozen branches battering the kitchen window. The wind might be able to sway the trees, but Sal had cemented his fate the day he'd tangoed with the EL6s—the notoriously violent East Side gang that knew a thing or two about revenge.

He and Gabe co-existed. A few nights a week they'd huddle around the TV for a game or a sitcom. They'd shoot the breeze like brothers did. But it was all on the surface, and Sal despised every minute of the pretense.

The house, at least, had been a stride in the right direction. Just last year they'd settled into the story-and-a-half craftsman with a master suite on the main floor for Gabe. He'd converted the sunroom at the back of the house into a studio for his brother to dabble with his interesting new hobby.

But as much as the space was clean, spacious, and comfortable, he always felt like the walls pressed in on him. Like he was a splinter trying to make a home in a place that would never accept him.

Maybe he hated being at home because it was the one

place he had no secrets.

Gabe knew it all. He knew exactly who Dorian was, and that, in its very essence, was unforgivable. Just as troubling was the way Gabe pretended like he didn't hold a grudge. But something told Sal it was all still there. The manifestation of all his mistakes had become a third person in the room neither would acknowledge.

"... Is that okay?"

"Huh?" Sal looked over at his younger brother by nine years, his face not at all like Sal's. Gabe favored their mother. Softer features, lighter, almond-shaped eyes. While Sal looked far too much like their father to be able to sleep at night. The man had been a monster. With his intense, deep-set eyes—almost obsidian, like they mirrored the darkness within.

There'd never been even a sliver of laughter in those eyes, not even in cruelty. One look, and the toxic hatred could pull you further and further into an endless deep of misery.

"Earth to Dorian." Gabe waved a hand to corral his brother's wandering mind.

Sal shook his head. "Sorry, what were you saying?" When he met the humor in Gabe's eyes something like pride swelled in his chest. In spite of all they'd endured, Gabe was remarkably well-adjusted. It was nothing short of a miracle Sal had been able to pull off raising a kid when he'd been nothing but a kid himself.

He stood, gathered their plates, and dumped them in the sink.

Gabe spoke at his back. "I said, I'm going to be doing a live recording at Archer and Sadie's church on Sunday. I was wondering if you'd take me."

"Sure." The word popped out before Sal thought better about setting his lying, cheating feet inside a house of God. Maybe he could just drop Gabe off and return when it was over.

"Awesome thanks! This will be my first on-site recording.

I was hoping you could help me bring in my soundboard and get all set up."

Or not.

"Absolutely." Sal grumbled, nudging the faucet lever and scouring the plates, burning hot water lashing at his hands.

The first few years of their lives had been plagued by so much lack. There'd been very few things Gabe had asked in the past ten years Sal had managed to deny him. Thankfully, since Gabe had such a good head on his shoulders, he hadn't ever manipulated Sal's guilt to get his way, which told Sal he hadn't destroyed the boy's spirit. Just his body.

"Thanks bro." Gabe coasted away from the table and halfway down the hall to his studio before he about-faced. "Oh, yeah. I forgot to tell you." He reared back and balanced on two wheels.

"Some chick was pounding on our door earlier. Didn't hear at first because I was mixing. When I caught sight of her through the sidelight she looked blazing mad. Even in the cold without a coat. And dude, her arms were pretty buff for a tiny little thing. I'm thinking she could've taken me. Maybe even you." He arched a dark eyebrow. "Figured you'd wanna fight the lovers' quarrel yourself."

Candice. The thought of an intimate spat with her curved his lips. He clamped down on his grin and turned back to the dishes. "It's not a lovers' quarrel, Gabe. It's a work thing. You know I'm not like that."

He hoped his brother knew. Sal wanted to be the right kind of role model. That meant never parading women around and never showing any weakness. It was a little exhausting, and it sure complicated his social life, but it was worth it.

"Whatever you say. But this chick ..." Gabe whistled. "She was smokin' hot. You might want to find something good to fight about."

That, Sal thought, was not going to be a problem.

It was well past midnight when the strains of music ceased from behind the studio door. Gabe was now in bed, and Sal clicked off the tube, not yet persuaded to venture from his sprawled position on the couch.

Still and dark, with nothing but the pale blue tint of the moon in his company, seemingly all the creatures but Sal had turned in. The whispered vibration of a motor passed outside, but no shift of light speared through the shades. The weighty blink of his eyes became more frequent. The soft pull of drowsiness beckoning him to the deceptive abyss of sleep.

With a final restless jerk, he reached behind his neck, tugged his T-shirt over his head, and slouched down the last few inches into the couch.

Sleep was only moments away, but rest, well, that was an entirely different tune.

"My wallet. My wallet is missing." The West County princess let the wide slouch of her Louis Vuitton tote gape open, the at-least five-carat ice on her right ring finger disappeared into the sac as she dug around for the soft leather wristlet Sal had skimmed earlier that morning. It was probably Italian. The leather. It had that kind of feel to it.

The hoity-toity kind of blonde with a bite was a bundle of tells. In addition to the cut of her skirt being a bit too short to be conservative for the courtroom—and yet intentional as it showcased endlessly long legs—she wore a shade of "maneater" on her meticulously penciled lips, both of which lured a look but warned a touch. Dorian's assessment said she was a divorce lawyer. A killer good one.

It was all written in the details. In the way she carried herself.

Women. Such fascinating contradictions of sweetness and sass, resistance and need, strength and frailty.

This woman put up a tough front. One that said she could devour every kind of man on earth for breakfast without smudging a single dab of her creamy designer lipstick.

Oh, but she had a weakness. And Dorian knew just what it was.

He was fifteen years old now. He'd grown ten inches in something like twelve months and actually looked like a man, instead of a scrawny, piss-poor minority from East St. Louis—the highest crime zip code in the entire Midwest.

The fact that he lived in a hovel on the wrong side of the river was bad luck. The fact that he was Hispanic and every other person in his school was black made luck an epic myth.

But Dorian didn't need to rely on the hand he'd been dealt anymore. He'd learned with a certain attitude he could become impervious to suspicion.

Now, if he could find a way to be impervious to pain then he'd really be on to something.

He wasn't invisible, per se, he was permanently pardoned. It was brilliant. There was a fool proof ace up his sleeve at all times, and it was all in the look on his face, the innocence in his eyes, the hapless tilt of his lips, the sweet, unassuming bumble in his tone.

Suckers.

Dorian bit into the crumble-topped muffin he'd lifted from the coffee kiosk. The sugary tartness of the fresh blueberries awakened his taste buds and flooded his mouth with saliva. He allowed himself one more bite before stowing the treat in his backpack.

There were a few occasions where he'd felt like maybe the scams, the little games, were just, well, wrong. But grumbling bellies were persuasive. And his conscience could justify the cost of deception because he was the man of the house now, and he'd do whatever it took to keep food on the table.

The lunch lady at school, Loretta Mae, had fallen for his undeniable charm. Okay, maybe the burn marks she'd noticed on his arms had moved her to load up his tray and refuse payment for the past three months. Because of her generosity, he'd been able to pack a few pounds onto his newly acquired height and finally had enough muscle to send his father packing once and for all.

But remove one problem and another ten found them.

Maneater continued to dig for her wallet, the trim sleeve of her blazer inching up to expose her own scarred forearms.

Making his move, he ambled backward from the courthouse stairs, turned, and crashed right into the leggy blonde. As planned, her tote went sprawling. She cursed, such a harsh sound coming from such a pretty mouth, and then she crouched to gather her things.

"Oh, I-I'm so sorry, ma'am." Dorian bumbled, reaching out to help retrieve the scattered cosmetics and making sure to expose the cigarette burns his father had branded along his arms. "I should have been looking where I was going, but I found this wallet on the steps here, and I figured I'd better get it to the police station before anyone tries to pass it off as their own."

He lifted the Tiffany-blue clutch, timid sincerity in his tone. "I hope I didn't hurt you."

Maneater was a cynic, so the moment her venomous eyes softened like Nutella on hot toast he knew he had her.

He saw the maternal concern awaken the woman's compassion when she took a quick inventory of the scrubby street kid fighting his own war for justice despite his noticeable poverty and abuse.

Her silken hand came to rest on his marred forearm, halting his continued assistance. "I'm fine. Are *you* okay?"

"I'm more worried about you, ma'am. I've been kind of clumsy lately." He shook his head, shifted his backpack over his shoulder, and embellished a wince. The very real bruises on his back weren't all that tender anymore but would assist in furthering the con.

He helped her stand, letting his shy, boyish admiration charm the Venus princess.

Women found him adorable. A blessing and a curse.

Maneater smiled, defenses fully breeched. His mother's freedom one pro bono case away.

Game. Set. Match.

Chapter 7

Shadows clung to the edges of the small two-story house. The gray siding blending with the murky fog lifting from the icy ground. The black wind chasing past like a ghoulish cloak in the thickening darkness. The clouds pressed back and a beacon of moonlight split the sky, highlighting the white smoke of each exhaled breath that dispersed as swiftly as the fog, as invisible as their very presence.

Anxious tension rushed in heated rivers beneath chilled skin. But patience was the hallmark of Vivaldi's perfection. He knew just when to wait and when to strike. When to emerge from the shadow and when to remain wrapped in darkness.

There was no learning curve in this. It had to be perfectly orchestrated each time, the tempo unforgiving and unrelenting. The consequences of even one uncorrected misstep too grave to think on. Because, if the mind was allowed to wander to that place, to the possibilities forever hibernating through years of seasons from beginning to end, all the cards would crumble. The notes would fall to the ground. Chaos would reign. And the grave would be a mercy.

The porch didn't bother to creak underfoot, almost as if holding its breath in reverent terror. The lock gave up without a fight, and the darkness inside the house replaced the cutting night wind.

A sip of warmth swallowed down on a hesitant breath, but there was no place for it to settle. A phantom touch led the way to the right position, and the pending score played in the silence. Though there would be no song today. No soprano scream. No plunge of the syringe awaiting its singer's refrain. Unless—

Something strained in the stillness. The groan of the floor like a splinter in unmarred flesh.

But despite the moment's reprieve, the prelude to death waited in the wings. The unblemished would be marked with the sins of another. The perpetual hunger sated for another season. For Vivaldi had vowed the song would never end.

Chapter 8

Candice Stevens

"Ehh!" Rolling over for the hundredth time, Candice pummeled the feather pillow into a lump and collapsed back down.

Sleep was a cunning target tonight. Not only because of her infuriating day, but because she hadn't been able to heft her mattress and box spring up the flight of stairs to her bedroom. The *only* room with shades covering the windows. Which meant she was sleeping on the stupid thing in the den where the windows were bare and the full moon was casting its Bat-Signal like a spotlight on Webster Groves's newest colossally idiotic resident.

Candice snapped her eyes shut. Again. Forcing each agitated breath to find a resting rhythm.

Dorian had the evidence. She didn't know how he'd managed to snatch it, but she knew he had it. Once she tracked the little weasel down he was in for a world of hurt.

A moaning sound tore a rift in the silence. The sound like pained planks of wood straining underfoot.

Old houses were achy creatures. She assuaged the reaction of her pulse with the knowledge.

She'd replaced the locks before she moved in. The door at the front was a heavy solid wood, and the only other entry door was in the room with her. It led out to a small stone patio and a modest backyard with a white picket fence.

Besides, Webster was Mayberry. Huffing out a sigh, she

wiggled further beneath the covers. *Paranoid much?* One of the downsides of living alone was no one else could tease you about your wild leaps. The isolation gave the paranoia power to slither deeper and weave its cancer-causing cells through your rationale to infect you with fear.

But Candice was tired of being afraid. Living afraid. There was no one in her house.

She crossed her arms over her eyes, burying her face into the crux of her elbow.

Breathe in. Breathe out.

Her breath hissed from her lips. The shushing sound like a crashing tide. In and out. Her fear ebbing away, each current an undertow carrying it further away until she finally felt adrift in sleep.

But then …

Something scraped across the floor just beyond the door. Hot on its heels was a faint high-pitched whine. The hall closet door made that noise. Unless this house was haunted that meant …

Jerking upright in bed, Candice's heart seized. A sharp gasp trapping a slice of air in her lungs. The dump of adrenaline inciting a conflicting riot of panic and paralysis.

She managed to turn her head and search the empty room for a weapon. The only thing she'd wedged through the office door had been her mattress, a pillow, and a soft blanket. Even her phone was on the kitchen counter.

She was normally prepared for this kind of thing. Since the day she fled the docks she'd never needed to rely on her emergency plan, but she'd always had one.

Except now. Now, when she needed it. Now, when her SIG Sauer was still boxed up with her office supplies. The irony didn't escape her that the very box holding her gun should have been in this room if she'd gotten any further into unpacking.

The house groaned again, further confirming the threat.

She had no means to defend herself. The mace on her

keychain was also on the counter. And not much could be hidden beneath the bursting seams of her cotton spaghetti-strap nightie from eight years and twenty pounds ago.

Helpless. Again. A vicious cycle.

She unfolded her legs over the edge of the mattress, testing her weight against the wood to check for protest. The blood rushing over her eardrums diluted her senses, but she thought she heard more searching sounds.

At least it didn't seem like they'd come to kill her. They'd have accomplished that by now. Had the floor just tilted beneath her feet? Oh, right. She guzzled down a much needed swig of air to keep from fainting.

She had to get out. *Now.* What if AJ had found her after all these years? What if her ex was still—

The creaking melody lurched down the hall. The dragging, dissonant refrain played like a villain's requiem. One usually punctuated by haunting strings and clanging keys. The kind of warning hidden in the score that said, "What are you waiting for? Run for your life, stupid girl!"

She tiptoed to the door; her cold, quaking fingers finding the deadbolt. Mercifully, the slipping metal unlocked without a sound. Now, if only the hinge would comply.

Each little task seemed to pass at a glacier's pace. It didn't help that her heart rate was dangerously tachycardic and hysteria threatened to bubble up from her throat in a strangled cry.

She forced down another breath and inched the door open. A wintery blast of air whistled through the crack. Sucking in her stomach, she wormed through the gap until her bare toes met the flagstone patio.

And the second she'd eased the door back to a sliver she hit the gas, sprinting over the Siberian stone tundra until her feet crushed through the frosted grass. Her fear burned so hot she scarcely registered the cold.

With more finesse than she thought possible, she vaulted over the fence. Her knee clipped the speared tip but didn't slow her progress. She scrambled up a few stairs of the neighbor's deck and assaulted the door. Kept banging. Couldn't stop. Couldn't even think until the door swung inward and she tumbled in uninvited.

"Candice?" The sleep-rasped voice of Dorian Salivas was the sweetest sound on earth.

Standing in his kitchen, the crisp wind still chasing in behind her, she fought to calm the breathless adrenaline so she could speak.

"Please ..." *gasp.* "Dorian, I ..." *gasp.* Her lungs refused to fill. The sound strangled and enormous in the quiet, calm of his house.

A hint of a smile curled on his lips as he grasped her forearms. "Shh. It's okay." His thumbs skimmed back and forth. His soft, reassuring stokes electrifying her obviously short-circuited nerves.

"I'm pretty sure it's not my birthday yet, so why don't you take a deep breath and tell me why you're standing in my breakfast room ..." He swallowed, and she was surprised she noticed. "... in your nightgown."

"S-Someone's there. My h-house. What I mean is, someone broke into my house." There. She finally got it out.

The warmth in Dorian's eyes froze over. "Stay here."

He was gone and back in a blink, armed with a Glock and a look even more dangerous than his firearm. Then, like a wisp of smoke, he'd disappeared before she could tell him about the back door. Without thinking, she dashed out after him. "*Dorian,*" she hissed.

Already at the back door, he whipped around, eyes furious black flames. He jerked his head back toward his place. *Go!* he mouthed.

She wasn't sure why she didn't listen. Moments ago she couldn't get away fast enough, but Dorian was here now, and she realized she had a senseless sort of faith in him that transcended her fear. *Him!* An injured, wiseacre FBI agent.

It was clear she'd lost her marbles.

Sidling up behind him, she felt the slight brush of his track pants against her bare knees. He shielded her with his arm, as if to push her out of harm's way. The other hand held his gun at attention and nosed open the door.

She followed him in, mimicking his stealth movements as he swept each room with ruthless efficiency. But everything was quiet now.

Long, unnerving silence reigned until a sudden creak came from the front of the house. In an instant, he'd tucked her into the powder room and vanished again before she could eek out a syllable of protest.

How irritating. Or was it noble? If any man-boy could pull off that particular dichotomy it was bumbling but oddly capable Agent Salivas. She held her breath, straining to hear what was happening. Something shifted above her.

Upstairs! Someone was upstairs.

Toiling for a half a second, and acknowledging it was a classic idiot move, she followed her gut and slipped from her hiding spot. She had to warn Dorian.

So she stuck to the shadows like a cat burglar in her own home, carefully skirting the strewn contents of ransacked boxes. Emotion prickled in her throat.

This was supposed to be her safe haven. And yet on her *first* night here it'd been violated. Not a great start.

Heavy steps poured down the stairs, and panic stopped her cold.

The innards of the "office" box lay in its own small landfill of junk. She peered through the darkness to see if she could spot her SIG 9 mm. But the only thing evident in the shadows was a Swingline stapler.

Better than nothing.

Once she had the weighty metal in her palm, she raised her hand over her head and waited.

A deathly stillness hovered like the Grim Reaper waiting to collect. You'd think that phantom feeling would be second nature for someone who spent her time in a morgue, but this was different. Her sweat-slicked fingers tightened on the steel. A quivery sensation hummed through her veins.

Lord, help. Plea—

"Ahhh!" Movement to her left triggered her reflex to start swinging.

A hand clamped around her wrist and sent her weapon clattering across the floor.

"Just me, Brat." His breath fanned over her cheeks, like he'd leaned close enough to offer comfort without forcing a touch.

All the tension drained from her. Her muscles, exhausted from the hysteria, liquefied until she went limp against him.

"*Oh.*" She told herself she wouldn't cry as she snuggled into his warmth. It didn't stop tears from testing the levee. Her hands curled up under his arms, pressing against his surprisingly buff back.

Somehow it managed to escape notice that he wasn't wearing a shirt when the threat of the intruder had befuddled her senses.

But she was much too aware of it now.

Tight, chiseled abs nestled against her. Strong, sinewy arms held her in place.

For reasons she couldn't explain, she needed this. Needed him to hold her together, if only in deference to those few moments when the danger had been so all-consuming.

But since the threat was now gone, why was she still clinging like a koala? Her rebellious hands memorizing striations of muscle as if she were stroking her favorite tune on the strings of a guitar.

Heat rushed to her cheeks. More so on the one smothered against his chest.

The comfort he offered was a convenient distraction. It was a silly sort of illusion, and it had to end.

She stepped away. "D-Did you check upstairs?" Without his warmth, a shiver tripped over her skin. She folded and rubbed her arms.

He nodded, reclaimed the space between them, and reached out to assist in rekindling the heat. Instinctively, she jumped back to avoid his touch, and something stabbed into the soft bridge of her foot.

"Ouch!" She leapt off the offending object, hobbled on her uninjured foot, and soothed the ache with a firm massage.

"Easy, Kitten. I'm not gonna bite ya." She could hear the twinge of humor lacing his tangy accent. His eyes were a mystery in the dark, but a peel of moon-glow flashed against the bright white of his smile.

"Whoever was here is gone. Left the front door wide open."

When she turned on the lights and exposed the damage a moment later, she bit her lip to restrain a whimper. More than anything she wanted to flip the switch right back, crawl beneath the covers, and pretend nothing had happened to shatter the hope she'd felt when she stepped into her new house this morning.

But even if she turned out the lights and hid behind the veil of night, she knew what would be waiting for her come morning. It was kind of like the past. She could shove it in a dark corner, but sooner or later, light always found a way in to expose the ugly truth.

With the light came the embarrassing revelation of her ratty, juniors' department, pink and white polka dot nightgown on display. She quickly rectified the situation when she spotted her fluffy lavender bathrobe ripped from one of the many ravaged boxes. Because of her stunted height the thing draped to her ankles instead of her mid-calves. One of the perils of being four feet eleven inches tall.

"Well, it looks to me like you got some help unpacking."

Now that she could see Dorian she wanted him gone. Every ripped bit of him.

"*Oh yeah*, nothing like a good ransacking. Loads easier this way."

Cinching the belt of the robe tight, she then clutched the

collar to be sure no single speck of skin was visible, praying the bulky mass of terry cloth would hide how much she was still shaking. She didn't want anyone witnessing her meltdown, least of all the goof troop next door.

Dorian had made a call, so the local PD would be by soon. She just wanted to get this over with. Wanted to piece her life back together.

She'd thought she'd been cleaning up her act, but the mess was everywhere. Literally and figuratively. And since everything she owned, aside from a few items of clothing and a toothbrush, had still been in boxes in her living room, she'd made it easy for the intruder to quickly and efficiently sift through all of her belongings.

What had they been looking for?

No sooner had the question formed in her mind, when the answer came with chilling clarity.

The evidence.

With the thought came the very real possibility that tonight while she'd tossed in bed, the Vivaldi Killer himself might have been inside her house.

Chapter 9

Dorian Salivas

"**Y**ou!" The accusation came with gale-force rage. Swallowed up in yards of that marshmallow PEEPS robe, with wild, sleep-tousled hair, and amber eyes like poison-tipped darts, he'd never seen a more disarming sight.

Okay, the tiny, baby-doll nightgown might've been worse. Or better, depending on how you looked at it.

Actually, the fleeting moment when she'd surrendered in his arms would carry him through the next couple years of her pandering politeness and was infinitely more thrilling than the slight exposé of her soft femininity.

Being touched by her … man, that had felt good. *Better* than good.

If only she could see how well they suited. How the past she'd never shared with him—the one playing before his eyes on every flit of her expressions—bonded them in a way even he could scarcely understand.

Before she got the chance to tear into him—and yes, he knew why—the police arrived and proceeded with the incident report.

For the next hour, except for a handful of dirty looks, she ignored him.

When they were once again alone, he preempted the impending verbal whiplash and insisted she traipse her stubborn self over to his house for the night.

For a few quarrelsome minutes he thought he'd have to

toss the ornery woman over his shoulder and haul her away against her will. He felt a twitch of a smile. Oh, wouldn't that be fun. She wouldn't make it easy for him. Then again, that was all part of the appeal.

But he'd made a solid case and rationale won the night. Her home—as the break-in proved—was unsafe. Under no circumstances would he be leaving her here alone.

"You're a real pain in the tookus, you know that?"

Dang, she was cute when she didn't get her way. All spit and steam and sass.

"Tookus?" He watched as she crammed her tiny feet into big, furry boots, biting his lip to quell an adoring amusement. Despite the fact that tonight had been dangerous, and obviously unsettling, he couldn't say he'd had a bad time. In fact, he was rather enjoying himself.

She hiked her purse on her densely padded shoulder and blew a matted clump of hair out of her eyes. "Yeah, you know? Pain in the rear, the buttocks, the hiney."

He tweaked a brow and didn't bother restraining his grin. "Hiney?"

"Man alive, you're obnoxious."

It was too fun to stop there. "Man alive? Quite the curious catchphrase, because, you know, you work with dead people."

With rolling eyes she shoved past him and flung open the front door. Following with a chuckle, he waited while she locked up and then walked beside her under the crystalline starlight.

It was clear she needed a respite from the heaviness of tonight, and probably today too because of the Vivaldi case and her missing evidence. He didn't mind playing himself a fool to distract her. He did it often enough, and the effects he had on her heart rate, the stress around her eyes and the tension in her body, were proof positive he eased her burdens.

He doubted she'd ever acknowledged it for what it was

and knew it was the main reason she saw him the way she did, but it was an act of service he knew she needed whether she'd ever see it that way or not.

And the price he paid was eternal imprisonment in the "friend zone." Or more likely the "kiddie corner."

Suddenly, he wasn't feeling all that humorous. He tucked his fingers into the cloth at her elbow to steady her over a lingering slab of ice on the sidewalk.

She tensed up, as if hating the thought of his hand on her. He got that. It was part of her story. But she hadn't seemed to mind one bit when she'd snuggled up to him earlier.

Good times and great oldies. It was a memory to cherish because he couldn't see it happening again. She wasn't the type to slip up, seeming almost fearful of any crack of weakness or need.

It wasn't the manliest of admissions, but sometimes a person just needed to be held.

He'd gladly be that guy if she ever fell off the wagon again. It'd probably kill him to keep it platonic, but he'd do it anyway. For Candice. Anything.

She tugged her arm free only to wobble on another slick spot. The ice bit at his bare feet. His body had been through the grinder the past year so a little cold was nothing to squawk about.

Steadying her again, he smiled to himself. Stubborn little sassy. "For Pete's sake, it's your elbow, Brat. I'm not trying to cop a feel if that's what you're worried about."

Expelling her resignation on a huff of white steam, she found firm footing and looped her arm through his as if to prove he'd miscalculated her reaction.

"Huh."

They were walking up the slight incline of his driveway. He watched her face for clues to the revelation she was indulging with that "huh." "Care to share with the class?"

She cleared her throat. "You, uh, drive that orange Dodge Challenger R/T Classic?"

Sal felt his mouth sag open, not remembering the last time someone had thrown him for a loop and literally loosed his jaw. Other than Candice, the first time he'd seen her in the morgue.

She quirked a smile his way, and the shock of it all was like a Taser to the chest.

"Marry me."

It sounded like she giggled. Could Candice Stevens giggle?

Stopping next to his car, she turned and swatted under his chin with the backs of her fingers. "You can close your mouth now, Dorian. Some women know their way around a hot rod."

"Would it help if I got down on one knee?" His pulse restarted, and the black wind whipped around him.

This laugh was humorless. Clutching her robe, her fist curling just below the little bob in her throat, she cast a skittish glance his way and then reeled it back as if he might bite. "You've gotta be freezing."

It was because he didn't have a shirt on. He was standing outside in February wearing nothing but a pair of sweatpants and a smile, and because he was standing a mere three inches away from the hottest woman on the planet he was almost on fire.

"I'll live." His voice was raw with emotions he could never utter in honesty. She'd bolt so fast not even the supercharged engine of his Challenger could run her down.

In a few moments they were inside. Candice Stevens, in his house, at three a.m.

No chance he'd get a wink of sleep tonight. Zilch.

She slipped off her boots by the door. Stubby little toes with red nail polish peeked from the hem of the oversized robe.

Sal swallowed. Toes, *ay dios mio*! Elbows and toes. Man, he was in trouble.

"So, are you going to make me yell at you now, or are you

gonna be a big boy and hand it over?"

"Ah, we're back to this now." He tugged at his neck, desperate to loose the raging awareness clamping tight around each vertebrae.

Her eyes sprang wide, and a sudden dab of moisture sparkled like caramelized sugar.

He winced, realizing he'd exposed the underside of his arm.

He'd taken precautions to keep his arms at his sides or crossed while the police were at her place and the lights were on. In the darkness there'd been no reason to hide. And even in the light most often he didn't bother concealing the evidence of his abuse. It reminded him who he was now and how he'd gotten here. But it wasn't something Candice needed to deal with right now.

"I'll go get it. Make yourself at home." A part of him wanted to be rid of the evidence, but tonight's break-in hadn't been a random snatch and grab. So that trouble he'd been trying to avoid? Yeah. It crashed right through his door and was now the marshmallow PEEPS clone parked on his couch.

After slipping into a long sleeve T-shirt, he retrieved the vial from his gym bag and went back downstairs to have it out.

She was slouched back into the microfiber sofa, hands laced over her tummy, one leg crossed over her knee. Hands, toes, and ankles the only skin in sight.

"Did you really think I wouldn't notice it was missing?" She stared long and hard, invoking intimidation to rival even the best interrogator.

"Maybe I was protecting you." He matched her stare. Only, he had more practice and held his ground until she caved. Folding in next to her, he made sure to leave a barrier of space between them. "I'm guessing this was what they were looking for tonight, so I suppose I did you a favor."

Those eyes darted back, blinking a staccato beat. Her lips

gaping as if to grapple for a response.

"You can thank me with gifts and compliments." He winked.

That seemed to help her get her sass back. "Thank you?" She snorted. "*Thank* you? Do you have any idea how important that is?" Striking like a cobra, she plucked it from his hand.

"If it was that important," he reached across her and took it right back, "why did you take it from the lab?"

If looks could kill …

Her eyes ignited like molten lava, teeth bared, and every muscle beneath that fluffy robe was ready to unleash the pit bull.

"Be careful with that, you Neanderthal!" She lunged at him, but he jerked his arm away. She was practically in his lap, so close the sparks in her eyes leapt out and scorched him.

"Candice …" He warned with his tone. The vial clenched in his fist.

Her rapid breaths warmed his skin. He watched like he was on death row of dehydration as her tongue snatched out to wet her lips. "This has something to do with Vivaldi. Tell me what's in the container, and we'll figure this out."

In a more controlled act of desperation, she leaned across him and covered his fist with her hand.

She just couldn't trust. Couldn't let go. She had to possess at least some of the power, or in her mind she'd failed.

If this was how she wanted to have this conversation, fine, he'd survive it.

And he did, barely. She explained about the scrap, the broken microscope, her careless and creepy coworker.

All tied up with the break-in meant this scrap of tissue could be a game-changer. It also meant Jensen could be right. Vivaldi might have a man on the inside. Or worse, Vivaldi might be the one working behind the badge.

It would explain why they'd never made any headway.

Why evidence and records would mysteriously go missing when they needed them.

Whether Candice liked it or not, it meant she and Sal would now be working together. He had orders from Director Jensen to do whatever was necessary to sniff out the mole. If this evidence was what they hoped, then his covert assignment would be a whole lot easier.

But it also meant he had another assignment he couldn't ignore.

And Sal had a feeling protecting Candice, and the sample, was going to be more trouble, and way more fun, than he'd bargained for.

Chapter 10

Candice Stevens

She couldn't say why she'd done it.

The past twenty-four hours were riddled with stupid and impulsive mistakes. Exhibit A: Taking the evidence without permission. But even that was taking a back seat to what she was doing right now. Exhibit B: Sitting on a man she couldn't stand.

In her bathrobe.

Why had she put herself in this position? And why, on God's green earth, was she still in it?

When Dorian came down with the evidence vial—and his shirt—he'd set up shop a fair distance away on the couch. A comfortable distance she'd appreciated.

And then aliens invaded her body and the belligerent tug-of-war over the tissue sample had somehow obliterated her sense of modesty.

So here she sat, her *tookus* on what must be his good knee. Her own knees digging into the couch on each side of his thigh. Her left hand clawing his right on the armrest.

How could a position feel nonthreatening and compromising at the same time? And what were her options?

As this exercise had proven so far, she couldn't very well finagle the thing from his grip.

But she also couldn't back down now. Even if her comfort was fraying like the threads on her ancient bathrobe. He'd have to pry her cold, dead fingers off the sample before she'd let him have it.

And yet, stranger still than the position she'd unwittingly put herself in, was the way they managed to have an entire conversation while playing this odd game of Twister.

"So, those are my terms. Take 'em or leave 'em."

Okay, so admittedly not the best way to converse, since she'd missed everything in the conversation for the past ...

Shoot, she didn't even know how long!

The speed-junkie drumming in her ears drowned out his words. Her breathing had gone fast and shallow. Her head felt kind of fuzzy, like her senses were all firing at once.

Had Dorian noticed? Did he think it was about him?

Oh, *swell*. That'd be a surefire way to discourage his little crush. She closed her eyes to keep them from rolling.

The long, crazy day was something she just wanted to put behind her. Maybe her body was trying to tell her it agreed. Time to power down.

"Brat ..." His voice pitched dangerously low and was ever so faintly seasoned with a spicy accent. He hadn't leaned in, hadn't touched her, but it felt as if that one potent word buzzed against her ear.

Was she closer than she'd been a few moments ago?

She gulped down a dry taste of air, one tinted with that warm spell of cedar and vanilla. Brutish, yet refined. Sweet, but undeniably masculine. Her stomach rebelled with little squirms. When had she last eaten?

"I'm sorry, what were those terms again?" Her eyes scoured for a safe place to land in a field of mines.

Eyes. Nope.

Mouth. Nyet.

Chest. Definitely no.

One side of his mouth edged into a slow grin. Funny, up close it didn't look so goofy. It looked almost—

"Distracted?" Again with the twinge of accent like Don Juan.

When a dark slash of eyebrow rose, her tummy rumbled.

She forced away the absurdity of her thoughts along with her reckless, wandering eyes. Hunger and post-traumatic stress were to blame. Perhaps she could pin the whole day's collection of stupidity on them. Especially the whole leg-straddling thing.

"I, ah ..." Before she could form the words, Dorian's left hand wrapped around her hip and dragged her toward him.

Brain function scrambled. A shriek trapped in her throat. Fire lit through her veins. Panic threatened to strangle her until ... he stopped? Just as quickly as his hand pressed against her back it was gone.

He'd only eased her forward an inch. If that.

Shifting his leg, his face scrunched as if pained. "Sorry, you're not heavy or anything, I'm just not quite back to full strength."

Not heavy? Well, perhaps not by normal standards. But for her, yes, she was quite heavy.

But why was that important? What she'd rather examine was even less fun than discussing your weight in front of a man.

The misinterpretation of his touch had frightened her, but her physical reaction had been complete compliance.

Perhaps you haven't come as far as you thought, her inner Jersey-girl taunted.

Put a cork in it, Jersey.

Candice tried to find her bearings in the conversation. Dorian was being uncommonly respectful, especially since she'd lunged across his lap—

Oh! His knee! Here she was terrorizing his injured knee out of sheer stubbornness, and he was worried about offending her.

She shrieked. Shrieked and vaulted off his leg rather tactlessly before scrambling to her feet. "Good gravy, Dorian, your knee! Why didn't you say something? That must have been torture."

"I'd hardly call it torture." He grinned again, and with the space between them, it was back in all its former moronic glory.

Without the contact she felt her breathing even. Her heart slowed and shuttered back in its rightful place.

"My terms, *Kitten*, were that I oversee your work dealing with the evidence."

"But—"

He held up his hand, the one with a firm grip on the bargaining chip. One no longer even remotely in her possession. "That way we can protect the sample until we confirm what it is and get it off for DNA testing. I think we can agree this is too important to take any risks. And tonight proves the sample might not be the only thing in need of protection."

"You can't be serious."

He stood. His height and miraculously well-hidden strength made a solid case for his argument. "Or I could always take this to the FBI." Something flashed in his eyes.

She wished she could say for certain it was a bluff. But those eyes, while kind of clueless and puppy-doggish, were also deeply dark and mysterious. They seemed endless, and she found herself funneling down into their beguiling depths.

Based on the burn marks she'd seen on his arms, she was guessing those eyes held enough secrets to gag an elephant.

"Okay." The word stuck like peanut butter in her throat, but she forged on. "Fine. You can tag along. But how are we going to explain your presence? You're not active."

He took a step forward. She wrinkled her nose, hating how much she liked the instant hit of his warm, silky fragrance and pretended she didn't.

So what, he smelled good. Big whoop.

"I'm consulting."

"In what capacity?"

He grinned again, and her empty belly signaled another moan of neglect.

"Don't you worry your pretty little head about it. We have

another reason to spend time together."

"We do?"

He reached out. The rough pad of his thumb sending a single blazing stroke over her cheek. "Of course we do. We're dating."

"We, ah … are *not*."

"Keep telling yourself that, sweetheart." With one well-perfected wink, he strode past her to the kitchen. She considered following, challenging the issue that was so blatantly absurd. Dating! Pfft! She didn't date.

But first off, he'd likely said it to get a rise out of her. And second, she really didn't want to get close enough to smell him again.

It was a strange, disillusioning scent. Almost parasitic in the way it seemed to burrow into her skin and wiggle around under there.

Only a minute or two later he walked out of the kitchen with a steaming plate of spaghetti, a crust of French bread, and a tall glass of water.

Her taste buds jolted awake. Dorian's earthy smell now overrun with something robust and spicy. He set the plate and glass on the scarred wooden coffee table.

"I'll go put some fresh sheets on my bed and you can sleep up there. I'll take the couch."

Sleep. In Dorian's bed? No way.

"I'll be sleeping on the couch, Dorian. Non-negotiable."

His jaw tensed. Did he think she might try to sneak out? Not without the evidence.

She crossed her arms, curled her chewed nails into the excessive terrycloth buffer, and held her ground.

With a sigh he went to the hall closet, pulled out an extra pillow and a blanket, and set them on the far end of the couch.

"You can come with me to the morgue in the morning." Shifting on her feet, she glanced down at her red toenails and then back up, squashing down the strange intimate quandary of being in Dorian's house with bare feet. And pajamas.

She hoped the offer was enough to assure him she'd comply. She had no reason not to, other than not wanting his obnoxious grin and tantalizing smell following her around all day. But it was just for one day. She could handle a kid like Dorian Salivas.

He nodded without a hint of that perpetual smile he loved so much. "Goodnight, Brat."

"Goodnight, Dorian." It hardly seemed adequate for all he'd done. Yes, he'd picked her pocket. But as it turned out, he probably saved the evidence. Kept the hope of catching Vivaldi alive. Saved her job and possibly her life. Twice. And all in one day.

She looked up, and he was already to the stairs. There was a stiffness in his gait, one she could tell he was taking great pains to conceal. "And Dorian ..."

He paused, his hand on the baluster, his back to her.

"Thank you. For everything."

The bang on the door came harder this time. Though the first seemed hard enough to shake it loose from its hinges.

Peering out the side-light, Candice saw her mother's *"Texan"* standing in the fading daylight.

"Torrie. Torrie, open up, I've only got an hour until I've gotta report back." The man yelled his plea. She knew what he wanted. "Victoria!" The violent determination in his voice made her shiver.

She was only twelve years old, but she wasn't stupid like her mama thought. Her teachers at school said she was really smart. That didn't mean squat in this household.

"Run and get your mama some diet cherry cola, would you Candi? Mama needs a few minutes to talk to her friend about a big audition for the opera."

It was always some variation of the same deal. Her

mother was one break away from being a big star, and every sleazebag that pounded the door was going to take her to the top. But even when Candi returned with the random item her mother came up with, it was always ignored and forgotten. Kind of like her.

After the first dozen or so times she finally wised up, stopped wasting the few dollars her daddy slipped her for allowance, and just made herself scarce. More recently she'd started sneaking over to her next-door neighbor Rosemary's house, where the tough old bird would harp on and on to Candi about all her life's grievances before she broke down and gave up another piano lesson.

Music helped mute out reality for an hour.

Before she'd started mooching off of Rosemary she'd heard some noises from Mama's room that could haunt a young girl 'til she turned gray.

And since she'd rather not hear or—worse—witness what went on in there, she opted to deal with the cantankerous old woman with magic, musical fingers.

But today, her mama was passed out upstairs on her bed. She'd worked late last night at what her mother always referred to as "The Restaurant." Though enough people at school had informed her the establishment in question didn't serve up anything but booze and live entertainment.

Another thing she made a conscious effort not to think about.

Candi peered through the opaque glass at the man in a spiffy-looking suit. Something about him screamed "cop" even though he wasn't in uniform. That was something you learned to sense young in these parts. He tightened his hand into a fist, twisted his wrist as if pulling on the reins of his patience. The simple tick made her tummy quiver.

She couldn't see his face in the shadow. Was sure if she locked eyes with one of her mother's "grand opportunities" she'd never be able to keep the deception from slipping past her own eyes to break her father's heart.

Oh, sure. He knew about Mama's men. He just didn't know Candi knew.

He and her mother weren't even married, so her mama didn't see much reason to hide her extracurricular activities, especially with her latest recurrent fling.

Candi's parents were roommates who despised each other, bound by a shared mistake, as her mother called her. Her father wanted to protect his daughter from the circumstances of her birth and the subsequent struggles of her childhood with an unfit, uncaring mother. But work kept him away far too many hours for him to protect her from her harsh reality that couldn't be brighter than how similarly dim her future seemed.

One thing was for certain. She would never be like her mama.

Not only did she not look a thing like her beautiful blonde-haired, blue-eyed Russian and Swedish mother, but she couldn't carry a tune in a bucket.

The banging stopped, severed by the sound of a pager. The man muttered a curse, mumbling something else about a crime scene until the clicking of his shoes on their sidewalk faded to silence.

Yep. Just as she'd suspected. Fuzz.

Candi wandered back into the kitchen only to stare at the bare cupboards. The musky scent of mildew scavenged any semblance of an appetite anyways. She vented open the window over the sink to clear the odor and breathed in a lungful of industrial grit and sea-salted air. The bridge workers were sandblasting today, as they were most days, but it didn't bother her none.

The heaviness in her chest eased. Now that the man was gone, she could stay here, in the rare quiet solitude of the decrepit space they called home. Tiny, cramped homes only a stone's throw from the shipyard where her father worked.

"Was someone here?" Her mother stumbled into the kitchen. Even bedraggled and hung-over she was stunning.

"Uh ..."

The effects of the previous night vanished. Her eyes cold and accusing and much too acute given the stench of alcohol clinging to her. "Did I stutter?"

"No, Mama. I—I mean, yes. Someone was here. He left."

"And you didn't let him in? Didn't think to wake me?" She crossed the room before Candi could form an excuse. Her mother's fingernails sunk into her arm. She jerked Candi close until the fumes of smoke and liquor made her eyes burn. "What's wrong with you?"

She tried to say that the man seemed angry and had frightened her. That the tone of his voice made her all prickly and nervous. Sort of like when the thuds of music signaled a late night cruise of the Gardallo boys down her street. But the slap came first. Stinging her cheek and ringing in her ear.

What was the use? Her mother didn't care about anyone but herself.

And this, sadly, was Candi's life. For now.

But maybe someday she could escape this God-forsaken place. She'd get a good job and never have to rely on anyone else to feed her or protect her or even pretend to care.

Because, let's face it, no one had ever been good at any of that.

A chill crept over her toes and cuffed around her ankles when she tugged up on the blanket and burrowed deeper into the softness. She drew in a deep, woodsy breath of smooth vanilla spice. In the quiet trance of morning her heart gave a little sigh. *Mmm.* Cozy.

Except for her toes. Those were cold.

The dream had been a rather unpleasant trip down memory lane. Was there any other kind? But in the here and now, wherever and whenever this dreamy haze of contentment was—pouring some sweet and savory concoction through her lungs—well, *this* was a bright spot on a dull canvas. Sleep had never been this good. But then again ...

Candice jolted upright. The insistent dawn lit the room with a none-too-subtle cheerfulness now at odds with her renewed disposition. The room she was in was not her own. And as the previous night rolled back through her brain she realized where she was, and, more specifically, *whose* smell she'd just been indulging.

Her feet peeked out from the plaid comforter strewn over her legs. Just beyond them was a stone fireplace rising to an oak-beamed ceiling. Each side of the stone column housed built-in book cases, sparsely filled with books and an anemic fake fern.

She hadn't taken the time to inspect Dorian's home last night after the break-in, but it was actually nice. Mature.

Surprising.

Warm beige walls, hunter green micro-fiber couches, and a metal-studded brown leather chair and ottoman. Swinging her legs over the edge of the deep sofa, she scooted forward until her feet touched down on an ultra-soft, Navajo-inspired rug over oak floors.

Nothing about the room provided any sort of revelation about the homeowner. No pictures on the mantle. No telling knick-knacks of any kind. Nothing except an oil painting of a hillside with swaying grasses and muted fall-hued trees surrendering to the pull of winter. It seemed more like a window to a different season. Almost as if an invisible wind breathed life onto the canvas, making the actual windows exposing barren branches seem more like an illusion than the art.

Candice tugged her robe tighter to confirm she was still covered and tiptoed over to take a closer look. She knew next to nothing about art, but the brush strokes seemed almost careless and unintentional, and yet when they all melded together it was so precise and breathtaking she couldn't make an ounce of sense out of what it made her feel.

It was a reality she wanted to immerse herself in. She wanted to step through the canvas, feel the melodious wind on her face, weave her fingers through the tall velvet grass. Be at peace. Far away from complications and dead bodies, past and present.

Someone cleared their throat, and Candice about leapt out of her robe. She clutched the lapels at her chin and turned, awaiting that dorky grin.

She got one. Just not the one she was expecting.

"Hi there." The boy was smiling at her. So much in his smile reminded her of SEÑOR Smells Too Good, but little else did.

He looked up from his wheelchair, a little bony but not at all weak. There was a teasing light in his toffee-brown eyes and a wry little twist at the corner of his lips. "I wasn't aware we had a visitor." There it was again. A new wattage of mischief in his grin that was a dead ringer for Dorian's.

"I'm sorry. I'm your new neighbor." Which still didn't explain why she was standing in his living room in her Michelin-Man robe at like seven a.m. "There was a ... ahh, break-in at my place last night. So, I umm ... crashed on your couch."

Pinching his lips together, he concealed another smile. One stating he knew something she didn't. She crossed one foot over the other, attempting to conceal at least one set of her naked toes.

What must this kid be thinking?

"You must be my brother's friend from work." His words

didn't match the conspiratorial twinkle in his eyes, but at least he hadn't called her Dorian's girlfriend.

She hadn't known he had a brother. She didn't know much about him at all, as this little exercise was proving.

She nodded rather than explain further. The case was confidential, so what could she really say?

Instead of providing an introduction he just nodded toward the wall. "You like the painting?"

Candice exhaled the ballooning pressure crowding in her chest, grateful for a distraction. Why was she so flustered anyways? Nothing happened. Yes, she was in her robe, but she'd slept on the couch.

Did Dorian make a habit of bringing women back to his house with his younger brother present? Did Junior here just seem so at ease because he was used to this sort of thing?

"Yes. It's … it's …" Biting her thumbnail, she studied the painting again, losing herself in the sweep and sway of the grass, the faint glimmers of sunshine dappling through the molting trees. "It makes me feel so much, but I can't figure out why."

The boy rolled his chair so he was next to her, examining the art from a few feet away as if in a museum. "It is sort of unconventionally beautiful, isn't it?"

"It is." She whispered reverently.

"The artist named it *Nowhere's Home*. Sometimes I think it's melancholy, but other times it just makes me feel free, you know? Like being there would make everything better."

"That's a good way to describe it." Tearing her gaze away from the riveting display of beauty and loneliness, she smiled down at the adorable teenage art critic. "So what's your name, Artie?"

Stretching out his hand, he issued another one of his big brother's grins. "Gabe."

"Candice." She returned his shake.

"Our casa, su casa." He wagged his eyebrows.

How old was this little Casanova anyways?

"Come on, sis. Let's go see what he's whipping us up for breakfast."

Chapter 11

Dorian Salivas

"Hey bro, whatcha got cookin'?" Gabe wheeled around the corner, stopped near the island, and plucked up a spear of red pepper. The grin on his face said he hadn't missed the sleeping beauty on the couch.

Was she up yet? Should he wake her? Wasn't that like, too ... something?

Too confusing is what it was.

Yeah, okay. So she had him a bit off-kilter. Last night was ... interesting.

For Pete's sake, his vocabulary was dwindling by the second! If the thoughts in his head were this scattered, what would happen when she actually waltzed into his kitchen. In her abominable bathrobe.

As if summoned on a prayer, she rounded the corner, unreasonably appealing in all that terrycloth, with hair teased in defiant little clumps, and fresh, dew-kissed skin straight from a Neutrogena commercial.

One slight blip in his brain had him visualizing what lie beneath all that fluff. Had him imagining a different morning scenario where he'd peel away the wrapping and greet her properly.

Not going there.

He turned back to the eggs, adding some spice and working the whisk. "Morning, Brat. You sleep all right?"

"Fine, thank you."

She was moving around behind him, at home in his kitchen. It was tempting to want to witness that, but he kept his attention to task until he went to grab the peppers, tomatoes, and onions he'd just chopped, finding both his brother and Candice predictably scavenging his ingredients.

"Hey, hey!" Swatting at both of their hands, he scooped up the veggies and tossed them into the skillet. "Patience, you vultures. Breakfast in three minutes. Gabe, why don't you get the OJ from the fridge. Brat, there's fresh coffee in the pot. Help yourself."

Sal finished preparing the Mexican-style sausage, egg, and cheese burritos, slid them onto the plates, and carried all three to the table.

He knew Candice was a big eater, so he made her a four-egg burrito the same size as his and Gabe's. Amazing how the woman stayed so small. He remembered at Archer and Sadie's rehearsal dinner she ate three-quarters of a double-decker JJ Twigs pizza. Like six slices of Titanic-sinkable pizza. Unbelievable. And totally hot.

"Wow, Dorian, this looks really good." She eyed the boat-sized burrito and smiled, looking like King Kong ready to pillage a banana stand. "But you didn't have to make a special breakfast for me."

Gabe was already halfway through his enormous burrito and spoke with a mouthful of eggs. "He didn't. My bro's an artist in the kitchen. Why else would I be up this early?"

Sal glared at his brother and issued a warning that earned him a stuffed-cheeked grin from the little terror.

He turned back to Candice just in time to see her first bite. Her eyes slipped closed, and—

Did she just moan?

Ay caramba! He needed out of this kitchen.

"Criminy, this is so good it should come with a warning."

She and Gabe continued to attack like wild dogs, and yet, under heavy hypnosis he couldn't tear his eyes off of her mouth to focus on his own meal.

"Should I leave you and the burrito alone, Kitten?" Sarcasm. An easy distraction.

She set the last little bit down, licked her finger, and grinned, bold and beautiful. "If you want."

Yep. If she stayed in his house for another ninety seconds he'd be full-blown certifiable.

"So he really cooks like this every day?" She asked Gabe.

"Umm hmm." He downed his last bite and started his post-meal stretch. "I have to fend for myself for lunch, but breakfast and dinner never disappoint. It's probably because we nearly starved growing up—"

"Gabe!"

"He gave me at least half of what little he got since I was old enough to gum solids. We make up for it now with hearty appetites and no shortage of—"

"Gabe, enough!" Sal's blood was boiling, burning hot spots in his cheeks. Nothing like airing out your dirty laundry over breakfast.

Candice had paled. Maybe only slightly, but Sal noticed. "Well, umm …"

He'd suspected she'd also gone hungry a time or two. Something about the way she ate seemed like an act of desperation.

She cleared her throat. A teasing gleam lit new fire behind eyes only moments before had been dim with dark memories

"*Mmm*. Neighbors sometimes cook for each other, right?" She popped the last bite into her pretty little mouth, chewing with her eyes closed in pleasure before dabbing the corners of her grinning lips with a napkin "Yep. I think this is going to work out just fine."

"Sweet Mama Jama, we're in business."

"You're just full of those, aren't you?"

Her eyes were still glued to the microscope, her odd little

sayings almost as adorable as she was.

She often wore scrubs in the morgue because of the messy work to be done. But every other time he'd seen her, whether at a crime scene, or leaving work, or just out socially with Sadie and Archer, she was impeccably dressed to the nines. And that wasn't even the right way to say it, because in Sal's mind, she was a perfect ten.

Some improbably perfect combination of imperfections. Cute and sexy in the most non-sensical way. A tiny turned-up nose, passionately expressive, perhaps slightly under-stuffed lips that unveiled her wit and under-riding emotions. She was ultra-short and curvy, with a mixed heritage he hadn't quite pinned down.

And then there was her hair. His chest rose and fell with a silent sigh. Like a siren song, her minky midnight-brown-and-golden-threaded hair tumbled around her shoulders, sometimes straight, sometimes wavy, but always begging his hands to run through.

Today it was in a ponytail. Also apropos of the girl-next-door look was that clean, glowing face with just the touch of mascara and some peachy-looking lip gloss. Seemingly approachable and yet painfully untouchable.

It was clear she'd missed his barb since she hadn't retaliated. No matter. He was too busy cataloguing all the intricate facets of her hotness.

She stood away from the microscope, child-like excitement sparkling in her eyes. "Oh, Dorian! I know I should be furious about the whole pickpocket thing, but I'm so happy I could kiss you right now!"

"Well I'm sure as heck not gonna stop ya." He winked to soften the blow because in another three seconds she was going to realize what she'd said and turn a blistering shade of red.

Right on cue.

"Get your head out of the gutter. That's not what I meant." Folding her arms was a clear movement of defense.

"Hey," he raised his hands in surrender. "You're the one who brought up kissing. I merely consented. And since when did kissing become gutter talk? I, for one, am quite certain I could contentedly kiss you all day without being relegated to *Gutterville*. Care to test the theory?"

She propped her hands on her hips, a surge of indignation bulging the vein in her neck. "Let me use small, easy words so you'll be sure to understand me."

Here we go.

"There will be no more kissing." So smug. So sure of herself.

So amusingly wrong.

"Are you referring to yesterday at your house? Please. That wasn't even a teaser."

Smug be gone, her narrowed eyes lit with unadulterated annoyance.

Touchy much?

He chuckled to ease the tension, and then nodded toward the scope. "What've we got?"

"Sebaceous glands. Have a look." She skirted back to accommodate ten people between them.

He moved into place, bent to see for himself, and pulled away. "Looks like a blob of nothin' to me. I guess I'll take your word for it."

"That would be wise."

He gave her the lazy grin she'd earned. "So now we just send this off for DNA, and bada bing, bada boom, we catch a killer."

She huffed her impatience. "It's not exactly that simple."

Of course it wasn't. This was the first shred of evidence they'd managed to hold onto in a Vivaldi killing for more than twenty-four hours. And the *only* DNA ever recovered. Plus, it was so slight there'd be no room for error. He'd make sure they'd send it unmarked to a different, private lab for testing. They'd have to do this under the table. Otherwise, he was sure they'd be facing another mysterious disappearance and yet another dead end.

The case Director Jensen made for an inside job seemed all the more plausible. Guess he'd need to go buddy up to Voodoo Veer sometime today.

"Ehh, you dames like to complicate everything." Which was true. "You just stick with your microscope. I'll handle the rest."

Ah, yes. Retaliation was fun.

"You know, Dorian, you are the most puzzling amalgam of cluelessness and arrogance. Trying to keep track is leaving me quite literally dizzy." She returned to the sample, set it back in its protective case, and then into an evidence baggie.

"Don't be too hard on yourself. I tend to have that effect on women." He extracted the bag from her hand before she could protest.

"What, nausea?" Arms crossed again. Another riot of frustration pounding noticeably in her neck, then inching up to the victory veins in her forehead reserved for Dorian alone.

"Denial." He tapped the tip of her nose. "That's cute, Brat."

She rolled her eyes and swiped the reminder of his touch from her cute little sniffer. Neither of which should have been encouraging. Then again, he wasn't sure he could misinterpret the grin flirting with her lips as she turned and stomped off.

He had to slip away if he was going to do some undercover "consulting" for Jensen. Didn't mean he was excited about leaving Candice alone at the morgue. Though she said she had an intern coming in for a few hours this afternoon.

Even less exciting was the way he would be spending the next few hours. With Garrett Veer.

It's not like much could rile an FBI agent. The profession demanded blending with some of the most treacherous human beings on the planet. And in St. Louis there was a dense population of them. Besides, with his unsavory upbringing, Sal had long ago built up a tolerance to scum. But nowadays, the creeps were usually on the other side of the interrogation table.

Having the perp on the same side of the badge and yet the opposite side of the law made Sal squeamish. Perhaps because he'd been the one playing people his whole life, and that made it feel like he had too much in common with a serial killer.

After being re-processed by Mary in HR and then rewarded with an unofficial clip-on badge of lameness announcing his "consultant" status, Sal strode through the doors of his department, shot back a burnt and bitter cup of sludge from the break room, and allotted a few minutes to yuck it up with the other agents under the pretense of normalcy.

He then ventured down to the second floor where the analysts' offices were located along with the strange specimen of Garrett Veer—one of their most skilled assets for cracking encryptions, tracking a tangled trace, and breaking through codes and firewalls. At least, he was until this Chrissick guy showed up.

Sal knocked on the office door and poked his head in. "What's up, Veer? Got a sec?"

Dark, shifty eyes tracked the intrusion. The guy's pupils were so dilated it looked like he was constantly tripping on acid. His behavior pretty much confirmed it, but somehow he'd never been called on the mat.

"Salivas." His lips barely moved when he hissed Sal's name.

Sal folded into the chair in front of the desk and lopped his ankle over his knee.

"There some reason you're here?"

The fluorescent light gleaned blue over Veer's reflective black hair and folded over the harsh points of his face stretched with pasty, vampirey skin.

"Naw, I just thought we could shoot the—"

Man, his eyes were so evil they could snatch your breath. Kind of like Santino Salivas.

Sal coughed. "Well, right, yes, I wanted to see what you've uncovered from those call logs from Stephanie Mueller's phone. Couldn't find the file and trying to play catch-up."

Of course, said evidence had gone missing two months ago, swiped from the system without a trace. But Sal had been recovering so he wouldn't necessarily have been privy to that information.

Veer's eyes never wavered. Shoot, he didn't even blink as far as Sal could tell.

Could Garrett Veer be a serial killer?

Well, it sure wouldn't surprise him.

"*Forty's* information vanished before I even touched it."

His eyes seemed to say "*But then again, you already knew that.*" He spared Sal the words. And Veer referring to a victim by number instead of name made him all the more sinister.

Sal dug a little deeper, needing to test Garrett's responses. "So you have no information on Vivaldi? You haven't touched anything on this case?"

"Not a thing." The name didn't evoke any reaction, voluntary or involuntary, as far as Sal could tell. Veer was as cool as a cucumber. So that meant he was either innocent or he was a sociopath. Difficult to say.

"Anything surface from the hard drive from the Landsdowne computer?" Different case. Same reaction.

"Nope." Perfect indifference. Not even a twinge of heartbeat in his throat. Maybe Veer really *was* a vampire.

Sal's lip almost twitched, but then he saw a few books on witchcraft, eckankar, and voodoo resting proudly on the bookshelf behind *Dracula's* head. Ick. If he spotted a little cloth doll with pins in it he was so outta here.

"Bummer. Well, I'd better get back to it." Sal stood and took three paces to Veer's door before turning back. "Oh, and hey, sorry about your girlfriend. A few of the guys and I might run out for a drink after work if you wanna come blow off some steam."

Please say no.

Garrett's face blanched to a ghastly shade nearly as blue as the gleam from his raven hair. The trigger in his jaw set, restraining his embarrassment or his venom. Sal prayed for neither, silently chiding himself for not lining his pockets with garlic.

"How did you know about that?"

Unusual darkening around his eyes—a subtle hint at sleep deprivation. The slight sag in the elasticity of his skin and the indentations at his fingertips meant he was a bit dehydrated. Like he wasn't taking care of himself.

There was also a certain sadness behind his eyes.

Something more profound than the *I'm-so-complex-and-misunderstood* doom and gloom storm cloud he carried around with him. To Sal, that meant heartache. It'd been a difficult cold read, a definite gamble, but a helluva good one.

Sal shrugged. "I can sense things."

Okay, that sounded a little creepy, even to Sal. It was true, but he knew Veer would interpret it differently. Sal didn't conjure any spirits, nor did he believe in telepathy. There was no such thing as psychics. Though he'd been called one more than once.

Then again, if Veer thought they had something in common, maybe it would help soften him up and make it easier to uncover the truth.

"I see. I always did sense something spiritual in you. You're *connected* to the other side. It's a gift."

The other side?

The words themselves were banal, but coming from the

source, they slithered around Sal like a sick little spell, making him want to retch up the few bites of breakfast he'd managed to cram down as they were now suddenly laced with Voodoo Veer's poisonous air.

"Yeaaahhh, well, uh … let me know if you ever want to get that drink. Though maybe you should start with some water. You're looking a little peaked, pal. *Adios*."

And on that note, he closed Veer's door firmly behind him, thinking perhaps it might contain the evil spirits flying around in there.

Sal didn't bother suppressing the shudder coursing through him. Yes, he was perceptive by nature, and sure, he'd caught on to those almost non-existent nuances in Veer's behavior. But something was off.

Either Veer was Vivaldi, or whatever spiritual mojo he was brewing in there called Sal's own lackluster faith to the front lines to suit up for battle.

The problem was, his armor had been decimated blow by blow for the first fifteen years of his life. And now, nothing but the gun at his hip remained.

Chapter 12

Candice Stevens

Conducting an autopsy with a shadow was tedious. And time-consuming.

As of late the shadow had been Blaine while he grew accustomed to his relocation from the county office. For the most part the lazy oaf stayed out of her way and merely observed in silence. But this chick? Laura something? Candice had forgotten already but, *oy!* She'd rubbed Candice's last nerve so raw she was numb.

"Eww, I mean, I didn't think there'd be so much blood. Is there always this much blood? Seems to me my last cadaver in med school didn't have *this* much. Though, I guess he'd been dead longer, huh? You know, packed on ice and all. I suppose that would make a difference. Though since it's cold outside, and fairly cool in here, I don't know if there'd be *that* much of a difference. Unless some people hold more blood, or maybe less blood was spilled depending on the crime. Man, that's cool. You know, like trying to catch a killer? I feel like a crime fighter already. I can't wait to tell …"

Blah, blah, blah.

While the intern blathered on about Lord knows what, Candice continued the autopsy for the forty-six-year-old construction worker who'd fallen from an overpass. Though cause of death seemed to have resulted from the fall, she discovered the reason he'd fallen had been a stroke. And since the deceased man's hysterical wife was threatening to sue a volatile coworker she was sure had pushed her husband over the edge, this information would be immensely helpful.

She blinked away the fatigue, straining to focus on the details of her report. The incessant high-pitched ramblings of the intern became white noise. Candice had already fielded nearly a zillion questions in the first three hours with this lunatic, so she decided whatever the girl was saying now didn't require a pressing answer.

"I think that's about all for the day." It was only four o'clock, but the tug of sleep was dire. She needed food, some really strong coffee, and then maybe an hour's worth of therapy with her punching bag before she retired early.

"Really?" The tall, rather buxom redhead stuck out her over-penciled bottom lip in a slight pout. "But I still have some more questions. And I wanted to maybe see those bones from that dead girl on the news."

"Listen, Laura—"

"Oh," she laughed. "It's Maura. With an M." Her lips smacked in illustration. She had really strange green eyes. Like grass green, though Candice was almost positive she wore colored contacts.

"Right, yes. Sorry about that. But I need to take a break and the serial case is sensitive. I'm not comfortable using it as a teaching exercise."

True. But she was also too preoccupied with the recently departed DNA sample to be handling critical evidence with an outsider present.

She was relieved she wasn't responsible for it at the moment. But at the same time, she hated relying on someone she didn't know or trust with something so significant. Neurotic with worry, dozens of worst-case scenarios tortured her tireless brain.

"*Another* break?"

The woman was truly ignorant of how exhausting she was. After being assaulted with questions for two hours,

Candice had called a bathroom break. Maura had wanted to stay behind, and from the look in her eyes, maybe snoop around the morgue. A normal compulsion for most newbies. Morbid fascination and whatnot.

Well, that didn't fly. Candice had shown Maura to the break room and locked up for those few precious moments of silence.

"No, not a break, Maura. We're done for the day. I'll sign off on your hours, whatever you need." Candice started her ritual cleanup routine, watching the dejected eager-beaver toss her smock in the bin by the door.

Jersey cheered, but Candice felt a pinch of her manners return. "Err, uh, good … questions today. Are you on the schedule to come back in soon?"

Please, Jesus, have mercy on me.

She shrugged. "Not sure what my rotation is. Thanks for being so patient with me. I know I talk a lot, but I'm just a curious person."

Well, bugger. Now Candice was sinking deep in her miry shame. She wasn't impatient by nature. She could appreciate tenacity and a desire to be the best—those were the same traits that had driven her out of the slums to rewrite her destiny.

She'd been where Maura was now. And people sure hadn't taken her seriously at first glance either. She was thirty-two, but she could still pass for eighteen. Well, perhaps not now that she'd forced on some pounds, most of which were clinging to more womanly places.

Aside from the talking, what was it about Maura that sat as heavy as a Crave Case of White Castle belly bombers?

Her stomach gave a greedy gulp at the suggestion.

"Well, umm, if you have any more questions feel free to give me a call. Or shoot me an email. That's usually easier." And shorter. "And once we get through some of the grittier parts of the investigation, I'd be happy to show you the remains. There's a lot to learn. So …"

Oh, criminy. She needed to shut up before she invited this chatterbox over for girls' night.

Without warning, Maura crossed the room and pulled Candice into a tight hug.

Stunned, she stood frozen, elbows bent, arms out. She wasn't a hugger, and since she had blood on her gloves it was awkwardly one-sided.

Even more awkward, since Candice was at least eight inches shorter than the Amazonian redhead, was the smothering placement of the woman's abundant chest. Strange, they were a bit spongy, like she *stuffed* or something.

Someone needed to tell this poor girl they were more trouble than they were worth.

Candice wiggled until she was granted some space. And some air.

"That really means a lot to me. We'll be in touch." Maura grinned, strummed her fingers in a little wave and was history.

Well, every last store of peace for the day was now shot to crap. But it wasn't just Maura. And it wasn't just today. She was beginning to realize the peace she was looking for might be as elusive as Vivaldi himself.

By the time she left work it was five-thirty and already dark. Rounding the coroner's office building, she strode toward her silver Jetta glittering under the streetlights. An echo of soles clapped on the city street behind her.

That old prickly premonition whispered over her. The steps were close. Much too close for coincidence.

Aww, come on!

As much as the fear filled her veins with a powerful intoxication, she was also kind of ticked. Sliding the safety from her mace, she felt overrun with a reckless sort of curiosity. She could almost hear her inner Jersey-girl's empty challenge *"You wanna piece a me?"*

Swallowing a deep breath, and a false sense of courage, she spun around, held her weapon at the ready and—

Was greeted by the cutting night air and an empty paper cup getting kicked around by the breeze. She wanted to laugh at the overreaction, but the panic's ripple effect had her shuddering so hard the keys slipped from her fingers.

And since this scene played in just about every horror movie ever made, she raked the bundle from the ground and ran as hard and fast as she could to her car.

Her lungs burned from the short sprint. Cardio wasn't her thing, but it should be because she always seemed to be running.

When she was safely locked inside, she clamored for the right key, jabbed at the ignition, and tore from the lot. It wasn't until she was on the highway that the fear unwound its shackles and her breathing leveled out.

Frustration pounced on the moment's reprieve, and she slammed her hand against the steering wheel. "You're right, Jersey, nothing's changed."

Fear had been her existence from the time she'd hit puberty until she left New Jersey.

Left. That's always how she put it. But in truth, she'd barely escaped. And even now, sixteen years later, she wondered how much longer she'd be running until the past caught up with her.

Her appetite was a distant memory, but she'd yet to stock up on groceries at home and knew hunger could strike at any time so she drove through Steak 'n Shake for a large cookies-and-cream milkshake. Ice cream might not be nutritious, but it sure never made anything worse.

Her breaks squealed to a stop in her driveway a few minutes and half a milkshake later. Heavy from all the drama of the day, she trudged like a zombie to her back door where the note from the security company technician informed that the new system was installed and armed with the passcode she'd chosen by phone. They'd also changed the locks per her request so she reached inside the storm drain, retrieved the bag with the magnetic key, and let herself into her home.

Funny, even with all the gadgetry and the new locks, it still didn't feel safe. But Rome wasn't built in a day. This was only day two.

Unloading her purse on the counter, shedding her winter coat, and sliding from her blood-red tennis shoes, she waddled into her living room and surveyed the anarchy.

"What a mess."

Everything lay scattered before her like a random, mountainous to-do list.

Just then, she remembered she had plans. And because she didn't want to deal with any more garbage at the moment, she knew she had the perfect distraction.

Chapter 13

Dorian Salivas

He'd worn a suit and tie every day for the past year aside from this current leave and a few weeks of undercover ops necessitating street clothes. Sal looked in the mirror, finished the single Windsor knot of his plain black tie, and then shrugged into his suit coat.

Each of his everyday suits were well tailored, but there was no denying these Calvin Klein duds were his best. A charcoal gray with a slight sheen. Ultra-trim with straight lines. His power suit. And right now, with the riot of butterflies ransacking his insides, he needed every ounce of power he could find.

Smoothing his hand down his tie, he exhaled the last of his nerves and slipped behind a cocky grin. "Showtime."

Gabe was closed up in his studio and saved Sal any further awkward questions about the ballet. Thinking himself the biggest idiot on the planet—and hey, at least he and Candice had that in common—he swept the bouquet off the counter.

Would she think they were corny? Likely.

Candice wasn't going to take him seriously, so in a way, he was setting himself up for embarrassment just by showing up. But when he walked past a window display after work, he saw the most unique bundle of paper flowers.

They were, themselves, a work of art. Folded origami petals of iridescent paper in every vibrant shade of purple, orange, and red created a mirage so real he could almost smell what they represented through the glass.

He might have kept walking by, but then he noticed at the heart of each bloom rested a foil-wrapped Godiva truffle in the same shade of each flower. And well, that sealed it.

It wasn't your average bouquet, but then, Candice wasn't your average girl.

The bitter wind nipped at his skin, but at least it helped to temper the nervous heat coloring his cheeks.

The day was going smoothly so far. The evidence was off to the secure lab. Sal had laid some groundwork on the reconnaissance mission at the bureau. Garrett Veer hadn't taken him up on his fake drink offer, so he hadn't needed to renege on that bluff. Bullet dodged.

And now, the icing on the cake, he just might be going to the ballet with the world's most beautiful woman.

Okay, so no man in his right mind gets all that jazzed about sitting through three hours of classical music and men in tights. But the second Candice mentioned the ballet, he saw a spark in her eyes. She'd obviously been teasing, but something in that look exposed a passion long dormant.

Was she planning on blowing off the date? He couldn't say. He'd mentioned it again at the morgue since last night's break-in had been plenty diverting. But she'd been so wrapped up in her little "sebaceous gland" excitement she'd barely spared him a glance.

Since he wasn't one to go back on his word, and he sure as heck wasn't about to miss out on the slight chance she might actually follow through, here he was, walking up the porch steps to Candice Stevens's door with two tickets to the ballet in his pocket and handcrafted chocolate flowers in hand.

Of course, at his back was his Glock. Not at all romantic, but a necessary hazard of his trade.

His cocky grin faltered.

It was a strange battle of illusions. The ultimate con

weighing confidence and insecurity, truth and perception. Except tonight there was no trick deck. He wanted this to be real. No scams and no pretending.

Deep breath, dude. What's the worst that could happen?

The echo of the doorbell drifted to him for the third time with no response. The lights were on, and Candice's Jetta sat in the driveway. Shadows shifted behind the sheets they'd tacked up over the windows last night.

She was definitely home, so why wasn't she answering the door? "Candice." He rapped his knuckles on the door until they stung. "Candice, it's Sa—it's Dorian."

Why the stubborn woman refused to use his nickname like everyone else was amusing. Clearly she thought the formality established a safe barrier between them.

A smirk edged against his lips. Epic backfire there. No one aside from his brother used his given name, setting Candice apart and turning each pass of his name on her lips into an unwitting connection.

After one final bang, intuition fired in his gut. His nerves stood on end like the scruff of a bloodhound catching a scent.

Leaning away from the porch he saw light bend behind the shade of the large front window. But not like the flicker of a television, more like the constant shift of bodies.

A struggle? The more he concentrated on the shadows the more they fine-tuned into violent choreography.

He stepped forward and pressed his ear against the door. Like a funnel of sound swelling from *Whoville*, he heard a crack of impact.

He whipped his gun from the concealed holster at his back, adjusted his stance, and eased the air out of his lungs.

This is gonna hurt.

In one powerful pounce he kicked in the door. The reverb fired through his good leg, flexing the scar running knee to ankle with shards of pain scattering like shrapnel through his nerve endings. His artificial joint about buckled, but there was no time to dwell on that.

The door crashed against the wooden banister. A spray of wooden flint peppering the entry foyer as he hurtled over the wreckage.

His pulse unloaded rounds faster than an AK-47. He heard the struggle again.

A grunt of pain.

The sickening thud of pounding fists.

For a single painful second he was a kid again, taking the brunt of his father's anger to shield his family. He blinked away the flashback, but his twisted mind produced an image even more painful.

Candice, bloodied and swollen, battling for her life. *Oh, God, please no.*

He couldn't remember running, or feeling much of anything from the waist down, though he was certain a world of pain awaited the impending crash of adrenaline. He didn't slow, though time seemed to pass like molasses through an hourglass.

The front was empty, but light speared through from the back room. Without pause, Sal bolted through the opening. "Freeze!"

Candice stumbled away from … a … a … *punching bag?* Her eyes enormous with alarm. Her boxing-gloved hands raised in surrender.

Sal couldn't breathe. Could hardly think to speak. His senses a virtual clog of adrenaline and panic, and none of the insanity was filtering down.

Her chest collapsed, and she used her gloves to pluck headphones from her ears. If it was possible, her eyes went even wider then, her irises drowning in the whites of her eyes.

She seemed to yell something at him, the vein bulging in her neck confirmed it though the sound was—

Oh.

His tunnel vision started to clear, his senses awakening to the realization that he'd set off the new security alarm. One so deafening, so painfully vicious, his ears almost refused to detect any sound at all.

Candice shoved past him, probably to go disarm the thing. Before he knew it he was standing behind where she'd halted in the foyer just short of the keypad, the tormenting siren still blaring. They'd likely start bleeding from the ears soon.

She stood stock still, sweat glittering on her skin like fairy dust as she stared at the battered remnant of her front door and entry foyer. Splinters of wood and broken glass had exploded to an astounding radius.

Sal finally came to enough to manage a conscious plan of action. He stuffed his gun back in his waistband and reached for Candice's hand, met instead with the cold leather of the dainty little boxing glove.

He wanted to smile at that, but then again, this was pretty much mortifying. You know, showing up to a date she'd obviously forgotten about—a date she didn't even want—only to destroy her house and be bludgeoned to deafness by sound.

Yep, here he stood, cementing his fate as the biggest idiot on the planet. Slowly dying to the sound of his embarrassment. And holding an artsy bouquet of flowers to boot.

Well, either way they needed to stop the alarm. He gently wrapped his hand around her wrist. She looked at him then, one second before he planned to lead her to the other entry door where they'd find another keypad—the one not obstructed by a warzone he'd personally created.

The look oozing from her honeyed eyes was one dazzling and talented display of anger and heartbreak and confusion. She didn't have to say anything, not that he'd be able to hear it if she did, her look packed enough punch. Just one more slight jab from her dainty gloved fist would end him.

He held her gaze a moment longer for punishment and then led her to the den with the spare door they'd snuck in through last night, waiting in prolonged agony while she removed a glove and punched in the code. The instant silence reigned, her phone started ringing and she was off to deal with the security company.

The rush of adrenaline fizzled until he was stripped bare of distraction and then clubbed mercilessly with raw, hot pain convulsing through his knee. Unable to stand, he crumpled to the mattress on the floor, pinched his thumb and forefinger above the ache and kneaded.

He winced, working the pain down, wrestling it into submission. At least, that's what he was trying to do. Jolting spasms sliced through to his nerves, pinning them down as they wriggled and writhed.

Sal sucked in a breath, ground his molars, and sank back into a pillow in wait of relief.

He didn't know how long he stayed like that. Heck, he might have passed out for a few minutes, he couldn't be sure. All he knew was when he opened his eyes, Candice was rolling up his pant leg, and wrapping a bag of frozen corn over the surgical scar.

Icy heat licked over him from the tips of his hair to the soles of his feet in wild contradiction. He was always the protector. A lifetime of practice made it an honest compulsion.

But this … this was so foreign he couldn't be sure it wasn't a pain-induced hallucination. The sweet illusion playing out said he was being Florence Nightingale-d by Candice. And that felt pretty damn good despite the languishing agony from his break-in.

"You all right?" Her words were a balm in and of themselves. Soft and serious.

The pain numbed enough to clear the fajita scramble of his brain. With it brought some much-needed clarity.

"Candice, I'm so sorry. I destroyed your house. I thought

you were in danger. I'm such an idiot."

"You're not an idiot." A small smile tipped the side of her mouth. "Okay, well, maybe sometimes, but this ..." She trailed off, and swallowed hard.

"This might have been a bit misguided. But you kicked down my door to save me." Her eyes cast off to some other place, hooking into something beyond the room. "Y-You were trying to protect me. I'm not sure anyone's ever done that before."

She looked so small. So vulnerable.

So completely unaware of the fact that everything he'd done, every stupid thing he'd said since the very first moment he met her was for that reason.

Of course most recently there had been the late-night intruder mission, the *Frogger* street dive for the vial, and the slight-of-hand snatch of the evidence too, all providing blatant illustrations of his protective instinct for her, but no need to bring those up.

She'd see it when she was ready.

He'd been expecting her to hand him his hide. Badger him endlessly about being so foolish and immature. But she just sat here at his side, holding the makeshift ice pack in place, showing him one broken little shard of the most remarkable shattered mosaic ever fashioned.

For the second time in his life—the first being the fateful day when he'd first laid eyes on her—he had no words, no sarcasm, no pretense to wield. Honesty would only drive her back into her shell. So he just watched her like some sappy, love-struck dweeb. Watched the roiling sadness of past memories rumble under the apparent calm.

Without thinking, he reached down to his knee, splaying the tips of his fingers lightly over hers.

Resurfacing, she turned her eyes on him, meeting him with another whispery smile. "Thanks for being such a good friend, Dorian."

Friend. Yep. Should have seen that one coming. But at

least it was a step up from coworker.

Of course, it was right then she seemed to take note of his spiffed-up attire. And then found the paper flower bouquet on the floor.

"Oh." Her fingers slipped from beneath his and touched politely to her lips. "The ballet. You tried to remind me today, and I totally forgot." She reached over, collected the bundle, and pressed her itty-bitty nose to the chocolate center. "Mmm. Hands down. Best. Flowers. Ever." Her smile stretched so wide he thought his heart might pop as it grew and grew to match the simple happiness on her face.

"They made me think of you." Unique. Lovely. With a sweetness that catches you off guard.

She smiled again, this time a little tighter with an extra dollop of warmth tinting her cheeks. Telling him it was a good thing he hadn't elaborated out loud.

"Well Brat, I've got some good news and some bad news. Which one you want first?"

She hugged one of her legs against her chest. With the companionable silence and the slight parlay of the blinding pain, he got to appreciate the view of her curve-hugging workout tank, and deliciously tight, cropped leggings just cresting her kneecap. Her hair was tied up, spreading from her crown in a palm tree fan of lush, dark locks dusting the nape of her neck. Her flushed skin still faintly dewy from sweat.

She was so close. And as usual, he was much too aware of her. What guy wouldn't be?

Yes, at the moment he was slightly crippled, but his arms and his lips still worked fine. His mind honed in to the powerful need to touch her. To slip an arm around her waist, tug her a few inches closer, and sneak one salty-sweet taste of that smooth bronze shoulder.

"Well, are you gonna give me the bad news or what?"

Oops. He brought his brain back on point. "The bad news is we won't make it to the ballet in time."

Not a huge loss, he supposed. He wasn't interested in watching people pretend to be swans and nutcrackers. Though he would have liked to watch Candice watch them. He smirked. He'd watch Candice watch anything. Besotted fool that he was.

"I can see you're all broken up about it." She twirled her flowers and again grinned, a coy, playful little ditty peeking from behind the bouquet.

Mercy. It shot through him like cupid's arrow.

"And the good news?"

"Looks like we'll get to have another slumber party."

Chapter 14

Candice Stevens

"Morning, Blaine." Candice shoved through the morgue door on Friday, spotting her coworker slouched back in his desk chair, on-time, possibly early, but completely useless.

"Hey." He spared her a glance and went back to staring at his laptop.

Not even her presence could make him act busy. Sure the dirty work with Vivaldi's latest victim was done, but since they'd sicced Soren Michael's flesh-eating beetles on Sarah Hoyt's remains yesterday they now had clean bones to work with. Bones unfolding Sarah's story from the broken fibula from childhood, to the tennis elbow from high school, to her final moments as Vivaldi's sculpture.

She suppressed a shudder, but as usual with this serial killer, the sickening familiarity balled her stomach into Jacob's ladder. A stomach otherwise blissfully full of another stunning culinary perfection served from Dorian Salivas's talented hands.

Plus she'd had another night of beautiful sleep. On Dorian's couch. Even though he'd offered the privacy of his bedroom, she just couldn't get on board with that. Maybe she was a serious freak, but she'd be perfectly happy to never slip even one limb in a man's bed again. The first one had been traumatic enough to swear her off the gender for good.

But there was something tantalizing and restful about the scent of that couch. Man, it was stupid, but the smell produced the most delicious form of hypnosis, lulling her into the sweetest surrendering sleep.

Stupid, stupid, stupid.

More idiotic was how normal it felt to sit at his table, chatting with Dorian and Gabe over a finger-lickin' breakfast of fresh apple pancakes and thick-cut bacon.

Even being tailed to work this morning didn't rankle. It was kind of ... nice.

He was kind of nice.

She shook her head to eradicate the phantom memory of his spicy vanilla and cardamom musk snuggling in her stomach with that delicious breakfast.

Nice in a kid brother kind of way, she corrected, warning her possibly bipolar alter ego to think on something else.

Ready to focus, Candice slipped her lab coat over her clothes. Last night while Dorian was hammering a piece of plywood to her front door opening, she'd done some light unpacking. Feeling semi-normal, today she wore a sheer black and pin-point red polka-dotted blouse that tied at her hips. A black tank kept it PG and stretched below the tie to cover the top inch of slim black cigarette pants cropped just above her ankle.

Below her ankles she sported her favorite suede wedge heels. Red. Because it was just one of those days when she needed to feel less like a blood-soaked zombie dwarf in pajamas and more like a *kick-A* professional woman sniffing out the scent of a murderer "The Wind Cries Mary" style.

She tugged on a pair of gloves and snapped the rubber at her wrist. She hadn't actually cursed this time, even in her head, but it was close enough. Her own form of classical conditioning was really quite helpful in retraining her vocabulary and smothering the bawdy Jersey accent that reminded her, and everyone else, where Candi belonged.

No. Not anymore, she reminded herself without much conviction.

Curling her fingers over the cold metal edge of the

autopsy table, she stared down at Sarah Hoyt's bones. She forced her breaths in and out, feeding her woozy brain enough oxygen to remain upright on the four-inch heels still only boosting her to five three.

Lifting the pelvis, she could see, even without magnification, kerf marks marring the smooth surface. The texture of the pubic symphysis showing her age, hinting at the vitality and beauty of what should have been wrapped around all of these lovely bones.

As if scattered with a careless toss of confetti, she examined the numerous marks Vivaldi inflicted, cataloging the angle, the length, the depth until the pain of each cut twisted like a knife in her own flesh.

Like all of his other victims, a pair of dark singes burned a place on her cervical vertebra, always dismissed as the signature of his torch. This was only the second victim she'd seen with her own eyes, the others she'd reviewed from reports. But something about those marks always poked at her.

What would cause that? Was there another weapon they were missing? Something more distinctive than his other untraceable tools of terror?

A pearl of sweat slipped between her shoulder blades. She craned her neck and bent her back to relieve the stiffness.

Her cell phone rang. Grateful for a breather, she set down the clavicle bone, stripped off the gloves, and hastened over to her desk.

"Candice Stevens."

"Candice, it's Soren."

Mmm, Thor.

Wait, really? She pulled the phone away from her ear and glanced at the unlisted number. "Hey, So—"

"Don't say my name!" His words came out in a rush.

Candice flashed her gaze on Blaine now unabashedly curious about her call. At least he was curious about something. Lord only knew what he'd been doing over there for the past few hours.

"So ... what's up, Joss?" Turning away, she pretended to leaf through the papers on her desk, wondering if Soren's gritty baritone was cutting through the clock-ticking silence.

"Is anyone in the room with you?" Soren growled. So cranky. And why was that hot? Perhaps she needed a psych consult. Jersey was taking over.

"Uh, yes, I could be up for a girls' night." Working the buttons on her lab coat free she slung it over her desk chair and breezed out the morgue door on a fake laugh.

When she tucked into the women's restroom she dropped the act. "Okay. I can talk now. What's going on?"

Soren was always agitated about something, but paranoid? Never.

"I dropped by the morgue this morning. It was before you or Blaine got in."

"All right. Did you use the key I gave you?"

He breathed out a little grunt. "Didn't need to. The morgue was unlocked."

"What? That can't be right. I was the last one here. I'm positive I locked up last night."

"I know you did, because I came back after you left. Most of the burned tissue was decimated. Basically carbon and nothing else. But I found a synthetic fiber on one of the samples you pulled. I'd left my scope there for you and I wanted to double check my findings, maybe run it through mass spec and see if I could pick up anything else."

More hope bloomed in her chest. An actual lead! Another surviving shred of evidence. "That's great news!"

"Yeah, it would be except I got called away on a family emergency just after I put it in the system. I locked it up in the evidence cabinet, locked the doors when I left. I was very careful."

Candice curled her stubby fingernails into her palms.

"When I went back early this morning the door to the morgue was unlocked and the fiber was gone."

Fighting the dizzy rush swimming between her ears, Candice sank down onto the toilet seat, not really caring what she might be sitting on.

"… Mackenzie."

She scrambled to catch up and connect the name. Mackenzie. "As in Agent Cara Mackenzie, of the FBI? What about her?" She was a shameless flirt and a bit flighty, but otherwise an adequate agent.

"You seriously didn't hear any of that?"

"I'm hanging on by a thread here, Soren. The Vivaldi cases are … they just get to me, is all." That was an easier truth than the questionable suspicions stirring within her. Binding her to this serial killer in a way that she wasn't sure she could accept.

Ignorant bliss, and all that.

"I said, I saw Agent Mackenzie leaving the building when I was walking in. So naturally, since the evidence was gone when I got inside, I followed her back to the FBI and confronted her about it."

"And?"

"And she showed me a signed order from the evidence team saying it was to be transferred and catalogued."

"But that doesn't make any sense. How did she get in? And you haven't finished analyzing it yet. They can't just take something as precious as hard Vivaldi evidence and put it in a storage room where everything else has mysteriously gone missing. Are they trying to sabotage our chances of catching—" She couldn't even finish the thought because the inkling clicked into place.

What if someone was working on the inside? What if Vivaldi was somehow imbedded in the FBI?

Her blood ran cold.

"That's what I was thinking." Soren's voice softened, his unspoken suspicions on point with her own.

"Holy smokes." She could only whisper the words, the implication too great, too scary to consider. No wonder all the evidence kept slipping through their fingers. No wonder Vivaldi was as elusive as the wind.

Her thoughts swirled, picking up speed to funnel down into the disheartening suspicion.

Soren kept talking. "Your un-trusty sidekick Blaine showing up early made me a little uneasy. He's not the type. I almost thought he might have slipped her the key or something. Maybe that's crazy, but I don't trust him. I don't trust anyone right now."

Except her. That felt pretty good.

"We have to get the evidence back before it vanishes for good." Candice stood, pushed her way out of the stall, and stared at her reflection in the mirror, seeing the person in front of her as if a stranger in her own skin. "We don't have much time. Shoot, we might already be too late."

She couldn't believe what she was considering.

Is this right? Or am I about to do something reckless?

Deep down she knew her answer was a little bit of both.

But could she pull it off? Did she know who to trust? Was there anyone she *could* trust?

She thought of Dorian, his face a mirage before her. His earnest eyes. His hapless innocence paring questionably with some impressive bravado. An act?

Had she been sleeping under the same roof as a serial killer? The very same killer who might have—

"I saw the code she punched in to the evidence lock up. Unfortunately, you need a keycard too. Otherwise I would have broken in there a few hours ago. I even tried cozying up to the little flirt to convince her to let me finish my analysis." She heard his sigh stretch over a long pause, knew he was probably forking his fingers through that long Tarzan hair. "Must have lost my charm, because she wouldn't budge." Firm, cold, perfect indifference reclaimed his voice.

What a confusing human being. Soren the Barbarian. Take one heck of a woman to tame that beast. Counterproductive tangent because she sure wasn't that girl.

Eyes on the prize, Jersey.

"I'm on it, Soren. If I manage to get it back, we won't have much time until it disappears again. Come get your microscope while I'm gone. Set up shop in a safe, unsuspecting place. I'll be in touch."

"Candice." His gravelly voice went smooth again. As smooth as it could for a man like Soren Michaels. He cleared his throat, though she got the feeling he was trying to reinsert more grit. "Please be careful."

And that was the end of it. A glimpse of a warm, melty center meant he wasn't all Grizzly Adams and jagged edges. Her safe, silly infatuation was over. Soren would now be quarantined into the kid brother/friend zone with Sal and all the other nice guys a girl could too easily fall in love with.

Because even Candice knew that while Vivaldi was the most decorated and deadly force walking around St. Louis, love was the most dangerous villain of all.

Candice belted her trench coat tight around her waist. Probably too tight, but her nerves were threatening to resurrect her delicious breakfast yet again, and the added pressure seemed to cage the wild, winged beasts swooping through her belly.

These were not your ordinary butterflies because this wasn't a very meticulous plan. Granted she'd concocted it in the five minutes it'd taken her to walk to the FBI building so, all things considered, it wasn't completely pathetic.

She needed to play this like an undercover op. The possibility of Vivaldi working for the FBI made that a no-brainer. But it also meant Vivaldi could be watching her. He'd already broken into her house for the DNA. Now he'd orchestrated for this "fiber" to be brought to him.

All the secrecy made her skin crawl, as if Soren had left a few members of his clean-up crew behind. She shivered, tugging the belt tighter still.

The FBI were supposed to be the good guys. They were *supposed* to be on the same team, and yet here she was preparing to sneak into the evidence room to snatch back what rightfully belonged in the lab.

A necessary evil, she'd convinced herself. Though whatever delusional courage she'd worked up on her way over must have hit a snag around the corner of Fourteenth Street and Market because now she felt the weight of her mission like an anvil in each shoe. Felt the shift of the odds stacking against her. Felt the consequences either way.

None of it was anything she wanted on her conscience.

And yet, what choice did she have? This was what she did. She saw what no one else could see. She fought for those little scraps that could turn the tide and prevent a vicious killer from claiming another victim.

And just maybe she'd help anesthetize the pain of a life without answers.

She might only work with dead bodies, but she liked to think she also saved lives.

Candice rerouted that confidence into her short-legged strut as she approached the front desk, flashed the right credentials, and was granted a guest pass. Having visited before she knew what needed to be said.

Reaching the correct floor she hung back and did a quick survey of the bullpen before entering. As usual, there were agents propped against their desktops in conversation, some engrossed in their computer screens, while others milled around … swapping reports … scribbling on a giant white board … flirting with the brunette in the corner—

The last one grabbed her for a double-take. It was Dorian. Just as dark and spiffy as he'd looked this morning in his trim black suit and standard black tie.

The brunette was tall and willowy. Candice hadn't seen her here before, but something about her struck a familiar chord. The way she twirled her hand when she spoke, her long manicured fingernails, the pursing at the corner of her lips.

Miss Runway leaned in and giggled, splaying her claws on Dorian's forearm. Good grief, how ridiculous. Why even bother with subtleties or subtext at that point.

She was the brunette version of the tactless redhead Cara Mackenzie, pawing all over a clueless and grinning Dorian.

Ick!

Candice's blood burned a little hotter. Her nerves must be getting to her. This was a colossally stupid stunt, but it was all she could come up with on the fly. So she loosened the tie at her waist, eased out of her coat, and folded it over her arm. It was as good a hiding spot as any.

Then, before she could talk herself out of it, she strode through the doors into the bullpen, disturbingly pleased to notice she'd snagged some attention from the suits behind their desks, especially with the waif and leggy runway model in the room.

She pressed her shoulders back to insert some steel into her rapidly deteriorating spine and added a little extra purpose in the soft stomp of her red suede shoes until they butted up to Dorian's stylish black loafers.

A midnight swath of eyebrow quirked with curiosity. His eyes, dangerously dark like hot fudge, poured over her, flashing with a little spark of something else nearly radioactive.

Her tummy rumbled, and though she was sure he couldn't hear it, his lips gave an effortless tug. "To what do I owe the pleasure?" His words were decidedly suave for a man of such little pretense.

Then again, perhaps it was a show for Miss January still crowding his personal bubble.

Giving her best imitation of calm despite the tremors pirouetting through her middle, Candice flashed what she hoped was her own flirt-ladened smile. Hmm. She wasn't sure she actually had one of those. Never used one, and couldn't decide why she was getting all territorial since her only point of interest was the stolen fiber.

Dorian didn't seem to miss a thing, and his smile stretched so wide she thought he'd split his lip any second. Or she could do it for him. It could certainly prove useful for her mission. Jersey pushed for the drama, but Candice shut her down. A physical altercation would draw too many perceptive eyes.

"Candice, this is our new analyst Jill Chrissick. Jill, this is Dr. Candice Stevens, medical examiner extraordinaire."

She hadn't detected any sarcasm, but something in the formality of his introduction pinched a nerve. "Nice to meet you." Candice turned another forced pleasantry toward the fair-skinned brunette and was greeted with an even more impressive saccharine smile than the one in her possession.

Again she was struck with something familiar. The angle of her jaw, the curve of her cheekbones, the soft prominence of her supraorbital ridge that made her eyes fiercely deep. The underlying architecture was as plain to Candice as an X-ray film, but the covering was all foreign.

"You too." Miss January Jill's eyes regarded her for a mere moment before she refastened her gaze on Dorian. "Sorry I bumped into you again. But at least I got a full introduction this time."

Lashes fluttered, and glossy lips curled in a predatory smile. Candice fought against the mother of all eye-rolls.

"Dorian, might I have a word?" Candice asked, salvaging the last shred of the brunette's pride before she started begging for some of Dorian's rolling r's against her lips.

You'll thank me later, Leggy. Now use what the good Lord gave you and run along.

When the "analyst" didn't take the hint, something possessed Candice at the thought of being so casually dismissed. Without thinking, she slipped her hand in Dorian's much larger one, weaving his fingers with her own. The touch was like match to fuse. An extremely short fuse that lit up long-neglected, decidedly female regions on her body like a freaking contrast CT.

His fingers clasped with a tender pressure, and with only a careless nod to bid adieu to the head of his fan club, Dorian led them away from a glaring Jill Chrissick.

Is this how friends hold hands, Candi? Jersey taunted, and Candice tried to reclaim her burning hand. But his grip tightened and something clenched low in her belly.

Can it, Jersey.

It felt like an eternity, but moments later they were in the deserted break room, the smell of blistered coffee strong enough to singe her nose hairs.

At least she couldn't smell the man in front of her.

"What's going on? You look troubled." From up close his eyes were no longer playful or amused. They were edged with concern and maybe a hint of anger. She floated in them for a long moment, trying to discern what might be hiding in their dark chocolatey depths.

A lust for blood? A collection of deadly knives and blow torches? All masked behind the smooth veneer of a psychopath?

Well, except Dorian wasn't really all that smooth.

His thumb traipsed over her knuckle with an almost imperceptible caress.

Tingles burst through the myelin sheath and threw a party in the synaptic gap of her nervous system.

Was his gentleness a manipulation? The kindness of a friend?

Or something else altogether.

Okay, maybe he was a *little* smooth.

A war of doubts threw down wagers in her head. How could she be sure about him?

She couldn't, Jersey reminded in a rare act of sensibility.

When it came to men, her barometer was busted beyond repair. So as much as she wanted to trust Dorian with this secret and put those skilled hands behind the wheel of this crazy reconnaissance mission, she couldn't know for certain she wouldn't be handing over the keys to the devil himself.

Sucking in a deep breath she did what she came to do. With a light squeeze of his hand, she tugged it back and leaned in as if to share a juicy secret. She was no better than Miss January Jill at the moment, but she put that from her mind. Distraction. This was about distraction.

She placed her simmering hand on his lapel, noting how the heat leaving her fingers was now revving up in his eyes, melting them down to Hershey's syrup.

She *really* needed to stop comparing the man to chocolate.

"I-I hate to impose, but I couldn't get a new door installed today." She swallowed down a hunk of air, forcing the grapefruit-sized lump past her windpipe.

Despite the intense concentration she was directing toward her hand to be seamless, a tremor shot to the fingertips trying to finesse his ID badge from his breast pocket. "I was wondering if it'd be too much trouble to crash on your couch again."

"You already know the answer." His gaze didn't even flinch when the clipped edged of the badge scraped and released the fabric of his jacket.

She couldn't breathe. Didn't know why that last breath had become a boulder in her throat. "Great." She strove for brightness, plastered a smile on her face, and tucked the contraband into the folds of her coat. "Thanks so much, Dorian. You're a lifesaver."

Or a double-crossing sociopath

Turning away so he wouldn't read her uncertainty, she took several steps to the door before she'd gathered the moxie to turn back. "I'll see you at home around seven."

Chapter 15

Dorian Salivas

What was she up to now?

Sal watched Candice round the corner near the stairwell and gave it another fifteen seconds before trailing after her.

He couldn't help but grin. *Ah, Candice.* The forced flirty smile straining on her lips was like clean lines on a Monet. If that hadn't tripped the trap door early it was the way she'd imprinted herself on him with her hand. Other than a few lapses brought on by intense stress, the Candice he knew kept a very strict distance.

And then, lifting his badge from his coat?

He'd have to teach her more effective ways of doing that. She'd been quaking all over, her fingers a little jerky and unsure whether she was committed to her cause or not—a cause that had her coining phony smiles and attempting party tricks well beyond her skill set.

Subtlety wasn't her forte, but the absence of her usual brash Jersey-girl told Sal she was about to do something stupid. And he was going to catch her in the act.

Because, well, even if she didn't want one, it was clear she needed a protector.

Sal reached the ground level, knowing where Candice was headed. She needed his badge to enter evidence lockup, after all. Though he wasn't sure how she was planning on bypassing the security-coded entry without him.

And without his badge, he wasn't certain how *he* was

planning on following her in there.

"Sal, my man!"

Ah, perfect timing.

"Moss. How's the cyber division treating you, pal?"

"Ah, you know. Same old grind."

Sal continued the conversation on autopilot. Kip Moss was a nice enough guy. It'd only taken about five minutes after meeting him to realize how "susceptible" he was, meaning he was uncommonly easy to hypnotize. It had proven helpful a time or two when he and Archer needed information on the fly. Procedure and red-tape were important for sure, but when it came to national security, sometimes the big picture was more important than rules and regulations.

At least that's what Sal told himself when he couldn't sleep at night.

Spying the badge clipped to his shirt, Sal lifted his hand and double-tapped the spot he'd established on Kip's shoulder. His eyes lost a little focus, his speech about their most recent identity theft came to an immediate pause. Man, he really was an easy mark.

Sal indelicately palmed the badge, stuffed it into his pocket, and tapped Kip back out of his trance.

"That's fascinating. But listen, I gotta run. Let's catch up again soon, okay?"

Kip blinked in rapid succession and then smiled an easy grin. "Cool. Later."

"Salivas?"

Hearing the name at his back, Sal froze before he could visibly flinch. *Jensen.*

Had he just been caught? Sucking in a calming breath, he sent a silent prayer heavenward. Considering what he'd just done to Kip, and what he was about to do for Candice, he was surprised he had the gall to direct any inclinations above where he was sure to be headed.

He turned and met his boss eye-to-eye. "Director Jensen."

There was a steely edge in Jensen's piercing blue gaze. He ran a tight ship. Tough as nails. No nonsense.

All of it worked for Sal except the no-nonsense part. Laced up and poised wasn't his style, but when it came down to it, he'd learned the hard way that laws were black and white. And any gray area fed straight into the dark side.

Sal flashed a glance at the evidence room door, feeling like he was sinking down into murky gray quicksand. He knew what side of the law he needed to stay on to avoid resurrecting the old Dorian. And yet right now, in this moment, he was being swallowed up in gray. Infested with it. It was sucking him down, bleeding out on every bent truth escaping from his lips.

It was becoming painfully obvious he hadn't learned a thing.

He had good intentions. In some way that made him feel that despite the unique skills he'd inherited from his father, Sal wasn't as slippery as a common criminal. And nowhere near a monster like Vivaldi.

But where was the line? Where was the distinction exactly? He told himself he was no longer a con man, but wasn't that what he was doing right now?

And what disasters might result from this little jaunt into his old life?

"Anything to report?"

"Working on it, sir." And he was. What else could he say?

Jensen's jaw tightened at the hinge, parallel lines skating between his brows. "Well, I expect to be kept in the loop."

Sal kept his eyes firm and fixed, not allowing Jensen any privy to his inner conflict.

"Of course." It'd only been two days. The Vivaldi killings had gone on for nearly a decade. If Jensen was looking for magic, he'd have to look elsewhere.

"All right. I was just curious because I saw Dr. Stevens here from the morgue. I assumed there might be something new on Vivaldi."

Fierce protectiveness swelled within him. "I've been following up there, sir. Nothing new as of now. And Candice was here at my request alone."

"Is that right?" There was something in Jensen's expression. A twinge at his lips. A subtle undercurrent of amusement.

Interesting.

Sal fired off one of his lazy grins and shrugged. "What can I say? I'm a sucker for a pretty face."

With a slight smile, Jensen morphed into a good ol' boy, nodding that Ed Harris head of his. "Aren't we all. Good luck with that one."

Once Jensen turned the corner, Sal returned to his mission. Whatever qualms he'd had obliterated by an irrational need to keep Candice safe, even to the point of his own reckless demise.

He really should have his head examined. Or perhaps find the sort of woman who would help keep him on the straight and narrow. Candice was obviously not that girl.

He scanned the card and flung it toward the bathroom door as if it had simply dislodged from Kip's shirt on his stroll. Then, punching in the code, he slipped behind the door and followed the long hallway to the back room where a labyrinth of shelves and cabinets held decades of evidence.

There were a number of ways Sal might miss catching his kitten with her paws in the paint back here. So he siphoned his breath to utilize the silence, hoping to expose her less practiced stealth, and soon heard soft sounds of rifling.

He followed like a hunter, not wanting to tip her off. More curious than angry that she'd taken such a monumental risk by breaking in. She was proving to be quite the little rebel. He was sure she had a cause, but it all blared a cautionary danger signal in his head.

One that begged he heed for his own good.

He grinned in spite of himself. Yeah, well, it was as good a time as any to acknowledge he'd never been too keen on rules. He wanted to be. Especially given all his knack for mischief had cost him. But right now he was that fifteen-year-old boy on the street, fighting his own battle, vigilante style.

Alas, he spotted her. Her body rigid, her breathing battered, her movements almost frantic as she scanned the long shelves and shoved at the bins before tugging them back into place.

It was absolutely adorable. She was desperate and emotional. And yet after she took out her frustration on each row, she had to go back and carefully eradicate the signs of her intrusion.

"That's a little counterproductive don't you think, Brat?"

She gasped, clutching her coat to her chest. "D-Dorian. You gave me a fright."

"I gave you a fright? Have you been watching late-night BBC? I'm not sure I'm subscribed to that channel." He closed the space between them. Noting how the fear and uncertainty in her eyes made them flicker with golden flashes of firelight.

She took a step back, as if … as if …

"Whoa, what happened?" His teasing evaporated. "Why are you acting like you're afraid of me?"

"I-I'm n-not." Her lips fumbled over each word. The wobble on them raising a new wave of alarm.

"Candice." He stalled his pursuit while she continued her retreat. "I don't know what's going on, and I might be critically senseless because of this, but I trust you. Let me help."

It was a long moment of just watching, analyzing, barely feeding the need to breathe, but she finally took a step forward. The frenzied pulse at her neck backing baby steps from the ledge. "I suspect Vivaldi might have someone working on the inside. Or maybe …"

She let that linger without completion.

Sal nodded, not knowing what possessed him to break his

silence on the subject—break his pledge to Jensen for discretion. "We suspect that too. It's why I'm consulting here during my leave. It's top secret."

The tension drained from her shoulders. A deep breath swelled within her, and he could now see clearly why she'd been afraid.

"You thought it might be me." The deduction crashed into his sternum like she'd made his chest her punching bag.

"No! I—"

He stepped closer, pressing his thumb against her lips. "Listen up, Brat. I'm not perfect. And I've certainly dabbled with the wrong side of the law a time or two." Or twenty. "But I'm not the mole. And I'm most definitely not a killer." Though deep down, he knew that wasn't exactly true either. He'd never murdered anyone, but that didn't mean there wasn't still blood on his hands.

She nodded, her eyes wide and unblinking. Did she really believe him? And furthermore, could he really be trusted?

"Look in my eyes, Kitten." And she did. Those gorgeous gleaming eyes searched him so deeply he was afraid she'd see all his wounds … and the ghosts of all those he'd left wounded.

"I believe you." She whispered against his thumb and pulled away. "But I had to be sure. And now I need your help. The FBI stole evidence from my lab this morning. Evidence from the Vivaldi case that hasn't been fully analyzed."

Which meant the information they had on it was useless, so why take it? "I have a bad feeling about this." Sal murmured. No wonder she'd gone all *Catwoman*.

"Me too. If we can find this fiber Agent Mackenzie catalogued this morning, we can let Soren finish his analysis. And then we can sneak it back, and Vivaldi can have it for all I care. I'm just afraid, if it stays here, it'll go missing like everything else, and we'll have lost another piece of the puzzle."

"You're right. I wonder who signed the order. Maybe we can track the paper trail back to the mole."

"Or back to Vivaldi." She shivered, and everything in him wanted to pull her close and shield her from her fear. Shield her from all the dangers sure to follow them now that they were here where there was no turning back.

"A fiber." Sal whispered to himself. "Catalogued today." He laced his fingers with hers just like she'd done before, chiding himself because even now, with the gravity of the situation, he was still thinking about how right it felt. How silky soft her skin was against his hard palm. He'd bet she was soft everywhere. His mouth watered.

"This way." Clearing his throat, he tugged her along, found the right container, and—*Praise the Lord*—the little fiber still in its place.

"Yahtzee."

Candice squeezed his hand, beaming at him with the kind of hero worship a man could only dream about for a solid five seconds until—

The door jerked open. The sounds of pursuit awakened all the exposing silence.

"You said you found your badge on the floor?" The voice asked.

Dang it! Should have left Kip Moss under hypnosis just a bit longer.

"Yeah." Kip said. "And when I went to the front desk, Sandy said it showed I'd swiped in here."

"And you haven't been in here today?" This voice was Jensen's.

No bueno.

Sal pressed his index finger to his lips, as if Candice didn't already realize she needed to keep a lid on it. He listened for the echoes of their shoes, positioned them by the bound of their voices, and took the route he hoped would lead them out undetected.

They managed to escape into the hallway without notice.

The naked length of white walls had only one door into a sort of supply closet about halfway to the exit to freedom. They made a run for it, still bound together by their hands. Only the careless slipping of the handle behind them gave a hint of warning they weren't going to make it.

With no other options, Sal forced open the supply room door, more than a little grateful it responded immediately without sound.

He let go of Candice's hand and wrestled the hinge to a silent close.

Their strangled breaths were amplified in the cramped closet. The sound of the evidence door clicking shut signaling they'd be discovered much too soon.

Think. Think.

Sal pressed his ear against the door.

"Someone's coming." He mouthed the words to Candice.

She trapped her unpolished thumbnail between her front teeth, nibbling down on the nail already bitten to the quick.

He thought of Jensen. Yes, maybe it was an odd time to be thinking about his boss, especially when he was in a tiny, dimly lit room with his crush. But any moment they'd be discovered, and the only Hail Mary coming to Sal's mind was tied to the amused little quirk in Jensen's nearly non-existent smile.

In truth, there was no time for nerves. No time for anticipation of any kind. But it ignited on his blood nonetheless. He ripped off his jacket, scrubbed his hand through his hair to give the right amount of hand-tossed tousle.

This was not at all the way he imagined this moment. But she'd gotten them into this mess. Now he'd do what was needed to get them out of it.

Without warning he knocked her hand away from her mouth, drew in a deep stuttering breath, and pressed his lips to hers.

Chapter 16

Candice Stevens

There'd been no time to react. Not really.

One minute she was chomping down her last meal of shredded thumbnail before prison, and the next Dorian was kissing her.

Her coat slid off her arm and puddled at their feet. Dorian's arm snaked around her low back, lifting her to her toes.

And to his lips.

She didn't know where her hands were. Couldn't even tell if her lips were responding. Her brain had obviously left the building.

And time stood still. The pressure of another body. That blasted delicious smell. The sure, tender strength of a pair of practiced lips.

Man alive …

Something bumped against her. Of course, it was Dorian, but—

It was Dorian! She was still kissing Dorian. The door at his back was open. The light from the hallway speared over them, dishing up a brutal slice of reality. And when his mouth unlatched from hers after … well, who knows how long really. Probably only a few seconds, but it'd been a very long time since she'd been kissed and neither her lips nor her brain could be trusted with an estimate at present.

"Salivas?"

He whipped his head around, granting Candice a view of their audience. Director Jensen stood beyond the door, his expression a conundrum. He was either going to yell or cut up with laughter. It was a serious toss-up.

"*Oh!* I, ahh ..." Dorian sounded appropriately flummoxed. And the ruse was complete when she got a good look at him. He'd shed his suit coat just before attacking her. His shirt a bit rumpled. And his thick black hair passionately finger-streaked. Had she done that?

She rubbed her fingers against her palms, desperate to recall any tactile sensation of his hair between them. Anyone's guess.

She'd barely registered the few words exchanged between the men. Something about trying to dig up old clues since there were no new leads. About her clearance to enter with an FBI escort. Which was true, she hadn't thought about that.

But then again, she hadn't wanted to ask Dorian, because, *her bad*, she'd thought he might be a serial killer.

Right about when she started coming out of her brain clog she heard Dorian say something about getting "*distracted.*" To which the older man with intense blue eyes and face carved of stone actually snickered.

Oh, har har. Unsuspecting woman was just mauled in an FBI closet. Yuck it up, clowns!

A few moments later she realized the door had clicked shut, leaving them once again in their cozy little kissing cubby.

That was it? No interrogation? No cavity search? No hard time?

Dorian turned back, looking unflappable and perfectly unaffected by their brief interlude.

And wasn't *that* a kick in the keister!

"At least we bought ourselves an alibi." His carefree shrug stomped on her self-esteem.

Here he was all smiles and lame jokes. Not a care in the world. And she still couldn't catch her breath. In truth she was shocked, not only by the ease of which Dorian had just talked their way out of a jam, but by the deep restlessness he'd stirred with his kiss.

She wanted to scream. Or cry. Or run a marathon. Or maybe just succumb to a deep obliterating sleep. Maybe the punching bag was her best bet. Because what she was feeling was—

Whoa. She stopped the thought right there.

She didn't *feel* anything because it didn't *mean* anything. It was a ploy. A cover-up.

And this was *Dorian*. Poor, clueless Dorian. What was he, twenty-five? A puppy, really. He didn't have any game. And he wasn't all that attractive, was he? It should've been like kissing a brother.

But it hadn't been. Not even close.

A delicious shiver shimmied down her spine, warning her nervous system was on the brink of a meltdown. And suddenly, amid the chaotic disbanding of her gray matter, those few vague moments rushed back with a blip of clarity.

The distinct texture of his kiss had branded her lips so curiously she could still feel it. One of his arms had surrounded her, molding her against him. The other pressing the pads of his fingers beneath her jaw, against her neck, trapping her lips in his possession.

As the haze faded, she could see it hadn't been an elaborate kiss at all. And yet, it was strange how knowingly and simply his lips had claimed her. How they'd anticipated every move of her stunned response, how—in one mingled breath—they'd shattered all of her defenses and left her utterly helpless.

Still coming down from the sugar rush, she forced her breathing to even out, praying her heart would stop being so foolishly runaway over what, Dorian? Ha! She wanted to laugh, but it *so* wasn't funny.

Looking up into his endlessly rich eyes, she took a moment to scour his face for a hint of recognition. Gone was the dopey-eyed child. The man before her had transformed into some kind of molten man chocolate!

It was then she realized the man in question was still holding her. Close.

Really close.

She couldn't help but tingle from the pressure of his fingers against her spine, the feel of the immutable, delineated muscles hidden beneath his suit. Sparks of desire fired their warning flare a little late for intervention. Her face burned with crimson heat he'd have to be dead to not feel diffusing into the space between them.

Son of a—

If she could move she'd reach for her rubber band. Instead, she was his captive. A fly in his web.

He spoke low. The smooth tenor of his voice dropping to a dangerous baritone. "Are we still pretending, Brat?"

His fingers shifted, circling on her low back. Her brain went fuzzy, her body seeming to lean into him as opposed to pulling away. What on earth had he done to her? Had he slipped something into that pancake batter this morning?

Suddenly enraged, she regained control of her hands. Ones she feared might have succumbed to Jersey's influence and started groping his lean muscled arms. "Nice play, but hands off." She shoved him back.

His lip curled. That tricky top lip enticing her with a slow, mischievous display of his orthodontist-ad smile. "You're not easy, are you?" Smoothing the hair near her ear, his tickly touch grazed her neck and then skimmed down the sheer fabric of her sleeve now dissolving beneath his touch. Her heart flipped over, rebelling with something like a swoon.

Good gravy, Jersey! Get ahold of yourself.

Right on cue the combination of his words and her response to him made her blood insta-boil. "*Easy? Me?* Listen up, Dorian, you use those hands to touch me again you'll risk dismemberment."

He actually laughed. Not hearty and arrogant, but a deep

and sexy rumble from his throat. Very non-kid like. "You know what I meant. You're difficult. But I love a challenge."

There was only one word for this moment. Smoldering. From the fire in his eyes and the dark, smoky tone of his voice to the embers stirring deep within her, flaring through every vein and artery until she was almost literally ablaze.

Man alive, the closet was on fire! Immediate evacuation was imperative.

Ignoring her threat—and risking life and limb—he bent down, touching his lips to hers so gently she leaned in to get the full effect.

Biology overriding common sense.

Some chemical misfire enslaving her to its fanatical whim.

It was a medical anomaly.

Just as quickly as his lips deposited that last whispered kiss, he pulled back, turned, and waltzed out the door.

Candice pressed her palm to her chest to make sure she hadn't slipped into cardiac arrest.

Oh, but she hated him. Hated what he'd just done to her. Hated how easily he'd just dismantled sixteen years of armor. For what? A cover story? How humiliating!

He poked his head back in, his expression so innocent she wanted to knock his stupid, perfect teeth out. "Are you coming? We don't really want them thinking we were getting-it-on in here, do we?"

Her inner Jersey-girl riled, and Candice wholeheartedly agreed. Her slap came hard and fast. The sound, and even the sting, of Dorian's chiseled cheek against her palm was the most beautiful soundtrack for the moment.

His eyes flung wide, surprisingly big and pretty. She'd never noticed how the sooty-black lashes were so dense and long they tangled at the corners.

So yeah, she was expecting some kind of backlash. Whatever it was, she knew she'd endured worse.

But then the most inexplicable thing happened.

Dorian wiggled his jaw as if shifting it back into joint and grinned that same goofy grin.

"Worth it." He winked. "But let the record show my hands didn't disobey. My lips, well, they have a mind of their own."

"That's ..."

You use those hands to touch me again you'll risk dismemberment.

True. *Drat!* Must be more specific. "That's not ..."

Full sentences, Candice.

She cleared her throat. "What I mean is, let's just consider everything you see off the menu. Mmm-kay?"

Lame smile melting away, Dorian's eyes suddenly took on a new kind of X-ray sizzle. Candice slapped her arms over her chest just to be on the safe side. The man was a magician's bag of tricks, and she was learning not to underestimate his unconventional talents.

"Yeah, whatever you say, dear. I've gotta run an errand. Like you said before ... see you at *home* at seven."

Turning off the ignition, Candice sat behind the wheel of her Jetta, staring out through the starless winter night at the dark outline of her house. It was only a quarter to seven, but in February, it might as well be midnight for the full fall of darkness.

Home.

Yep, she *had* said that about Dorian's place. It'd been a slip, of course. Because her *home* was ...

Nowhere.

She couldn't help but think of the painting in Dorian's living room. *Nowhere's Home.* The sadness, the loneliness of the approaching winter. And yet the hope in that waning sliver of light through those fragile trees emitted an overriding sense of belonging.

She blinked away the reverie of the scenic hillside and stared again at her fresh start. With the boarded entry and the desolate cast of deep shadows, her new house—along with her dream of creating a haven—seemed hopelessly grim.

Of course, having her nest broken in to twice in the two days she'd lived there hadn't been a promising start. But she did her best to keep things in perspective. These were the suburbs of St. Louis, not the slums of New Jersey. What else could go wrong?

Vivaldi.

His name slithered through her subconscious on a whispered premonition. A queasy little quiver started in her stomach, rippling out with tremors so vehement her muscles seized and locked her in the prison of her own feeble body.

No. She gripped the steering wheel tight. She wasn't that same weak, little Jersey-girl. All talk, no action. There'd be no more playing along, cowering in fear.

With one resolute breath she crawled from the driver's seat, hiked her purse on her shoulder, and started toward the back door. The whistle of the wind played a haunting tune on the brittle branches. Her heart joined nature's deranged elegy, fumbling on the keys and racing off tempo.

The air speared into her throat, dry and crisp, and then escaped into the night on a breath of white. The cold was so smothering she knew she couldn't croak out a single, stale note if she tried.

Fear had always been a player in her life. It almost always took the melody. And yet, for years she'd managed to compose a new score, one where the notes created a sound she thought she could live with. But just when she was sure the tune had changed for good, she'd find herself back on the blacks, in the land of sharps and flats, fear and running.

Here she was, thirty-two years old, thousands of miles from that same old music, and even here, fear replayed its own relentless dirge. She couldn't escape it.

Except ... now she heard something ... else. She turned

toward the source of the sound. Dorian's saucy hot rod wasn't in the driveway, but a warm swell of light and sound parted the dark cloak of night.

Drawn like a heartbroken woman to the promise of chocolate, she redirected her course to the addition on the back of Dorian's house where she walked up a handicapped ramp and rapped on the door.

A low shadow passed behind the curtained glass before the fabric drew to one side.

Gabe grinned like his big brother and opened the door. The music unfolded from behind him, and she was instantly smiling. Why? It had been years since music had done anything but make her sick with memories of the past.

"I'm already jealous of my brother, Sugar. You don't have to make it worse."

"Huh? No need to be jealous, Cutie pie, you're both too young for me." She patted his shoulder and welcomed herself inside.

The room was small and scant on furniture. A compact gray couch rested against one wall, and a tall stack of amps stood adjacent to it. At the center a long table with dual computer screens and an extensive soundboard pressed up against what looked like an interrogation mirror.

"Dorian's gonna be twenty-eight tomorrow. You can't be a day over twenty-five."

Tomorrow. Hmm. She filed that away. "Pretty slick, kid. If I were fifteen years younger you wouldn't stand a chance of escaping me." She winked at him.

But fifteen years ago she'd been the one without a chance.

Gabe's mouth hung slightly ajar and then slid back into that easy smile. "Don't tease me, Candice. I'm handicapped. It's cruel."

God, I love this kid. Can I keep him?

Candice bent down, pressed her lips against his smooth cheek, and then ruffled his hair. "Can I hang out with you for a bit? My house is all *Nightmare on Elm Street* over there.

Spooky."

"Gorgeous, after that kiss, you can do anything you want." Still with the Dorian-grin, he wheeled past her back to the mixing board. "Pull up a seat."

She snagged a rolling desk chair from the corner of the room and sidled up next to Gabe.

"I could hear the music from outside. Sounds great, what is it?" It did sound great. And wasn't *that* confusing. Nowadays her mind was all science. But years ago, each wavelength of thought had been coded with a musical score.

"It's actually from a local church I'm mixing for. Pretty sweet, right?"

"Totally." She couldn't help but smile. "I just started going with Sadie and Archer. The music there is similar." Though most often she made sure to show up when the music portion was over.

"No way! I'm recording there this weekend." He toyed with a few dials while lines resembling heart tracers squiggled across the screens.

"I guess I'll be seeing you then."

"Lucky me. And lucky Dorian."

"Dorian's going? I didn't take him as the church-going type." And now she sounded like a snob. What exactly was the "church-going type?" *She'd* been attending church so apparently they'd let anyone in.

Gabe studied her for a long moment. "You should give him a chance, Candice. There's more to Dorian than meets the eye."

"Dating advice? From a teenager?" She nudged his shoulder in hopes of easing away from the topic, but he was just as stubborn as his brother.

"Yeah, well, I was raised by a pretty smart guy."

"That's great, Gabe. Believe me. My father wasn't around much." Again, another opportunity to segue the conversation. No dice.

His caramel-colored eyes were deadly serious. And much

too wise for his age. "I wasn't raised by my father. I was only six when Dorian ran him off. Probably saved my life."

She didn't really know what to say. What did that mean? Dorian raised him? Could he have been old enough to do that? Was he even old enough now?

"You see, our father was a mean drunk. Just mean, period. He was quick with his fists, but he usually preferred something that could do more damage, like a baseball bat."

Her throat ran dry. Her own painful shadow suddenly less paramount.

"Dorian could always sense the storm brewing. He has a gift that way. Though growing up I'm sure he saw it as a curse. We were both scrawny and half-starved, but Dorian made sure he took it all even if he had to pretend to screw up to guarantee the bat, belt, boot, or cigarette butt wouldn't fly any other way."

"I, uhh … I'm sorry. That must've been awful."

Gabe nodded. "Awful for him, yes. Broken ribs, ruptured spleen, burns, you name it. Most of which were undertreated at the free clinic because all of Dorian's money was spent putting food on the table."

A quick comparison of their pasts had Candice's insides shriveling to nothing. She could relate like few could.

"I didn't know any of that, Gabe. He just seems so …"

"I know."

And she was sure he did. None of Dorian's past came across in his personality.

"He's crazy tough. And resilient. In every way but one."

She felt sick. Literally. Like the nothingness churning in her stomach would retch up bile and her own bad memories. Everything in her rebelled against the knowledge of what Gabe was going to say, but she couldn't help herself. "And what way is that?"

"He can't forgive himself."

I know the feeling. "For what?" She whispered the words, praying he would just let it go unsaid.

He waited a moment, watching in the same calculating way Dorian had that made it seem like he could snatch away the thoughts you'd left unspoken. Then he rolled the wheels at his sides back an inch and then forward before he confessed ...

"For *me*."

Chapter 17

Dorian Salivas

"Lucy, I'm home." Sal slipped out of his suit coat and draped it over the banister in the foyer. "Sorry I'm late, I got stuck ..." The rest of his sentence fell off when he spotted Gabe and Candice on his couch. Looking snuggly, shoulder to shoulder, swaddled under a shared blanket.

There were two open pizza boxes on the coffee table. All but a few pieces had been consumed, from the looks of it, without plates. A pair of sultry red heels held a seductive and carelessly discarded station just beyond the couch.

"Well, don't you two look cozy."

They finally deigned to acknowledge his presence. Peeling his laughing gaze away from *Real Genius* playing on Comedy Central, Gabe issued a nod in Sal's direction. "Sup, bro? There's some pizza left if you're hungry."

Candice spared him a glance and the faintest crack of a smirk. It should have looked smug, and he was guessing that's what she'd been going for. Instead, it was so enticing he had to douse the urge to cross the room, haul her up from that blanket-sharing nonsense, and taste it right from the source.

Those lips ... not fashionably full, but so silky and expressive, tart and tender, they held the bewitching power to both soothe his soul and cut him to the quick, usually in the same breath. Lips he had just barely sampled only hours before but was certain he wouldn't stop thinking about even if the EL6 crew lit up the living room with a drive-by.

He was a slave to them. Studying their every nuance. Desperate to pull from them her every secret, including how he might persuade her to use them on him again.

Not likely, but a man can dream, can't he?

All right, time to stop thinking about kissing.

Walking to the back side of the couch, Sal sidled up behind Candice. "Kitten?" He slid his hands down the cushion until they came to rest on her shoulders, the gauzy fabric of her shirt stamping his palms with the warmth of her skin.

And, he was thinking about kissing again. And maybe a few other things off the menu.

She didn't shrink away, but became perfectly still. The slight tumbling of her breathing the only tremor of movement that touched her. He was just beginning to discover how receptive she was to his touch. It made him supremely happy.

And everyone knew turnabout was fair play.

Bending at his waist, he leaned in until his lips nearly grazed her ear. He could almost feel each of their nerves standing at attention, firing impulses across the splinter of space between them. "Might I have a word, privately?" He hadn't needed to whisper, but it sure was more fun this way.

She launched off the couch like his words had poked her with a branding iron. Interesting, since his touch had glued her in place.

He closed the door to the studio once she slipped past him, noting how carefully she avoided any brush of contact.

"Where were you?" She folded her arms under her bust.

Sal refrained from indulging in a cursory glance.

Well, *that* failed. He wasn't leering like a lifer devouring his last view of a flesh and blood woman. But he was male and he was breathing. And he was, above all else, pathologically observant. What else could he do? Talk to her with his eyes closed?

She glared up at him with those golden-embered eyes. Her

lush black lashes blinking with her irk.

Stepping forward, he realized, again, just how short she was without her shoes on. How short she was even *with* her shoes on. There was just something about coming home to the woman you're crazy about that drove even a sane man a little bit mad. Add to that the sweet teasing temptation of their kiss today, and he was so far off the canvas he didn't trust anything about himself at present. Least of all the wayward flicker of his eyes, the itching on his lips to taste her, and the thoughts of what could be, drugging his acute senses with more testosterone than a frat house.

"I took the fiber to Soren."

She gasped. "*Val Kilmer in bunny slippers.*" The murmur was so slight he'd almost missed it. "How could I have forgotten?"

Love might be for dopes, but idiocy was looking more appealing every day.

"I guess your mind was elsewhere." The grin overtaking him was meant to be playful, but it grew from a soul-deep satisfaction. Perhaps the tides were finally turning. Maybe she was starting to see him as more than just a goofy kid playing cops and robbers.

Man, he wanted to kiss her and set the record straight. *Really* kiss her. No holds barred, no trick deck, no audience, just—

"All right, Skippy, mama needs you to focus for ten seconds. Think you can handle it?"

And she was back to scolding him like a toddler. *Confounded woman.*

"Sorry. I was remembering something deeply delicious from a few hours ago." He wagged his eyebrows to be sure she caught his drift.

She huffed. "Does someone need a time out?"

"Only if someone needs a reminder of our *seven minutes in heaven* in the closet?"

The snarl loading on her lips meant she could start spitting bullets at any moment.

He corralled a laugh. It'd be a fun way to go, but it'd be smarter to curb the wrath ready to erupt from his feisty sprite before he earned himself another slap. He held out his hand. "Okay, truce?"

Doubt and a myriad of conflicting emotions flipped like schizophrenic flash cards on her lovely face. She shifted her hands, tucked them more firmly into the folds of her arms, and nodded. "Truce."

Oh, yes, he was getting under her skin. The revelation was even better than touching her.

He smiled again—this time with considerably more effort to appear aloof to her inner conflict—and let his hand drop untouched. "I called Soren so we could get to work on the fiber. Archer met us there."

"Why didn't you tell me? I was going to do that. Or at the very least, we could have gone together." She propped her tiny hands on the swell of her hips. Fragmented thoughts crumbled in his brain and slid back down a throat now starchier than his shirt.

Maybe if she put that puffy robe on over her clothes he'd be able to concentrate long enough to formulate a full thought.

Without thinking he reached out and cupped his hand around her upper arm. "I probably should have, but I wanted you safe in case Vivaldi, or someone from the FBI, came after it."

"I would've been safer if I'd been with *you*! You let me leave the FBI by myself. What if he'd been watching? What if he thought I had the evidence, not you?" Her nostrils flared, her cappuccino skin scalded with twinges of red, and that telltale vein bulged against her neck. None of that vitriol could stain what she had just unwittingly revealed.

She feels safe with me.

Well, hot dang! Progress.

"I had Archer follow you home, Brat. He waited until you

got inside, and then I had my security company arm the alarm after he called. You were safe. I made sure of it."

"You—" Her accusation screeched to a halt.

He was about 99 percent positive she was about to go all girl-power/gloves-off/*that's-just-like-a-man* and rip him a new one for overstepping. But she stopped herself, her little flush turning crimson. "Thank you." She whispered, perhaps because she realized they were now standing very close and there was no need for volume. Or perhaps she was shocked by the revelation that he'd been looking out for her. Again.

I always will. No matter what.

He rubbed his thumb over her arm, not really knowing what to say and not wanting to shatter the moment with words.

Her gaze locked with his, hinting at all those unspeakables he wished she felt in return.

Love me.

His heart hit a snag, bumbling all on its own, without the affront accompanied by his practiced unassuming manner.

There were moments, precious few in a lifetime, that possessed the power to wake something long deceased. Potent moments that could resurrect a sprig of hope amid the ashes of the past and the ravages of the present.

In this moment, Candice's eyes told him a story. One of desperation to belong. One of crushing devastation and clawing through the pain to the surface for another agonizing breath. And one of hope against all odds.

More intimate than a kiss, he bathed her with his steady focus, exposing his captured heart and confessing an unspoken promise. He willed her to see it. To see *him*. And not just what he seemed. Or what his past said about who he'd been. But who he was now, underneath all the stains and scars. And perhaps even because of them.

Surrounded by all the gray in his little brother's studio, without a single uttered eloquence, but with only an unspoken bond of yesterday's pain and a platonic touch, his careful world burst wide open, gushing every unfathomable shade of Technicolor. Black, white, gray all blending into the vibrant and hopeful chaos.

And right then and there, Sal plunged into the deepest trouble of his life and fell in love with the girl next door.

"I, uhh ..."

Love? Really?

Someone had super-glued his tongue to the roof of his mouth and pressed pause on any intelligible response percolating in his brain.

He loved her. The realization was both liberating and terrifying. Like leaping out of a plane at 10,000 feet. Like envisioning something beautiful and daring to put that first stroke on a blank canvas.

Sal had been beaten, nearly to death, no less than a dozen times in his life. He'd run scams against thugs no one in their right mind would dare tango with. He'd untangled the minds of some of the most sadistic killers on the earth. He'd even stared down the barrel of a gun into the eyes of a murderer. And yet, right now was the first time he'd ever felt truly terrified.

He had no business falling in love with Candice Stevens. He barely knew her, aside from what he'd gleaned from his always handy insights. She'd made it clear his interest was unwelcome, even if it wasn't as one-sided as she wanted it to be.

But what was the point of kindling the fire? She was practically sizzling, and yet she'd deny it with her last breath.

"Dorian?" The *maternal* concern in her eyes shoved him back in his place.

Ay caramba! It wasn't an act. He really *was* an idiot.

Letting his hand drop away, he forked his fingers through his hair, gripping the strands so tight his scalp ached.

"Por favor perdóname." Why his Spanish always eked out when he was embarrassed, he didn't know. "I was trying to tell you what Soren and I discovered. That was my intention for pulling you aside, that is. The fiber was from carpeting used to upholster trunks and floor mats in *Maseratis*."

Candice whistled, and Sal found his smile again. "Oh, baby, we could be so happy together."

She grinned back at his quip in the same way she had when he'd proposed over his Challenger. One part annoyance, one part amusement, two parts flattery. A subtle victory.

"There can't be *that* many people who can afford to drive a Maserati in St. Louis. I mean it's not like we'd be looking for a Chevy. We could probably track down everyone who owns one in a couple of hours. That's as good a place to start as any."

"Already got the list." He pulled it from his back pocket. He and Soren and Archer had made good use of their time. Sal had every intention of sneaking the fiber back into evidence tomorrow. Archer promised cover. Hopefully, no one had noticed it was missing. And hopefully, it would drum up a viable suspect.

Peeling open the folded paper, Sal tapped the name that had leapt out at him and Soren right away.

"Preston Bradley?" Candice leaned in to peruse the list. Mercy, the scent of her swirled around him like a spell. She smelled like … like warm island magic. Like sugar-dipped, pheromone-charged petals leaching a sweet, sticky poison that made rational, and even exceptional, minds either singularly obsessed or stark raving mad.

He straightened away a step to clear his head. "Yep. Preston Bradley. British millionaire steel tycoon. And, as Soren informed me, Blaine Attwood's uncle."

"Blaine? As in, my coworker? You think he had something to do with this?"

Sal shrugged. "Maybe. But there's only one way to find

out."

Chapter 18

Candice Stevens

"That stupid smile is telling me I'm not gonna like this."

Okay, the smile wasn't really *that* stupid. It was actually making her a little squirmy. Why? She wouldn't go there. Nor did she want to consider why the charged suspension of time passing between them moments ago had felt like she'd laid her soul bare without even spilling one word.

Or even why, only a split second before Dorian pulled away, she'd almost buried her face in his chest and held on so tight she wouldn't have worried about breathing.

Ugh, her stomach hurt. That fifth piece of pizza lodging unnaturally between her ribs.

"Aww, come on, Brat, where's your sense of adventure?"

"Tucked away with my Wonder Woman cape from grade school."

"I'm getting a nice visual."

Criminy, that smile was growing on her. Before today it had made him seem naive and juvenile. But having learned how early his innocence had been ripped away she had a whole new respect for it.

It didn't seem right knowing something so personal without ever having shared an ounce of her story with him. Or anyone. Isn't that how you made friends? You gave up a little something of yourself?

"Dorian." Her fingers curled into fists, preparing to go to battle with herself to free the imprisoned words. "Before we risk our lives on whatever undercover mission I know you're planning, you should know something about me."

The laughter faded from his eyes. "I'd love to know anything about you, Candice."

That didn't help. She tried to swallow. The air, as brittle as her confession, scraped down her throat. "I-I'm not strong. Or brave. It's all a front, you see. I'm ... weak."

She couldn't look at him. Couldn't stand the way her hands started fidgeting so she nibbled on her thumbnail and let her admission soak in before mumbling against her finger, "I just thought you should know, because well, you won't be able to ... to rely on me."

All the muscles and curves were an illusion. A clever little facade. Underneath she was hopelessly fragile.

Without lifting her eyes, she sensed him cross the room. Perhaps his scent had alerted his approach, or maybe some of his psychic insights were rubbing off on her, but she was surprisingly prepared when he pulled her down onto the couch beside him. He waited, and she wished she had the courage to look up and read the script in his eyes.

So gently he lowered her nail-nibbled hand to her lap and covered it with his wide, warm palm. "You don't see what I see."

She shook her head, speaking to their joined hands. "You don't understand. It's not about what you see. I overeat to keep my weight up. I'm practically skin and bones. Seriously, if I didn't gorge out every meal I'd be back down to ninety pounds in a week. I'd blow away on a stiff breeze—"

"Brat ..." The word was an endearment, achingly sweet on his spicy voice. It was growing on her too. And that made her hyperaware of the thin line she was dancing on. "I know." His thumb swiped over her knuckle. "You went hungry growing up too, didn't you?"

Her head came up. How did he know? Was she that transparent? Did she look like some rabid, gluttonous badger when she was eating?

"It doesn't matter anymore. What you look like on the outside doesn't matter. Your strength comes from within. I know weak women, trust me. And you, Kitten, are the strongest woman I know."

His eyes were so steady she couldn't help but want to believe him. But it was pointless. She'd always been weak. She'd abandoned herself, her conscience, her gifts. Surrendering without a fight, she'd become someone else's property.

Looking away, she whispered again. "You don't even know me, Sal." The words were slight, but the punch in them slammed back through her. *No one* knew her. No one even knew her real name.

"Don't call me Sal." He lifted her chin with rough-tipped fingers, searching her eyes so thoroughly he might as well have stripped her bare and catalogued her bones. "And though I don't know everything, I know enough to trust you to be my wingman."

"Your wingman?" What she really wanted to ask was what he *did* know.

He seemed to sense that because he said, "I know that, like me, you had a lonely childhood. You felt weak and helpless and abused."

Her throat clogged, emotion burning behind her eyes. *Oh, God.* Did she really wear her hurts like a coat of armor for all to see?

Can't old things pass away? Haven't I performed this self-autopsy enough times to lay the old Candi to rest for good?

Apparently not.

"Someone hurt you. Controlled you. And you blamed yourself."

Tears leaked down her cheeks until the salt invaded her mouth. It was all true. But there was so much more to it than that.

"You lost someone. You blame yourself for that too—"

"Can we stop now?" Slipping her hand from beneath his, she covered her face with both palms to mask her silent cries.

He muttered a curse in Spanish, and then she was being drawn against him, her hand-covered face to the heat of his neck.

"I'm an idiot." His breath stirred her hair. His hands rubbing long, soothing strokes against her back.

It was too much. She was, once again, too vulnerable. Imprisoned in her own shame and dangling the keys in front of a man who could very easily own her.

Bolstering her will to pull away she smeared her hands down her cheeks. Instead of having the desired effect, her damp face soaked up the heat of his neck like butter on a hot skillet.

Oh, man alive. He smelled so good she was tempted to lick him.

And then there was the way he was holding her, lending his strength and his heartbeat like some pacifying lullaby. It was too easy to forget this was Dorian Salivas—man-child with a badge—when his touch made her feel so pieced together.

But it wasn't just the novelty of a comforting embrace.

He was more than a pair of arms. He was solid and dependable, resilient, as Gabe had said. Everything she wasn't and wanted to be. All wrapped up in smoke and mirrors, he was the finest contradiction. And she was putty. The second he touched her she melted.

Was she reverting back to her old ways?

After all her running, was she still destined to become her mother?

The fact that she was slurping down his scent like some man-starved leech didn't grant her any peace.

Down girl. She prompted, and with another rare act of willpower, Jersey obeyed by leaning out of his embrace.

"You should probably tell me the plan now." Silently

cheering her sense of composure, she went for more by slouching back, propping her elbow on the arm of the couch, and bracing her head against her palm. The chord was complete when she slung one knee over the other and let her leg bob casually between them.

He dug into his back pocket and pulled out a white card. The calligraphy was unreadable from her position, but she wasn't about to reclaim the space she'd just battled with herself to gain.

Frowning a little, he tried to smooth out the creases and then shrugged. "Ehh, it'll still do. This is our ticket to Preston Bradley's Valentine fundraiser tomorrow night. All proceeds go to the American Heart Association. What a guy."

"Sadie mentioned something about that. Her mom is like the head-honcho for most local charity events. I heard it was invitation only."

He slapped the card against his hand, his smile getting more ridiculous by the second. "It is. Archer called up his mother-in-law and, as luck would have it, they had an invitation returned to sender. She happens to know for a fact Mr. Bradley has never met the intended recipient."

"And who was the intended recipient?"

"Mr. and Mrs. Sylvester Gutiérrez." With a quick raise of his eyebrows, he added, "Sylvester and Katarina. Sly and Kitty." That ridiculous smile resurfaced with all its asinine gusto. "Has a nice ring to it, don't you think?"

"Oh, crap sandwich."

Now he was nodding, eyes wide, grin plastered like a five-year-old at the question of candy. Candy not *Candi.*

"And speaking of rings, don't you worry, Kitten. We'll go make it official tomorrow."

"Please. *Please.* All I want to do is sleep," Candice whispered the words aloud as if they might help her cause.

Dorian and Gabe had retired to their rooms hours ago. The specter of moonlight and the Dorian-scented couch cushions were her only companions in the still quiet room. No ticking of a clock. No quiver of heated air. Not even the refrigerator hummed a little ditty as far as she could tell.

She wiggled down deeper into the couch, stirring up a fresh morsel of his intoxicating redolence. With everything going on, she should have been overloaded. Sleep should have been a swift and beautiful release. Instead her mind would not be silenced.

Nagged first by thoughts of her poor violated house. Of her crumbling security here. Then of Sarah Hoyt, and inevitably the victims that lay scattered in her own past.

When she forced her Energizer Bunny brain back to the present she was reminded of the evidence. A single fiber from a lavish sports car. A mere shred of DNA to be devoured by the test and lost forever.

What might they discover if they played their cards right tomorrow night? A suave British millionaire with pounds of flesh hidden in his basement? A blood stain in the trunk of a $150,000 car?

Tomorrow night they would parade themselves behind enemy lines. As man and wife. That part was still tough to muscle down. And she was used to cramming all sorts of junk down her throat.

Sure, they were just pretending, but how much pretending was required to be convincing?

Before she could stop it, the memory she was desperate to forget played on the top note in her mind like an unrelenting aria.

Dorian's kiss … the sensation continued to dance beneath her skin like water in a swirled glass.

Why hadn't he tried to kiss her again in Gabe's studio? Would she have kissed him back?

No, she wouldn't toy with any notes in that melody for even a second. But maybe just the one adagio in the closet.

Just for a moment. *Seven minutes in heaven*, she smirked to herself, remembering Dorian's childish jab.

She'd been surprised by the contact. But even more surprising was the kiss itself. It wasn't the kind of kiss that made a good spectacle for their little ploy. In fact, it wasn't at all what she'd expected from someone like Dorian. And nothing like the kisses she shared with AJ.

Dorian's kiss was … an aberration.

She couldn't unlatch from the exquisite memory. No wonder she couldn't sleep. She was so stirred up she was practically frothing.

What was a woman to do with such a mystery? What *had* she done?

Some secret storehouse of self-consciousness dumped heated shame into her bloodstream. She tossed off the covers and jolted upright on the couch.

How, *exactly*, had she responded?

Had she put voice—or rather, *sound*—to her little swoon?

Candice cringed, feeling with certainty that he'd nudged a shameless moan from her throat with his gentleman's kiss, and that her fingers had curled into his skin-heated shirt and toyed with ideas that might even make Jersey blush.

Something was definitely wrong with her. Or perhaps she'd simply reached the threshold of her resistance against a touch and a kiss. Maybe now she could go another sixteen years.

Pressing her thumb to her lips, her blood stirred up a feverish heat.

She knew Dorian had a sort of "gifted" mind. And now, having experienced what she feared was merely a sample of his gifted lips, she knew he must have a few tricks up his sleeve that went beyond simple perceptiveness. She was bewitched. Bamboozled. Maybe even intoxicated. From an innocent little kiss!

It was a psychic's illusion. Or didn't someone say Dorian was a mentalist? What was that? Like a magician?

No, she didn't believe in any of that. What she could wrap her brain around was the possibility of some trippy endorphins. Faulty hardwiring from her twisted childhood. Of course, genetics weren't on her side either. So perhaps it was a perfect storm of factors short-circuiting her senses.

No more. No more kissing. Or touching. It robbed her of her intellect and her defenses. She knew better, but as usual she was weak. And the only way she would survive this, catch Vivaldi, and get on with her new life, would be to remember why Candice Stevens *had* to be alone. And drive a final nail in the coffin.

"Have you been practicing?" Rosemary seemed like a sweet old lady name, but Candi's neighbor didn't fit the bill. She was equal parts bark, bite, and snarl. With nary a sugared bit to be found.

"Umm, not since last time I was here. How could I? I don't have a piano."

"I know, but I just showed you this piece last week. And you just played it … perfectly." What might have actually been admiration came across as disgust.

"So?"

"It's 'Für Elise.'"

"That s'posed mean somethin' to me?"

"Let me get this straight. I just put the music in front of you, and you can play it? You? A little ten-year-old mixed-blood skinflint?"

Cranky old bird. And she was twelve, thank you very much. Almost thirteen. And she'd been so bored in middle school the guidance counselor had helped her test out of her regular classes and apply for consortium credit through the high school. So she was technically a freshman. She'd been researching grants for college credit classes too.

If Candi didn't want to play this piano so darn bad she'd give this bitty a piece of her mind. *Ten-year-old mixed-blood. Pfft!* She was going places. Just not fast enough. "Ain't that what I'm s'posed to do? Play the notes?" She said instead, through grinding teeth.

Rosemary's wrinkly old mouth hung open like an attic door. She hadn't even blinked, and for a few moments Candi wasn't certain the woman wasn't dead.

"Umm… Miss Rosemary?"

Now she blinked. Once. Twice. Her eyes curtained with excess skin, and the clouding from her cataracts like fog rolling in off the steel-gray waters of the Atlantic.

"Wh-what about without the sheet music?" Rosemary's age-spotted hands ripped the pages from the ledge and flung them to the floor.

"I, ah, well, I could give it a shot. Do you need to take some kind of medication before we go on? No disrespect, but I really don't wanna be here when you croak. My life is traumatic enough as it is."

"Quite the lip on you, kid. Doesn't your daddy beat you like the rest of the parents on this block?" She didn't wait for Candi to answer. "I sure ain't croakin' today, not now that my curiosity is about as aroused as your—" She clamped her saggy mouth shut, shaking her head. Her silver, cotton ball curls didn't budge an inch. "Never mind."

Candice exhaled a grunt. Yeah, yeah. Everyone knew. Why sugarcoat it? The guys at school started saying things too. Wondering if Candi was anything like her mama.

As if!

She turned back to the piano, thinking about the crash-course Rosemary had outlined so far in their lessons. The crabby old broad must be pretty lonely to let a "mixed-blood" like Candi into her house. She'd never once seen anyone visit here. There were even half-a-dozen signs on the door warning solicitors they were "in range" and to "knock at your own risk."

She felt sorry for the old lady but pushed the sympathy aside and threw all her focus into the scant information Rosemary deemed important enough to mention.

So far, learning music theory was like her first gulp of fresh-air freedom. Like, despite the structure, there was room for what she brought to the table. A place for her.

She closed her eyes to blot out the present. The smelly old lady furniture. The mirror layout of her horrible rat-trap next door. The air of prejudice and old hurts and disappointments in this place more polluting than the thick grit the dockworkers left clinging to her tiny slice of the ozone. She kept her eyes squeezed tight, desperate to see something else for a change.

Maybe *be* somebody else.

And then, like an apparition, she could see fresh notes chart out in her mind. The combinations that would ring and resonate. Those clashing notes that could be sprinkled in to tug out unexpected emotion and create beautiful chaos.

She could feel the shifting melodies dance around each other, feel the drive of the tempo calculating in her pulse to rush and withdraw, the conflicting urgency dueling with the lingering promise in a sustained pause. A *fermata*, Rosemary had called it.

Theory crashed and tumbled in her brain, stirring up some untapped reservoir of creativity straining against the levee.

"Okay, I might have something. I'll give it a shot." She shrugged, curled her fingers over the soft ivory, and felt the music begin to crackle and waltz beneath her skin even before she'd struck a key.

It was strange. But the music seemed to possess her. Its voice chanted in her head. Its energy humming through her veins. She opened her guarded heart and let the voice sing over her. Let it take over everything she was down to the marrow.

With a deep breath, and something like a prayer, she unraveled all her tightly wound expectations and just played, shocked by a symphony of sound exploding from the work of her skinny brown fingers.

She played and played. The new song like an old friend, embracing, warming, soothing away everything wrecked about her life. It was as if the music had always been a part of her, buried inside and slumbering until it was ripe.

"What's going on here?" The shrill voice pierced her moment. Candi's fingers froze on the keys. Her mother's bloodshot eyes spewed a poisonous mist into the room. "So this is where you've been. I was worried sick!"

Yeah, right. There wasn't a soul in the bi-state area who would buy that crock of—

"You think it's right to keep secrets from your mama?"

"I—I didn't think you wanted me in the house when you had guests over. And Miss Rosemary was just giving me a few piano lessons to pass the time."

Her mother stomped over to the bench and ripped Candi up from her place at the keys, Victoria's fingers pinching down into the tender skin of her arm until she trembled from the unrelenting dig.

"*Piano* lessons. Well aren't you *special.* If you're going to play piano, you're going to play for me while I practice. I want you out of this house this instant! You come back here, I swear, Candi, you'll wish on every star in New York City you hadn't."

A hollow threat. As if things could possibly be any worse.

But then again, whenever she would think that, it was exactly what would happen.

Chapter 19

Dorian Salivas

"Are you sure you don't wanna hitch a ride with us?"

Please say no.

After three days and two nights of close contact with Candice, Sal could use a break. Not that he really *wanted* one. But the more time he spent with her the more he realized just how much he was drowning. Sinking so deep, the surface, and any sense of sanity, slipped further from his reach every minute.

Yeah, love stinks.

He tucked the last of Gabe's sound equipment into his trunk, resting his hand against the top of the door still ajar.

His little cupid jutted her curvy hip to one side and propped tiny hands at the waist of her jacket. A waist so cinched he'd bet he could encircle her with his hands. Not that she'd let him close enough to test the theory. But he liked the image and the thoughts that rabbit-trailed from there to a very happy place.

"Listen bub." Her sunlit eyes sparked with playful energy, and he sank a little deeper.

Here we go again.

"I know you've, like, come to my rescue a couple times in the past few days. But I'm not completely helpless, okay?"

Man, she was cute.

With her ponytail, skinny jeans, and those same hot red heels that had made a guest appearance in his dreams last night, she looked part vixen, part girl next door. If the wind could pick up the song, "Dream Weaver" would be the soundtrack of the moment.

Slamming the trunk door, he tried desperately to tune-in to a different station as he bridged the space between them.

"I'm glad you took my pep talk to heart." He smiled down at her. No wonder she thought him an idiot. His face was paralyzed with a love-sick puppy grin every time he looked at her.

Real smooth, ya chump.

"What pep talk?" Craning her neck, she stood her ground.

He took her chin in his thumb and forefinger. Her pulse accelerated at her neck and her pupils dilated, just the way he wanted. "The one where I reminded you that you're my tough little cookie. But even the toughest guys I know need backup once in a while. That's me. Your safety net."

Her expression went blank. Wiped clean of any telltale lines and not even a flicker of motion to tip him off. Why? Had he said something wrong? And if he had, knowing Candice, wouldn't she have, with great delight and impressive smugness, pointed it out?

Her lips finally quirked. "You're really annoying. Anyone ever tell you that?"

He threw his head back and laughed. Not because her words were particularly funny, or even all that comforting, because let's face it, it wasn't really the thing a man wants to hear from the woman he loves. But at least his read had been right on the money.

"Yes, dear. As a matter of fact, *you* tell me that. Daily."

"Just keeping you humble." Scrunching her nose, she stuck her tongue out in an act of defiance. "And I'm still taking my own car." She took a step back and crossed her arms, her eyes challenging him to tango.

But as much as he wanted to dance—maybe wrestle would be a better word—church was starting soon, and they needed to get there early to set up. "I know, Brat. You're very predictable."

She lobbed over a smile riddled with mischief. He ground his jaw to keep it together, love and infatuation twisting his heart into a tangled mess even more confusing than the coded messages behind her eyes.

"Good. That's just what I want you to think. See you at church, buddy." She turned and swaggered away victorious.

Belittling him had been her emergency flare. But the fire in her eyes told him the match she was trying to smother had just touched the wick.

Sal turned back to his car with a little smirk.

Game on.

Church. Even the word made him squirm.

Who in their right mind would let a con man into a church? Okay, reformed con man turned law enforcement agent, so that might make it more palatable, but he doubted God saw any difference. Sin was pretty black and white, as he remembered from childhood. And then there was something about penance.

Well, he'd been paying those for a long time, but he was sure the statute of limitations on his crimes had yet to run out.

Wasn't there some kind of get-out-of-jail-free card? What did they call it … absolution?

He'd sign up for that in a heartbeat if someone would pass him the clipboard.

But no, life was one giant ongoing collection plate. No free passes. Loretta Mae always claimed there was. Grace, she'd say. Like it was some extra-strength bleach pouring over all the mess.

But even that didn't seem right. Fair was fair. He dug his grave, right alongside his mother's. And now it was his burden—no, Gabe was no burden. It was his *responsibility* to right all the wrongs he'd dumped on his baby brother.

Who would he be if all that went away? What purpose would he have?

"You're in it pretty deep right now. Care to share?"

Sal jerked his head out of the trance. Gabe was waiting for him at the entrance of the sound booth.

"Oh, uhh, nothin' really. Just been a long time since I been in a church."

Gabe nodded. "When was the last time? Mom's funeral?"

"No. Loretta Mae's."

"Ahh." Gabe paused, seeming to measure his words. "I'm sure she'd be real sorry to hear that."

She would. Gabe was right. The only shred of faith Sal possessed had come from that woman. He'd told her countless times he didn't have faith like hers. That he couldn't rationalize God cared for him when no one in his life ever had.

"I do." Loretta Mae smiled, warm like butter on hot grits. "And don't cha go thinkin' that's a coincidence. Besides, you think ya need some great big pompous faith and a long list a mighty deeds? Pshhh! That ain't what it's about, young'un. All ya need is a surrendered heart. B'cause deep down inside us all there's a measure of faith, ya see. It's in you whether ya want it or not. And the Good Book says if you have faith the size of a mustard seed, you can move mountains."

"But—"

"There ain't room for any more buts in here. Besides, if you can move a mountain with ya puny faith, knockin' that chip offa ya shoulder should be no problem."

"I think we're about all set up. Could you help me into the booth?"

"Yeah." Sal turned away, a little shaken by the flood of memories evoked from simply standing in a church.

The urge to run for the exit was strong. Or maybe if someone came up with a shaker of holy water and pronounced him "unclean" all would feel right in the world.

Because right now he felt like a raging hypocrite.

He'd been a crook. A killer. He already had a nice, toasty spot reserved down south. And he was okay with that. It would be the final act of his penance ...

As long as Gabe made it through to the other side.

Candice was late.

That information made Sal's already tremulous focus wane even further from the sound of Gabe's work.

The music portion of the service had started about ten minutes ago, and his *chica* was still a no show.

His mind spun off into possible scenarios she could've encountered on her way here. He knew Vivaldi was watching their every move, yet he'd still let her ride alone.

What could he do, really? Force her? Cuff their wrists together?

That could be fun. He smiled at the mere thought of her. What a fool he'd become.

As if materializing from his mind, Candice stepped through the back corner door. With one glance, he sensed something amiss. Almost as if something in the music slammed into her.

She wrung both hands around the purse strap on her shoulder. Her spine was stiff. Her jaw tight. Signs of stress, not fear. She was rattled but proud. He'd let her save face.

Sal settled back into his seat next to Gabe in the sound booth. The last of his immediate unease swept away on the melody.

This place didn't fit his perception of what church should be: robes and rules and scowling faces spewing God's wrath.

Amazingly enough, there was nothing inherently stuffy about it, or even the people, as far as Sal could discern. For the first time in a long time he saw beyond the condemning finger he was sure would be pointing straight at his lying, murdering, lusting heart and felt a genuine peace in this unorthodox sort of holy place.

"Huh. A church. Go figure." He muttered to himself.

Well, chalk it up to an off day. Not promising since they had a very important mission tonight.

He'd sensed Candice's hesitance to his plan. Playing married was going to be tricky, for sure. She was as skittish as a stray kitten, and with Vivaldi there was slim to no margin for error.

Always the multi-tasker, Sal observed the musicians and those in attendance, alert to any blip. He also watched Candice. Her body language a virtual tug-of-war of angst and passion, restraint and longing. Not for him, of course.

But was it the music, like he thought? Was it God? Was He as much of a contradiction for Candice as He was for Sal?

Her eyes slipped closed, and her hands balled together, clutched to her chest.

Unlike everyone else in the room, she didn't look at peace in the swirling sounds.

She looked like she was at war, fighting for it.

The sight stirred beneath his skin. Something like pride, respect, maybe even jealousy was the potion poisoning him. After everything she'd been through, she was still fighting for peace.

And until this moment, Sal hadn't realized he'd given up on that very thing a long time ago.

Chapter 20

Candice Stevens

She'd done it for Gabe.

Instead of her planned weekly tardiness, she'd arrived nearly on time for church to see Gabe do his thing. Moral support, she told herself, while she focused on deep breathing and mumbled prayers for the songs to end.

Once upon a time, music had been her sole joy in life. Each note had illuminated every cell of her spirit, soul, and body with pure wonderment.

Shoot, she could still feel it ensnared within, inexorably woven into every fiber of her unfortunate DNA. An inherited gift. And curse.

Her mother had been a beautiful singer. A *coloratura*. The things she could do with those rafter-high notes could make grown men weep and bulletproof glass shatter. But those lovely notes only haunted Candice now.

And being in church, knowing forgiveness was the bedrock of this place, she always felt like she was grappling for a handhold but could never quite grasp the concept. *Forgive and forget*, she reiterated in case Jersey missed it, for the role she'd played in those two deaths still stalking her like the reaper anxious to collect.

Perhaps God could overlook her past. But to the Candice she had to face in the mirror, there were some things that were simply unforgivable.

And so many things she just couldn't forget.

"It's too short." Candice shook her head, plopped down on the chaise outside the closet, and gobbled down another handful of peanut butter M&M's from Joselyn's stash.

Joselyn's five-year-old adoptive daughter Kendi climbed up onto the chair with Candice and reached for a handful of her own. "I think it's pwiddy." She dropped the "r" in favor of an adorable toddlerized "w" and gazed at the dress as if it were Cinderella's ballgown. Then she shot a glance back at Candice with an innocent accusation. One that said "How could you wee-fuse the faiwee godmudder's dwess?"

"It is pretty, sugar. It's just too short." And not only that, but just one more inch down the backless black dress would reveal the mortifying "tramp stamp" tattoo just above her tailbone. One she'd been branded with in high school and had yet to remove.

Compared to back then this *was* like a fairytale moment for Candice. Not because she was being stalked by a serial killer and preparing for an undercover op. Yeah, that part didn't fit the fantasy. But here she was, surrounded by girlfriends, trying on the most decadent kinds of dresses in preparation for a date on February fourteenth.

No! She halted the thought right there. Even shook her head in confirmation. Not a date.

Sadie shifted her glare over at Joselyn, the challenge in her eyes stating she was about to stage an intervention since Candice had found fault with each of the thirty-some dresses she'd perused so far.

Joselyn, the tall, gorgeous, and leggy waif Candice should probably hate, raised her hand to hold up further argument. "It's not that short. Besides, *you're* short. If you wear one of the knee length dresses it'll drape down to your ankles. And you'd trip over a floor-length gown so short is really our best bet since I don't have any petites."

Candice huffed out a sigh and raked up another handful of candy-coated "stress-relievers," dropping half the morsels into Kendi's outstretched hand before she threw back the rest. "Is this supposed to be cheering me up?" She spoke mid-munch. "I mean, don't get me wrong, Joss, your clothes are fabulous, no doubt about it." And they were. Joselyn owned a boutique clothing store and had probably hand-selected this piece straight from New York's Fall Fashion Week.

Yes, it was dynamite. So simply lovely Candice really, *really* wanted to slip in and take it for a spin. And actually, it *was* pretty conservative from the front, with a boat neckline and solid black shift under a layer of black lace with elbow-length sheer lace sleeves.

The back was another story.

Trouble was what the dress was.

"But come on, you guys, I'm already dreading this thing at super-snob Preston Bradley's mansion tonight. The last thing I wanna do is draw extra attention to myself."

Candice flung her hand toward the stunner begging to be worn. When she was met with matching exasperated eye rolls from her friends she stood, marched over to the dress, and spun the hanger to expose the back to further her point. "Exhibit A. Really, guys? You could count my vertebrae from my C1 to my L5 in this contraption. It's practically an anatomy lesson."

"What'sat mean? Dat some kinda *gwown* up code?" Kendi piped in looking adorably confused.

"Sorry, sugar. It means you would be able to see all of my back bones from my neck to my ... umm ..."

"Booty." Sadie supplied, and Kendi giggled.

"Seriously," Candice held it up higher. "What about this dress says undercover?"

Not to mention she'd have to go braless. Talk about being subtle.

"That's exactly the point. You are going to be schmoosing

with the who's who in St. Louis. In this dress, you'll fit right in. Just try it on, okay. If you hate it, I promise, we'll send it into exile with all the rest, no questions asked." Sadie held up innocent hands.

Candice shook her head again, then pinched the bridge of her nose.

Joselyn crossed to Candice and laid a soft hand on her arm. "The dress really isn't that scandalous. Is this about something else?"

Looking up, she saw her tight little group surrounding her, amazed by how much comfort she drew from having friends.

"I just have this terrible feeling I'm gonna screw the whole thing up. I don't belong in a place like that. My mother was practically the town prostit—umm, bad girl." She amended for Kendi's ears. "My whole house growing up could fit in this closet. These kinds of people can sniff out trash a mile away."

"You are not trash!" Sadie and Joselyn defended in unison.

"And where you came from, or who you once were, doesn't define who you are today." Sadie's gaze was unyielding. "You're the strongest, smartest, most tenacious chick I've ever met. You're drop-dead gorgeous, and sometimes you're so unflappable you scare the cr—poop out of me."

"You can say *cwap*, Aunt Sadie. I'm almost six now; I've hud it befowa." Kendi fairly squeaked with pride.

Joselyn bit her lip to hide her grin, touched the cheeks of her child, and tilted Kendi's head back. "Let's stick with poop for now, okay, munchkin?"

"Mmm-kay, Mommy." Kendi smiled so big her cheeks went round as apples, her crystal blue eyes bright with love before she buried her face in her new mama's legs for an impromptu hug.

All three of the adults in the room were instantly foggy with tears. Kendi had come such a long way in just a few short weeks since the adoption. She was gaining weight after years of malnourishment, talking almost non-stop, and her smile was now effortless.

What a difference a loving family could make.

Candice did her best to quick-stitch the wounds tearing open in her chest. But without thinking, she stroked the sandy-colored puff of tight curls spiraling out from Kendi's little Afro.

When they were all out together people mistook Kendi for Candice's child because of their similar mixed heritage.

To have a child …

Her thoughts roamed the well-beaten "what-if" path for an extended moment before she snapped her attention back on point.

"Thanks, Sadie. You too, Joss. I don't know what I'd do without you. For the first time in my life I'm not completely alone. You don't know how much that means."

They pulled together in a group hug, poor little Kendi getting smushed between their legs. "You were never alone, Auntie Candice." She mumbled. "God is always wiff you."

Oh, to have faith like a child.

Breaking away from their huddle, Candice bent down and smiled at the wise little girl, hoping it didn't look as forced as it felt. "You're right, Kendi-girl." She tweaked her tiny button nose and straightened.

"Whaddya say, Dr. Stevens? Ready to make jaws drop and tongues wag?" Sadie wrinkled her nose. "That didn't sound right."

Candice smiled in spite of herself. "Fine." She grumbled and snatched the hanger. "I'll try it on. But don't get your hopes up. There is no way I'm wearing this dress."

The doorbell rang.

Candice's breaths bordered on hyperventilation as she

stared at her reflection.

No, it wasn't technically too short. Not obscene at least.

But the delicate lace was like a spider web, snaring her almost immovably as if to restrict her next necessary breath.

Death by cocktail dress. Who would perform the autopsy on that one?

Blaine Attwood sure wouldn't be able to determine "cause of death."

At least they'd been able to confirm her coworker would not be in attendance to blow their cover tonight. That *should* have made her breathe easier.

No dice. The feisty little dress pinched tighter, protesting Candice's lack of appreciation for it, no doubt.

"Just breathe." She forced air in through her nose and out past her bold red lips.

How had she let Dorian talk her into this? And furthermore, how had she let the girls talk her into this gorgeous black contraption that probably cost more than her first month's mortgage?

And why had the dress felt fine before but was now wringing every last scrap of air from her lungs and shrink-wrapping her butt?

A knock came this time, with a warning that he didn't want to have to break down the door again.

"Be right there." She managed a fairly convincing holler. One she hoped would save her new door the abuse.

She didn't look at all like herself. Though if she squinted and pretended she was seeing someone else, she could admit the chick in the mirror looked pretty snazzy.

Her breathing started to even, the silky threads loosening their grip. Released from the illusion of the Chinese handcuff trick dress, she spun on her toes and shot a final regret-ladened glance over her shoulder at the reflection of her exposed spine. "Thanks a million, girls." She sighed, feeling self-conscious but grateful that the dress covered her tasteless tat.

When she whipped open the front door, she immediately turned away. "Just need to grab my coat and I'll be ready." She gathered her coat and clutch, managing not to wobble on her trusty red-suede wedges. "Okay, all set."

Dorian hadn't spoken, his jaw dangling slightly slack and askew. "You look—"

"Let's not talk about it, okay? This dress is already exacting its vengeance. I'm suffering from enough regret as it is."

Pushing him out the door, she armed the alarm and locked up.

"What? Whoa! Whose car is *that*?" Candice gazed out at the sleek black Ferrari f430 parked in her driveway.

She felt a hand press the small of her back, guiding her toward the decadent display of Italian engineering.

"Why, it's ours, Mrs. Gutiérrez." His words brushed against her ear.

Despite the cold, a warm shiver tripped over her skin. It earned him a glare. "You already briefed me on your Chip Foose-custom-automotive-designer cover, *Mr. Gutiérrez.* Whose car is it really?"

"You know who Chip Foose is?" He shook his head, one strong hand grinding a massage into his neck as he muttered something in Spanish. "Forget it. It's Joselyn's dad's. You know Declan Whyte, billionaire, runs the world. His fleet of exotic cars makes Preston Bradley's collection look like a used car lot."

"And he let you borrow his swanky Batmobile because?"

Dorian ventured ahead and opened her door. "Because regardless of the fact that my efforts weren't very effective, he seems to think I did a good job sacrificing myself as roadkill for his daughter's safety. Watch your head."

After she lowered into the supple black seat, she inhaled the dazzling aroma of the Italian leather, stroked her hand reverently over the plush extravagance and the precision stitching. *Oh, Jersey, if you could see us now.*

It was surprising how natural Dorian looked sliding behind the wheel.

Framed by all the decadent black of the Ferrari's interior, he looked just as dark and intense in his trim black tux, steel-gray shirt, and black bowtie.

He completed the sophisticated 007 look with a parted and combed jet-black mane instead of his usual perfectly imperfect tousle.

She forced herself to swallow just before the dome light dimmed and plunged them into near-complete darkness behind the tinted windows. With impressive strength the engine roared to life and then purred like a big bad kitty.

The zenon glow from the dash carved over Dorian's jaw, illuminating the sheen of an extra-close shave.

He looked good. She was just about to mention it when he finessed the stick into reverse and glided out of her drive, turning his head to afford her more than just a profile view.

Okay, fine. He looked better than good.

But really, how hard was it to look good behind the wheel of a Ferrari?

"Do you need me to go over the plan again?" His eyes never left the road as he shifted gears. The thrilling hum of the powerful engine charged, zipping through her veins like liquid speed and pumping her nerves into fifth gear right along with it.

"Nope. I got it." Adjusting in her seat, she tugged at her skirt. Was it just her, or was it getting shorter?

"Okay, well, just remember, we lay low if possible. Staying under the radar will make it easier to sneak around. But if Bradley takes an interest in us—"

"Dorian, I got it, okay. I can be bait if I need to be. Don't make me more nervous than I already am."

"You are not bait!" His intense reaction surprised her.

"Bait, distraction, whatever you wanna call it. I know what I'm supposed to do."

The blue cast from the dash highlighted the muscle

flexing in his jaw. A tense silence fell over them. For once Candice wished for some of Dorian's wisecracking, or even one of his dopey smiles. Because in the next twenty minutes they could be walking into Vivaldi's lair. And neither Candice, nor her shrinking dress, were thrilled about that.

Chapter 21

Dorian Salivas

It took all of five seconds to conclude this op was *not* going to be played under the radar.

Lord, have mercy, Candice looked so smokin' hot she might as well be the sun. He could hardly even look at her for fear of going blind. That and the very real possibility he might be tempted to act on impulse and do something he'd most definitely regret.

Hands to yourself. Mouth closed. Eyes on the prize. Well, the one that *wasn't* wrapped in black lace.

A waiter stopped and offered the last two flutes of champagne from a silver tray. Sal collected the pair and passed one to Candice, singed when their fingers grazed and their eyes met.

All right, Salivas. Game face. You can do this.

"You've got quite a few admirers in this room, *mi amor*." He laid into his accent to embody his character. Unfortunately, he also leaned in, detecting a wisp of that mind-bending sugared scent. He forced a hard swallow, chasing it down with a slim sip of the champagne. "One of whom is Preston Bradley, two o'clock." Who was leering at Candice like she was sex-on-a-stick.

With impressive nonchalance she breathed out a laugh like he'd said something amusing and swept the room with a glance.

Preston Bradley shifted his gaze from the little missus and

tipped his head at Sal in acknowledgement of his competition. *Somebody's classy.*

Sal raised an eyebrow, a superior smile gripping his mouth. *Eat your heart out, Bradley. She's all mine.*

Dang, he wished that were true.

He scraped his fingers into his palm in hopes of deadening his senses and then touched a hand to the enticing little sway at Candice's low, breathtakingly bare back in plain view of the millionaire. The smooth, firm skin caught him by the throat and strangled it dry. Much the same way the sight of her had when she'd opened her door tonight.

Breathe, buddy.

He gazed back at his "wife" with a look of adoration that wasn't at all forced. As if possessed, his thumb skimmed the scoop of her spine and he felt her skin pebble in response. Heat rocketed from his hand and punched him straight in the gut.

"It seems our host is coming to pay us a visit." He locked eyes with hers, gorgeously golden and sprinkled with uncertainty. "It's showtime, Kitty." He winked to put her at ease and she leaned into him, her arm sweeping around his waist and holding tight.

His smile came straight from his heart. If only for the moment he would let himself believe the charade.

"Mr. Bradley." Sal extended his hand. "Sly Gutiérrez, and I'm sure you've noticed my beautiful wife, Katarina."

Candice's arm tightened for a fraction of a second before she let it drop away and offered her hand with a gracious nod. "This is quite the party. Thank you for having us."

Preston trapped her hand between both of his, his eyes roving over her too luxuriously. Sal dug deep for restraint and smirked his amusement at Preston's bold appreciation for his wife. It was the best he could manage when all he wanted to do was plant his fist between the guy's slithery gray eyes.

None too intimidated, Preston took his time memorizing Candice's curves before he relinquished her hand and did a quick inventory of the room. "I dare say it's not too bad." His words spoke of modest deflection, but his tone was as pompous as his smile.

And "not too bad" was *not* the right description of Preston Bradley's crib.

Opulent and regal, every surface of the ballroom was covered in a gleaming white marble. Crystal chandeliers leapt in intervals on the molded ceilings from the wall of windows opening to a stone terrace and across the room to the three-story foyer big enough to hold Sal's entire house. Corinthian columns stood like Buckingham Palace guards throughout the giant room, flanking each of the six sets of double doors swinging out from the ballroom into another large space, hosting something like a library on one side and a parlor on the other.

St. Louis's elite mingled in the grand open space, bustling and fluttering their feathers like a bunch of proud peacocks touting their importance just by being present in all their finery.

The real Sylvester Gutiérrez was a bi-coastal creature, splitting his time between New York and San Francisco when he wasn't overseas or working in his shops. From what Sal had read about him, Sylvester was quiet with his business, usually drafting models and fabrications for his custom cars from home. Hopefully his solitary life would help procure their cover for the evening.

Sal went on autopilot, chatting up the host about anything from business and cars, to bourbon and poker. Their strong accents clashed as if discussing foreign affairs from opposite sides, and yet, when the conversation loosened up, so did Sal's peeve with the Brit who'd ogled his wife.

He might be an arrogant British playboy, but Sal's meter wasn't reading "serial killer."

Not that he knew for certain. Preston Bradley had the resources to cover his tracks, and he sure looked slippery enough with his almost predatory perusal of all things female. He was old enough to be Sal's father, but his wealth and classic good looks meant the man could afford exquisite taste.

But what was Preston's preference? He sure didn't disguise his fascination for Candice. All of Vivaldi's victims were young and beautiful.

And blonde, Sal reminded himself.

Now was the time to act, before their host excused himself to mingle with other guests. They'd discussed this possible scenario and numerous others, but leaving Candice with Preston went against every protective instinct in his body.

What if he'd read Preston wrong? It was virtually impossible to cold read a sociopath since they didn't fit a traditional mold. They weren't affected by a conscience or reliable emotions.

What if he ran their scam right now, like he knew he should, and left Candice in the arms of a killer?

He caught her eye. Almost imperceptibly she nodded, accepting what was coming and granting permission, as if she could sense his hesitance. A mix of pride and fear knotted in his chest. She was so much tougher than she knew.

Slipping his hand into his pocket, he sent the signal. "Well Preston, it was nice talking with you but I promised my wife a dance." Sal wove his fingers through Candice's small, strong hand.

The ring chimed right on cue. "Ahh." He withdrew his phone, made a show of eyeing the screen. "*Mi amor*, I'm afraid this cannot wait." To Candice's acting cred, she actually looked disappointed. "Preston, I don't suppose you'd be a gentleman and push my wife around the dance floor while I take this outside?"

A reptilian grin slanted across the man's mouth, and Sal's blood burned as hot as Candice looked.

"It would be my pleasure." Preston issued a semi-respectable nod in his direction and then cast ravenous eyes on Sal's woman.

A battle warred within him as his phone droned on, his mind scrambling to weigh the odds. Short-term loss versus long-term gain.

Candice would be in a room with hundreds of people. She should be perfectly safe for a few minutes. The plan was solid. Wasn't it?

He didn't want to startle her and tip their hand, but he also didn't want to leave without marking his territory. So he did the only thing he thought she might accept.

Ever so gently, he touched her face, letting his thumb skim over the lovely curve of her cheek. "Save a dance for me, Kitty."

And with that he turned and strode from the room without looking back, leaving his fake-wife/real-love in the arms of a suave Bond millionaire who might just try to steal her heart … by carving it right out of her chest.

Silencing the ringer and talking one-sided nonsense into the phone while he wove through the party toward the nearest exit, Sal kept walking until the winter wind chilled his face.

Once he was out of earshot of the last Secret Service type guard, he shoved the phone into his pocket and melded with the shadows, slipping through a dimly lit drive-thru portico toward the garage.

The distant chime of laugher and classical music exposed the weighty silence. There were eight separate carriage doors flanked by lanterns with bulbs flickering like flames.

Having researched the blueprints for the property in advance, he knew where he was going, knew which lock to pick, and the best route of escape if things went south.

The only problem was, if he got caught, he couldn't fall back on his classic bumbling innocence act. He was the dignified and brilliant Sylvester Gutiérrez.

He just hoped he'd be as sly as the name implied.

Something didn't seem right about the silence. And the flickering lanterns made the shadows dance, creating illusions that he wasn't alone in this empty courtyard.

And speaking of dancing …

His mind wandered back to Candice. And Preston. How close were they standing? Where were Bradley's hands? No. He shook away the image. *Focus. Get in. Get out. Go get your girl.*

The wind chased around him in a directionless fury, prickles of sweat dotted his neck and nearly froze on the turbulent breeze. Yet the faster he went, the harsher the clack of his shoes bounded off the cold stone.

Sal shivered, checked his rearview once more and disappeared around the side of the garage.

Extracting the lock-pick from his pocket, he went to work on the door. By last record, there wasn't a security system wired here. The inside of the garage, on the other hand, was safeguarded with all sorts of antitheft rigs. Including a biometric fingerprint safe housing all the keys like a tricked out valet stand.

Sal was playing his luck, hoping the Maserati doors wouldn't be locked so he could gain access to the trunk. The car was already in a locked garage. And the keys were as secure as Fort Knox. How paranoid did you have to be to keep the doors locked as well?

The soft slide of the deadbolt clicked against his steady fingers, and the door eased open with only the faintest brush of the weather stripping at the base.

He held in a whistle. Preston's collection gleamed like pretty maidens all in a row. The soft pulse of lantern light through the carriage windows made each sleeping beauty look all the more dangerous and exotic.

His breathing remained even, but his heart rate ratcheted up a notch. He practically glided over the glossy epoxy floor. The hard soles of his nicest pair of shoes clicking a clean, rhythmic cadence as he worked his way down the line in search of the Maserati.

The garage was full, and he'd gotten to the last car, a bronze Bentley. No Maserati.

Hmm. The car had been licensed in Missouri only two months ago. And this was Bradley's primary stateside residence. So where was the Maserati?

Sal started back the way he came, the pivot of his soles squeaking on the floor when a shape shifted behind the half-glass entry door. A key crammed into the deadbolt he'd thankfully locked behind himself.

Now what? Crouching behind a car could prove to be a monumental mistake. If he tried to outmaneuver whoever it was, his shoes might squeak on the epoxy. He only had a few seconds to decide. Only a moment of sound from the weather strip before the silence could expose his search for a place to hide.

As the door peeled open, Sal collapsed down to the floor on his stomach, wrapped one arm around a tire of a—*hey, whaddya know*—a Challenger like his. Only older and classic. And way, *way* nicer. With the brushing sound of the closing door, Sal dragged himself in unison beneath the car, trapping the pain screaming from his knee in his throat with his last breath.

Heavy steps beat a path toward him.

The slow measured march of someone with suspicions.

Aww man, he was toast! What possible reason could he come up with for hiding under Preston's car? And in a locked garage, no less!

At least the lights were still off, though that tossed the option of hypnosis out.

The pursuer passed him. Sal fed a much-needed breath into his lungs, cringing slightly at how much the tension was trashing his system. His leg throbbed. His chest banded tight. His—

Keys collided on a key ring; the sound a welcome relief in combination with a growling, "All clear," that followed.

When the door clicked and locked behind Sal, leaving him alone on the garage floor with his twisted knee and banged up lungs, he let his breathing resume and allowed relief to tumble through him.

And yet, when he pulled himself upright and surveyed the cars again, fear raced right back in. Because if the Maserati wasn't here, Preston Bradley—the man at this very moment in possession of one of the few precious things Sal cared about in this world—most definitely had something to hide.

Chapter 22

Candice Stevens

If this were any other time, Candice would tell the charming British Pierce Brosnan exactly where she might shove his wandering hand if it "accidentally" groped her rear again.

But this wasn't one of those other times. This time, a delicate balance of factors all hinged on her keeping him placated and occupied.

His pampered hand slid up her bare back. Shivers having nothing to do with pleasure chased over his slimy path. *Stupid dress!* She'd known it'd be a magnet for trouble.

"You're a wonderful dancer, Katarina." His heated breath misted over her temple as he pulled her tighter.

She strained away to reclaim the space, smiling sweetly. "You're not so bad yourself, Mr. Bradley."

"Preston, please." He hiked a suave eyebrow toward a resilient hairline, everything about his grin screaming "debonair," and yet she couldn't help but feel her stomach lurch with every tip of his lips, every suggestive twinkle in his cold, gray eyes, and every liberal skim of his too-soft hand.

All she could think about were his victims being deluded with that charm just before he sliced them open. He could be Britain's Ted Bundy, for all she knew.

Of course, there was always the possibility he wasn't Vivaldi at all. Perhaps he was just a giant flirt. Maybe she should be flattered someone like Preston Bradley, who could have his pick of any female partner in the room, wanted to dance with her.

She just needed to make sure the dancing continued, controlling Preston's presence so he couldn't wander off and stumble upon Dorian's search for Sarah Hoyt's blood.

"So, rumor has it your husband has interest for very little that doesn't run on four wheels." He didn't say it directly, but his tone begged the question, "Aren't you lonely?"

Candice Stevens was lonely. By choice. Because men were dominators by nature. Possessors. And as much as she wanted to be brave and risk giving her heart to someone again, she knew she was far too easily manipulated to trust herself with a man.

"Things that move on two wheels as well. He's also a fan of what moves on these two legs, so that works out well for us." She playfully reprimanded him with a smile.

"Who could blame the chap for that?" He eased her into a dip. She let her head fall back to avoid an intimate gaze and laughed.

"Smooth, Mr. Bradley. But my husband is very gifted. I completely support his interests."

"I see. And what, may I ask, are your interests?" Light on his feet like Fred Astaire, Preston twirled her around the floor, the twelve-piece band embellishing the scallops and scotch-scented airwaves with an instrumental version of "What a Wonderful World." Breathing deeply, she focused on charming the millionaire and matching his steps, turning a deaf ear to the elegant strains of music.

"Why, cars of course." She winked. *Like the one you stash bodies in.*

His steps slowed. "Is that right? What's your preference?"

"Maseratis." The word slipped before she could think. Her heart stumbled in the same moment her toe stubbed against his foot, nearly doubling her over the arm he extended to steady her.

With a wicked smile and a precise hand, he swept her

back into a slow waltz. "O-Of course, I like Ferraris too, or anything my Sly designs. And I'm a sucker for some old American muscle." She was babbling. Nervous heat from her blunder charging through her body to accumulate in an explosive blaze against her cheeks.

She needed a specific diversion, something less exotic and American. Dorian's macho Challenger came to mind. "Maybe I'll have Sly doctor up a sweet old Challenger. They always were my favorite."

Great, Candice! Maseratis and Challengers. Preston Bradley and Dorian Salivas. In a nut shell.

Stopping midstride Preston swiveled out from under her hand at his shoulder and tugged her toward the door. "In that case, there is something I'd like to show you."

No! She forced herself not to scream the word as fear boiled up in her throat. Go somewhere alone with Preston Bradley. To see his, *gulp*, Maserati?

Dorian would be *made* and this whole night would be over.

Digging deep for a naughty little vixen role, she tugged him back, laced her hands around his neck and folded in her bottom lip. "But we haven't finished our dance, Mr. Bradley. And I'm finding I rather enjoy being the envy of every woman in this room."

Gag me.

Preston dragged her flush against him, easily persuaded to stay entwined as he barred his arms around her back, locking her in place. Fear rioted in her veins, and without a moment's notice the suffocating memories came flooding back.

"Don't you get it, Candi. You belong to me now." The sadistic twist of AJ's lips looked nothing like the smile he'd used to coax her into his bed the night before.

His fingers pinched against the pulse point at her throat until he'd wrung tears from her eyes. "I don't care how extraordinary that mind of yours is. You're mine, and you'll do what I say." His lips slammed against hers, her choking sob smothered under the brutal beating of his mouth. And then, he softened, the healing stroke of his lips a balm to the damage he'd inflicted.

Unable to respond, she stood stock still, tense as the beam against her back.

"Kiss me." He demanded. Her mind reeled. Her fear so palpable she was shackled to the wall with it.

Leaning against her with the fullness of his weight, she sucked in a breath at the pressure. The reminder of his strength. His size. His complete and total advantage. "Kiss me." He growled. His hard fingers sinking back in for a bite.

She cried out, and he gripped a fist full of her hair, cranking her neck back to meet his black, soulless eyes.

How had she missed those before? They'd been so deceptively sweet. And she'd been so lonely, so desperate for connection she'd unwittingly compromised the bright future—the escape—she had fought tooth and nail to pave for herself.

"AJ, you're h-hurting me."

Tears leaked back, collecting in her ears. He let go, and for a moment she thought he would free her. But without warning his fist slammed into her eye. An explosion of pain ripped a broken cry from her lungs, nearly collapsing her knees before his hips pinned her against the beam. "I'll teach you about pain. This is your life now, Candi. Get used to it."

"Is something wrong?" The honeyed British accent chased away the reverie. The final whine of the violin strings bringing Louis Armstrong's classic to a close. "You're shaking—"

"May I cut in?"

Relief rushed out of her lungs on a sigh when Dorian's spicy accent took down Great Britain. She looked up, seeing the tension in his smile drain off when their eyes met.

"By all means." Ever gracious, Preston stepped back, dragging one of her hands to his mouth for a perfunctory kiss before he released her. "Your wife is a marvelous dancer,

Mr. Gutiérrez. You're a very lucky man. Though it seems I might have worn out her tires a bit." He winked back at her.

"Everything all right, Corazón?" *Sweetheart.*

Candice nodded and smiled, not ready to trust her voice.

"Thank you for keeping my wife company. I owe you one."

"The pleasure was all mine." Preston scrunched his pompous nose. "Do I smell motor oil?"

Candice laughed for no apparent reason. "That's my Sly. The stuff practically runs in his veins." It was a knee-jerk reaction. But at least it meant her brain had kicked back in gear.

"Well, I was just about to offer your wife a glimpse at my small collection. You interested?"

Interested in seeing his murder-mobile? Only if she could use it to lock him away for the rest of his life. After she ran over him with it.

She looked over at Dorian, desperate to read his reaction. What had he found? Had he used the Luminol she'd given him? Had she explained well enough how it could detect the presence of blood that might have since been scrubbed away?

And just as urgent was the question—had she just been dancing with Vivaldi? Had a murderer's hands just slithered all over her?

The thought alone could induce vomiting.

"We'd love to." Dorian offered his arm, a conspiratorial gleam in his dark chocolate eyes.

Were they anything like AJ's? Could they also be sort of melty and puppy-dog sweet one minute, and then morph him into Lucifer's minion the next?

Candice threaded her arm through Kitty's husband's and let herself be lead through the house and out to a lantern-lit courtyard. A large carriage house was separated from the main residence by fifty yards of creamy white stone.

They made their way out into the brisk night, the men talking engines and horsepower. Worthy topics but not enough to distract Candice from what they might find behind the garage doors.

Had Dorian not been able to break in? And how would they be casual about asking to scope out the trunk. Maybe mist some Luminol over the back seat and shine her special black light on it. Or maybe a Kastle-Meyer test with her prepared swabs of phenolphthalein in her clutch.

No way he'd find *that* suspicious.

As if hitting a wall, her head suddenly hurt, her feet ached, and the chilled air withered away her hard-earned insulation.

Before she'd even shivered, Dorian was draping his suit coat over her shoulders and tucking her beneath his arm. Drugging her with his smoky sweet scent, he squeezed her against his side and dusted his lips against her hair.

Despite what they might find, with one comforting touch—that was most likely for show—she felt safe. She was wandering off to a secluded garage with two men, one of whom might be a serial killer, and she felt … safe?

How stupid was that? This was precisely why she avoided men. And relationships.

Candice sidled away from his hold but kept his coat and wrapped it tighter.

"Aww, thanks, Sly." It probably sounded as saccharine as it felt. Like a verbal pat on the head. But his touch disturbed her. And her response to withdraw, undercover or not, was a mechanism of survival. Besides, Preston was too enrapt with car jargon to notice.

Dorian's slight puzzled frown said he'd detected the shift in her. There were no such things as psychics, she reminded herself, hating how it felt like he was reviewing her thoughts on X-ray films.

This Dorian was an illusion. Every action was calculated for their ruse. He was only pretending to be this sophisticated, brilliant businessman.

Though the serious act looked good on him, she could admit it.

But even pretending to feel things for Dorian was dangerous. She was starting to rely on him, in dozens of tiny ways over the past few days. He'd been right. He was becoming her safety net.

She could feel the tread beneath her feet slipping. Could feel herself spiraling down to that place of entrapment. She'd learned the hard way that safety nets were actually spider webs. And they weren't safe at all.

Sylvester Gutiérrez was a good-looking, Ferrari-driving, affectionate husband. But Candice had a feeling Dorian could play any role he was given to perfection. Who even knew who the real Dorian Salivas was?

Was he the guy in the closet at the FBI? The guy who'd kicked her door down? That guy was code-*blazing*-red. Impulsive. Dangerous. Maybe a little bit delicious.

Or was he the goofy, skillet-wielding big brother who'd taken the wrath of his father to shield his family? And couldn't that guy be just as dangerous to her heart?

In truth, she didn't know who Dorian Salivas was. He wasn't a killer but he could very well be Sly Gutiérrez underneath it all. Or perhaps even a skirt-chaser like Preston Bradley. Or worse yet, AJ.

It just wasn't worth it. Her life might not be a dream. But she'd rather be laid out on her autopsy table, or be alone every night for the rest of her life, than wake up in another nightmare.

"Criminy. What on earth possessed you to say yes!" Candice was trying hard to remain calm. It felt like she'd even managed to keep a smile on her face while she spoke the strained sentiment to her idiot husband.

Dorian finessed a lemon tart from a passing tray and popped the miniature sweet into his mouth. She'd give him points for keeping his mouth closed, but he smiled as he chewed.

Always with the smiling. This wasn't amusing in the slightest.

His languishing consumption of the tiny dessert stirred the coals of her frustration. Well, if he was going to act like a child she would treat him like one. "I'm putting my foot down." She even pointed to her red shoe to drive the point across. "And the answer is no. We will find a suitable excuse and graciously decline."

"But I already accepted. He's expecting us for the weekend. How else are we going to check out the Maserati? He told us it's at his new lake house. And you know darn well we don't have enough for a warrant."

Their voices were low enough to avoid curious ears, but the tension between them was as polluting as the scent of motor oil on his jacket. What had he done, rolled around on the garage floor? *That's some impressive sleuthing, you big dope.*

"Kitten, perhaps we should discuss this at home later. Privately." With a sense of calm she couldn't find in her own bag of tricks, Dorian scanned their immediate company to be sure no one overheard, nodding politely at a gorgeous blonde devouring him with her eyes like she'd starved herself a week just so she would fit into her dress and was now ravenous.

They'd been stuck talking to some of Preston's cronies after they'd returned from the garage, and Dorian had agreed to a group getaway.

Talk about sleeping with the enemy. They'd be over three hours from home—from back-up—and down the hall from a murderer.

Sweet dreams.

And of course, there was absolutely no chance of them sleeping together, but under the guise of a married couple they couldn't exactly ask for separate rooms.

She was going to kill him!

"What a generous offer. We haven't gotten away in a while, have we Kitty? We'd love to."

Moron! Stronger words vented silently in her head.

Of all the times not to be wearing her rubber band ...

"Come on, sweetness, let's dance." He tried to tug her out to the dance floor, but she dug in her heels.

"Not on your life, pal."

It just shot out. A teensy bit too loud.

Chapter 23

Dorian Salivas

This was obviously too much for her to handle. A nervous current stirred shrill peaks into her usually smooth alto. Her body language was so rigid and cold if she fell off those sexy heels she would shatter, her shards of ice would skate to the edges of the enormous room.

Even *that* would be more subtle than her big sister act.

Since their cover was a married couple, he'd been looking forward to having an excuse to hold her hand, touch the small of her back, feather a kiss over the wrinkles in her forehead when she frowned at him.

She did that a lot.

The night held so much potential. A possible break in the case. A date of sorts with the woman of his dreams. A reason to escape reality for a few short hours and test the waters of a relationship.

But no. From the moment she'd opened her door, she'd been in babysitting mode. As the night wore on he assumed she would find her rhythm and loosen up; let the ruse play out if for no other reason than to catch a killer. Instead, it had gotten progressively worse. The real turning point had been when they were walking to the garage. She'd been fighting another one of her internal battles. Losing, from the looks of things.

Her comments had become increasingly condescending and dismissive. Back to the old Candice who'd plowed him down on the sidewalk not even a week ago. The one whose polite smile seemed to pity his sad little crush.

He'd thought they'd made some headway, especially after their confessional in Gabe's studio when the walls between them crumbled from the shared pain of their pasts.

He hadn't imagined it. He remembered feeling the surrender in her body when he'd held her as she'd cried. The needy look in her eyes that spoke of a lonely little girl still fighting to overcome her past. The undeniable sadness and regret that broke on her voice as she tossed away her armor and laid herself bare. *"I'm weak."*

Darn woman had him all tied up in knots. At this point it might be less painful if he climbed into a long black box and let her saw him in half.

Ladies and gentlemen, your magician this evening is the constantly emasculated fool, Dooorian Salivassss!

Downplaying her belittling comment, he issued a rueful smile and placed his hand over his heart. "You wound me, Kitten." Sad how accurate the statement was.

"Dor—" She stopped herself. "Darling, I'm … I'm …"

He pressed the pads of his fingers over her lips as her punishment. The soft touch did something to her. In the same way his innocent kiss in the closet had unraveled her.

If he took it further he just might make her whole house of cards tumble. All that pretense and denial. But he didn't really want them to fall in front of an audience. He wanted to free her from her chains, not humiliate her.

"It's fine, *mi amor*. We don't have to dance."

Something flagged on his senses, and he let his hand drop away. Candice started back up on the strings of her apology. The worst of it was it still sounded like she was consoling a preschooler who'd lost his dollop of ice cream to the pavement.

A sparsely landscaped head of hair came into view just beyond Preston and a young, fawning socialite. The head was familiar, but the face eluded him in the shift of bodies.

Closing his eyes, the details sketched in his mind. The arctic blue eyes, the lined face, and the subtle hint at adolescent acne. Jensen. His boss was here.

Handy. Sal could bring him up to speed.

But ...

His boss was here. *Sal's* boss. At this party. In roughly thirty seconds their cover would be history.

The head of the FBI had some influential friends. He was a regular at these types of fundraisers. Sal didn't know why that important tidbit had slipped his mind when he'd concocted this plan.

If he'd thought this through, he would've informed Jensen of his covert op. But it'd been thrown together so last minute, and on a Sunday no less, Sal didn't see the point of setting himself up for a fall if this turned out to be a dead end.

That certainly wouldn't inspire the kind of confidence he needed to regain his badge.

And he couldn't utilize many FBI resources if Jensen wanted him to sniff out the mole, now could he. So it wouldn't have changed a thing. He'd still be flying solo.

Well, solo plus his big sister/wife. Not the Mormon kind. One brat was plenty.

Maybe he could intersect Jensen before he got to Preston. Or preferably before he spied Sal just over Preston's shoulder. Maybe if he gave him a quick rundown Jensen could play along.

No sooner had a plan drafted in his head when his boss found their illustrious host and hastened right into the fray.

Fine. Plan B.

Sal turned, angling his body to hide Candice. "We gotta go before we're made. I'll explain later." He grabbed her hand and bee-lined toward the nearest exit. Except, in his haste to leave the room to keep out of sight, he'd taken the wrong door. They were now much farther from the valet and still had to weave through the mass of snobs to the coat room.

Candice didn't utter a word, though she still had that annoyed look on her face that said he was a count-of-three away from a timeout.

Sal tried not to focus on that. Tried to keep his eye on the ball as he raced to the end zone. But Candice jerked her hand away. He turned to find blazing anger in her eyes.

"What?" He snapped. "What now? Do I get a spankin'?" Oops. That didn't sound right.

"I do *not* need a leash. And I won't have you dragging me around this place like your poodle."

Somehow he'd hit a nerve. Well, fine. She'd struck more than one tonight as well. His retaliation was prepped and ready when he spied Jensen and Preston emerging from the ballroom doors near the foyer. Sal uttered some colorful Spanish.

Plan C.

Preston Bradley was scanning the crowd. Candice wasn't gonna like it, but she'd just have to deal. Grabbing her wrist, Sal turned back and spotted a closed door leading from the library. Her leash was tighter this time, his grip a bit stronger to ensure her compliance.

His pulse hammered away on his clumsy lung, each breath a fraction of what he needed until he closed them behind the door. Another dark closet. From the smell of it, this one had cleaning supplies.

Slipping his phone from his pocket, he pulled up his flashlight app and set the phone on the shelf at waist level.

Candice was rubbing her wrist, the flashlight casting her with "ghost-story" shadows from below. But despite the dim illumination, her glittering eyes seemed to possess a light of their own.

"Jensen showed up, all right!" His attempt at whispering failed. "I was trying to protect our cover so we'd still have a shot at seeing the Maserati, but you just had to go all independent on me, didn't you?"

She huffed, still rubbing her wrist. "How much longer

would it have taken you to say, 'Hey, Director Jensen is here. We'd better go before we blow our cover.'"

"A lot longer. And I wasn't trying to drag you, I was trying to help you along. Those short little legs of yours don't move very fast. Especially in those heels. What would you rather me do? Throw you over my shoulder and carry you out? In that dress, that'd be about as subtle as setting myself on fire."

"You think it was subtle the way you nearly yanked my wrist out of socket!"

"Oh, you wanna talk subtle, do you? *Great*. Since we are on the subject, we might as well discuss your lousy acting skills."

She crossed her arms over her chest. The hesitation in her rebuttal gave him free rein.

"We're supposed to be pretending to be in love. I know that's like your Everest, but you said you could handle it. Well, you can't. You're blowing it. If everyone doesn't leave here thinking we're brother and sister I'll be amazed."

"What?" She shrugged. "Maybe we're just not an affectionate couple?" Holding on to her sass, she jutted her hip and kept her sunshine eyes on full blast. They were so beautiful it should have been blinding, but regardless of the way she weaponized them, he kept on looking.

Come on, Sal, feel the burn.

He cleared his throat. "Well, that would be sad and boring, but it's not what I'm talking about. You simply refuse to see it."

"See what?"

The darkness should have been a shield, but somehow he was more tuned in than ever.

He was right. He hadn't imagined it. It was there.

But it was her blazing sun, and she just couldn't bring herself to look at it.

"Somebody really did a number on you, Candice. But here's a news flash. I'm not him. I'm so done with your patronizing big sister act. So ditch the shades and take a good long look because here it is, Kitten ... I'm a man."

"Yes, I can see that. The he-man testosterone you're putting off is as potent as these cleaning agents. I'm getting asphyxiated by that almighty Y chromosome. Congratulations. You're a credit to your gender."

He wanted this to be a serious moment, but his lips curled in defiance. "No, Brat. You might see that I'm male. But what you refuse to see ..."

And here it was. The loaded gun. He couldn't wait to see the look on her face.

"... is that I'm sexy."

Chapter 24

Candice Stevens

"Oh, brother!" She rolled her eyes, waiting for his next quip to follow, but nothing came. Admittedly, she wasn't feeling particularly sisterly at present, but a little more scolding should do the trick. She met his eyes to do just that.

Bad move. They were magnetic, probing in his psychic way that made her want to close her eyes, click her heels, and pray to be whisked away to anywhere but here.

He couldn't be serious. *I'm sexy.* Who even made a declaration like that? No, he was fishing for something, but she wouldn't give him the satisfaction. Candice tilted her head. "You about done with your tantrum?"

"Not even close." His voice had gotten thick and rumbly. A sliver of light melted the centers of his eyes to dark chocolate ganache. Her stomach reacted first, grumbling and shrinking in want. Then little spirals of heat trilled outward on a faulty pump of her pulse. She checked herself before a nervous schoolgirl giggle snuck out into the scant inches between them.

What kind of scam were her emotions running? All she knew for sure was they were running amok because some confused chemical imbalance told her Dorian suddenly looked different.

Gone was the hapless class clown with the boyish smile. The man standing before her was rugged and serious and kind of ... hot.

Huh. Dorian, sexy?

Was it a trick of the light? She was tempted to seek out a switch, but she was frozen in place, fully consumed by his stare.

He took a step forward. Then another. Frustration and something possibly more dangerous defined the angles of his face. Sculpted cheekbones, large espresso eyes, strong straight nose, and his lips ...

The lips usually delivering bone-headed lines were sensuously full and downright drinkable.

"What are you doing?" The words were hers, but the voice belonged to some breathless wanton fool.

He pressed the pads of his fingers over her mouth to silence her. With a slow tender stroke he traced the crest of her lip. The tickly touch shivered down to her toes. A stuttered breath dragged in the cool air wrapped around his warm fingers. And then he ventured south. Which should have frightened her but for some reason, anticipation injected into her veins.

His hard fingers shimmied with the gentlest touch across her jaw. Callused knuckles continued the caress down the side of her neck to her throat.

He didn't speak. His eyes patiently roaming her face. His fingers stirring up goose bumps spreading to regions far beyond the respectable planes he touched.

When he leaned in, she could do nothing but wait. Surprisingly, the thought of his kiss was too exciting, and confusing, to turn away. Closing her eyes, she gave herself over to the inevitable.

Only, his lips didn't land. They touched just beyond the corner of her mouth, traced the same shivering path over her cheek, down her jaw ...

Oh mama ...

He wasn't kissing her, but his lips, so soft and molten melted her defenses, and apparently her kneecaps. Heck, all her joints were liquefying under his heated assault. Soon she'd be nothing more than a puddle of longing.

The silk pads of his lips continued to work their magic, painting her neck with nothing but the tantalizing skim of his mouth. Without realizing it, she tilted her head back to grant him better access.

He took that as his invitation, and she felt the first kiss press into the hollow of her throat. And then another on her collarbone, and up her neck. Each kiss teasing and tempting until her heart nearly shattered with exertion. She swallowed a whimper, taking with it a heady breath of his sweet and spicy intoxication. Her head swam, hints of the woman she'd denied for so long escaped into her bloodstream on a needy rush of estrogen.

"Are you trying to seduce me?" She couldn't believe she'd breathed the words because, at the moment, the last thing she wanted him to do was stop.

He ignored her, which was just as well, and placed one last kiss on the sensitive flesh by her ear, before he nipped gently on the lobe. She heard herself gasp, though her voice seemed so far away.

And then, perhaps sensing her knees about to buckle, he steadied her hips, dragging her close until no sliver of space could be found between them.

Lifting his face from her neck, she could feel his eyes on her again, as if they could touch her as perfectly as his mouth. She opened her eyes and met his.

Man alive, they were an easy mark. He wanted her. Not shocking since he'd always been clear on that, but more surprising was … she wanted him too.

"No." He finally answered, and with one word squashed her surge of desire. "I'm not trying to seduce you, Candice. I'm changing the way you see me."

Oh. And it had been a wildly successful exercise. One she desperately hoped wasn't quite over.

He bent down until his lips tickled hers, and without kissing her, he angled his head, letting his motionless mouth caress hers, as if to memorize the contours of her lips without giving in to them.

She couldn't take it anymore. Her need had become a force stronger than she could restrain. In one swift move she dug both hands into his thick hair and pulled him to meet the full force of her kiss.

She strained against him, and he surrendered to her request. Melding together, just lips and breath and soul. Still just teasing her mouth with his, he released her hips, slipping one arm around her waist to anchor her low back. The other hand skimmed up her naked spine to pull her tighter to his chest where their heartbeats raced in unison.

Surrounded by his strength and his lips was the most exquisite sensation, she had to have more. Easing her mouth open, she tilted her neck to deepen the kiss.

But he pulled back.

Stunned, rejected, justifiably confused, Candice stood bereft, feeling the cool air wrap around what had been kindled by Dorian's warmth. She wanted to scream. That or throw herself at his lips and beg them to finish the conversation.

With bunched fists at his sides, and labored breathing, it was clear stepping away hadn't been an easy decision for him.

It was a small sort of consolation. Much preferred over a blatant rejection, especially since she'd basically attacked his mouth and demanded his kiss. Not her style. So… why had she done it?

And furthermore, now that the smoke of his seduction act had cleared, why did she want to kiss him again? *And then some*, Jersey added. It had been more than a decade since she'd willingly touched a man, one who wasn't dead, that is. Why now? Why Dorian?

With AJ the only times she'd acted on her own had been with the less than brilliant idea that she'd at least have the illusion of control. She'd been tired of being used and hurt and degraded. She hadn't realized how deeply wounded she'd become until she stopped fighting it, handed over her will and her body, and enslaved herself.

Just like her mother had.

But this ... this felt different. Never before had she been touched with such tender control. Such adoration.

As much as physical contact in general might make her want to head straight for the nearest confessional and purge her ingrained filth, this awakening with Dorian gave her the smallest hope that perhaps not all men were like AJ.

She couldn't help but think that, despite his provocations, Dorian's actions, while counterproductive to what she'd wanted in the moment, were actually noble.

Dorian's always carefree face was strained as he raked his hand through his hair, mussing Sly Gutiérrez's perfect coif. "That was chapter two. I survived." He huffed under his breath, "barely."

"Chapter two? When was chapter one?"

What did that even mean? The sensations of the past few minutes were finally fizzling enough for her head to clear. But there were still too many questions swirling around for her to pinpoint which answer to seek first.

He feigned looking wounded, and she was disturbed to note how cute it was. "You don't recall our first romp in the closet? Apparently it's our version of Lover's Lane."

In an instant the cute was gone, the sultry lift of a dark eyebrow fired over the mother of all hot flashes.

Good gravy! How had she never noticed how freaking hot he was?

Lord, she better not swoon. At least not outwardly. And she most definitely needed her rubber band stat.

Grappling with her last blip of gumption, she propped her hands on hips that had, only moments ago, been in Dorian's full possession. "Romp? I don't recall anything of the sort."

He winked. "It was just an appetizer. We'll get to dessert, eventually."

Whoa. Bumbling little Dorian was a ladies' man?

Indignation flared. Chapters and dinner courses? What kind of game was he playing?

Bloody brilliant, Dr. Stevens! She wanted to slap her forehead. Maybe the whole thing had been a manipulation? Sneaky, using tenderness instead of force. She'd played right into his hands. How could she be so stupid? AJ Gardallo had seemed charming at first, too. Tortured and misunderstood.

Oh, how easily you forget. Jersey tsked, as if she didn't have something to do with it.

"Don't get all huffy, Brat, I'm not the hit it and quit it kind. These aren't bases. I'm not looking to score. At least, not the way most people use the analogy."

Slightly comforting. Though she hated how quickly she'd been persuaded by his touch. By his words. Even all his quirky analogies. To think, an hour ago she'd thought of Dorian as a brother. Nothing in that vein was coursing through her now.

"Well, I'm flattered, really." Though the words were laced with enough sarcasm to buzz that sexy, tousled hair right off his head. "But, I won't be engaging in any romping until … I'm married." It was a safe call. Because to willingly, legally bond herself to a man? *Never gonna happen.* "Sorry Dorian, this restaurant doesn't serve dessert."

"I'm fully aware of the menu, sugar. And my comment stands. We'll get to dessert, eventually."

It was a threat. One she didn't want to decipher. Less than ten minutes in a closet and her world was back on its head.

Seven minutes in heaven, my eye. More like seven circles of hell for how much torment would follow her first slip of affection since she was sixteen and escaped AJ.

Why had she let him touch her? Why had she kissed him? Wanted more? Why, with all his arrogant and annoying banter, was she practically smiling inside?

She didn't have an answer to any of those questions. But they almost didn't matter. What mattered was the answer to a single terrifying question with a million wrong answers. Why on earth did she trust Dorian Salivas?

Chapter 25

Dorian Salivas

She kissed me!

Sal relived the moment of triumph as he maneuvered the Ferrari out of Preston Bradley's long driveway.

Perhaps he'd pushed it too far. But her skin was so petal soft, her sugary fragrance so maddeningly sweet, he couldn't help himself.

She'd had it coming, throwing down the gauntlet with all her patronizing.

He had to find a way to break free from the exasperating confines of the friend zone. Or the kid-brother zone. Though, he'd never heard of that one before. It seemed he was the exclusive member.

But, and this was the greatest but of all time—no pun intended, at least not intentionally—when she'd taken matters into her own hands ... *ay dios mio!* He'd indulged in the taste of her long enough to know he'd never get enough. And he knew better than to try.

Besides, he had, in a way, been trying to seduce her. Not to take it too far, but to strip away her fear and her misconceptions and allow her to be seduced by her heart and all those repressed emotions.

Even thinking he'd *manipulated* her into that kiss made him want to take a sledge hammer to his knee.

Absently kneading the ache, he thought about how hard he'd tried to shut off his inner *Rain Man*. But when he passed over the pulse at her neck, his fingers had lingered there and read her reactions to his roaming lips like a treasure map. The same way he'd strategically placed his fingers on her in the FBI closet. That time had been to make sure she wasn't about to knee him in the groin.

But this time … this time hadn't been for show.

Helpless to the memory, he was back in the closet, Candice straining against him, her lips the most dangerous detonator he'd ever encountered.

And he still hadn't allowed himself to kiss her properly.

A most difficult exercise in restraint. But when she kissed him for real, he wanted to be sure it was because she wanted to, and because she trusted him, not because he'd hotwired her touch receptors with his tricks.

Glancing though the jet-black interior of the Batmobile, he saw her rubbing her wrist. Without thinking he snatched her palm and lifted it to his mouth, placing the softest kiss on the tender spot.

She stilled, her pulse point jumping gears. Because he couldn't seem to help himself, he rubbed his lips over the satin skin, kissed her wrist once again, and returned her hand to her lap, where he let his hand remain on hers.

She didn't pull away, so that was a good sign.

"You okay?"

"Yeah. I'm just glad we got out of there before we were discovered."

"Me too, Brat. I'd hide in a closet with you anytime." He glanced over at his gorgeous date and winked. He didn't want her tense and stressed so he did what he did best. Annoyed her.

Only, for once, she didn't look annoyed. With a small laugh, she smiled. Actually smiled. "Better not get used to it. In fact, I'm fairly certain I can pin the blame on the dress. I warned the girls it would be trouble."

"I like trouble." He forced his eyes over the dash. "Though I can't bring myself to say a single bad thing about that dress. On anyone else, it might be ordinary. On you?" Glancing back at her he smiled, unable to see the dress beneath her coat but not needing to as he had every stitch of black lace and amaretto skin committed to memory. "On you that dress is a gift to humanity."

He was being a sappy idiot, but he couldn't wrestle back the words when the compliment marked her with such genuine surprise and disbelief. "Candice, I notice a lot of things. Things others might miss, but things that fade quickly. Your beauty tonight, in this moment, will stay with me until my last breath. Of that, I have no doubt."

Her breath heaved in her chest without a sound. She wetted her lips, and he had to pin his gaze to the road lest he be tempted to pull over and wet them himself. "I'm not sure I believe that, Dorian. But thank you. That's the nicest thing anyone's ever said to me."

"What in the world?" He glanced at the dash.

"What? It can't be that hard to believe. I mean, you already know my childhood was tough. And I haven't even told you the worst of it."

"No. Not that, Kitten. This." Pointing to the gauge, he eased the Ferrari to the shoulder of the wide, deserted road. "This was the last thing I thought would go wrong tonight."

"Car trouble? With this car? I'm with you there." She slipped her hand out from under his and was out of the car and tapping on the trunk before he'd cut the ignition.

Sal popped the latch and stepped out into the brisk, black night.

"Ferraris have mid-engines and they're air cooled so it's not a leaky radiator hose or coolant issue. Let's see what we got." Candice braced one arm on the strip of rear fender and leaned over the vapors billowing from the overheated engine.

Sal stood practically paralyzed in awe when his Wonder Woman stripped off her coat, wrapped a sleeve around her palm to protect it from the heat, and braved her hand to the smoldering beast.

"Looks like …"

He tried to focus on her words and not the sight of this gorgeous car-goddess bent over a Ferrari, but when she twisted a small scrawl of ink peeked from the open back of her dress—from that tantalizing little sway at the base of her spine.

The gulp he forced down his throat was unmercifully resonant. He fastened his gaze to the immaculate chrome of the engine glistening in the moonlight. The sight not even slightly interesting in comparison, but at least it didn't burn him up from the inside. Just the outside. He swiped at the moisture misting his brow.

"If we let it cool about twenty minutes, we should be able to make it home as long as we keep the heat on full blast to draw the hot air away from the engine." She propped back up, dashing the back of her wrist over her forehead.

"That was, hands down, the hottest thing I have ever seen."

"What, the engine?" She winked. Winked!

It seemed the real Candice had come out to play. Dang, if that didn't make him one hundred kinds of happy.

The icy wind had free rein across the open plain, but the unfurling fumes from the engine wrapped them in a cocoon of warmth.

"Looks like we've got some time to kill." Sal refrained from rubbing his hands together. Instead he grabbed her coat and helped her slip back into the soft black wool. "Come on." He jerked his head toward the front on the car.

Following with timid curiosity, she let him lead her to the hood, where he scooped her up and deposited her on the incline. She squealed in protest, her hands refusing to touch the gleaming black surface.

"Okay, I take it back. *That* is the hottest thing I've ever seen." He tugged off his coat and draped it over her legs before he sat carefully beside her on the hood, leaning back to cup one palm behind his head.

"Are you nuts? What if we scratch it?" She still hadn't moved.

"Ehh." He batted his free hand, then touched her shoulder to coax her back against the windshield. "Live a little, will ya?"

Settling beside him, she clasped her fingers over her tummy and sighed. "All right. It's your funeral."

"Well, at least I got my dying wish." Riveting his eyes on the onyx canvas pierced by countless silver bullets, he let the thought percolate and felt her eyes on him hotter than the recalescent engine.

"Should I even ask?"

"You could, but I'm not gonna tell. Haven't you heard that told wishes don't come true?" He looked at her then, hypnotized by the starlight reflecting in her eyes.

Her teeth snatched a corner of her lip, her forehead pinching in that quizzical way saying she was trying to figure him out. That or she was annoyed again. Hard to say. "You said your wish *already* came true?"

"Ah, yes." Gazing back at the oblivion of stars, Sal felt his heart grappling with its rip cord. It was too early to deploy, but restlessness mixed up an impulsive little cocktail flavored by her sudden nearness, her rarely unarmed defenses, and as always, her disillusioning beauty. A potent array of Candice that was lovely and sweet and strong, and just … not yet his. "I can see how that might cause some confusion. Let's just say my wish is a work in progress."

"Wishing is a waste of time, Dorian. Praying works much better."

Sal didn't have a response to that, so they fell into silence, the stars whispering the song and splendor of all God's most beautiful things seemingly laid out at his fingertips, but actually billions of miles away.

"So, who's Al?" Sal stole a glance at her neck, watching her heart bring calamity upon her body.

"Al? I don't know what you're talking about." Threading

one arm through another, she hugged herself tight, searching the skies for safe haven.

"I sense there is someone from your past you haven't quite gotten rid of. Is his name Al?"

"You sense? What is that, some sort of psychic mumbo-jumbo?"

Sal shrugged, letting the silence expose her evasion.

"Fine, Houdini. There *was* someone who, at one time, had a pretty good hold on me. His name was AJ, not Al. And because of him, no one will ever have a grip on me again. So if that's your wish, you might as well forget about shooting stars and start praying for a miracle."

I believe in miracles. The words were on the tip of his tongue, though he couldn't say he agreed with them. With the hand he'd been dealt, praying for a miracle seemed about as sensible as casting your last few dollars for food into a wishing well and crossing your fingers for the skies to rain down enchiladas.

"You know, growing up as my father's punching bag didn't exactly inspire my faith in humanity. But sometimes people surprise you." Sal crossed his ankles, careful not to scuff the Ferrari, and decided to peel away a layer of mystery in hopes of reciprocation.

"My father was a snitch—an informant for a dirty cop. Money was patchy in his line of work, but even before I forced him to leave we went without food several days of the week."

His voice was distant, isolated in its frailty on the lonely wind. "If my own father didn't care if I was fed, who would stop to care about a scrawny, Hispanic kid from East St. Louis when even a moment's hesitation at the wrong intersection could lead to a .38 in the head."

Closing his eyes, he blocked out the pain rushing in with the memories. Tried in vain to eradicate the reminding aches of his father's rage hiding just beyond the dawn of the approaching spring. Even new seasons unearthed old wounds, just ask his bones.

"But there was a woman."

Candice sighed. "Isn't there always."

He nudged her shoulder with his. "Mmm, honey, your jealousy is music to my ears, but it wasn't like that. She was seventy."

She kept her eyes on him, but he looked beyond the stars, back at the life he was still trying to leave behind.

"She was really something. Aside from sneaking me free lunch every day at school, which I later found out she'd paid for with her minimum wage, she actually talked to me. Seemed to genuinely value what I had to offer." He shook his head. "It didn't make any sense. No one had ever acted like anything I did mattered. Instead of acting out to get noticed, I decided to go unnoticed. And I did. By everyone but Loretta Mae."

"She sounds like a special lady." The words were soft upon her lips.

"She was. But the truly amazing thing about her was her faith. The kind that seemed pretty blind to me, but so strong, when she prayed you'd swear the walls were trembling. Armed with all that firepower, she prayed for me. Every day." It'd made him feel like a gladiator equipped with the king's armor.

"For a time, she inspired me to pray too. Thought I'd gained some perspective. So I put my own cross on my shoulders, to remind me of Loretta Mae. And the God she convinced me cared about my life. The one who would bear my burdens." The tattoo burned against his skin at the mention of it. "That sure was foolish of me."

"You're talking about a tattoo? You have a tattoo of a cross on your back? I don't think I noticed that."

He issued her a rueful grin, knowing since he'd changed the parameters of their game, if she ever caught him without his shirt on there'd be no way she wouldn't notice now. "Why does that not surprise me?"

She shrugged, a wicked smile on her lips. "Maybe you're just not all that."

"Ha! Well, we both know *that's* not true."

"Have you ever seen such arrogance?" She spoke to the stars.

Sal wished he could say for certain brilliant burning gases weren't all that was up there. Something told him Loretta Mae hadn't been beyond her sensibilities. That those stirrings he'd felt with her back then, and if he was being honest, maybe even a little bit now in remembrance, weren't simply parlor tricks or smoke screens. Was it really so absurd to believe in something bigger than himself? Something greater than chance?

Maybe. Maybe not.

"All right, Brat. We've talked about my tattoo. Now let's talk about yours." Even in the dark he could see the rich pigment drain from her face. Letting his hand skim over her sleeve to warm her to the idea, he then found her hand, dovetailing each finger with hers.

"You saw my tattoo." Pressing her lips together, she shook her head and then exhaled a mirthless laugh. "Wow, those are some impressive psychic vibes, Obiwan."

He let his thumb traipse over the heel of her hand, watching as she warred against the wave of truth building inside her.

It wasn't just about AJ. It was about her. Who he'd made her. "You can tell me, Candice. I promise you I've done worse."

"Oh, yeah? Try me."

She was close but still wouldn't budge.

"Well, let's see." Sal sat up, gazing out over the long desolate road into the past.

"It's all your fault, Dorian." His mother was a puddle, a perfect specimen of human weakness lumped on the stained linoleum of the barren pantry closet, sobbing until the sound was hoarse and thin. "If you hadn't sent your father away,

we wouldn't be living like this. Why'd you go and do something so selfish? Like I would divorce him for you? You're my biggest regret. I hate you! I hate what you've done to us."

The incoherent spewing of her desperation continued on her sobs. She'd always been weak, blind with adoration, and completely dependent on the monster she'd married.

Dorian's heart split. One side with anguish for the hurtful words he could never erase. The other with determination to make things right for the sake of his kid brother.

He didn't know which was worse. His father nearly killing his son with his anger, or his mother effectively signing the death certificate with her cowardice. He tried to drudge up an ounce of sympathy for her. An ounce of love. But nothing came.

Here he'd used his gift to give her, all of them, a ticket to freedom. A clean break. A free divorce, a new name, a fresh start. All swag from his brilliant con of the beautiful divorce lawyer.

And yet, she refused to stand on her own two feet. Refused to fight for her sons.

Leaving her to wallow in her misery, he grabbed his jacket from the banister, whipped it over his shoulders, and flung open the front door.

If she wouldn't step up, then he would. It was time to escape this pit before Santino Salivas came back and killed them all.

Or forced Dorian to drive a dagger into his cold, black heart.

"Hey, bubby, where you goin'?" Gabe's eyes were wide and innocent, untouched by the life of agony Dorian bore for him.

Tears prickled in his throat. He sniffed them away and scanned the street for trouble. "Just gonna run out and get some food, all right buddy."

His little brother tugged on his sleeve, forcing Dorian to look at him. "Can I come? Mom's acting crazy."

Yeah, crazy was right. "Not today, okay pal. But could you do me a favor?"

His face lit up with a grin, and he nodded at hyper speed.

"Could you go down to our room, get out that coloring pad I got you, and draw Mom some pictures? I think it might cheer her up. Oh, but wait until I get back to give it to her, huh champ?"

"Okay, cool!" Gabe turned and barreled down to the musty basement where they both slept on a twin mattress on the cement floor. Dorian prayed the task would keep a six-year-old occupied and out of harm's way until he got back with his score and enough food to snap his mom out of her depressive spiral.

Flipping up his hood, Dorian checked to be sure his knife was in his pocket, just in case, before he locked up and climbed onto his bike.

He'd overheard the EL6s bragging about their latest pull—an Audi A6 with a shaved off vin. Having fashioned a homemade Slim Jim two weeks ago, researched exactly how to hotwire the luxury car, and made arrangements with a crooked old codger on North Grand to flip a sale, Dorian's plan was set. Now all he had to do was sneak in undetected, stow his bike in the trunk, get the car out without being seen, and collect enough bank to press reset on their lives.

"What happened? You get caught? Is that the worst thing you've ever done, stole a car from some gangsters?" Candice's question jerked him free.

Sal let the memory fade, just enough so he could choke out the words. "No. I pulled it off. Got twenty grand for the car. Brought home this giant bucket of KFC and all the fixins. I'd never seen Gabe so excited about anything in his life. Not even Christmas. After our feast, we even took some over to Loretta Mae's house and watched *The Goonies*."

"So, it's guilt that's plaguing you? Because I gotta tell ya, as an FBI agent who risks his life daily, you've probably more than paid off your debt to society. You were just a kid trying to survive."

"Yeah." Nodding, he closed his eyes and pinched the bridge of his nose. "I *was* just trying to survive. But then I got greedy. You see, I was good at flying under the radar." *Good at manipulating people.* He let that one go unspoken. "So I started working more scores. Bringing in more money. Eluding every suspicion. Almost everyone I met was a mark. Pickpocketing, mind games, eventually hypnosis. Countless little scams that kept food on the table and a stockpile of cash hidden in my mattress."

Blinking fast to clear his eyes, he braved a glance at Candice's face for a final glimpse of the tenuous trust he was about to shatter.

"But I didn't know my father had returned to the East Side, with a vendetta against the son who'd finally gained enough muscle to retaliate. I'd beaten him nearly to death and sent him packing with a threat of finishing the job if he ever came back." He forced an icy spear of air down his throat, wishing it would sever the approaching words.

"He'd caught on to my scams. Tipped off the EL6 gang of my involvement. His final snitch." Sal shook his head. "I'd covered my tracks well, and the gang couldn't confirm the story, but they wanted to send me a message anyway. They jumped me, but I managed to escape before they'd made a proper example out of me. So they went old school with a drive-by.

The moment the shots rang out, he'd been shoving fistfuls of cash into that damn mattress. He'd dropped it all and tripped up the stairs to find a yawning puddle of blood swallowing his baby brother.

"They shot Gabe." His words were flat, but the storm pummeling from within tunneled down to the deepest depths of his despair. Every breath was another blow of his father's bat testing his ribs, each blink shaking him with a wrinkle of time and choice that could never be restored.

"My brother is paralyzed because of me. And two weeks after the shooting, while Gabe was still in a coma, my mother left a letter blaming me for it all and signed it with her blood when she took her own life." Sal crammed his hand through his hair. "The sad part was I didn't even care. She'd abandoned us long before she made it official."

"Oh, Dorian." The heartbreak in her voice exposed his own emotional void for the woman who'd left uglier scars than his father's fury. "That must have been horrible. It's always the ones we love most that wound us the deepest."

Sal shook his head. "No. I didn't love her. Who could love a woman who wouldn't fight for her own child?"

Chapter 26

Candice Stevens

His story shattered her, and his heartbreak over his mother speared straight through her heart. He couldn't know how the truth both bonded them together as wounded soulmates of misfortune and yet tore them oceans apart.

He might be the only person she'd ever meet marked with scars such as hers. And even though his pain seemed as raw as her own, he somehow managed to exude this cheerful, and yes, sometimes naïve, magnetism.

How? Short of some dynamite happy pills, she really couldn't say. All she knew for sure was she wanted what he had.

Candice looked over at Agent Dorian Salivas, taking the time to *really* see him.

He was a gorgeous man. Funny how she'd missed it. Not really all that bumbling, but confident, effortless. Even just looking at his face put her at ease.

But right now, with his wounds torn afresh, his heart and his shame bleeding before her, she felt something warm and golden rush through her veins. A kinship, yes, but something more.

A fierce protectiveness overwhelmed her. *Not* the motherly kind.

And before she knew it, she was holding him. Arms bracketing his burdened shoulders, his face cradled to the curve of her neck.

He held on, wrapping her up in him. Both of them sitting on a quarter-million dollars of precision steel, suspended in time, and lost in the rare comfort of an honest embrace of two broken souls.

Not completely honest, Jersey reminded. Some wounds could slash so deep, not even the most skilled surgeon could stop the bleeding. Unbidden, tears streamed down her cheeks, memories of her own torment resurfacing from the grave and twining with Dorian's pain.

It wasn't true, what everyone said. Time didn't heal all wounds. It could only numb the ache. The pain was always there.

Some days she could revisit clumps of her history without breaking down. There were even days she could embrace the concept of forgiveness for the part she'd unwittingly played in her mother's death. In the same way, Dorian's rebellion had backfired and resulted in bloodshed.

But another death had been at her hand alone.

She held on tighter, feeding off of Dorian's strength and warmth and honesty, savoring a moment of absolute physical comfort in the midst of their emotional agony.

It was improbable their pasts had been so similarly tragic. How much they'd both had to overcome. But there was one main difference, and it was all that mattered.

Dorian had been a survivalist.

Candice was a murderer.

He pulled away as if sensing the truth about who'd been in his arms. But then, his palms cupped her face and his forehead bowed against hers. His thumbs stroking away her tears. Nothing between them but a single white breath and her darkest secrets.

"You don't have to tell me. But if you ever want someone to talk to, I'm right next door." He smiled, and her heart piled in with lead bricks.

So she told him about AJ. About how easily she'd been

wooed by his attention. How easily she'd been deceived. How he'd manipulated her into giving herself away, convincing her his love could help her numb the pain of her horrible life.

How he'd turned her into her mother.

And finally how when he'd flipped the switch, it'd been too late.

Each layer of the story lifted off onto the cool night air with one of those bricks. Though one remained. One too heavy to ever be moved.

As they drove back to their quiet little street, hand in hand, blasted with heat from the air vents to keep the engine cool, Candice knew she felt happier, lighter, and probably hotter than she'd been in ... maybe ever.

It had to have been the moonlight. Or maybe the stars, all twinkly and optimistic as they shone undaunted by the darkness. The only way she could rationalize it was that they—the conniving moon and stars—had somehow cast a spell, wooing a cynic from the toughest part of Jersey with their radiance.

Of course, the Ferrari hadn't helped to rebuke the spell. And the tall, dark, and tender hunk of man-candy might have played a teensy part in her psychotic break.

Wait, the dress! Definitely culpable.

Candice leaned back against her headboard, munching a cuticle till the skin was probably pink and certainly raw.

The moon was still playing its sappy little tune as it peeked through the shades and taunted its victory over her. Not just over her apparent lack of sleep. The clock was complicit in that taunt, blaring 3:17 a.m. in an obnoxiously cheerful lime green that cut through the room with a citrus glow.

It was night. Why wasn't it darker? Why couldn't she

keep her eyes shut? Was it because it was her first full night's sleeping in her new house since the break-in?

Yes, that must be it. She nodded to herself in the dark, slid back down beneath the covers, and decided if that was all it was, surely she could go to sleep. The house was now secure. There was nothing to worry about. Mind over matter.

It definitely wasn't about that other thing she wasn't going to think about. Nope. She would just pretend it never happened. Denial. She could live with it. Denial and perhaps some electric shock therapy to delete the memory. How dangerous could that really be?

Not nearly as dangerous as the thing she wasn't going to think about after the count of three.

One. Two. Three.

Crap. Still there. Maybe a hundred.

One. Two. Three. Four …

She felt her eyelids weigh down, her breathing deep and even with each number scanning through her mind like floating sheep on a mobile.

Eighteen. Nineteen …

"You really don't have to walk me to my door. It's late, and we've already been out in the cold long enough." Candice tucked her clutch under her arm and stepped away from the Ferrari so Dorian could close the door he'd insisted on opening.

His lips quirked but didn't quite split, and yet his eyes crinkled in a way that made the hint of a smile light his entire face. "Maybe I want to."

This was the time when he would wag his eyebrows and make some lame remark about a possible nightcap, but neither followed. Just an offered arm to hold.

Which she took. Who could say why? It was polite, sure, but she could walk just fine.

Her feet, even in heels, weren't the problem. It was her heart that was skidding on ice.

The cool night had its own sort of serenade. A clear,

resonant high note of hibernating stillness. A soft purr of a distant motor painting the middle. And an almost absent base of warmth on the wind crooning a warning of change.

There was music in everything, even silence. She just couldn't escape it.

These were the thoughts she entertained instead of plotting a game plan for their goodbye. And before she could blink they were standing at her door, facing each other, an arm's-width between them and her keys still tucked in her purse.

Talk about unprepared.

But instead of being nervous, or even desperate to duck out of his possible attempt at a goodnight kiss, it was she who bridged the space between them.

She who crossed her wrists behind his neck.

And she who leaned in, replacing the uncertainty in his eyes with what looked like hope.

Their lips weren't yet touching, neither were their bodies, just her forearms resting on his wide, strong shoulders.

Why did she always let the heaviness of the past weigh her down? Maybe just once, just for tonight, she could see what it felt like to be free. After what he'd shared it seemed they both struggled with the crushing weight of guilt. Only he was strong enough to survive it with a smile.

Her hand was stroking his neck now, slipping beneath his collar to touch where she guessed the ink marked his skin. She kept her eyes open, riveted on his and the look so enthralled by only her she wanted to lock it away in her memory for the days when reality returned.

Nuzzling her nose to his, she whispered against his lips, "Happy birthday, Dorian."

And then she kissed him. Their lips melded with the sweetest tenderness, slow and deliberate. And when she coaxed his lips apart and deepened the kiss, a groan ached from the back of his throat.

He drew her closer but didn't press. His hands skimmed

up and down her back but didn't part her coat to warm her skin.

They kissed. And kissed. And kissed with no sense of urgency. Like they could burn through the night savoring every second.

She kept expecting things to escalate. Expecting him to shove her against the door and replace all that was achingly tender and out-of-this-world with something rough and predatory and greedy. Any minute now he would try to force his way inside and take advantage of her weakness. Of an ever deceptive physical craving that led to nothing but pain, manipulation, and endless echoing emptiness and regret.

If that was his intention, he was in no hurry to execute his plan.

Gravy, it was too good. She never wanted it to end.

Never in her life had she been kissed like this. Never in her life had she imagined such a kiss existed.

And yet, here it was. Hers to keep forever. Pressure built behind her eyes, a tiny whimper escaping into his mouth. Repositioning her arms, she threaded them up under his, flattened her palms against his back, and melted into him, arching her neck to offer up the fullness of her kiss. Which he accepted but didn't take, as he gave much more than seemed possible with the loving caress of his mouth.

His big, warm palms cupped her face, his thumbs doing that thing they did so well in the closet. He explored some more in a way so thrillingly the same and yet enticingly different. She was sinking fast, his lingering kiss like quicksand.

After an eternity in heaven, he broke away to breathe, and then leaned back in and kissed her again. Repeating the act over and over like he just couldn't stand the thought of stopping.

She knew the feeling.

His lips moved to her cheek, and it was only when the wind touched her face that she realized she was crying. And

Dorian was kissing away her tears.

He didn't ask what was wrong. After tonight's stargazing confessional, he knew.

Most of it, anyways.

Instead he just took her pain in the sweetest way imaginable, held her close, and vowed, "Never. Never will I hurt you."

Chapter 27

Dorian Salivas

Yep. She was avoiding him.

Tricky to do with someone as perceptive as he, but she was doing a bang up job. Sneaking out of her house early. Spending long, busy days cooped up in the morgue. She'd acknowledge his stake out by her car at the end of each work day with a nod as she strutted past in those come-and-get-me red heels.

After her escort home, she would issue a painfully polite thank you and rush at her door as if to duck an approaching meteorite.

It had been three days. Three miserable days of giving her space.

Well, as much space as he could tolerate and ensure her safety. He kept a tight surveillance on her house. He also dropped a plate of dinner on her doorstep and waited on his porch until she cracked her door and pulled it in like a captive pouncing on her food ration. Watching again when she slipped out an hour later to return the clean plate to the back door by his kitchen.

The kiss had scared her. To be honest, it'd scared him too.

He'd known his feelings for Candice were real. But when he'd held her in his arms, tasted the sweetness of her surrender and her tears, his love came alive. It leapt out into the great hopeful unknown, and for those perfect minutes— and there were a lot of them—he'd soared.

But it was more than just skill on either part. It was perfect compatibility. Each stroke of her silken lips, the gentle folding of her body, the little sighs of contentment ... spellbinding.

Sal braced his elbows on his knees and dropped his head into his hands, desperate to shake it away and stay focused. But the delicious memory played on the most wonderful and infuriating repeat, teasing him every moment, waking and asleep.

Not that he'd gotten much of the latter.

Tomorrow they would be visiting the lab to check up on the DNA results. And they'd be doing it together.

If he happened to walk her to her door to sneak a kiss, well, then, she'd just have to deal with it. Her childish standoff had to come to an end eventually. And he'd been more than patient since she hadn't even bothered to ask for the space she so obviously needed.

She hadn't asked for it ...

The thought tooled around, stirring his irk. More so with himself than with her.

Yes, she was being evasive and immature. But he was letting her. Why? What if what she really needed was reassurance? Honestly, how often did women know what they wanted?

Shoot! And here he'd wasted three days being "considerate." When all this time they could've been making up for years of loneliness and giving their endorphins a sugar rush.

It was late, but he had half a mind to go bang on her door right now and kiss her senseless.

You know what?

Not stopping to bother with shoes or a coat, Sal burst through his door, marched a direct route to her front door, and set his knuckles to wood. She wouldn't want to answer, but the flicker of her TV proved she was up. He knocked again.

Finally, only moments before he was sure to lose his nerve, she peered out the sidelight and then eased open the door.

"Dorian, what the heck?"

Mercy, she looked edible in that cotton candy robe. Her hair piled up in a messy knot, her eyes like sunbursts of golden topaz lighting up the night.

"It's almost midnight. What's so important it can't wait—"

Bending forward, he cut off her protest with his lips. Cupping her face, he kissed the stuffing out of her, tasting the sweet mint of her toothpaste, breathing in those candied flower notes from her skin, not wasting a single moment in reminding her why she was being so ridiculous.

Without a beat of hesitation she was up on her tiptoes, her hands sliding up his back. One of those delicious little whimpers flavoring their kiss as she took it all, the longing, the frustration, the need, and returned it with such eagerness and generosity his heart could have grown three sizes in the span of a second.

This is so not over.

He pulled away an inch but then dove back in to pepper her lips with a dozen more furious kisses before he forced himself out of her embrace.

Her eyes were glazed, as lost in the phenomenal sensations as he. Her lips, even in the moonlight, were swollen and pink and beckoning.

So he answered with one last slow kiss packed with all the words begging for freedom, then pressed his cheek to hers and nuzzled her face, drinking in the memory with his eyes closed tight for fear he might wake to find it all a dream.

"Good night." He whispered, forced a hard turn, and made the agonizing trek home, turning back only when he reached his door. Just in time to see hers click shut behind her.

He'd thought a goodnight kiss would have eased his frustration, perhaps uncoil him enough to help him sleep tonight. Instead, his body hummed with sugar shock. And his brain was now fully-caffeinated and even more intensely preoccupied with the girl next door whose kiss still flavored his lips.

His tongue snatched out to drink in every last morsel of her lingering there.

At least he'd given her something to think about. Maybe even dream about. One could only hope she wasn't banging her head against the back of the door with regret.

Why did women always make things so complicated? Love sure wasn't supposed to be. And even though she'd opened up the other night about this AJ, she still held the ace in her pocket. The thing she was certain made her unlovable. But what she'd had with that jerk wasn't love. Love didn't use you up and wring you dry.

Not that Sal was an expert on the subject. But he'd seen enough false examples to know what love wasn't.

With this revelation of his budding love for the daring and spunky medical examiner, he was discovering the wonder of falling for the first time.

What she couldn't yet see was his love didn't come with prerequisites. There were no strings, no conditions. All he needed was her heart.

"You think you need some great big pompous faith and a long list a mighty deeds? Pshhh! All you need is a surrendered heart." Loretta Mae's voice mingled with the wind, invisible and yet unmistakable. It was as if she'd become his conscience, and an echo of the only part of his past that didn't sting.

It was strange, but ever since the other day in church her voice was as near as his very breath. Almost as if her prayers were still ringing in the heavens, waiting to find purchase with a lost soul.

But why was his non-existent faith tangling with his thoughts about Candice?

Sal closed himself behind the door, hoping to shut out the

voices wreaking havoc on his rationale. Loretta Mae had been his guardian angel, if there was such a thing. And there were times he knew life would be simpler if he could just trust. Believe.

But it'd been nearly impossible to believe in anything after Sal's father beat up his six-year-old son for the first time. After he and Gabe huddled together, night after night, on that tiny mattress for warmth, unable to sleep for the loud aching of their empty bellies. After his circumstances drove him, a child, into a life of crime. Only to be punished for all those things forced into his hands.

And to be punished by destroying the one thing he'd been trying to protect.

Dragging himself up the stairs to his room, Sal stripped down to his boxers and crawled into bed. Laying in the dark, he couldn't help but think about all those ghostly words hounding after him. Were they simply shadows of his past taunting him for yet another failure? Or were they resurfacing now because his trusty perceptions were trying to tip him off about something bigger?

He didn't really want to think about it. What he *did* want to think about while he drifted off to dreamland had melted caramel eyes, silk spun hair, and the most stupefying velvet lips.

Whatever she thought she needed to work out in that beautiful head of hers, well, she had about five more hours. Because before the first press of dawn awakened the skies, he'd be waiting. They might both be running from their pasts, but tomorrow, come hell or high water, they were gonna find a way to kick fear and guilt in the *keister* and start building a future.

The connection finally clicked into place. For the first time in his life he *did* believe in something.

Love.

Perhaps Loretta Mae's words were meant to remind him that falling means surrendering your heart and taking a leap of faith.

Candice was the type of girl who kept her feet firmly rooted on solid ground. But he'd make a believer out of her. He would just wait at the door of her heart and keep knocking like he had tonight. Eventually she would open up. He'd be ready to catch her.

Until then, there was no better material on earth to occupy his dreams.

"Morning, sunshine."

Caught trying to sneak out, Candice flinched at his greeting and craned her neck over her shoulder exposing an extra-large everything bagel clutched between her teeth. She re-hiked the dueling straps of her purse and briefcase with a shrug of her shoulder. Her hands were otherwise occupied with keys and a to-go mug with what smelled like coffee.

Sal smiled up from his lazy perch on her porch swing, the gentle lapping of the extra chain chiming with each gentle sway. "Boy, you sure are leaving the house early. Big day?"

He was rewarded with a muffled groan and an exasperated eye roll.

Standing, he stepped closer and tugged the bagel from her mouth, eyeing the impressive missing mouthful with the pride it was due. He turned it slightly and took a neighboring bite oozing with cream cheese, chewing and swallowing at leisure, and not bothering to alleviate her of any other items.

"Care for another nibble?" He held it out as if to feed her, knowing by the deadpan expression on her face she'd rather starve than be hand-fed. "Good, because I've got something better." Holding up another bag he wafted it beneath her cute little nose. A nose that, to her apparent annoyance, eagerly followed the salivating scent of homemade cinnamon-sugar donuts.

"Someone's in a chipper mood today?" She snarked,

hopping the slipping straps back onto her shoulder.

He relieved her of each bag, smiling as she continued to scowl at him from those sleep-deprived eyes. "Slept like a baby. You?"

Shaking her head, she tried to hold on to her peeve, but a slight smile twitched the corner of her lips. "We're not talking about this. In fact, I prefer it if we didn't talk at all."

"I know lots of ways we can pass the time without talking." He quirked an eyebrow, enjoying the crimson wash of her skin.

Her shoulders collapsed a little. "I begged for that one, didn't I?"

She'd set herself up again. Pure delight curled on his lips. "I'm thinking of something you don't have to beg for. Care to guess what?"

"Ehhh! Gimme that donut." She ripped the bag from his hand and stomped toward his car. "You're driving." Folding into the seat, Candice sank her teeth into the hot, fresh donut, serenity cleansing all the tension from her face as she inhaled sharply on each bite. "Mmm." Keeping her eyes closed, she licked her lips and swallowed. "Stop watching me eat and drive, Salivas. Your silence is mandatory."

A chuckle bubbled up from his chest. "Yes, ma'am. Wouldn't wanna miss the sweet sounds of your appreciation anyways."

Throwing a wayward backhand that connected with his bicep, she forged ahead with another bite, holding back her satisfaction.

Something, he was pleased to note, she just couldn't seem to do when they kissed.

"Let's hope this all ends today." Sal pushed through the double doors, a sugar-dusted Candice close on his heels.

"How'd you find this place?" She kept a stiff distance and

then glued herself to the opposite wall of the elevator they'd entered as if he might pounce on her at any moment.

Not that he wasn't tempted.

Even with bags under her eyes, a flippy little ponytail, and a frown, she was the sexiest creature he'd ever laid eyes on. It was obvious by the initial freeze out, and now with the attitude, she was unsure of how to navigate the redefining of their relationship.

So he kept things light. It was what she needed until she could come to grips with her change of heart. At least, he hoped it was changing.

Perseverance. He reminded himself of one of his strengths before the memory of her lips and the softness of her curves brought him to his knees.

"Earth to Dorian ..."

"Oh ... yes, my uh, buddy from Quantico was a U.S. Marshall before he retired to teach. He took a special interest in my abilities to cold and muscle read. Anyways, he suggested this place. And he's definitely a guy who knows about discretion."

He knew he'd divulged too much the instant a whole fleet of questions paraded across her face. He wouldn't lie to Candice about anything. He just hoped there were things she might not ask. Like, for example, how good he was at manipulating people.

That might not inspire the trust he was hoping to build with the woman he was trying to woo. One who'd once been someone else's puppet. Something he knew still scared her enough to self-inflict a lifetime of loneliness to avoid a repeat performance.

Just thinking about what that punk did to her made his fists bind and his blood blaze with murderous heat.

"What are cold reading and muscle reading?" The elevator jerked into action. Candice stumbled a step, but the flats she wore kept him from having to intervene.

Tugging at his neck muscles, Sal willed his words to come

out right. "Well, it's a bit like an ingrained polygraph. Cold reading means you can tell if a person is trying to deceive you. Or if you've hit a nerve. And muscle—"

"So you can tell when I'm lying to you? Or when I'm uncomfortable or, like, frustrated?"

Oh, yes. Among other things.

Sal smiled to sweeten the truth. "Now, Brat, don't act like you don't try to make your feelings known. You're very expressive. Every quirk of your lips fascinates me."

That earned him one such enticing little quirk.

"It's not an exact science, and some people are more difficult to read than others."

"But I'm easy."

It wasn't a question, and the fire in her eyes burned a strong message of displeasure at being transparent.

"I didn't say you were easy. I said you were fascinating."

"Whatever. And muscle reading?"

Mercifully the elevator doors separated, bringing them to an underground level not noted on the marquee in the lobby. Sal took her elbow and shouldered out into the dark, dank space. Unlike last time, a prickly premonition raked over him.

"Stay close." He shifted her behind him and withdrew his firearm.

"What is it, Dorian?" Her fingers curled into the tough leather of his jacket at his sides.

Forcing a practiced calm to take over, he drew a deep, even breath, tuning in to the silence to detect the threat stirring bone deep.

"Something's different. Wrong. I can feel it."

Chapter 28

Candice Stevens

The second Dorian tucked her behind the cover of his back, those heebie-jeebies hitched a ride on an adrenaline surge.

Sinking her fingers into the leather of his bad-boy jacket, she clung to his shadow, feeling reckless and terrified and oddly intrigued by his premonition.

The basement of the very generic building they'd entered looked like a long enclosed parking garage. A solid concrete structure with spaced out rows of dim florescent lighting that left alternating lanes of abrupt darkness in the underground tunnel. At the far end there were several doors, only evidenced by a shank of light pressing a thin line against the epoxy gray floor.

It was very *Underworld/Matrix-y*. Creepy. Even without the added suspense of Dorian's Spidey-sense. And as if a spider had slipped beneath her blouse, a squirmy little shiver traipsed over her skin.

Dorian swept them behind one of the cement pillars. Turning to face her, his eyes only a glitter of moisture in their slice of the dark, he whispered, "Brat, I don't want you to fight me on this."

She swallowed, the sound like the plink of a stone in shallow water.

"Take this entry card, swipe it in the elevator, and wait for me in the lobby." He pressed the cold plastic key card into her palm.

"But—"

"Please."

The pleading in his tone went to work on her stubbornness. He was trying to keep her safe, and threat or not, it had a heated little coil springing in her tummy. But not being able to see the desperation in his eyes helped her cause. "Dorian," she leaned in to whisper close, just in case they weren't alone. "What if there really is trouble? How will you get back out? And don't even say you'll call me. Because there is no way in tarnation you get reception down here, other than your spooky psychic vibes."

After a long moment, his warm fingers wrapped around her wrist, pressing against her racing pulse. "Fine." He growled. "But you stay back. First sign of danger, you run, understand? Run as hard as you can back to the elevator with that." His fingers tightened to indicate the key card still in her grip. "As soon as you surface call Archer. I'll find a way out."

It wasn't likely she would leave him behind, but she nodded anyway. He released her wrist, and she went back to clawing his coat and mimicking his stealth maneuvers through the shadows.

They approached the first door, and she saw immediately that Dorian's "feeling" had been right.

This would be the moment she should start her survival sprint. But her legs were glued in place, a vital breath frozen in her lungs, the loud drum of her heart overwhelming her ears.

The coded entry panel dangled toward the floor on a tangle of wires. Char marks streaked the concrete opening where it had been—like some small high-tech explosive had rendered the industrial steel door and top-of-the-line security system useless.

Said door hung open a wisp, the handle blown to smithereens, and shrapnel littered the surrounding floor like its own small battlefield.

Dorian's eyes moved like trained soldiers, absorbing every angle and calculating his plan of action on the fly. He shot a glance at her, tipped his head toward the elevator and mouthed the word "Go" on a command. "Now." He added on the slimmest whisper.

Terror clutched her by the throat. More at the prospect of running off alone than facing what lay behind the door with Dorian. She shook her head, then jerked a nod back toward the lab door.

He must have sensed her fear, weighing the dangers ahead against the threat lurking in the dark march back to the elevator behind them.

Squeezing his eyes shut for the briefest moment, she saw a deep breath expand his chest before he raised his gun.

On his final signal to enter she drew her fists in preparation, which, by the wry twist of his lips, must have granted him a moment's levity. She wrapped her knuckles tight and winked, if for no other reason than to rally more confidence than she felt.

With a slight smile, and a look she didn't have the time or nerve to decipher, he crossed the last few steps to the door, exposing himself under the harsh cone of light for the first time. Her confidence fumbled, and flimsy little prayer burst from her soul.

Oh God, help.

Dorian edged his ear against the door, nosed it open with the tip of his gun, and disappeared inside the lab. Candice waited for the pop of gunfire. When none came after thirty seconds, she peeked around the door.

Blood.

Everywhere.

Her stomach shriveled down to nothing, her silly fists trembling like leaves on the wind.

Fresh sprays of hot red blood splattered against the row of stainless steel cabinets. A sickening path smeared across the floor around the side of a large commercial freezer.

A dark figure emerged from the last office door in the back corner. A startled scream cracked from her throat.

Oh. Candice clutched her hand to her heart as the light confirmed it was Dorian picking his way back across the wasteland of crushed lab equipment.

"All clear."

The words should have been a sedative to her bludgeoning pulse and violent tremors, but as she watched a glob of blood drip slowly down the front of the freezer, terror seized her anew.

"H-How ma-many bodies?"

He was still in FBI mode, his gaze sharp and instinctive, reconstructing the scene similar to the way she mapped out a murder with bones, flesh, and particulates. "Four. Each shot at close range with what looks like a .45."

"Where? Where are they?" The words were numb on her tongue. Every crime scene had its challenges. But from the oxidized sizzle of the keypad outside, to the rolling drops of blood, it would seem they had just missed the killer. And either just missed catching Vivaldi, or missed joining these four in the morgue.

The shakes were fully enslaving her now, threatening to release her to the blood-drenched floor.

"There are two in the offices, one by the vent hood, and another by the freezer."

The blood smear. Had someone gotten away? Or …

Vaulting over the rivers of red, Candice jolted into action, nearly slipping when she rounded the toppled steel table and saw the man slumped against the freezer.

A deep garnet wash saturated his lab coat and hands, the smear on the floor leading to this spot meant he probably hadn't died instantly. He may have dragged himself to cover to try and stop the bleeding. But were they too late?

A ghostly white had stolen the man's color, and the stillness gripping him snatched her hope. But when she pressed her fingers to his carotid artery, life still beat through his veins.

"Man alive!" Sliding the man to lie flat, she put pressure on the wound to slow the bleeding. "Dorian, did you hear me?"

She heard him approach, though she could tell he was preoccupied, mumbling something about jacketed hollow point bullets.

"Yeah, I heard you. What's up?"

Looking up, she blew the wispy pieces of hair from her eyes until they stuck to the clammy sheen of perspiration on her forehead. "I have a live one here. If none of the lab phones are working you need to go up and call for help. Now!"

"Candice, I won't leave you. The lab is clear, but he may not be far. I can't risk—"

"Dorian Salivas, you go call for help right now or this man dies. He might be our last surviving link to Vivaldi. I'll be fine."

Would she? It was absolutely the right call, but the old, weak Candi wanted to beg him not to leave her. What if Vivaldi hadn't left? What if they'd interrupted his massacre and he was lurking in the shadows waiting to finish the job?

A war of indecision scanned over his face. Courage and fear brewed a similar battling tempest in her conscience. He'd already checked the office phones. He was thorough and would have tried to call it in right away.

And that meant he had to leave. Had to leave her here in this death lair where Vivaldi just claimed up to four more victims.

Alone. Defenseless.

With no guarantee the killer had ever left the building.

Her neuroses were working overtime.

Every silent creak, every ghostly shift of stillness made

the nauseating fear gurgle up in her throat. Her heartbeat had slowed considerably, which meant there was a solid chance she wouldn't stroke out before help arrived.

The man wedged beneath her palms was still unconscious. His pulse thready and powerless. His breathing just as shallow.

The silence seemed to scream at her, reliving the terror this room had seen moments before she'd arrived.

With a gun-toting psychic FBI agent. That'd been the difference.

Now she was in the lab alone, soaking her knees in a stranger's blood. Practically dangling herself as prime Vivaldi bait.

All at her own insistence that Dorian get help!

She forced a deep breath in through her nose, out through her mouth. Repeating the act to pass time and remain vertical, and chanting an internal reminder of Dorian's gun hidden between her knocking knees. So she wasn't *technically* defenseless.

But what about Dorian? What if he bumped into the bad guy on the way out?

She tried not to think about it or anything aside from keeping this man alive. He might be the only person who has ever survived an encounter with Vivaldi. She prayed he'd live to tell the tale. And then live out the rest of his days knowing he'd helped silence the unrelenting song of a serial killer.

A phantom score, invisible but as palpable as the blood coating her fingers, aligned with the rhythm of the man's heart in her hands. Those old haunting notes swiveled mercilessly in her mind. Such grace and surprise in each arpeggio. A unique blend of dissonance and rhythm creating something achingly beautiful to the ear and yet devastating to the soul.

She forced a deaf ear to the silent taunt and set her ear to hear something that might actually help.

God, I could really use a miracle here. But even without one, could you send one of those big, burly angels of yours to stand watch until Dorian gets back?

The whimsical yet intentional prayer was a tether to another time and place. One full of childlike musings about angels and spirits, fairies and magic, and faraway fairylands and frog-prince kisses.

There'd been this one night. Another of so many teeming with the nightmarish truth of her lot. Her mother had been working. And after he'd tucked Candi into bed, her father slipped out back to tinker with his beat-up old Mustang she'd affectionately named "The Rustang."

The house was quiet despite the riff-raff usually littering the neighborhood streets. Her bedroom, not much bigger than a closet, sat just to the right of the front door. She'd heard someone test the knob on that door, jiggling to find it locked but not difficult to pick, or break down.

At age seven, knowing her father wasn't in the house, knowing she was all alone, she felt as if the monsters would burst through the door any moment and devour her.

She slipped beneath the covers, a quivering blob of limp pillows, thin blankets, and one scrawny little scaredy-cat.

The rattling at the front door grew more deliberate, the wall quaked, and then it suddenly stopped. Scraping soles darted away from the door until all fell back into silence.

She sensed something in her room. Her fear was so raw it should have poisoned her with salmonella, but somehow she folded back the cover and peeked out.

The room seemed brighter than before, though no lights were on. And in the span of a heartbeat her fear had vanished. She sat up, scanning a large shadow reaching to the ceiling. One that should have scared the tinkle out of her. But she wasn't afraid.

"Thank you." She'd whispered to the shadow and snuggled back down under the blanket, confident her angel had scared the bad man off the porch and then returned to his post as her protector.

Years later, she remembered it. More clearly than made sense, since she'd never told anyone who could help keep the childhood memory alive. It had to have been a product of her imagination. That, and the impressionable whimsy of childlike faith since that angel failed to show up again for the next ten years, leaving her to fend for herself when she'd needed him the most.

But in all the years since, she still took the memory to trial on occasion. Curious about her white knight. Wondering why she'd just accepted his presence and not bothered with a closer look.

Had he really been there? And if he had, why had he not returned? Or perhaps she'd been too skeptical to see him when reality drove off with the final thread of her innocence.

She was thinking about that angel now, praying her faith would regenerate and root deep, maybe summon him back to her aid.

The warm pool of blood beneath her knees cooled as it dabbled the length of her shins. It wasn't until the frigid syrup permeated the toes of her cloth ballet flats that she realized the man's chest no longer rose and fell under her compression.

Removing one bloodied hand from the wound, she checked his pulse, smearing more crimson paint on the man's chalky neck.

She held her stained hands away from herself and sat in the silent song of his death. Knowing if Vivaldi had his preference, he'd have turned some beautiful composition into a river of red notes in this concrete tomb.

A rush of tears fell over the loss of the stranger who died in her hands. Using her forearm to wipe away the first drip from her nose, she let a sob escape as the suffocating memories of her mother's blood dragged her down beneath the surface.

And through the haze of the present death she was

currently sitting in and the past agony she kept drowning in, Candice failed to sense she wasn't alone.

Chapter 29

Dorian Salivas

The second he ended his call with Archer, Sal was back on the elevator, pacing like a lunatic and wishing this underground express was a little more *express*.

If anything happened to her he'd ...

He let the thought hang unfinished in his mind, knowing full well there'd be no recovery.

By the time the elevator doors opened, Sal had worked up a full blown panic attack. Sprinting through the lanes of darkness, he wasn't sure whether to scream out her name in desperation or remain silent in case she was in trouble.

All he knew for certain was that nothing felt right. Insufficient slivers of air pierced his lungs. He was simultaneously dizzy and maddeningly still. Cold sweat burned his eyes. It was taking too long. It was too quiet.

Abandoning all sense, he barreled through the lab door. Unarmed and unprepared for a fight. It didn't matter. He needed to see she was safe more than he needed his next breath.

The sight of her sobbing in a scarlet puddle kicked the last scrap of breath from his chest. Allowing only one glance away to scan for immediate danger, he went to her, making it just as the pain from his sprint buckled his knee.

From the drenches of blood he couldn't tell if she was unharmed. But he knew she was alive. And in the moment it was all that mattered.

Unconcerned with the gory mess, he tugged her toward him, curling his blood-soaked beauty against his chest.

He wasn't sure how long they stayed like that. Her painted hands held away from his back. The strength of her arms clamped around his ribs with the sweetest ache.

Despite the fact that this felt right—Candice safe and snug against him—the case was spiraling downward, deeper than this bleak basement of death.

They no longer held a single scrap of material evidence. The DNA was history. And since the Maserati fiber had been swapped back into evidence, more than likely it was gone too. All was lost.

But as the death toll brimmed to new heights, and the dangers seemed only to snare them deeper into Vivaldi's web, Sal felt an overriding calm amidst the crash.

They were close. Vivaldi was getting nervous.

And Sal was already in his head.

An hour with this crime scene could be very enlightening once he knew Candice was somewhere safe.

There was also the Maserati lead insinuating not only Preston Bradley but another short list of players Archer was working on.

Nope, on the surface things didn't look good. But if you scratched past the vanishing evidence, and the tragedy of four more souls lost to Vivaldi's collection, there was a riddle waiting to be solved by someone who could see beyond what was, to what could be.

He'd always claimed he wasn't a seer. But this was his gift. Taking fragments of scattered trivialities and piecing them together.

"Thank you, God," he whispered against Candice's hair, for her safety, for his gift, and for another chance to atone for his mistakes.

This may not be how he would've plotted out his suburban dream, but somehow he knew he was right where he was supposed to be. Right where he could make a difference. Not in spite of what he'd endured, but because of it.

And as sure and finite as the high-octane charge of love racing on his bloodstream, he knew, with an uncanny certainty, someone was on his side.

"Maybe we should request another patrol car?" Stalling at Candice's curb, Sal's fear sank its teeth back in for another taste. He didn't want to leave her, but he couldn't very well ask her to stay at the crime scene while he did a more thorough investigation. It'd been traumatic enough wading in a stranger's blood until the cavalry arrived.

Archer issued an emphatic throat clear over the phone. "I'd say the 5-0 parked in her driveway and the other one circling the block should send the right message for the next hour or so."

Training his gaze on her front door, Sal wished he could be sure. Closed. Locked. Armed. Facts that should be comforting. Especially with additional manpower from *outside* the FBI on watch. Just as a precaution.

But he'd kicked down a similar door only last week. Without his full strength and with a bum knee to boot.

The knowledge made unease stir on the whispered warmth sweeping through the Challenger's open window. The sun teased with platinum brushes of springtime, and that hint of heat on the breeze should have sweetened the pot. But while the weather boasted the hopeful intro to spring, the day held only the devastated melody of Vivaldi's latest winter score.

Sal wrestled with his options, tapping his phone against his forehead before shoving it back to his ear. They really did need his eyes on the scene. If they caught Vivaldi, he'd no longer need to worry about her safety.

Besides, after all she'd been through today, she needed a shower, a super-sized nap, a double-decker pizza, and possibly a relaxing dose of hypnosis. They'd be leaving for Preston Bradley's lake house in a few hours, and her A-game had been patchy enough the last time. Let alone now, only hours after a man died in her hands and Vivaldi redefined all the rules of his twisted little game.

"It was wise you took her home, pal. I've worked with Webster Groves PD before. And the guy in the driveway is Connor, served in Afghanistan. One heck of a Ranger."

The tightness banding his chest loosened a smidge. He speared his fingers through his hair, and piled an extra breath in his shaky lungs before pulling out on to the street.

"Fine, you're right. I'm on my way. Don't let CSU haul anything away until I get back." An incoming call beeped. "Arch, I gotta go. Jensen's calling. See you in a few."

"*Salivas.*"

"Sal. Director Jensen here."

"Yes, sir, I was just about to call you." Sal couldn't say why he felt like he just got caught lifting a cop's wallet.

"I would hope so. I would also think a piece of hard DNA evidence might have been important enough to mention."

Ah, yes. That's why he was feeling guilty.

"Sir, I—"

"You think I want your excuses, Salivas?" Jensen's voice was so even he might have been talking about golf. A heated reaction would be more telling. But this? He didn't know what to do with this.

"No, sir. But if you'd indulge me just a moment, I wanted to tell you while I have had a few small leads in this case, with the potential breech inside our walls, I thought it best to keep the whispers and speculation to a minimum. At least until I confirmed if they had merit." Sal held his breath, unable to gauge his boss's silence without a visual.

"Fine. I suppose this mole could be anyone. If you thought informing me might somehow tip our hand, I get it. I don't like it. And I certainly didn't like getting the call that we have four more bodies on our hands, and another—and the most significant—piece of evidence as collateral for those lives."

Sal took a full breath once he was certain he wasn't about to lose his job. Even the lame temporary one.

"But this has got to stop here."

His tone made Sal question if Jensen meant the secrecy or the killing. Both would be preferable, but his boss didn't wax passionate about much. And being lied to seemed to have struck a sharper nerve than the collective work of Vivaldi's reign over them.

"I understand, sir."

"Will you be leaving the lab soon?" There was an extra shake of gruffness to Jensen's voice.

"Uhh, no, actually, I'm on my way back now."

"Good. I'm sending over our new analyst Jill Chrissick. She needs some field experience, and I don't want Veer anywhere near those computers. Make sure she has everything she needs on site before we haul it all back here."

"Absolutely. Whatever you need, sir."

He could picture Jensen nodding that shiny head of his. Crossing his arms in the way that said he was satisfied with Sal's contrition.

"I expect you back in office later for a full briefing of your progress."

"Ahh, I can't tonight, sir." Silence ticked down like the final countdown to his termination. "Another one of those small leads I mentioned. I'll be working out of the office for a few days. I'd tell you, but I'm just pulling back up to the crime scene. And I'd rather not discuss any leads over the phone. Playing this one safe."

"You're on thin ice, Salivas. Losing material evidence is bad enough. If I find out you've mishandled this investigation in any other way, you can kiss your badge goodbye. We clear?"

Sal cleared his throat, desperate to dislodge the unsavory implication that he'd just dug his own grave. He'd stolen both pieces of evidence. Lost one. Possibly both. Lied to his boss and broken at least a dozen rules in the process. The line, if he'd ever known one, lay buried with all of his common sense.

But he needed this job. And not just for his conscience or for the money. But for Gabe. Insurance that any surviving influences from their father would remain in check.

"I understand." He said the words, knowing full well the moment he set off on his weekend reconnaissance mission he'd have signed his termination. Unless …

Unless he delivered Vivaldi on a platter.

It was a daring move. All or nothing. And pulling this off could be the greatest scam he'd ever run.

Even the thought of what lay ahead for the weekend put his blood on ice. Because the consequences of his jaunts on the other side of the law had always led to pain and suffering and death.

Who would pay the price this time?

"There won't be any prints." Sal spoke absently to the forensics team dusting for fingerprints. One guy halted mid-swipe; wide eyes magnified through his thick glasses with a look that said Sal had just crushed his lifelong dream of being the nerd who nabbed Vivaldi with a feather duster.

"I mean, don't stop. Just don't get your hopes up, kid."

He went back to dusting. The scene bustled with an overpopulation of CSU and Major Case Squad personnel. The other ME, Blaine Attwood, was zipping the corpses in black body bags, and the FBI forensics team wove between the chaos.

Sal picked silently through the mess—noting trajectory of the shots fired based on blood spatter, determining the position of the gunman for each kill, and then observing how and what equipment had been thrashed afterward. The information he downloaded constructed the scene as the killer entered it and mapped his course of action, telling Sal the height of the gunman, five-ten or taller, and some insight into his personality.

"Hey, can I see that camera?"

The forensic photographer tiptoed through the streams of blood and handed it over.

Flipping through the images, Sal focused on the shots of the floor. By now the crew of professionals working the scene had smeared any discernible marks. And aside from what he saw were his and Candice's footprints in red, the pictures showed the scene untainted by escape.

Vivaldi had been careful in his destruction, leaving in haste due to their interruption but without placing a single print on the hemorrhaging floor. With the multiple rounds of jacketed hollow point bullets used to ensure fatal wounds, there'd been no shortage of bloodshed.

A calculated assault. Vivaldi wasn't slipping up and getting careless like Sal had hoped. Everything, from the tripped security feed, to the dismantled access box, down to every last detail of this crime scene, had been meticulously planned out.

Except for the delayed death of the technician and …

Sal scanned ahead to the pictures of the victim in the second office, zoomed in. Despite the vulgarity of the image, a smile bloomed on his face. "Well, I'll be darned."

"Not much can make a man smile like that. Especially not at a crime scene." A cashmere voice sliced clean through his concentration.

Sal tore his eyes away from the screen, grasping at the details and theories still swirling in his mind. He'd delved over each of the autopsy reports with a fine-toothed comb. But now finally, he'd hit pay dirt.

"Care to share what's making you so happy? Because that's information a girl can use."

Eyeing the source of the flirtatious quip, Sal spotted Jill

Chrissick, new analyst extraordinaire. In a snug gray skirt and blazer with a crisp robin's egg blue shirt matching her icy eyes, she raised an eyebrow in wait of his response.

Sal shrugged. "I'm working a theory."

She drummed her fingers on the table by her stuff before stepping forward with a smile. Her eyes level with his and boldly unflinching. "Anything I can help out with?"

FBI agents were excellent manipulators and, like all newbies, Miss Chrissick could add the task of proving her worth to her case load, but flirting at a crime scene?

Okay, to be fair, he'd probably flirted with Candice at one before, but this felt different.

"Not at the moment, Jill. But I'll be sure to let you know."

Her face fell with a slight pout. "I'll need the equipment to see if anything scrubbed from the hard drives can be recovered. Where should I set up?"

When she tilted her head, the light scooped against the deep contoured dimple in her chin. He wasn't sure why he noticed. Normally he found dimples endearing. And Miss Chrissick was easy on the eyes in a lanky and generic sort of way, but something about her tripped his caution sensor, casting her in a less than endearing light.

Though her insight could be helpful, and they certainly could use a fresh perspective with Vivaldi, her placement at the FBI met Sal at an odd juncture of life and circumstances. Was jealously rearing its ugly head? Or was he picking up the scent of another weasel in their midst.

"You find something, Biggs?" Sal redirected his attention, though Miss Chrissick didn't bug off. He'd caught sight of the head of the CSU lifting what had to be a hair into an evidence bag. A long hair.

A stout, balding Kyle Biggs stood, swiped a smattering of sweat from his deeply receding hairline, and stepped over a puddle of blood. "Probably not. Got a hair. Auburn." He shrugged. "One of the lab workers was a ginger."

Sal snatched the bag and held it up to the light. "No, make

this top priority. This is a deeper shade. Not by much, but the victim's hair had a coppery sheen to it. This one, look at the root," Sal held it out. "I'd wager anything it's synthetic."

Biggs reclaimed the bag, an odd smiling frown tug-of-warred on his face. "Nice catch, Salivas. I see why they keep you around."

Yeah, be sure to mention it to my boss.

Biggs headed off, but Jill remained in his airspace, though no trace of fragrance accompanied her presence. The expensive cologne wafting from his left, however, meant Blaine Attwood was approaching.

"Hey, Agent Salivas."

Stupid how much the title meant to him, even though at present it wasn't entirely accurate.

"I don't suppose Dr. Stevens will be returning here, but did she mention coming back to the morgue today? I could use some help." His eyes shifted to Miss Chrissick and bumbled, rebounding back to the woman who issued a tight smile and a repellent gaze.

Something bristled. The vibe between them as awkward as a public breakup. "Do you two know each other?"

Jill scrunched her face, darting another quick glance at the gawking ME. "No." Shaking her head, she swiveled back to Sal. "And you're obviously busy. I'll just—"

"I swear you look familiar. Something about your face." Blaine took a step closer. "No, but your eyes are blue. And your ..." Surveying south of her throat, his eyes narrowed. "Huh. You don't happen to have a redheaded sister, do you?" Blaine's smile was so slimy it should have slid from his face. Unprofessional flirting or not, Sal had half a mind to usher poor Jill away from the tactless ogler.

She saved him the trouble and left.

Tilting his head, the ME's gaze followed her departure.

"Hey, Blaine. You're loaded right?" Sal elbowed the idiot in attempts to spear him with at least a hint of integrity.

Smugness lined Blaine's grin as he unlatched his leer

from Jill's backside. "You got that right."

Sal patted his shoulder, and before parting, left him with a nugget of wisdom. "Good. You're gonna need it to buy an education on how to talk to women."

Chapter 30

Candice Stevens

"Candi," her mother pleaded. Her voice resonating over the phone with such vibrato she was surely putting on an act.

And the Tony Award goes to Victoria Bristol.

"Bravo, Mom. Really convincing."

"Candi, please. I need you to c-come h-home. To … to practice." The words were muffled, almost a sob. Not shocking since she played this violin last week, successfully guilting Candice into playing for three hours without even the courtesy of a bathroom break. AJ hadn't been pleased to be kept waiting.

She nibbled down on her stubby thumbnail, muting out the overdramatized pleas. The constant manipulations soured the few precious morsels of nutrients she'd snuck into her stomach when AJ had gone out to meet with his dealer.

Manipulations from her pathetic and selfish mother who'd stolen all the joy of Candice's precious rare talent.

Abuse from her violent and obsessive boyfriend who took everything he wanted and left Candi depleted and lonely, though never alone.

One would think sixteen years was enough time to grow a backbone, or at least let her lippy inner Jersey-girl off her leash.

Yet every time she spoke to her mother, and every time she looked into AJ's wicked dark eyes, her weak little stomach shrank inward. Proving her eighty-eight pounds of musical prodigy and super book smarts were useless without any guts to back them up.

Actually, in the past few months she'd managed to gain a few pounds. A ticket to freedom? If she packed on some padding maybe she'd be strong enough to put some oomph behind her protests, or perhaps become so unappealing she'd be left alone.

Nah. She'd once foregone showering for days in hopes of a similar outcome, but it'd backfired when AJ took it upon himself to personally monitor her hygiene. A shudder ripped through her, squeezing her stomach until bile flicked the back of her tongue.

"Okay, this isn't about my music. I need help, and I can't call the po—" Another award-winning blubber cut her off. "I just thought you'd come if—"

Candi swore under her breath as the cries wailed on. Despite everything, she loved her mother. Shoot, she loved AJ too. But love wasn't just blind. It was stupid. Likely fatal if things continued the way they had.

Sure, she could slip home right now and get back before AJ returned. But it wasn't enough to spend an hour playing for her mother. If you gave her an inch, she took a mile and then some. And Candice was sick of it. Sick of the way love only damaged her. Something in her snapped.

"You know, Mom? I made you a stupid tape with all your precious songs, use that. I don't wanna see you. I hate what you've done to this thing I used to love. You're a leech. A vampire. A wretched, miserable soul-sucker, and as long as I live I'll never play another note for you again!"

Well, that didn't taste too bad coming up. Not like the

taco she'd pilfered from the guys' fast food run yesterday that had made a second appearance. She sat a little straighter, glowing with pride from her first stab at defending herself.

"No! Please. Candi, he's here! I need you to call—" Her throat collapsed on a whimper.

A gruff male voice cut through the airwaves. "There you are, *Torrie-love*. No more escaping. It's time for your final song."

Ick!

A rustling brushed against the earpiece. The sound like restless limbs on smooth sheets. The man laughed, a sick, sinister sound on his gritty southern bass. Older and wiser, Candice now understood the horrors happening behind closed doors. This was not something she wanted to hear. Something she prayed she'd never be party to again. Fate wasn't that kind. Her prayers proved to be wasted breath, her songs wasted melodies.

She pulled the phone from her ear to hang up when she heard his final farewell.

"Say goodbye now, love. The show's over."

"Hey Brat." The words a caress as soft as the feathered touch smoothing over her hair, grazing her cheek. "Come on, Brat. I need you to wake up."

Wake up? Mmm ... not from this dream.

Curled up in a cozy block of warmth, Candice burrowed deeper until the softness snuggled all around her, breathing in the crisp scent of fresh laundered cotton.

Sleep. *Good.*

She became aware of the light warring with her eyes but ignored the intrusion, resting instead in the calming lull of her breath. Her old life, this morning at the lab, all a bad dream. This. *This* was real. Her safe and solitary Mayberry.

An enticing little slip of heat, spice, and vanilla awakened her senses. That smooth stroking hand electrifying her hair follicles. A prelude to more stirring within.

Oh. Maybe not so solitary.

"All right Sleeping Beauty, if you don't open your eyes, I'll have no choice but to awaken you with a kiss." That saucy accent swirled through the voice so meltingly rich it was like luscious waves of melodic chocolate.

She felt the bed shift, deducing Dorian had decided to sit. Minty breath, and that absurdly delicious scent of his, wafted closer. But before his lips could set off a spark she was flooded with realizations.

First of which was he was in her house, that should have been locked.

Second of which was he was in her bed, which was off limits.

And third of which, and most critical, he was about to kiss her. And she was about to let him.

Panic jerked her upright.

A sharp pain splashed white behind her eyes and then ballooned with dark, dancing spots.

"Ouch." She cried, eyes still pinched as she rubbed the place her forehead had connected with his. Squinting past the ache, she peeked up at Dorian, a comical tilt tipping his lips, a keen little sparkle in his eyes.

"I, uh … sorry. I meant to set an alarm."

A slow grin swept across his lips.

Good gravy, when did he get so good looking? It had to have been recent. He sure hadn't looked like this two weeks ago.

"Didn't want to scare you, and I also didn't want to break your door down, but you weren't answering or picking up your phone." He held up a key. "Found your spare in the storm drain. Magnetic. Smart." Leaning forward he placed it on her nightstand. "Probably not the best place for it though.

I found it in like three minutes."

His eyes latched on her face with intense focus, as if he were avoiding looking elsewhere.

She glanced down at her well-worn cami sticking like cellophane to her braless chest and jerked up on the covers.

"My bad," she winced, perhaps a little impressed he'd abstained from groping her with his gaze.

But then, for reasons unknown, she pinched with insecurity. Why hadn't he looked? Was she so unsightly with the extra weight he wasn't even tempted?

She loosened the sheets she'd twisted between her fingers. With her self-esteem circling the drain, she let the impulse to drop the sheet tool around in her head. How would he react?

Before she could test the theory he stood, stuffed his hands into his pockets, and stared at the wall above her head. "I'll let you pack your stuff. Holler at me when you're ready, and I'll carry your bags down."

Nodding, she was once again twining the cover, unsettled by the urges whipping through her. "Hey, Dorian?"

He paused at the door, his shoulders squaring before he glanced back. "Yes, Brat?"

"The code. How'd you know the security code?"

Hesitating a moment, he issued a slight shrug. "It's what I do."

"So, what's the plan?" A bit nonplussed by his silence, Candice found it difficult to not blather on. He'd been his usual happy-go-lucky self when they left on the almost four-hour drive to the Lake of the Ozarks. They'd stopped for burgers since she'd slept through lunch. Laughed together at his horribly tone-deaf renditions of the oldies he crooned along with on the radio. And talked everything from high school woes to favorite movies and guilty pleasures.

But when she'd brought up the painting in Dorian's living

room, prattling on about how deeply it touched her emotions, he'd gone mute.

She couldn't blame him. She'd practically romanticized the thing, nearly tearing up while she spewed about her feelings and the beauty hidden in the desolation of it. He must think her a complete basket case. Basically every man's nightmare.

So absorbed in her rare emotional purge, she hadn't caught on to his stiffness until she'd begged to know where he'd bought it.

"It's the only one." He'd said. Case closed.

So Candice escaped to the sights beyond her window. Barren trees packed against endless rolling hills stood guard in the distance while a white line and a brittle grassy ditch streamed alongside their sexy Ferrari.

The silent moments ticked past like deafening screams until she could no longer stand it.

"Dorian, are you listening? I asked what the plan was. For Preston Bradley's?"

He turned to look at her, his eyes blinking out of a deep trance. "Right. Sorry." Shaking his head, he focused back on the road. As did she.

"So the plan is to act like house guests, charming Preston Bradley and his snobby friends with our cover as a busy married couple in need of a getaway. I'm hoping he takes the opportunity to show us his cars since I'm a car guy. That way I'll know what kind of security to bypass to sneak into the garage after everyone turns in."

She looked back in time to see him weave a hand through his hair, dislodging a clump from his slicked back "Sly" look to stand adorably on end.

His tan knuckles flushed white on the steering wheel; his eyes pinned on the road as he scooped around a sharp curve in the car made to savor the road.

"With any luck, we'll get what we need tonight for a warrant. Then we can head back and finish up with the bodies from the lab. Oh, that reminds me."

A sparkle flashed back into his eyes. He met her gaze, that old stupid grin splitting his lips. This time, it wrenched a smile right out of her. "What is it, Sly, darling?" She smoothed back his rebellious lock of hair and wagged her eyebrows, hopefully instilling some confidence she'd do better this time around.

In fact, it shamed her how excited pretending to be happily married to Dorian was making her. Shamed her doubly how much she wanted him to pull over so she could run her hands through his hair again, and then—

Not the time, Jersey.

Criminy. Her brain cells were shrinking by the second. All because of his good humor, his stupid smile, his talented lips, his protective instinct …

And well, the Ferrari. It should probably shoulder some of the blame for her sudden swoon.

Her heart was treading in dangerous territory. But she couldn't deny Dorian seemed trustworthy. When they were together, everything about him felt honest and good. Safe. Did such a man even exist?

Was he really what he seemed? And how could she be sure?

The last time she handed over her love she'd been beaten into submission with it. There were so many valid reasons why allowing herself to feel was a terrible idea. But was she strong enough to stop it? And was it naive to hope it might be different this time around?

It won't matter once he finds out what you've done.

Her secret felt so much bigger since learning of Dorian's childhood. If he was feeling anything for her, it would all change once he learned the truth.

"Vivaldi has an accomplice."

"What?" Her thoughts screeched to a halt. "An accomplice? How do you know?"

"Because of your incredibly detailed reports on his

victims." He smiled, and she all but melted into the Italian leather. "The way you catalogued each of those cuts in the bones, you indicated Vivaldi was right hand dominant."

"Okay. And his accomplice is left handed?

"Yep."

As if that would be enough. He peeked playfully from the corner of his eye and then zoomed around another deeply wooded curve through the Ozark hills straightening to expose high, muddy water hugging the shore.

She raised her arm as if threatening to backhand him, but he caught her hand, and with nimble fingers, slipped a ring on a very important digit. Well, wasn't that some impressive sleight of hand.

Catching sight of a twinkle, her breath caught, but she couldn't tear her eyes from the happiness curving his mouth. He twined their hands, brought the bundle to his lips, and pressed a kiss against her ring finger.

A flood of warmth raced through her. The ripple effect starting at that one small finger enough to wipe out the whole Eastern seaboard if it wasn't contained in her body.

The ring was just for their cover. And they'd forgotten to buy a decoy before the fundraiser. So why did it feel real? It was just a sliver of cut glass masquerading as a promise, but the significance felt as enormous as a ten-carat weight.

She spared a glance at the fake bling to find a tasteful round solitaire wrapped in a delicate halo of pavé sparkle. Sparkle that continued around an eternity band.

Using their joined hands, he shifted into the next gear without letting go. Emotion clogged in her tear ducts, pressing until she was sure the flood gates would break and pronounce her the world's greatest fool.

"*Oh*, Dorian. Too bad it's not real. It's so perfect I can hardly breathe."

He said nothing, only tightened his grasp and tickled the back of her hand with his thumb. The gentleness was like a spell. It tumbled through her, awakening and unnerving every last cell. "I'll be sure to nominate you for fake husband of the year." She heard the quip escape on a nervous laugh. Self-preservation kicking in to ease the tense emotional rush.

His chuckle melted over her like heated honey, and her erratic heart simmered to the sound. "You think I got a shot?"

"You're a shoo in." She was instantly uncertain about the subject they were dancing around but couldn't squelch the hope rising to match the swollen waters of the lake in the distance.

When he glanced back at the road, she cleared her throat and trained her eyes forward. "So, the lefty ..."

"Ah, yes. We did get a bit distracted there, didn't we?"

"I'd say." She mumbled under her breath, but his little huff of laughter said he hadn't missed it.

"When I reconstructed the scene at the lab, I noticed something about the last victim we found in the office. She was the only one shot in the head, and when I zoomed in using the camera at the crime scene, I could see where the shooter had pressed the gun barrel against her temple."

"Okay."

"If you can picture it, the woman was sitting at her desk in the small office, facing the door, back to the wall. The only reason the killer wouldn't have shot her from the doorway would be if he needed something from her. My guess—something from the computer since she never left her chair. Because of the size and configuration of the room, I could tell where he had to have stood to both keep the gun to her head long enough to leave an impression and be able to view the computer screen."

Focused on visualizing the scene, she hadn't sensed he was looking at her.

When she caught him he smiled again. Always with the smiling. "Even when you're frowning you're cute."

She rolled her eyes but couldn't refuse the grin squirming for release. "Cute?"

"My bad. Devastating." He winked, then eyed the road.

"I'd sketch you a diagram, but well, I'm driving."

"A diagram of my devastating cuteness?" Oh, duh. The crime scene. The office layout. Why was her brain on scramble? Heat burned in her cheeks. She considered hiding it, but Dorian would know either way. Besides, he was already grinning like a gorgeous dope. "Never mind."

"From the way the victim fell back and to the killer's right, and by the angle of the entry wound, he was holding the gun with his left hand. Something a righty wouldn't do."

"Huh, you're right. That's strange. So, what else do we know about the accomplice?"

He shifted again, the thriving rumble of the engine and the rev of information supercharging the blood coursing through her. She squeezed his hand tighter.

"Five-ten or taller, ruthless marksman, meticulous, highly intelligent. You know, the norm."

He was downplaying his skill, but he was incredibly insightful to have gathered those clues at the scene. Especially with the competing commotion of the other investigators and the emotional pendulum of their discovery just before.

He did that a lot, she was realizing. Not demanding attention, but reading each situation and responding with calculated intentions. Sometimes with a well-placed blunder to cast him inept, sometimes with a joke to diffuse the tension. And sometimes with calm direction, instilling absolute trust she'd once thought irrational.

But he'd taken her by surprise. He was humble and self-sacrificing. Driven by something other than success and recognition and power.

He fought his own battle of redemption, on his terms alone.

In her eyes, it made him the most noble, dependable, and honest man alive.

And if only for the next three days, she'd delude herself with the fantasy that she could be worthy of such a man.

The Ferrari slowed and descended a long steep drive. "Here we are, Kitty."

A stacked modern white stucco estate rose to the tips of the trees four stories high. A pair of glass and metal balconies graced each level as if floating in the fog-frosted air. The posh house belonged on some cliff in LA and seemed out of place on the quiet hill in the Ozarks.

The grumble of the engine ceased, and Candice realized they were already at the end of the drive. Frigid fear plunged through her middle as if she'd been dropped into the icy lake with an anchor.

It'd been far too easy to forget the real dangers that lay ahead when they'd been joking in the car. When it was just the two of them it felt like they were all that existed in three dimensions, everything else around them, all the dangers and the obstacles, simply folded up and tucked away, too flat to notice.

But now, flashes of Vivaldi's victims scanned through her mind. Beautiful women carved and burned for a decade. The middle aged man who bled to death in her hands mere hours ago.

She swallowed a lump of nausea, thinking she'd need another burger and fries, and perhaps a whole pan of brownies before she could walk through the opulent entry and paste on a smile for Preston Bradley.

Dorian was opening her door, and her legs nearly went liquid when he pulled her up to meet the pavement. Good thing he held on to her waist or she and the asphalt would've become much better acquainted.

You'll be fine. Keep it together. The words looped in her head as they walked to the door.

And then Dorian tugged her closer, melding her to his side. "Stay close, Brat." He whispered in her ear as if sensing her dwindling courage. "I won't let anything happen to you."

Oh, please God let that be true.

Chapter 31

Dorian Salivas

"How do you take your scotch, Sly?"

The brunette temptation next to Sal was intoxicating enough, adding liquor to the mix wouldn't assure a clear head. And it sure wouldn't help him keep his hands to himself. But he knew it would be an insult to refuse Preston's offer. Especially since the scotch in question was a sixty-two-year-old Dalmore, a nearly $60,000 bottle of Scottish whiskey. Preston was showing off.

"Just a single. Neat. Thanks." He slipped his arm around Candice, who was snuggled up against him on an outdoor chaise for two overlooking the lake. Dusk was settling in. The cool air tempered by rows of high-end propane heaters and a cozy knit blanket thrown over their legs.

A chef was currently whipping up some culinary exhibition fit for a king, and the Gutiérrezes, as well as the other six house guests, were being entertained by their host on the expansive tiered deck.

Replacing the stopper on the etched glass decanter, Preston carried over the inch of amber liquid and handed it to Sal. "I'm so pleased you and your lovely wife could join us. Working as much as you do, I know it mustn't be easy to get away on holiday."

As far as undercover work went, it was pure luxury. They were welcomed warmly into the modern mansion, the greeting with Preston much less awkward than he'd been anticipating, even if the guy unabashedly ogled Candice like she was the prime rib for dinner.

They'd been escorted to their guest suite by the housekeeper instead of Preston, which helped to ease any awkwardness there. At least until they'd bid her farewell and carried their luggage into the room unchaperoned.

The stark white accommodation was like a lavish hotel suite. A wall of sliding glass opened to a terrace with a lake view, and the glass and white subway-tiled bathroom boasted absolutely no privacy since it didn't even have a door but a curved wall for an entrance. Though it had a shower like a carwash a family sedan could actually drive through.

And the bed, well, Sal wasn't going to think about that right now. He'd be spending torturous hours on the floor, pining away for the woman he loved tangling all that smooth, caramel skin between those pure white sheets.

"It's a pleasure to be here. This is some place you got." Thankfully, his synapses aligned enough to form an intelligible response. Though his mind was still fastened on the fantasy that had Candice wrapped in different layers of white. A fancier version just preceding the white sheets. She was that kind of girl now. And he'd do anything to be worthy of such a prize.

Small talk abounded, Candice surprising Sal with her clever drop-ins and quips that kept their audience in smiles and stitches.

Sal was normally the funny one. Very often at his own expense. He was proud to have a woman by his side who could run the show. But he also felt the urge to maybe diminish her charm, just to keep her safe since she'd magnetized every person here. If anyone so much as touched her, he'd be in agent mode so fast he'd probably have them cuffed before he realized he'd dislocated their arms in the process.

Reaching beneath the blanket he laced his fingers with hers, squeezing a bit in warning. Except she didn't quite catch the hint to draw less attention to her ultra-fine self. Instead she angled her body closer, sliding her leg over to entwine with his.

Hot tamale! His brain did a belly flop off the deck. Whatever was left behind the wheel relished in the feel of the soft curves imprinting him with her heat while he dusted his lips over the satin skin of her cheek and drowned in the intoxicating scent of her hibiscus hair.

Yes, it all rendered him inept, which wouldn't be helpful if Vivaldi was in their midst. But at least it shut her up for a few minutes while the conversation turned to the other ostentatious wines and liquors in Preston's cellar.

The wine collection didn't interest him. Neither did the small fleet of speedboats, yachts, and jet skis lining the dock. Those were the topics of conversation. And there had yet to be a natural segue to the discussion of cars. Specifically a Maserati used as a hearse.

Might be a buzzkill.

Finally the topic turned when someone asked what Sly was working on. To which Sal regaled them with all the details he'd studied up on, providing a very convincing, if he did say so himself, outline of his latest automotive creation.

Just when he'd prepped the atmosphere for a shift to Preston's collection, Ariana, one half of the pair of Preston's Norwegian blondes, proved she could speak English.

"Could you draw us something, Sly? I'd love to see how all that creative energy looks on paper."

The question caught him off guard, and a heavy pause lumbered through the quaint party.

Candice tensed beside him, grasping his upper thigh with the hand he wasn't holding.

Well, if he'd come up with anything to say it was gone now!

"I made Sly promise no work this weekend." She stroked her hand over his leg as if to assure him she'd handled it. But the act was pure seduction. Sal's tongue must have swollen to twice its normal size and was rendered uselessly mute, just like his one-tracked mind.

All was still quiet in wait of his response. *Come on!* He urged his willpower to overcome the electric shock, but Candice's touch proved too debilitating.

Slipping his palm from hers, he trapped her wandering hand and shot her a pointed glance. *You're killing me here.* Her cheeks blazed as red as ghost chilies when she caught on.

"Sorry, blondie, no work tonight. Though I would love to see your Maserati, Preston. That might be something I could render for you. A keepsake as a sort of thank you for this weekend."

And an hour alone with your getaway car to uncover your murderous secret.

Surprise lined their host's face. He slung each arm around a blonde and leaned back into his chaise. "Oh, yes, yes. That would be splendid. Perhaps, after dinner?"

Yes, yes. Perhaps before you make one of those blondes number forty-two. Or whatever number he was up to after today.

The tension from Candice's body melted away along with his own as she exhaled the stress and nuzzled closer. The gentle sweep of wind carried a breath of soggy moss and freshwater fish from the tangerine ripples of sunset painting the surface of the lake.

Sal took his first sip of scotch, letting the wisp of the kerosene slip past his lips. Another coil of tension dissolving as the heat scorched a trail down his throat.

They would play their little game through dinner. Enjoy the time he got to con himself into thinking Candice wasn't merely pretending to crave his touch. Then, they'd do what they came to do.

And until then, because the other guests all excused themselves to freshen up before dinner, and because Sal suspected Candice wasn't anxious to close herself in a bedroom with her fake husband, Sal got to watch the brushstrokes of the sunset sink behind the trees with his wife, and watch the sherbet waters turn to stone.

And then, because he could, he put the brilliance of the sun to shame, pulled Candice closer still, kissed her eyelids, sank his fingers into the cool velvet bounty of her hair, parted her lips, and kissed her until neither one of them could remember their names.

Real or fake.

Dinner was the bomb. A full spread of prime rib, lobster tail, some sort of fancy mousse-looking twice-baked potato, and sautéed asparagus as the main course. Lots of delicate little finger foods Sal couldn't pronounce nor recognize went down easy before that, and by the time they plopped a fat slab of crystal-glazed Carnegie Deli cheesecake in front of him, he could scarcely recall even a hint of those old pangs of hunger he'd known most of his life.

All the women at the table pecked at the food like baby chicks, rearranging their plates to allude to some sort of consumption. All but Candice.

A smile warmed from his chest, and he found he'd been grinning at her most of the meal. She seemed to sense his admiration. And by some miraculous turn of events, after a few chews with her eyes closed, she'd peek over at Sal, letting a secret smile curl her lips, making him hungry for something so much better than the gourmet cuisine.

Once her plate was clean, and after she'd smeared it with her finger and lapped the last of the sweet cream from her fingertip, he'd had to fight the urge to throw her over his shoulder, gun it to the nearest courthouse, and make it official—by federal mandate if necessary. He wasn't beyond hypnosis at this point. He was desperate for her with a soul-deep hunger he knew would never find its substitute.

He'd have to tell her soon or he'd burst. He loved her.

And he wanted to spend the rest of his life proving just how much.

Maybe he'd even start tonight.

The vision skipped through his mind, teasing and tempting with possibilities that burned beneath his collar as hot as the hunger now restless in his veins.

But why did it feel as if Loretta Mae was viewing the captions of his thoughts and shaking her head with shame.

Love, Loretta Mae! The real deal. This is my chance for a do over. My chance to do something right. To make up for everything I've done that was corrupt and selfish.

Even though she was gone, and it was irrational to think otherwise, he could hear himself pleading with her.

What makes you think your love for Candice isn't rooted in your own greed? Loretta Mae asked.

His mind sputtered. What? How could it be?

Because it makes you feel good. It builds you up and gives you hope for your redemption. This time the voice was his.

Was he a Candice-junkie, taking what he wanted … the affection, the laughs, the friendship, and leaving her feeling empty and alone, like AJ had? Or could his love actually *give*?

"Hey?" Her hand touched his neck, smoothed lovingly over the back of his hair with enough zing to make it stand on end. When he looked at her he got swept away in those sparkling cognac eyes more decadent than the finest spirits in Preston's priceless collection. "You okay?" Shifting her hand to his cheek, her thumb tickled over the faint stubble.

Either she was reaching for an Academy Award or she was finally unlacing the boxing gloves and allowing the moment to strip away her reserve.

Turning his face, he pressed a kiss to her palm, then kissed once more at her wrist, feeling the rev of her pulse against his lips before he caught her hand, and rubbed his thumb over the evidence. "Never better."

When she flashed a smile the world around them

dissolved to nothing. She wove their hands together and brought them to rest on the table, in plain view of their guests.

He didn't know why it felt significant. They were supposed to be married. Holding hands. Harmless, right? Wrong. It felt like her heart was finally creaking open. In all his life, he'd never been better.

"Well, Sly, you've been showing off with your gorgeous wife all night, now it's my turn."

"Huh?" Sal's head jerked around so fast his neck cracked, rather loudly.

A devious grin tilted their host's lips, his eyes lingering on Candice a moment longer than Sal thought necessary. "My automobiles, of course. Care for a glance?"

A bit more than a glance.

"Love one." Sal pressed the white linen napkin to his lips, set it down on his plate, and assisted Candice with her chair.

They took three flights of what appeared to be floating steel and glass stairs ensconced in an atrium wall of windows to the ground level. Weaving through a rec room with billiards and ping-pong tables, they then entered a long, dimly lit hallway.

When he realized none of the other guests had followed, tension tiptoed down his spine. With his Glock holstered at his ankle to safeguard from any accidental touches, he felt ill-prepared for an ambush.

What if Preston was on to them? What if this was a set up? What if, at this moment, Sal was ushering Candice right into Vivaldi's operating room.

His steps slowed while his mind raced to plot out an emergency plan. Candice must have sensed his hesitance because she tightened her grip on his arm. A sick rumbling feeling roiled in his chest when he looked at her.

Her eyes—so much trust there. Trust he couldn't help but feel like he hadn't quite earned since he'd utilized his skills to read and manipulate her more times than he was proud to admit.

Why should she trust him? And while he was on the subject, why on earth did he think he could earn forgiveness after all he'd done? Everything he touched withered and died. He *was* being selfish.

If he'd considered something other than the way she made him feel, or what it meant for his redemption if he could find someone to love, or even the way catching Vivaldi would solve all his problems at work, he would have realized he'd only been thinking of himself. His needs and desires. He didn't deserve forgiveness. Or the gift of her trust.

His love, as fate would have it, was fatal.

Too bad psychics weren't real, because at this critical low point in his life, the man who was supposed to use his gift to help people and atone for his sins, had unwittingly led the woman he loved like a sheep to the slaughter.

Chapter 32

Candice Stevens

Whatever flashed in Dorian's eyes a moment ago had snapped the leash of her fear. Grasping for refuge from the runaway terror, she squeezed his arm like a tourniquet.

Why had the others not followed? Why were all the other women here blonde? Why was this hallway so dark and harrowing in this strange house of glass?

Despite the cool drift of air, a bead of sweat tickled her low back.

Dorian's steps slowed, and she clenched him tighter, feeling a phantom press against her back nudging her forward, whispering a sense of security into the fray of uncertainty.

Steps emboldened, she tugged him along, suddenly driven by the need for truth. When they reached the door, her heart hit a speed bump, fumbling through her like a fighter plane plunging toward the ground. "All right Preston, enough suspense. Let's see what all the fuss is about." Her voice was strange to her ears, the sound as fragile as a wafer crumbling in the silence.

Preston turned his chin over his shoulder, a hint of a smile etched in the shadow. "Wait until you see. It's to die for."

Her pulse was thick in her ears, slow and drugging. Whatever had urged her forward now seemed like the devil's pitchfork poking until she teetered on the edge of the earth. Her foot crossed the threshold from carpet to concrete, and she breathed a slight sigh when she hadn't fallen through to Vivaldi's fiery hell.

Preston disappeared into the darkness without a word. And Dorian released her, stooping to pluck what she hoped was a gun from his ankle.

Were they actually in his garage? Or had he lead them somewhere else?

"Preston?"

No sooner had Dorian called out when rows of lights rippled to life, reflecting in cannon off the gorgeous gleaming gems.

Candice released the trap of air she'd smuggled into her chest and strode ahead to view the fleet of insanity hidden away in yet another basement tomb.

Actually, no. Undeniable relief sedated her nerves when she spotted a wall of garage doors at her left. And glowing pads of openers mounted on the wall to her right, so not a tomb. Not like the underground lab still tormenting her thoughts after ten hours.

Dorian discreetly stowed his piece back in his waistband. And Preston was already weaving through his collection, presenting his arm like Vanna White in reference to each ostentatious ride.

The speech was lost on her. From the looks of it, on Dorian too since they were both preoccupied scanning for the murder-mobile.

"Dude, where's the Maserati?"

The reason they'd come was suspiciously absent from the ranks.

So absorbed with showing off, Preston hadn't seemed to notice anything amiss. He stopped and turned full circle. "Hmm, that's odd."

"Yeah, odd or convenient." Candice whispered to Dorian.

"I'm sure it was here." He ruffled his hand through his perfectly styled hair. Did that count as fidgeting? Indicate nerves? She wished she could tap into Dorian's brain and see what he discerned from all those subtle leaks of information.

"Guess I'll have to check the biometric safe and the guest log."

"Guest log?" Dorian was running the show so she kept her mouth shut lest she spew any of her doubts aloud.

Shaking his head, Preston crossed back between a Lamborghini and a vintage Mercedes. His distress not nearly as evident as she'd have thought a missing Maserati merited.

Unless …

Subconsciously her hands balled tight, like her meek little fists might somehow take down Vivaldi by sheer force of will.

"Yes. I don't just hoard all this beauty for myself, Mr. Gutiérrez. Part of the joy of having such exquisite things is *sharing* them with others." Thus, his generosity with their weekend visit, he seemed to say during the pause. But then his eyes held on her, his gaze like an unwanted hand copping a feel. "Something I'm sure you, a designer, would understand."

Preston shrugged and continued. "A few close friends and family members are permitted to borrow a vehicle, granted they return it in the same condition with a full tank of gas. I am a stickler on that one."

Sal nodded. "So, who are the lucky few on the prestigious list?"

It was an odd, perhaps inappropriate question, but delivered with Dorian's charming smile, Preston's flit of suspicion was replaced by a wry grin of his own. "Only those with exemplary taste in automobiles. If you are ever interested, Sly, I can get your prints added to the biometric safe holding the keys. Perhaps in exchange, you'd consent to take on my recently acquired 1925 Rolls Royce Phantom for one of your marvelous custom refurbishments."

"Hmm." Dorian slipped his warm palm into her cold one, skimmed this thumb in that toe-curling way over the back of her hand. She shuddered with relief. They wouldn't be dying today.

But then she watched his eyes memorize the layout of the garage. Watched them narrow a fraction when he spotted something important. Why he thought he needed to sneak into the garage now, she didn't know. But she knew something was brewing in that relentless brain of his.

Just when she'd convinced herself they'd dodged a bullet, or maybe some knives and a blow torch, she felt something else peak on her radar. Perhaps it was all the nagging loose ends of the case. All the missed opportunities. Or perhaps it was because they'd just lost their best lead and were no closer to finding their killer.

Or maybe, it was because she knew with terrifying certainty Vivaldi was on to them. Wherever he was.

"You got yourself a deal." Dorian released her hand and formed a gentleman's agreement with the arrogant Brit. One she still wasn't sure wouldn't try to cut into her flesh and serenade her to death the first chance he got.

The shower switched off, and Candice fumbled with the Bible in her hands—the only thing in Preston's nightstand and perfect material to squelch the thoughts and images traipsing through her head.

At least, it would have been if she'd actually read any.

Light from the bathroom of their suite puddled out into the bedroom, a wicked sort of reminder that nothing but space separated her from the man she couldn't stop thinking about. A man who was currently dripping wet and—

She shook her head. Not going there.

Too bad it was exactly where her mind had been for the past ten minutes "reading" to the soothing sound of falling water. Soothing, ha!

Seriously, what kind of bathroom doesn't even have a door? It was criminal!

Fighting her nature, she dug her nose deeper into the filmy pages.

Yes, read this! You obviously need it! She told Jersey.

But Jersey was the victor of their match since Candice's mind was right back where it had started. In the gutter.

Dropping the Bible to her lap, she flung herself back onto the pillow and succeeded in banging her skull against the headboard. "Ow." She squeezed her eyes tight, then stared up at the stark white ceiling.

"Everything okay out there?"

Without lifting up, she turned her neck on instinct. Dorian was poking his head out of the bathroom. Well, his head and a pie slice of his chiseled chest. His wet dark hair even more inky than usual. The concern softening his features assuring her he was taking his job as her guardian very seriously.

I give! Send back the old angel. This one is much too tempting for a girl like me.

"Uhh, yeah. Fine. Peachy." Wrapping her arms around herself, she drove her eyes back to the ceiling, wishing his image could be bleached from her mind.

His chuckle was like an all-you-can-eat buffet, something she could gorge out on for hours on end. "You're a terrible liar. Then again, I've got mad skills in this area."

Don't look at him. Eyes averted. Stay strong.

"Listen, I know things aren't really going as we'd hoped. And Preston wasn't exactly forthright with a list of possible suspects. Not that I could demand a name without getting us a one-way ticket back to the Lou. But as soon as everyone's turned in for the night I'm heading down to the garage to find the safe. I've a pretty good idea where it's at. Plus I brought a prints kit along. At the very least we can try to see who used it last and see if it gives us any hits to go on."

"Dorian?" Propping up on her elbows, she braved a long look, feeling a blistering blush of red fill her cheeks. "Do you think it's Preston?"

He stepped from behind the curve.

Holy scrap of towel! A soft drape of white clung low on muscled hips, steam still lifting away from his perfectly honed body. He leaned against the wall, his gaze somewhere beyond the room as if his all-consuming thoughts left him clueless to his near-naked display.

Candice was now sitting up, every muscle twitching with tension. She was her mother's daughter. A curse she couldn't outrun.

Finally, after he'd catalogued his insights—and she'd catalogued every dip of muscle and every scarred badge of courage—he shook his head, his eyes landing back on her. "I dunno. We're working with virtually no evidence. My gut says no, but something's not right. I don't want you here any longer than necessary. My heart crashes into my ribcage every time Preston looks at you like you're something to be devoured."

The sweet sincerity in his eyes carved a fresh wound into her heart. "I can't be with you, Dorian." The words escaped on a brokenhearted whisper. "You deserve better. And I—"

He stepped forward, wearing only terrycloth and sizzle. Would that little knot at his hip hold? She swallowed, unable to stop the forbidden fantasy of a different kind of weekend getaway. A different past. A different life.

"Brat," he moved beside the bed, looking down with those dark chocolate eyes that tortured her appetite. "There is no one better."

Just tell him, Jersey balked. *Get it over with so you can crawl back into your shell.*

The purge bubbled up in her throat, words she'd never uttered straining for a cathartic release.

I can't do this. I'm still weak. I can't forgive myself, and I'm surely not to be trusted.

All the what-ifs battled in her mind. She opened her mouth, but the words snagged like a breath of broken glass. Probably because her heart was shattered beyond repair.

She shook her head, tears burning behind her eyes at the

look of hope shining in his.

Sal's phone beeped, breaking the moment. Candice turned away and scraped her knuckle against her wet cheek.

With a sigh he crossed the room and grabbed his phone. "I tapped into the security system. Someone just entered the basement door from the garage. But no one's left that way since we got back. I need to check it out."

She nodded with too much enthusiasm to be rid of him and trapped her gaze in the blurred pages of Song of Solomon. Funny how Vivaldi's weapon was also a song. A sick, deadly one. Not a saucy ode to lovers in the middle of a holy book.

"Hey."

Fitting a breath through her trembling lips, she managed to look at him, her heart a twisted score of longing and agony. If only life was simple. Forgiveness might be possible. Love would be within reach. And Vivaldi would be in eternal torment.

But nothing was that easy. Her hands were stained. Her forgiveness, unattainable. The obstacles, insurmountable.

Not to mention her involvement in the disappearing evidence a surefire career-killer.

And the case, her chance to absolve one painful strike on her record, was a sinking ship she and Dorian—and the next few unfortunate blondes—would be riding down while Vivaldi continued his sadistic serenade.

"We'll finish this talk later." He disappeared behind the wall and returned a moment later in black track pants and a gray T-shirt, looking just as delicious as before.

How was that even possible?

"Lock the door the behind me. This could take a while." Slipping into his tennis shoes and stashing his gun at his back, he edged open the door. With one foot out he turned back. "And Brat," his attention flickered to the book in her lap. "I'll need some backup. Might wanna flip to a different chapter and start praying." With a wink and a grin he was off, but not before firing the parting shot that shaved past her defenses and struck the very heart of her weakness. "But don't worry. We'll save that book for later."

Chapter 33

Dorian Salivas

He was almost to the kitchen when he heard hushed voices.

"... got in later than I wanted. Been a long night ... wanna crash." The voice was familiar but, Sal couldn't place it from a distance.

"I'm just ... car back. Did you remember ..."

Snippets of the conversation found Sal as he wormed silently through the halls. He placed them by their voices. Their position impossible to see from this angle. One of them was Preston. And the other ... Vivaldi?

Hmm. Seemed like a good time for a late-night snack.

A smile tipped the corner of his mouth. He peeled out of his shoes, because really, who puts those on to wander to the kitchen past midnight? About to step from the dark cover of the hallway, a thought flashed through his mind. Vivaldi knew who he was.

If Preston was Vivaldi, Sly and Kitty Gutiérrez were mere pawns for amusement in his sadistic game. But if the other voice was Vivaldi, then Sal's late-night rendezvous would not only be a surprise, but a threat.

He envisioned each scenario, watching the players react and retaliate. If he walked out as Sly, things could escalate before he could draw his gun. And if he prepared his gun and stalked around like Agent Salivas, he could blow his cover for nothing.

Sal jammed his hand through his damp hair, squeezed his

eyes shut, and tried it Loretta Mae's way.

All right, I'm game. Show me what to do.

Before he could open his eyes his thoughts shifted to Candice, that clear desolate vision of defeat when she murmured, *"You deserve better."*

Unworthiness, a feeling he knew too well. Her body language and the tremor in her throat spoke of regret. But it was her eyes that haunted him. So broken, so absorbed in her pain he wondered if her nightmare of guilt could be worse than his own.

She was stronger than she gave herself credit for. But she wasn't strong enough to carry the burden alone. If she'd let him, he would gladly be the one to shoulder it for the rest of their lives.

He'd make her see it didn't matter what she'd done or who she'd been, only that she love him in return.

The air around him stirred, a warm breath chasing the chill from his wet scalp. His skin pebbled, and a little jolt snapped him back on task.

Back from the useless time-wasting tangent.

Wow, some focus you got there, genius.

Shrugging his shoulders, stray thoughts appropriately quarantined, he did his best drowsy trudge toward the kitchen. Right now he was Sly Gutiérrez out to retrieve a glass of water, no matter what it cost him.

He entered the cove to the kitchen where he'd approximated the voices to find it empty. All was quiet now, and frustration nipped at him. Those thoughts had cost him a glimpse of their killer.

Great.

For the first time in a long time, he wished someone would beat him senseless. Because right now, reaching out to a God who never seemed to care felt like a pretty pointless exercise in naivety. Add Candice to the brain clog, and it was clear he didn't have a lick of sense left.

At least not enough required to catch a cunning predator

like Vivaldi.

Going through the motions, Sal chased down a glass of water and slunk back into the hallway. The stairs would be tricky since everything was made of glass, but after a cursory search Sal slipped unnoticed down three flights and raced across the rec room.

His knee gave a little quiver from the sprint, pinpricks firing down his shins. Creeping down the hallway, he scrubbed his hands against his pants to wipe away the nervous heat and pulled out his cell phone. It'd been eleven minutes since the door opened to welcome the visitor.

It shouldn't take long to locate the safe, and since he'd tucked one of Candice's earrings into his pocket he'd have a feasible cover story if he got caught snooping around.

But if the Maserati was back, and he was discovered with his prints kit, flashlight, and luminol spray, well then, he'd be blown but he'd have Vivaldi in a deadlock.

He stepped into the garage and flipped on the lights. A wintery chill hung in the room. A thrumming buzz from the florescent bulbs unsettled the stillness.

It was easy to spot the one that hadn't been there before. A blood red Maserati, the paint nearly bleeding against the glossy sheen of light.

His heart tripped ten steps ahead as he crossed the space and stood before the beast, its venom and exotic beauty fighting for the high note. The quiet exposed the threads of his breath like frayed edges in a line of stark precision.

Squatting down, he inspected the freshly waxed door.

Yahtzee.

The car might be squeaky clean, but whoever had driven it back left a perfect fingerprint near the seam of the door. Working quickly, he extracted the rudimentary kit he'd put together and brushed the carbon dust over the print. Next he peeled back the tape from the sticker sheet and rubbed it over the dust. With practiced deftness, he pulled it away and pasted it to the card before stuffing everything back in his pocket.

Using his shirt like a glove, he lifted the handle on the door, relieved when the latch gave without protest. Phantom noises seemed to lunge at him from every direction. The rush of blood in his ears diluting his senses like foam plugs. He shot a compulsive glance over his shoulder every five seconds, a necessary precaution, but one that stunted his ability to focus solely on the details.

One thing was for sure. The interior was spotless.

Sal bent down and plucked at the trunk latch, each minute of his search ticking in his brain like a detonator.

He scanned the garage again and stepped around to the trunk.

Something flashed. And before the shift could register Sal had drawn his Glock and aimed to kill …

At the light over the Rolls Royce that flickered and buzzed out.

Excited breaths expelled in heavy spasms in his chest, his fingers still clenching the trigger while he let his aim rove over the still, reflective fleet of cars and the seemingly unoccupied space.

He stalled for another minute before concealing his piece, shaking the nerves from his hands, and getting back to task.

The trunk was clean, even after he'd sprayed the carpet and cast his light to detect blood. Upon closer inspection, a small scored edge traced a rectangle in the trunk carpeting, showing it'd been replaced.

Fighting not to slam the trunk door, Sal braced his palms against the lip of the trunk. He hung his head forward, taking a moment to breathe through the fury, and let his mind revisit his observations.

A niggling suspicion told him to check the interior again, but before he did he caught the reflexive curl of his fingers about to leave his prints on the inside wall of the trunk.

Hmm. Sarah Hoyt's body had trace evidence of a Maserati carpet fiber, indicating this was the most likely place her body had been. But wouldn't it have shifted during the drive? Meaning the carpet might not have been the only thing the body touched.

Grabbing his luminol and his light, he leaned into the open trunk, feeling the prickle of danger stir the hair on his neck before he sprayed the seemingly clean interior walls of the trunk … and lit up ultraviolent blue smears of blood.

He stumbled back, a spearing breath stabbing through his chest.

Excitement and terror wrestled within, flipping his stomach and barring his windpipe. He may not know who the killer is, but he now had a big piece of the puzzle in his grasp and a short list of players for death row.

A warrant would be nice security right now, but since Preston had invited Sal into his garage to explore hours before, he wasn't about to risk losing the only piece of evidence they had on a serial killer because of a technicality. He'd figure out a way to nail Vivaldi to the wall. Even if they couldn't prosecute with the evidence, they'd have their first clue to his identity. And once they knew who he was, there wasn't a place in the world he could run where Sal wouldn't make it his personal mission to track him down and make him pay.

Protocol blurred in his mind, finding the old gray area where vengeance and justice overlapped.

Using a swab, he took two samples from the walls. He clicked a picture of the blood smears with his cell phone and eased the trunk shut with his elbows.

Part one of his mission was complete. Or was it?

He'd started toward the house when something else tugged at him. Every alert in his body warned he was pushing his luck, but the call was strong. Inching back toward the driver side door, he pried it open for one last look.

The supple tan leather was meticulous, and not even a speck of dust rested on the dash. It was late, he was tired. He must have misread the signs. The split second before the door caught the latch something on the floorboard snagged his eye.

Pulling back the door, the little fleck of silver caught on a miraculous glint of light. Sal cast a quick look over his shoulder to be sure no one held a flashlight, or perhaps even a gun, behind his head.

He bent down, scooped the cuff link into a baggie, and stuffed his pockets full of ammunition against Vivaldi. The moment should have been marked by a surge of victory. Instead he was sinking in fear.

He'd been on plenty of dangerous ops before, tangled with more than his share of vicious killers and gangbangers and crime lords. Logic should be telling him this was no different, especially now since he had two pockets full of material evidence. The cuff link protected against illegal seizure since it'd been in plain view.

But Sal's unease wound deep until he was too ensnared in fear to move. While he'd been snooping around in the garage, he'd left Candice all alone in a house with two murder suspects.

He'd never gone toe-to-toe with a killer like Vivaldi. And he was about to.

With a dicey hand, and with everything to lose.

Chapter 34

Candice Stevens

What was taking him so long?

Candice paced the length of their room for the hundredth time, chowing down on her thumbnails until absent shards nicked her throat.

Restlessness raged through her, making her tense and jittery and nearly explosive to every creak in the silence.

What if he was hurt? What if someone caught him? What if—

Her stomach turned over with an unattractive gurgle she was a lotta bit glad he hadn't heard. Several hours had passed since the delicious dinner, but anxiety had chewed an ulcer in her gut and her metabolism had devoured the rest. Sinking down to the edge of the bed, she leaned forward on her elbows, raking her hands into her disheveled hair. Her stomach moaned again.

Good gravy! She wasn't even hungry. After all, she'd savagely consumed sixteen ounces of steak. And that mountain of cheesecake had gone down like smooth crème brulee heaven.

Her mind screeched to a halt. Her stomach settling as if—having made its point—it was thankful she'd finally caught on.

Steak and crème brûlée.

Steak knives and a chef's torch.

She felt the blood drain from her face as if Vivaldi himself had just slashed her throat and released her vitality. Before she could think it through she jerked on one of Preston's white silk guest robes, shoved a handful of phenolphthalein vials into the slim pocket, and left the safety of her locked room.

The house was quiet, unnervingly so for the number of guests in occupancy. With concentrated caution, she crept down the flights of thick glass and steel that looked like something out of a sci-fi flick.

Strange how his house in St. Louis had been sort of classic and warm and grand, while this one was stark and harsh and modern. But both very, very white.

She tried to construct a reason why those details could peg him as Vivaldi in some way but couldn't come up with anything on the fly, especially when she was taking such pains to monitor the sounds of her steps, her breathing, and her wild, maniacal pulse threatening a meltdown.

The kitchen was lit only by a subtle glow from the under-cabinet lighting. She stepped into the space. The moment the cold touch of the tile floor met her foot it slithered up her legs with a silent warning to go back to her room.

White cabinets were shadowed in shades of gray. The soft track of lights gleamed off the white marble countertops ... as well as the magnetic strip holding a dozen deadly looking knives against the subway tiled backsplash.

Her pulse gave a little surge of fear and curiosity as she crept across the nipping floor and stood before the wall of blades.

Most of the kerf marks on the victims' bones had been made with a non-serrated edge, so she would start with those. Casting a glance over her shoulder, she then stared again at the display of metal before stretching her hand forward, hating the way her fingers trilled as if to create a tremolo on the ivories.

Blinking hard, she silenced the ominous notes playing in her head, peeled the weapon off the magnet, and laid it on the counter. She dug out one of the swabs dipped in phenolphthalein, quickly painted over the edge of the blade, and dipped the swab back in the clear gel looking for a pink indicator.

Nothing.

Candice wiped the excess on a paper towel and replaced the blade on the magnet strip, repeating the process with another potential murder weapon. And another. And another. Almost frantic with the need to pin this on Preston Bradley.

Vivaldi couldn't kill again. It wasn't something she could have on her over-loaded conscience. If she sat idly by while another life was taken, she'd be no better than the man who'd stopped their hearts.

The vision of her parents' bedroom came flooding back on a sharp spasm of her heart.

Her mother's remains on the bed, hacked to pieces, her dismembered bits left on the blood-drenched mattress that had served as her cutting board while the music—

Something stirred behind her. A whispered premonition bristled against her nerve-endings.

With only a moment to act, she dropped the test vial back into her pocket, left one hand on the blade she was about to swab, and spun around.

A gasp pierced the air in her lungs. "Preston!" She wheezed. "You scared me."

His eyes were steely and intensely focused. His lips a hard line. "I beg your pardon, Katarina."

What had he seen? Was he on to her? Was he Vivaldi?

"It's late." His accent made the two small words almost elegant, though they possessed a darkness capable of stopping her heart.

She could only nod in agreement.

He took a step forward. Then another. Like the man on a hunt for …

For what? For blood? For information? For sex?

Her fingers curled around the handle of the serrated knife

on the counter at her back as Preston closed in.

"There's something about you, Katarina."

Something sneaky? Something deceptive?

Beads of nervous heat pressed from beneath her clammy skin until she was certain she would start sweating droplets of her blood. She swallowed a breath somehow laced with that old grit from the docks, knowing by the shift of his eyes where his thoughts were heading.

No. Please no. Not again. Not ever.

He lifted his hand and touched the silk tie at her waist. "This robe has never looked so fetching. But it isn't taming my imagination of what lies beneath."

Candice tried to step back but was pinned in place by the wall of cabinets behind her and the seemingly immovable plank of muscle crowding her front. Preston placed his hands on the counter, bracketing her waist as white hot fear slithered around her on the potent breath of his peppery musk.

"Mr. Bradley, I'm flattered by your attraction. Truly. But I'm married."

Undeterred he leaned in, and in an act of animalism, stroked her cheek with the chiseled edge of his own. "Yes, I know." His voice became a moan. "Sly seems like a very satisfied man." One hand tugged at the tie to her robe, and before she could blink or breathe, he'd parted the silk and his slimy hand touched her cotton sleep-dress at her waist.

"Preston, stop." She braced her non-weapon-wielding palm against his chest.

Her hesitance seemed to genuinely surprise him, and he froze, searching her eyes to see if she meant it.

Oh, she meant it, all right. But when he looked at her, towering and strong with selfish hunger in his eyes, she wasn't the tough medical examiner who could take care of herself. She was Candi, her mother's daughter, someone's used toy.

Emotion bubbled up in her throat. Preston's leer as

strangling as AJ's grip. Tremors bumbled through her, her knees nearly collapsing as tears bloomed in her eyes. "Please." This was the time to shove him away, go all *Carrie* on the creep and show him she meant business. But the old familiar chains wrapped around her, reminding her of the futility of all her struggles. How they'd only made matters worse for her in the end.

Sure she could say no right now, but would it matter? Were a knife and some fake muscle and bravado enough to stop a man from taking what he wanted? And furthermore, could she really stab a man? Was his unwelcome desire punishable by death? Could she live with any more blood on her hands?

Please. I don't want to be the victim anymore.

"Back away from my wife, Preston."

Dorian's command brought relief so strong it loosed her grip on the knife and sent the sheaf of metal clattering to the counter.

Preston's eyes shot wide, and he jerked away. "You were going to stab me?"

Though her trembling made it almost impossible, she curled her lip to soften the moment. It's what Dorian would do. "I would've given you fair warning." She braced her arms on the counter behind her, hoping the added support would help reinforce her bluff.

Dorian crossed the room with long, confident strides and stepped nose-to-nose with the ruthless Lothario. She saw a moment of indecision flicker across his face, a little twitch tightening his jaw. "Listen, we appreciate all your generosity, and I know you just can't help yourself around a pretty woman. But hear me when I tell you, if you breathe too close, brush her in passing, or so much as look at my wife sideways again, I'll pour you some concrete shoes and drop you for a swim in your lake. *Comprendes?*"

The men were in a standoff, equally matched for height and muscle, but the intensity in Dorian's eyes, his voice, his body language, made him Samson and Preston a mere gnat.

Preston's gulp sounded through the room. "My apologies." With a curt nod, he turned tail and fled.

Dorian waited until Preston was long gone, his fists clenched, his face tight with torment. He closed his eyes, working shallow and erratic down to deep, even breaths through his chest. "Are ... are you okay?"

"Yes." She whispered. "Dorian, I—I prayed for help the second before you showed up."

His eyes reluctantly opened. In an instant he closed the space between them and gathered her to his chest. His hand sifted through her hair, palming her scalp, holding her against his heart.

A heart betraying how rattled he'd been.

"I think we've finally got someone on our side." The words were little more than a vibration.

"Maybe we always have." Her lips brushed his shirt, and she dragged the heady heat and spice of him into her lungs to cradle her lonesome heart.

Easing away only slightly, he lifted her chin with his knuckle. "I'm not so sure about before." His voice creased with all the hurts he'd locked away in the most magnificent vault ever made.

"Maybe we just couldn't see it at the time. Sometimes it's hardest to see what's right in front of us." The words grappled for intention. She'd started with her thoughts on God, the one who always seemed just out of reach. But with Dorian so close, his touch so different, so perfectly right, she lost her head.

Raising up on her tiptoes, she curled her hands around his neck and urged him to meet her kiss. The second his lips landed, her capillaries exploded. That essence she'd hoarded close to her heart now flooding her chest and blitzing to her toes. The sweet heat pouring through her a stark contrast to the fear that had paralyzed her minutes before.

Dorian's kiss was the eighth wonder of the world. Patient

and eager, reckless and safe. Perfect and uncanny. He breathed deep into the kiss, meshing her infinitely closer still, and she wanted to invade his every breath, reside in his very heartbeat.

For the moment this was real. More real than anything she'd ever felt. Right now, she wasn't the abused doormat who'd once belonged to a thug. She was Dorian's wife.

One of his hands left her back, and she faintly registered the sound of the knife reconnecting with the magnet. Then he lifted her and set her on the counter. Their level height was more manageable. She wrapped her arms around his strong shoulders, hooked her legs around his hips and drew him closer, every fiber of her being a helpless filing to his magnetism. His lips, his touch, he was wholly intoxicating, and she drank it all in. All the beautifully foreign tenderness and passion telling her she might be loveable. That she was no longer damaged. It was the most exquisite illusion. She never wanted it to end.

In the same way she'd possessed a sort of blind faith in the angel in her bedroom as a child, Dorian Salivas was the first man who felt completely honest and selfless. Never once had he pushed the limits. Every single action, even from the first moment they'd met, considered her first, giving what she needed over what he so obviously wanted.

Desperate to be closer, she rocked against him, tearing an achy groan from his throat that supercharged his kiss into the kind of indulgence she could binge on until nothing remained of her brain but drunken need and rampant hormones.

The muscles in his neck strained against her arms, and she became aware of a blip in the silence. His lips unlocked from hers, and he scanned the kitchen.

The kitchen! They were still in the kitchen. As if reading her thoughts he lifted her off the counter, swept his arm under her knees, and carried her like a princess to the stairs, up the stairs, and to their room.

"That's really distracting, you know that?" The smile in

his voice made her heart rebel with utter delight so she kept on distracting him, pressed another one of a dozen nuzzling kisses against his neck and massaging her fingers through the thick mink of his hair while he carried her.

"I might have a vague idea." She nipped softly on his earlobe, smiling when his breathing hitched.

Once they were in their room, he eased the door shut with his foot and set her down. He wrapped his big, gentle hands around her upper arms, looked at her with such adoration and love she tried to sandbag the tears fighting to steal the moment.

"Brat, I—"

"Don't." She whispered, skimming her fingertips over his full lips until she tugged him back down to speak without words. She didn't know what she'd read in his eyes, something steamy and delicious but also something like regret. Right now she didn't want to know. Didn't want to dredge up all the reasons he was too good for her. Didn't want to think about why this was a colossally bad idea.

So instead all she could say was, "Don't ruin it."

Chapter 3.5

Dorian Salivas

Kissing Candice was a dream. The very best kind that often warranted a hard slap back to reality. Only this was real, even if the kiss was out of this world.

Burrowing against him, she held on tight, exploring the contours of his back with her strong little hands, a new slip of desperation in the seduction of her soft mouth. Sal cupped her face and dove in like a man on a rescue mission, pouring his heart and his halted confession into a language all its own—a dance of two broken pieces of humanity finding the perfect fit, against all odds.

"Candice." He broke away, trailed a line of kisses down her neck, tasting the sheer decadence of her skin.

Her hands plunged through his hair, trapping his face to the apex of her chest, to the thrilling serenade of her heart.

For a man so high on his perceptions, he barely noticed their racing breaths nor their slow maneuver across the room. And he hadn't really noticed the reason his lips had sampled the *skin* directly over her heart was because she'd shed her robe by the door.

Or had he done that?

With the questionable state of his brain, he just couldn't be sure.

He pulled back, so as not to push too far, and raised his head to kiss every surface of her enamoring face before he intended to tuck her in and steal another lingering bedtime kiss. Or two. And then retire to a cold shower.

But before he could continue to test his willpower, she inched away a step. A shy little smile curling on her mouthwatering lips. Crossing her arm across her chest, she hooked a thumb around the strap of her nightgown and stepped back again. He reached out before she moved beyond his grasp and traced his fingertips over the elegant curve of her cheek. "I love you."

The proclamation burst free before he could think of a gentler preface. Then again, he wasn't one for fancy words, so he supposed it was just as well he throw it out there.

A look of pure joy alighted on her face, in her eyes, like she'd been freed from a dark past. One that had so viciously beaten her into submission with just how unlovable she was.

As quickly as it came, her expression faltered; the indecision so slight he'd almost missed it. A faint whispered thread wove through his mind—a subtle warning, but as plain as East Side neon against the night sky.

He shut it down unheeded. He was all in. "I do. I love you."

Before he realized what was happening Candice had used her thumb to slip the modest nightgown from her left shoulder, then her right. The mint green cottony fabric slinked down golden brown skin to the floor.

Suddenly suspended in liquid, the room swam around him in a blur. A line of tunnel-vision the only thing keeping him from face-planting into the carpet and having a heart attack. At the end of that line was the very thing inciting the vertigo and palpitations. And the catatonic paralysis.

Have mercy.

Not even a fraction of thought scanned through his overzealous brain before he erased the space between them and crushed his mouth to hers. His hands treasured the warm, smooth skin of her waist and then pulled her closer until her softness melted against him in all the right places. Her kiss was eager and abandoned, and it fueled him. No, it burned through him, eating up tangles of thought until all was lost to the flame except the all-consuming need. He wanted to touch and taste and explore and savor every inch of this woman he loved. And here she was. Finally his.

The kiss catapulted into the stratosphere. Luscious and deep and deeper still, he was mesmerized and completely undone by the sensual stroke of her tongue, the maddening suction of her lips, the seductive scrape of her teeth. Before he knew it, the bed hit their entwined knees. She lifted a leg and hooked it over his thigh, unmasking her desire and matching his own.

He'd wanted to go slow and savor every moment, but his control was rapidly unraveling. He broke the kiss and tugged his shirt over his head, desperate for the contact of her skin. *Bliss.* He eased the nearly naked bronzed goddess down onto the plush white mattress before he settled over her, taking her mouth again.

He let his lips trail down her neck, giving into the demand to caress her generous and supple curves with his hands until his mouth could take over.

But everything seemed … quiet. Only the charge of his breathing marking the silence.

More than anything he wanted to stay out of his head and revel in the moment, but why was she so still? There was no moan of pleasure. No arching into him with her own need to take or taste him like moments before. Her beautiful body beneath his, that had laid waste to his control like wildfire to parched earth, was now stiff and cold.

He paused before that first taste, felt the quiver in her belly echo in his chest, felt the tremor from her center ripple down the legs cradling him.

The truth slapped him.

She was afraid.

And in this suddenly vacant fermata he realized he was alone in this. Recalling now that she hadn't returned his declaration of love in the delusional duet playing in his mind.

After all she'd been through, she still couldn't see how what he was offering was any different than what she'd been victim to before. The brutal reality of it diced and sliced was, in this moment, he was no better than AJ.

He looked down at his hands holding her so gently and then back up to read her numb expression. Numb except for the terror resonating in her eyes. Shame splashed over her open wounds, and he felt every searing slice of her pain as his own, wincing at what he'd caused.

She's not ready. Loretta Mae's voice cut through his conscience like a bat to the skull. He was pretty sure he'd experienced that once before on one of his dad's drunken binges, so who could say what kind of traumatized madman was steering his brain-ship.

Gently shifting off her, he helped her to a seated position, watching the apprehension expand with her pupils. He tipped her chin, trapped her gaze to gauge the truth, and saw the vulnerability take hold of everything she was. She was offering her body because she'd convinced herself it was all she had to give. Or someone else had convinced her. It was the only form of love she'd ever known. And it hadn't been love at all.

So as much as he wanted this, he didn't want it this way.

"Oh, honey." He held her face in his hands, praying she would see his sincerity. "We can't do this."

She flinched. "I thought this was what you wanted." Her eyes filled, conflicted, tormented. A darkness falling back over her like a veil of shame.

"It is, believe me. You're remarkable. So perfectly lovely. Smart, funny, tough. From the first moment I saw you I was struck speechless, appropriate because no words could do you justice. And there are parts of my anatomy quite literally screaming in protest right now because you are *everything* I want. But not like this. More than your gorgeous body, more than hours upon hours of pleasure," her eyes bulged when he paused there, and his lips softened in a smile. "What I want is your heart, Candice. Everything else is frosting."

Somehow he'd known the words would zap her. She jerked up to stand and wrapped the bedsheet around her chest. He stood too. Knowing the bed was now out of the equation.

"My heart?" She practically spit. "My heart is dead, okay. Lifeless and weak. Just like the two people I killed by choosing to live in fear. You think you love me, Dorian? You don't know who I am. You don't even know my real name. Love is poison. It pumps you up with fizzy little endorphins, and then it breaks you down from the inside out until you are nothing but a shell. And someone else's shell at that."

She'd just dumped a truckload of questions into the middle of the road, but none of those things were what this was about and now was not the time for a detour.

He wanted to reach out to her but knew she'd only retreat further into herself, so he planted his feet and shoved a breath down his throat. "It's okay to be afraid. I am too. But what you had before wasn't love. Love doesn't take. It doesn't leave you feeling vulnerable and used and insecure. Which is exactly what you would have felt tomorrow morning if I'd taken you to bed tonight without telling you that you deserve more. Without making sure you know you're worth the wait."

He honestly didn't know where all the words of wisdom had sprouted from, but he had a feeling Loretta Mae had sowed some seeds on rocky soil all those years ago, and they had finally found roots in his heart.

Don't you go taking what doesn't belong to you, Dorian. Not even if someone is 'bout to hand over those goods. Because them are stolen until your name is on 'em. And I sure as heck ain't talking 'bout anything money can buy. Well, except here on the East Side, but you better not go buying down there 'less you want your dangle to fall off. Sho' nuff. Somebody who knows a thing or two 'bout love better teach you 'bout lovin' a woman, because it sho' as heck ain't all about you.

None of it had made much sense at the time. But right now, the fog of his youth long diminished in the rearview, he could see how Loretta Mae had thrown some heaters. He hadn't even bothered to swing; all of her lessons had just sailed right past him. He was more than a little grateful—and maybe a touch annoyed, but mostly grateful—they'd come back to sober him now.

Being with Candice meant more than some basic need to scratch an itch. She wasn't a convenient distraction, and he was done with cheap imitations. This time, he wanted the whole enchilada.

"I don't need to know your name to know I love you. If I didn't mean it, and just spouted the words to *get some*, we wouldn't be talking right now." He nudged her chin to keep possession of her gaze. "And even though I probably won't sleep for weeks fantasizing about what could have gone on between those sheets tonight, I won't steal from you. I won't be the guy who takes what he wants and leaves you hollowed out. I'm willing to wait as long as it takes to prove this is the real deal."

She crossed her arms under her bust, the white sheet doing little to hide what had already been gloriously seen. And felt.

Dio, she'd felt good.

The shuddery breath he grappled to consume didn't feed nearly enough oxygen to his waylaid brain. Which was more than likely because the taste of her skin was still on his tongue.

"Even if it kills me." He added. *Which it might.* Which he didn't.

Her steam lost its edge, lines of tears still damp on her face. "Y-You said we'd get to dessert. I thought … I'm not like this, you know. I don't go throwing myself at men who need a fix."

"I didn't mean—"

"This is why I'm supposed to be alone. I'm no good at

this. I can't read people like you do." She touched her hand to her throat, and then her eyes shot wide, spearing him with some shocking revelation before she spoke. "You *read* me, didn't you?"

"Candice, I—"

"Muscle reading, right? That's how you conned me with your kisses. You felt my pulse. In the closet of the FBI. You measured my responses. You manipulated me!"

"The first time in the closet when we were hiding with the Maserati fiber, yes, something like that. I wasn't sure you'd play along because you always looked at me like some pimple-faced freshman with a crush on the prom queen." He cupped his hands on her arms, relieved she didn't shrink away but desperate to erase the tension in her body and the shattered trust splintering pain through her eyes.

"But after we left Preston's fundraiser, and you told me about AJ, I realized if I ever had a shot of winning your heart, it'd have to be on your terms." That was the night she'd kissed him on her porch. The night they'd kissed for an hour straight, each of them discovering real intimacy meant more than pawing and possessing. More than shed clothes and gratification. Though those things were nice too. When the time was right.

"I can't believe this." She whispered under her breath. "I thought you were different." Tears magnified the brilliant sunbursts of her eyes, her lip wobbled, and he fought the urge to persuade her with his kiss.

Counterproductive at the moment, buddy.

"How do I know every touch hasn't been a lie? How do I know you're not still playing me?" Her arms readjusted around her middle, and the sheet slipped.

He caught it, trapping the fabric between his palm and her heart. "Because you know me." He took a small step closer. "This isn't a scam. There are no trick plays here. No smoke and mirrors. Just me, a man who didn't believe in love, crashing into it heart first."

The trill of his phone vibrated in his pocket. The hum severing the expectant pause.

He was holding her heart, watching a plague of doubts parade through her honey-glazed eyes, praying for perhaps the first time in his life that he could be trusted with something so precious.

Only a second after the call stopped, the phone trilled again.

Archer.

The events of the past hour snapped back into place, taking momentary precedence over their conversation.

He closed his eyes, breathing one more prayer. Then using his free hand, he unfolded hers from her chest and replaced his where it had been holding her sheet-covered heart.

"Archer. You get my message?" He'd called from the garage with an update, knowing he'd need back-up if things went as far south as he was expecting.

"Yeah. I called Jensen, and we're sending tactical support. I'd be there, but Sadie's been sick all night, and I have to testify on the Westwick case at nine." Archer's sleep-rasped voice reminded Sal it was nearly four a.m. "Are you guys safe until morning?"

Define safe.

Like a bad habit, Sal's gaze traipsed over Candice while she stepped into the puddled sage cotton and shimmied back into her nightgown. Little did Archer know this bedroom was proving more dangerous than any other place else on earth. Whether Vivaldi slept down the hall or not.

"Sal? Something you're not telling me? If you're under duress use your code word."

Candice caught his gaze, the pronounced chug of his Adam's apple slurping back the salivating sight of her.

Heaven help me.

"Nah, sorry. Everything is quiet. We're gonna lay low till morning." *And lay separately.* "Then I'll try to sneak a peek at our late-night party crasher before he sees us and potentially blows our cover." He remained riveted while he spoke, desperate to decode the riddle locked behind her expression. It dawned on him that he'd yet to detail his recon mission so she didn't know what he'd found.

He'd stumbled upon Preston cornering Candice in the kitchen and fought every fiber of his flesh wanting to separate the guy's head from the lower half of his body. But since they needed to be here in the morning when the Maserati-driving guest unveiled himself, he'd called upon years of being a punching bag and doled out the most gracious warning he could muster.

After the blinding rage had simmered there'd only been Candice. Her touch like a vortex, sucking him down into the best version of reality and leaving everything else in a latent cloud of dust.

"Okay. Just be careful. Vivaldi is slippery. Try to hold off as long as you can. SWAT should be there shortly after first light."

"Sounds good." And yet some small tentacle of unease slithered around him and squeezed his windpipe. "Uhh, and it, uhh, might be a good idea if you check in every hour or so. If I don't answer and SWAT hasn't arrived you should alert local authorities. It's a small force, and I'm not sure they'll know what to do with Vivaldi, but I'd like some back up on hand just in case things get dicey."

"I was gonna anyway, pal. Stay safe. And don't let anyone lay a finger on our favorite medical examiner, you hear?"

Sal exhaled a sigh. "Doin' my best, Arch."

"See you later, dude."

"I'll be the one escorting Vivaldi in cuffs."

Chapter 36

Candice Stevens

The cool gray hint of dawn parted the stars, though twilight still hovered in the room. Candice rolled over for the fiftieth time in maybe an hour, knowing her need for sleep wasn't enough coercion to surrender to it after the night she'd just had.

She squeezed her eyes tight, desperate to obliterate those fragments of memory, or better yet, zip back a few hours and do things differently.

For starters, by keeping her clothes on. Liquid fire filled in her cheeks in remembrance of her weak moment. He'd said he loved her. To Candice, that had only ever meant one thing. And while the euphoric feelings snuggling around her heart from his confession were new, her response had been the same.

Automatic. Resigned. Enslaved to the same old brainwashing she now knew she'd never escape. Like Pavlov's dog, AJ would snap his fingers and she surrendered, or suffered a much worse fate.

But Dorian was nothing like AJ. Why did that truth never seem to solidify?

And why, when Dorian shut her down, had she felt both relieved and restless?

After he'd hung up with Archer, she'd climbed into bed alone while Dorian plotted out his strategy for their morning encounter. Wanting to be full strength she'd given it a solid go, but sleep hadn't claimed her.

Archer's check-in call had come about twenty minutes ago, and shortly after, she'd heard Dorian retire to the floor.

There were no tell-tale sleep sounds like tossing or heavy breathing. As the minutes ticked by her curiosity nibbled away at her faster than she could devour a thumbnail. She'd done both and then started in on an index finger—a sure sign she was at the end of her rope.

Today was the day. She could feel it in her bones. Today they would unmask the enemy. And despite how long she'd craved vindication for all the lives he'd stolen, and all the atrocities he'd committed, the thought of looking into Vivaldi's soulless eyes shrank her stomach four sizes. In fact, it let out an unfortunately loud gurgle to confirm what it thought of the gut-churning confrontation.

Biting her lip in mortification—as if she hadn't already had her fill—she stared at the shifts of gray bleeding onto the ceiling in decreasingly ominous shades.

Almost time.

Was Dorian asleep? What was he thinking about? Did he regret what he'd said? Especially now since she'd proved what a hussy she was down to the marrow?

Crossing her arms over her face, she tried to mute out the expanding prism of light awakening the room like a ticking time bomb to their mission.

Come on, think of something else.

She flung her arms back down on the bed, dragged open her eyes, and exhaled the anxiety building in her chest.

Before rational thought could return, she rolled onto her grumbling tummy and wormed quietly across the king-sized mattress to peek over the side.

Eek! Caught. Flipping to her back at mach speed, she squeezed her eyes tight, and heaved against the breathless rush crowding her lungs.

You're being ridiculous, Jersey tsked.

Swallowing down some courage, she rolled back and

hung her head over the mattress, digging her chin into the edge. "You're not sleeping either, huh?"

A subdued smile quirked on his lips, and he shook his head.

"A-Are you okay down there?"

He thought on the question a beat before answering. "There are moments when I think I might be. But then I'll hear you toss again, and I've all but had to cuff myself to the nightstand to keep from climbing up there just to hold you."

Oh, melt. Her heart really was the most foolish dunce of all because she loved him. She really did. And that wasn't the foolish part because Dorian was a catch.

What was foolish was believing he would feel the same when he learned who she really was. And what she'd done.

But, hey … today they were going against the most violent criminal in their city's history. They could die. It wasn't an unreasonable leap.

So, for just one more moment, just in case she didn't have many more to ride out, she'd let her foolish heart indulge one last delusion.

Still looking down at him, Candice lifted the sheet to invite him in. To cuddle. *Only* to cuddle, she reminded Jersey just so she didn't get any more ideas.

So much sparked in his rich brown eyes. Excitement, love, temptation, indecision.

Hope.

The last one scared her. She shouldn't encourage him. The last thing she wanted to do was break a heart of gold like his. But if she had a dying wish, this would be it.

She waited, her heart dangling on a line, the sheet of shame still lifted in invitation.

"I better not." The spice in his voice alone about made her break out into a sweat.

As far as she could tell she had two choices. She could accept his need for space and set the cold, rigid Candice back in place, or she could ditch the past, and roll the dice on a love that could break her more than AJ ever could. A love destined to fail.

She waited, uncertainty joining her under the Egyptian cotton. The voice in her head wasn't Jersey, and she wasn't sure it was hers either until she took charge.

Lowering down off the mattress, Candice scooted until she could rest her head against his shoulder, drape her arm around him, and twine one leg with his.

"Don't try anything fresh. You may not recall, but this restaurant doesn't serve dessert." She snuggled closer, letting her breath sync up with his.

He placed his hand over her arm on his chest. She didn't look to confirm but she felt his smile warm all the way to her toes. "Oh, we'll get to dessert. Eventually."

"Do I have to?" Candice crossed her arms, feeling remarkably like a fifth-grader sassing her father. Great, now she was the one of them acting childish. She'd come full circle.

Dorian finished buttoning his pale blue shirt, bent to grab his Glock, and stuffed it in the concealed holster in his dark jeans just posterior to his hip. He crossed the room, and tipped up her chin. "Listen, Brat, I promised to keep you safe. But there are too many unknown variables here. We don't know if this is Vivaldi, or his accomplice. Either way we can assume he knows our real identities." The stroke of his thumb over her cheek made her next protest dissolve on her tongue.

"If you're with me, I'll only be concerned with your safety and he could get away. And neither of us will be safe until Vivaldi is behind bars."

Huffing, she hugged her arms tighter. "I know, but I'll go stir-crazy in here. And besides, I'll be a sitting duck. You can't even leave your gun this time." She shivered, and

Dorian hauled her to his chest.

Her arms were still crossed between them, his lips dusting his words into her hair. "Could you just not fight me on this one?"

He wasn't playing fair. He was so warm, his heated scent so disillusioning she would agree to just about anything right now. "Fine. I'll stay put."

He pulled back and tweaked her nose. "That's a good girl. Be sure you lock up." Before she could blink he had placed the most sensual kiss on her lips, gave her backside a playful little slap as if to stake his claim, and was slipping out the door.

For some reason it felt like the conversation ended too abruptly. Like he should have said something more. Like, maybe, "In case I die tell Gabe where the Fritos are." Or perhaps, a renewed sentiment of his love with one of those great movie lines like, "I'll come back for you. I'll always come back for you."

Candice sighed, fell back onto the bed, and felt the fear spread like poison.

"Where I am weak, you are strong." Words of faith she'd heard before. Man, she wanted to be strong.

Grabbing what might be a serial killer's Bible from the nightstand, she decided there was no better time than now to stock up on some of that strength. But before she'd even cracked the cover, someone knocked on the door.

After a minute the knocking ceased. And with a little jiggle of the knob the visitor left.

Candice let the air pop from her chest, and then resumed feeding intentional gulps back down her throat to remain conscious. If it'd been Dorian he would have at least tried to say something through the door. And it was a bedroom door, not a hotel door, so there was no peep hole. No dead bolt.

You're fine. Dorian's fine. It's all gonna be fine.

The minutes passed like hours. Candice checked her phone every thirty seconds or so to realize only fifteen minutes has passed in the span of a lifetime.

She'd replaced her pajamas with a pair of red skinny jeans and a new slinky black crocheted sweater. Taking a few minutes, because really, she had some to burn, she went to work concealing dark circles, brushed on some mascara, a smudge of smoky eyeliner, and lip gloss. Any distraction was a welcome relief from worry.

For perhaps the tenth time she went and flattened her ear to the door in hopes of catching a slip of sound. A scuffle, an argument, a gun shot?

Silence as bland as the stark white house echoed back at her. Not much could have easily found its way up the two flights of stairs, she supposed.

Another knock, just two inches of wood beyond her ear, startled a squeal from her throat. Her heart flatlined, then jump-started into a sprint with the jolt of the next knock.

"Excuse me?" The voice belonged to a woman. "I have fresh towels for your room."

The knot in her throat slipped loose, and the fear holding her immobile released her. She locked her knees to refrain from sagging into a pathetic heap, swiped damp hands down the front of her jeans, and pulled open the door. She collected a stack of pristine white towels from the rotund, possibly Bosnian woman with heavily salted black hair.

"Thank you." She felt heat creep into her cheeks as the woman muttered something in her native language and wandered off down the hall. With the door open, Candice heard the faint tickling sound of laughter. Laughter? Was something funny about this? Was it safe to go down?

No. She wouldn't be stupid. Dorian might be charming the killer into a confession.

She started to close the door when a shadow passed the doorframe and a tall figure halted.

"Dr. Stevens? Is that you?"

Chapter 37

Dorian Salivas

"Are you sure I can't get you something to eat, Sly? My housekeeper, Ana, may not be as skilled as Chef Roland last night, but she makes a smashing eggs benedict." Preston shoveled another bite of poached eggs into his mouth, impressively unfazed by their confrontation in the kitchen only hours ago.

Sal stood by the center island nursing an excessively creamed and sugared espresso, eyes on alert for any flinch of suspicion. He raised his cup a fraction. "This is fine."

"Suit yourself."

All the players from last night were around the table. The mystery guest had yet to make an appearance, and Sal's unease ratcheted up another notch each minute he waited for the big reveal.

His phone buzzed in his pocket signaling a text. Either SWAT was in place or Archer was checking in.

You were right. The hair was synthetic. Looking for trace DNA or a way to track the wig. —Biggs

"Everything all right, chap? Seem a little tense." Preston dropped his plate into the sink then braced his palms against the counter in the same place he'd come on to Candice last night.

Sal stowed his phone and balled his hands into fists,

nearly crushing the mug in his left grip.

"Yeah, everything is fine." That word again. Fine. Everything was so not fine. "We just might need to leave a bit early is all."

"Oh?"

"We'll see how it plays out." Sal shrugged, brought the mug to his lips, and slurped back some artificial energy. "So when do we get to meet your mystery guest? I did hear someone sneak in last night, did I not?"

"Ahh. Yes." His eyes, cold like the murky waters just beyond the panoramic windows, narrowed.

Sal shrugged again. "I'm a light sleeper."

Preston nodded slowly, studying his guest. "I see. My nephew and his girlfriend were supposed to come up for the weekend. He had to work late and mysteriously, his girlfriend vanished, so he arrived a trifle late. He'll probably sleep in."

His girlfriend vanished. Preston's words slithered under Sal's skin.

Keep him talking, Salivas.

Adopting the appropriate good ol' boy persona, Sal elbowed the Brit chidingly. "Does he favor blondes like you?" *You know, besides when you're making a play for my brunette.* Sal's smile gripped tight, though he hoped it looked rueful.

"Actually, no. This one was a redhead. A real firecracker with a motor mouth on her. He brought her up here not long ago. They didn't stay but the afternoon. I was gone when they left but it would seem they'd checked out the Maserati for the week. Women love that car."

A redhead.

And wait. *Blaine*, Candice's coworker. He was Preston Bradley's nephew. He'd been working late because he'd been at the crime scene.

Blaine Attwood and a redhead. Vivaldi and his accomplice?

Yep. There was a mole all right. Just not one in the FBI. One in the morgue. With unlimited resources, easy access to knives, and evidence. And ...

Not at all squeamish about slicing into a person's flesh.

"What room." Sal demanded, once again shocking his properly improper host.

"I don't understand. Do you know Blaine?"

"As a matter of fact, I do. For a few months now. Though I've been familiar with his work for years."

Ten years. Dozens of victims. Immeasurable pain and suffering.

Sal saw Preston shiver, which was odd. Then he pinched his lips together until impressions of his bite blanched white staples against the seam of his mouth. "I-Is there some sort of trouble?"

Training his expression, Sal ground his molars. "Which room, Preston?"

"Uhh, just next door to yours."

He tried not to run but found himself dashing up the two flights of stairs to the top-tiered balcony. Gun drawn, he tapped the nose on the wood twice before he flung the door open. One glance, and the room proved empty. He slipped through the opening to the bathroom before lowering his weapon and leaving the way he came.

He turned his head toward the room he and Candice shared. It was then he heard the sounds of a struggle.

Candice!

He raced down the hallway, his heart a frantic spasm in his throat, his emotions threatening to boil over. But despite the weight of grief like a stone around his neck, his training kicked back in, keeping his head aboveboard.

The door was cracked, a little wedge of light shifting the shadows. A body hit the floor with a thud. Drawn back for a split second, the sound of his failure popped in his ears like the rounds of bullets emptying into his childhood home and robbing his brother of his legs.

Oh, God, what have I done?

He crashed through the door, gun poised, lunging into action to save his damsel in distress.

Except …

The damsel was Blaine.

"Freeze."

Candice followed his command, stalling, arm cocked, bloodied fist drawn back like a bow ready to release another zinger.

Moaning on the floor, blood oozing from a crushed nose and chest pinned beneath her legs was Blaine Attwood. Down for the count. Blaine groaned, thrashing his head against the carpet.

Resident serial killer gets whooped by a girl?

Sal lowered the barrel of his gun. "You all right?"

Candice relaxed her arm, shook out her fist, and dragged herself off her victim. "Yep."

"Is *she* all right?" Blaine rolled into the fetal position, steepling his fingers over his nose. "Jeeze, Dr. Stevens! I was just trying to grab the tag still dangling from your sweater." Mumbling into his hands, he levered up to a seated position and braced his elbows on his knees. A flow of red poured from his nose and bubbled together with the saliva he spit from his swelling lip.

"What is the meaning of this?" Preston Bradley stepped over the threshold, fists on his hips like Superman. His nephew looked up and sprayed a mist of the blood seeping into his lips onto the pristine white carpet.

"Is that …" Preston washed whiter than every colorless thing in his house. A second later his eyes rolled and he flopped like a cooked noodle straight into Blaine's mess.

"Oh," Blaine's fat lip tugged to the side as if caught by a hook. "Oops, I forgot. My uncle Pres is hemophobic."

"He fainted?" Sal cast a suspicious glance at the grown man indulging in a spontaneous nap—in an unfortunate spot for someone who gets queasy around blood. "Okay, yeah.

That fits." Preston had gotten all fidgety and pale when Sal mentioned he was familiar with his nephew's work.

Of course, Preston would have been assuming Blaine's work as a medical examiner, not as a sociopathic butcher of blondes.

"Are you guys together?" Blaine winced and touched his nose. "Wait," he shook his head, more droplets of blood went airborne. "Why do you still have that gun pointed at me, Agent Salivas? And why the heck did Dr. Stevens just go all Bruce Lee on my face?"

"Because I am about to arrest you for the murder of Sarah Hoyt. I'm sure I'll be tacking on at least another forty homicides soon enough. Hope you enjoy your concrete cell." Sal pulled a pair of cuffs from his back pocket, belatedly wondering why SWAT still hadn't arrived before he dangled the cuff on his index finger. "Would you like to do the honors, Brat?"

She smiled, little crystals of sweat glittering on her skin from the intense boxing session. He'd seen the way she'd frozen up last night with Preston. But today she'd kicked some serial killer can. He swelled with pride, knowing she'd had it in her all along.

"With pleasure." Candice swiveled the metal link off his finger.

"Whoa, whoa, whoa! I didn't kill anybody!" Blaine held up bloodied hands, one sleeve of his collared shirt flapped open. "If you think I'm Vivaldi, you're barking up the wrong tree."

"Oh, really? I see you're missing one of your platinum cufflinks." Sal pulled the evidence bag from his pocket. "Look familiar?"

The handcuffs snapped into place, Blaine just sat there looking dumbfounded. "Yeah, but ..."

"You make me sick." Candice growled and stepped away.

Preston stirred nearby. Candice retrieved a white hand towel from the bathroom and chucked it at Blaine to cover his nose before she went to assist the wussy millionaire off the floor.

A serial killer with a fear of blood? Missed the mark on that one by a landslide.

Blinking hard, Preston let Candice drag him to his feet. "What happened?" He pressed his fingers against his forehead. "What's going on? I demand—"

Sal saw the color funnel from Preston's cheeks when he caught a glance of the blood he'd just unintentionally wiped from his face.

"Here we go again." Sal mumbled a second before Preston's lights went out and slapped him back down in the same spot. "Candice, honey, we might need another towel."

It might have been relief that she was okay, or it might have just been Candice's unique effect on him, but her smile turned him inside out. Man, he loved the heck out of that woman. She nodded like a happy little helper while she marched off again.

Blaine watched the display, darting his attention back and forth. He must have come to some conclusion because beet red heat sprouted in splotches on his cheeks. "You're making a mistake. I didn't kill anyone. I don't even understand what's happening."

Under normal circumstances Sal could set his watch by the accuracy of his insights. Right now, something wrestled in him, skewing just beyond the mark.

When Candice emerged a moment later he motioned her over and handed her his Glock. "Keep it aimed at his chest, understand?"

White knuckles curled around his gun, and she nodded without a word.

Sal crouched down by Blaine, stared into his steel-blue eyes, and wrapped two fingers around the man's wrist just above the metal shackle.

"What's your name?"

"Blaine Preston Attwood." He nodded toward his

namesake. "After my uncle."

True.

"What high school'd you go to?"

"Whitfield Prep."

Also true.

"Have you recently ..." Sal leaned in to whisper the rest discretely in Blaine's ear.

Blaine jerked back. "What? No! Who said that?"

False.

Sal smiled, having found the deviation for his pulse.

And a solid pocket ace if Blaine ever decided to tick him off.

"Did you borrow your uncle Preston's Maserati this past week?"

"Is that what this is about, the Maserati?" Blaine's pulse revved up a bit but not enough to signal a lie, his pupils dilating ever so slightly in his frustration. "I don't know how you knew about the scratch, but I swear I don't know how it got there. I had it fixed before I brought it back. That's why I kept it a few extra days. I was gonna tell my uncle Pres, but I figured, you know, no harm no foul."

"Just answer the question, Attwood." Sal remained calm, reading Blaine's surge of life like an owner's manual.

"Yes. I borrowed it. It's not that uncommon. I've done it before. Some girls are impressed by nice cars. I mean, most girls are pretty stoked about my Beemer but it was in the shop, and I could tell Maura had a more exotic taste. I thought, I dunno, after a few weeks it might finally, you know ... seal the deal."

"Maura?" The gun shook in Candice's hand as she lowered the tip a fraction. "Maura the med student?"

Sal looked between Candice and Blaine, seeing the confused exchange.

"Med student? Maura Masterson? No she told me she worked in real estate. She's kind of ... mysterious. We've been going out for a couple weeks, and that's about the only thing I really know about her. Oh, and she said she wanted to see the inside of a morgue, but I thought for sure, if I took her there, we could bury my chances of getting lucky with the next dead body that rolled in. You know what I'm sayin'?" He chuckled a little, sweat still dotting his brow, but his pulse confirming the truth in his statement.

That is, unless he was a sociopath and could trump Sal's lie detector.

"How do *you* know her?" Sal cocked his head at Candice.

"She was a last-minute addition to the intern schedule the other day. I got an email from the coordinator at Wash U. She was a med student. Dark red hair, about five-eleven, six-feet, high cheekbones, green-colored contacts, stuffs her bra."

Blaine's expression fell on the last one. "I wouldn't know."

"She would *not* stop talking."

Sal knew excessive chatter to be a good tactic for distraction.

Blaine volleyed back with an enthused nod. "Lotta talk, very little act—I mean ..." He cleared his throat and shied away from Candice's power-packed glare. "Very little *said*. That'd be Maura."

"With an M." Candice smacked her lips, Sal guessed in imitation of the source.

"You're dating *her*? How on earth do you stay sane? She drove me—" Her words cut off on a gasp. "She *was* pretty insistent on seeing Sarah Hoyt's body. And almost desperate to snoop around. I had to lock her out of the morgue just so I could go to the bathroom."

A few scraps dovetailed in Sal's mind, snippets of conversation weaving like fine threads on a loom.

Long, dark red hair. Synthetic.

Green-colored contacts.

Stuffs her bra? Sal shook the image from his head.

"I swear you look familiar. Something about your face."

... "No, but your eyes are blue. And your ..."

Blaine hadn't said it, but he'd checked out Agent Chrissick's rather non-voluptuous bust and dismissed the possibility.

"You don't happen to have a redheaded sister, do you?"

"Blaine." His head snapped back, and he met Sal's eyes. Serious and yet genuinely confused. "Do you remember what she smelled like?"

Most women had a smell, even if it was just their shampoo or a scented body soap. Men tended to notice. But Sal hadn't detected a single note when Jill Chrissick had invaded his space. Not even the first time she'd crashed into him outside Jensen's office.

"Yeah. Nothing. Like literally nothing. I asked her what scents she liked because I was thinking about purchasing a little surprise from the perfume counter at Sak's, but she said strong scents bother her."

Yeah, or give her away despite her disguise.

Blaine shrugged. "I even cut back on the cologne when we went out. Lotta good that did me."

Sal heard Candice's huff and knew without looking she'd just rolled her eyes in annoyance.

"There was a point to that, Attwood. Remember when you showed up at the lab yesterday and you thought Agent Chrissick looked familiar, except the details were all wrong. The brown hair, the pale-blue eyes, the small, umm … yeah." Sal cleared his throat, trying not to react to the memory of what Candice had unveiled last night.

Darn woman! You can't just show a guy those! How was he supposed to erase an image like that?

"You know," Blaine sniffed, twitching his busted nose with a wince, "there was something about her face that seemed familiar. Plus she was just as tall, which is rare."

"January Jill? That new runway-model agent pawing all over you at the FBI?" Candice practically spit the words.

Ahh, somebody *was* jealous. My, that shouldn't be so

satisfying but it was just too tasty not to savor for a moment longer. He turned his smile on Candice.

She sputtered. "I, mean, I knew something wasn't right about her. Let me think." She closed her eyes, nodding to herself as if imagining the details. "You're right. Maura and Chrissick are one and the same. The deep set of her eyes, the structure of her jaw. You can change the dressing, but bone structure doesn't lie. Neither does the dimple in her chin. Those are inherited and difficult to disguise without prosthetics."

"So you're saying my girlfriend was playing dress up? Why?"

"She probably laid the ground work at first so she could sneak into the morgue and cover their tracks in case anything went wrong. Vivaldi's not sloppy, but he knows how to make things disappear. Later on it was to steal your car and use it to transport Vivaldi's last victim. Your BMW would have been much more difficult to track, but the somewhat rare collectible made it easier for us to follow the evidence here."

"What!" Preston had managed to stand. "You transported a dead body in my Maserati?" He looked away when the sight of Blaine's dried blood started invoking sleepy-time again.

"I didn't, I swear! But Maura did come up to my place for the first time when we got back from the lake. She poured me a glass of wine, and then," he shrugged. "Nothing. When I talked to her the next day she said I fell asleep when things started heating up." With wide eyes, Blaine shook his head in adamant denial. "That sort of thing does not happen to me."

"She must have drugged you and taken the car. Did you feel weird the next morning?"

"Yeah. A brutal hangover, with double-vision, a monster migraine, the whole nine. Of course, then I got a call saying I needed to relieve Dr. Stevens for a few hours since she'd been at Vivaldi's crime scene all ni—" Blaine's face blanched. "Oh, man. I was dating Vivaldi?"

Sal shook his head. "More likely Vivaldi's accomplice. Vivaldi's profile doesn't fit for a woman. Plus, it would take a lot of muscle to do what Vivaldi does, down to the bone, with a knife. I'm guessing that's part of the thrill for him. I could be wrong, but it doesn't happen very often."

Their host's face scrunched into a knot, all his features puckering around a blood-stamped nose. "Wait, who *are* you?"

Dorian released Blaine's wrist, stood, and turned to look for the key. Instead of wasting time he plucked a bobby pin from the little tuft of hair Candice had secured away from her face and released Blaine from the handcuffs. "I still don't want you to leave town. Well, not any further than we already are, *comprendes*?"

Blaine gave a salute and went to go clean up his face.

Now that Sal had the man's nephew out of cuffs, he extended his hand. "Special Agent Dorian Salivas, FBI. Everyone calls me Sal. Everyone except my girl Friday over there, Dr. Candice Stevens, St. Louis's finest ME."

Preston's eyes flashed with renewed interest when they settled on Candice, who was obviously not Sal's missus.

Sal squeezed Preston's hand until the bones practically whimpered. "Still mine, Mr. Bradley. Still mine."

Chapter 38

Velvety soft peels of spring-ripened air curled through the crack in the driver's side window, tossing wisps of hair around her neck. She breathed deep, desperate to feed something beautiful into her soul, but the sweetness seemed to dissolve before it invaded her chest. Only withered breaths of the dying winter prickled like shards of ice in her throat.

She'd needed air. Needed escape. Needed so many things she couldn't name. A shiver of warning crept down her spine. A warning she wanted to ignore, but she couldn't squelch the tremors that started in the epicenter of her stomach and rippled out, making her grip the steering wheel hard enough to dislocate a knuckle. She slowed to a stop at a traffic light; the vibrant splendor of the wind dying to a feeble whisper. The warning blooming in her gut said to turn the other way. To run.

She lowered one hand to her thigh, tracing the faded scar hidden beneath the fabric of her pants. Resounding aches from all the badges of surviving life chimed in canon.

Something was wrong. She sensed it. Sensed she was being followed. Sensed she already had a bull's-eye on her back.

The light turned green, and she stared through the empty intersection. Stared ahead to witness the awakening energy of the cityscape finding first light after being swaddled in night. The resilient dawn cutting away the shadows like curtains crashing to the ground. A new day. With the promise of spring creeping closer each morning. The remains of winter in full decay. Soft strains of music pulsed from the stereo speakers, interrupted by the blare of a horn from the perturbed driver behind her. She stayed frozen, letting her thoughts about life, death, cycles, and seasons consume the moment.

Maybe she was imaging the disquiet in the wind. But then why was she stalled? Nothing had changed, and yet, maybe everything finally had.

Like the last fracture rending the ice beneath her feet, fear plunged through the barrier of insulating numbness she wore as Kevlar. Repressed tears rained down her cheeks. Hiccups of anguish siphoned from her strangled lungs as the few angry early morning drivers drove around the roadblock she'd created.

Her phone rang, but she couldn't answer. Instead she moistened her lips to shakily sing along with the words on the radio and accelerated through the intersection. Sniffling back the wasted tears, she turned around at the next street and headed back toward home.

For years women of a certain age in the city of St. Louis tended to live in fear, with the uncertainty that they might be next. Glancing in her rearview mirror, she swallowed her due. They needn't worry. The dénouement was drawing to a close. Only spring remained. And Vivaldi had already found his mark.

Chapter 32

Candice Stevens

"It's seems weird we're just leaving it there." Candice fidgeted in the passenger seat of the Ferrari. This would be their last ride since the jig about Mr. and Mrs. Sly Gutiérrez was officially up.

Dorian lifted one hand from the wheel and kneaded his neck. "The evidence response team is on their way to collect more samples. And I still don't know what the heck happened to our SWAT backup. Archer is in court, so he didn't pick up his phone. But we need to get this stuff back to the lab." He gestured to their stock pile of evidence in the back seat obtained from the Maserati, now even less questionable since they'd gotten full consent from Preston Bradley.

"I sent an image of the fingerprint back to get analyzed already. Maybe we'll luck out and get a hit on it, find out who Jill Chrissick/Maura Masterson really is. And who she's been linked to in the past."

Glancing around the pokey older model Cadillac piddling at thirty miles an hour just inches beyond their front bumper, Dorian shifted gears and passed the Sunday driver, revving the engine until the needle announced they were going to make *really* good time back to St. Louis. "I've got several agents on the hunt. Hopefully they'll have tracked her down by the time we get back. I'll interrogate her until she cracks and gives up Vivaldi."

His phone vibrated in the cup holder. He frowned at the screen. "Voodoo Veer? That's strange." He pressed the phone to his ear. "Salivas."

While Dorian chatted with someone named *Voodoo*, Candice reviewed his plan. They finally had some substantial evidence so things should be looking up. But her ever trusty growling gut signaled trouble when something besides hunger churned from the pit of her stomach.

She closed her eyes to mute out the nauseating mirage of passing trees, letting the nervous energy eek out with each deep breath. When her fear was a safe distance off, she opened up, just in time to spot a Crown Vic pull a u-ey and inch up behind them.

"Umm, Dorian?"

He raised one finger.

She glanced at the speedometer, watching the red needle bump past sixty in a ... Scanning the shoulder, a sign posting the speed limit at forty whizzed past.

Yep. Not good.

"Uhh, honey-pie?" Leaning closer, she batted her eyes. "I hate to interrupt, but you might want to cool it on the lead foot." No sooner had the words left her mouth when a siren bleeped on their tail, rotating strobes of red and blue reflecting in the mirrors.

"Aww, man. Listen Veer, let me know as soon as those prints pop up, I'm getting pulled over ... No, we're just leaving Horseshoe Bend, it'll be a few hours ... Will do."

Dorian dropped his phone back into the cup holder and started his jog to the slim shoulder of the two-lane road. Not the safest place to be pulled over. She sure hoped no one took that curve too fast or they'd turn the Ferrari into an accordion in the roadside ravine.

Then again, the only car they'd seen for miles until now had been that pokey old Caddy they'd left in the dust.

"So," Dorian cast a quick glance in the rearview mirror and turned in his seat to face her. "That call was one of our top analysts at the bureau. Now bear with me here. Jensen thought Garrett Veer was the mole, and the dude is seriously creepy, but he just sent me some info he hacked from Jill's server. Seems she's been keeping tabs on our phones. GPS, messages, internet searches. He also said she'd run a search on custom upholstery less than a week ago. We tie those prints to her, we've got our smoking gun."

His words tumbled out quickly, his eyes darting to check for the approach of the cop who still sat in his vehicle.

"Not exactly sure how we are going to justify having vials of bloody swabs and a fingerprint kit in the back seat since I don't have my badge."

"I do." Digging into her purse, she pulled out her credentials, hating the way something as silly as getting a speeding ticket was making her shake like a Preston's *Bond*-style martini with dinner.

She watched Dorian's eyes shift back to the mirror, the sound of a car door slamming meant they were done waiting, thought they would likely end up wasting more precious time trying to talk their way out of a ticket.

Since she couldn't see from her mirror like Dorian, she turned and watched the Highway Patrol Officer approach from the corner of her eye. Wide brimmed hat, dark aviators, something distinctive about the cut of his jaw.

Dorian kept both hands on the wheel. Tilting his head, he craned to look out at the cop, but the man stood without bending, their low, wildly pretentious ride wasn't doing them any favors right now.

"License and proof of insurance." The voice growled. The edge in it seemed to scrape over her skin like a blade. Something inside her screamed a warning.

"Listen, officer. I'm Special Agent Dorian Sal—"

Dorian's words snapped off on a strange buzz of an electric current. His body slumped like dead weight into the seat, his head collapsing on his shoulder.

Terror seized her by the throat. A strangled scream

escaped into the eerie stillness. Not knowing what to do, she pressed her fingers against Dorian's neck, feeling only one thud of his pulse in assurance before the imposter-cop ripped open the driver door and dragged Dorian's limp body out onto the road.

"No!" The words wrenched out from the puddle of darkness quickly filling her lungs, drowning her in a frantic sort of slow-motion as she grabbed Dorian's phone, shoved open her door and hit the ground running.

Always running.

"Let there be a car. A good Samaritan. A real cop. Anything." Her legs burned with adrenaline. "Run and get help, Candi. You have to get help." She chanted to herself, fumbling with the phone as the sound of Dorian's attacker clipping on the road behind her.

"Help! Somebody help!" The broken cry scattered like a flock of birds in the dense woods, catching on the cold and vanishing with the wind.

Her legs slowed without her consent. But suddenly something clicked in her mind. Whoever was chasing her had to be Vivaldi. From her observations in the car, it sure wasn't Jill.

Why would a woman like Jill be an accomplice to a serial killer? Like a Rubik's cube her brain turned and twisted a few scenarios until the colors seemed to line up. In an instant her feet planted on the asphalt, and she turned to face her attacker.

He slowed now too, walking the last few paces, hidden behind his disguise but not fooling Candice any longer.

"She's your daughter, isn't she?" Candice eyed the cattle prod in his hand as his wrist twitched, then she scanned the road behind him, pleading with God for a car to come—but maybe one that wouldn't run over Dorian who was prostrate over a dash of yellow road paint. "I don't know how I didn't see it before. The arctic blue eyes, the sharp features, the chin dimple—those are genetic you know."

She didn't know how her words were escaping with such composure, but she knew she couldn't outrun him. Knew, even as she tapped her fingers against Dorian's phone at her back, the chances of her blindly managing an emergency dial on a touch screen were about as likely as her escaping this scenario with Vivaldi alive.

His lips turned in a wicked smile, the skin of his cheek twisting like knots of barbed wire. But he didn't advance so she did her best to stall.

"I'm guessing that cattle prod left those two parallel burn marks on your victim's vertebrae. Everyone else attributed them to your way of wielding a blow torch, but somehow I knew better."

Come on, Dorian, wake up!

The likelihood of him recovering so quickly was a pipe dream. Kind of like the one swimming around in her head all morning about a white dress and a little chapel. A fresh start. A clean slate. An impossible feat of forgiveness.

A strange tendril of heat stirred in the air, and that little tide of change somehow sedated her pulse with an uncanny calm despite the terror of facing down a serial killer. Her fingers continued to fiddle, trying a vague assimilation of the emergency dial trick she strained to recall until she swore she heard a barely audible, "Hello?"

Vivaldi's eyes were still masked behind the reflective lenses, but she sensed them shift. She had about two seconds to scream something into her phone before he could rip it away.

In an act of boldness, one of few in her life, she jerked the phone to her lips, pivoted and ran while she screamed to whoever was on the line. "Call Archer Hayes, FBI. Vivaldi is—"

Lightning struck her brain. And whether it was the old familiar dream, or a new nightmare, the only thing she heard before the lights went out was …

"Say goodbye now, love. The show's over."

The glow swaddled like a blanket, warm and cozy in all its heavenly softness. She breathed in the sweet elixir of light and heat and joy while the tiny weight wiggled against her chest. Tucking her chin she breathed deeply again, memorizing the perfect way he felt before her arms loosened their tender grip and held out all she'd lost.

Drip.

Please.

Drip.

Please, just—

Drip.

The sound funneled through the noise in her head. Darkness billowed over the resplendent light signaling her curtain call. She wasn't ready yet. But time had always been the enemy. Too much of the angry crash on the blacks, never enough of the brightly tickled ivories.

And now, like a metronome conducting her swan song, the dripping measured each prolonged moment of dread. Even a single, miniscule drop at a time was enough to shatter the silence. Kind of like her mistakes. You didn't need to add them all up. They were just as devastating on their own.

Candice blinked, or tried to. Her eyes webbed and smothered in the dense black space. The water clicked in her ears like a death rattle, stimulating her awareness of receptors now too weak to rally. Same old story. All brains, no brawn.

She'd been taken by Vivaldi. That much she remembered. Wherever she was now, well, that part was trapped in an unconscious fissure of memory she'd rather forget unless it could save her. Or at least refresh her eyesight.

She kept on blinking, wondering if she was simply immersed in total darkness or rendered blind from the jolt to her brain.

A cattle prod. Interesting choice.

The finer fragments of her brain started to line up despite the drummer in her skull. Little pulses of gray light teased her eyes while the water dripped on nearby, a painful reminder of how every leak of her conscience in the past justified where she would meet her end. Her skin tightened, a violent shiver crawling over to claim every inch.

"Candice?"

"Dorian." Her voice emerged thin as a reed.

The relief he exhaled trembled from somewhere nearby, exposing the emotional torment he'd been suffering for however long they'd been … here, wherever here happened to be.

Had anyone seen them? Was anyone even looking for their soon-to-be skinned and carved bits?

"Oh, Candice, honey, are you okay? Are you hurt?"

She tried to take inventory, but the reassurance of his voice clogged her response with a swarm of tears. She sniffled, desperate to hang on to even a smidgen of the strength she'd found in the past week.

"I-I think I'm all right." She tugged at her wrists, bound immovably to some kind of incline. "I can't see anything, and I'm stuck like an unwrapped mummy to a table or something." Testing her restraints again, she managed to raise her head. The nauseating swish of her brain met with a sharp jab through each temple.

Other than the allowance at her aching neck, she got only the slightest lift at her hips, fearfully noting the absence of the clothes she'd been wearing. "I'm stuck pretty good." She omitted that last piece of info, sure it foreshadowed the horrors awaiting her. "W-What about you? I'm not sure my heart beat at all from the time he zapped you until I woke up here."

Another knot of air escaped him. If only he was close enough to smell, she could use a little fix of something sweet right about now. Anything to mask the stale mustiness and the faint, yet very near scent of blood cloying at her nose.

"My head hurts, it's too dark in this tomb to see, and I feel like I just wrestled with an electric eel and lost. Otherwise I'm functional."

Something rattled the stillness. "Well, except for the fact that I'm chained up, each arm strung out from a thick cuff to a sort of Medieval pulley system, giving me the illusion of movement, but I can't get anywhere. Least of all to you. I thought I could hear you, but the echoes keep toying with my mind." He stopped, drew in another deep, shaky breath. "Thank God, you're here."

She didn't want to say it. Didn't want to think it. But here wasn't a good place for either of them to be. Especially now since it seemed they were waiting on death. And if Vivaldi's track record was anything to go by, a really, *really* unpleasant one. "I don't suppose you've come up with some sort of brilliant plan to get us out of this."

"Workin' on it." She heard the clinking of his chains.

"Hey Dorian?" She looked out into the plague of black that might very well be the last thing she ever saw.

"Yeah, Brat?"

She smiled at that, the unexpected happiness about to squash her confession. "I umm, I appreciate what you said to me last night. It took a lot of courage." Not only to say the words, but to believe in love after all they'd both been through. "And if things were different ..."

She shook her head. None of it was coming out right. It wasn't just if this moment were different, it all hinged upon her having a different past. The one she'd lived was one Dorian couldn't possibly forgive. Why should he? She couldn't forgive it either.

How did I find my way back here, once again at someone else's mercy? Why are you silent? Why can't I feel you here, when I need you the most?

The dripping silence mocked her. The entrapping bonds only seemed to tighten their strangling hold. The panic, held miraculously at bay thus far ripped from its cage and flooded through her system. The consuming darkness permeated so deep she was drowning in it, drowning in the doubts of her soundless soul.

"I'm sorry. But once I tell you the truth about who I am, you couldn't love me, Dorian."

"Try me."

The hurt swelled in her chest like that old unrelenting song, pounding out its painful melody until she was too bruised to move or breath.

"You said you couldn't love your mother because she never bothered to fight for you. I didn't fight either." The sour taste of the words siphoned the acid from her stomach into her throat.

"Thinking back I *knew* I was weak, but worse yet, I was hopeless. I submitted to my cage and cowered in fear without even trying to escape. If I had …" A sob punched through the silence, her whole body convulsing in her straightjacket as the pain—still so raw she was gushing red—cut her to pieces all over again before Vivaldi had the chance to do the same.

She closed her eyes and remembered the vision of light and softness floating above the tenderest lullaby. Treasured the sugared breath of the powdery soft skin she'd never known. And then, as if being granted one wish to make it right, she'd extended her arms. Not to unload the burden of what she held, but to surrender the lingering hurt once and for all.

It was a beautiful illusion. But it hadn't played out that way in real life.

"I … I killed my child."

She let the admission hang like a toxic vapor, breathing it back in so it might claim her, releasing her from the eternal prison of torment.

For weeks after finding her mother's body in a butchered heap, she couldn't stop vomiting, wasting away even more from the guilt of her involvement. But when the sickness lingered on, she'd discovered the life growing inside her. A gift bringing equal measures joy and fear to the weak little punching bag from the docks.

"It wasn't a good situation to begin with. Sixteen years old. Pregnant by an abusive boyfriend." She shook her head, squeezing her eyes tight against the flash of memories.

AJ's rage when he'd discovered her deception. His solution to the problem. One she'd known would come when the little life bumped out her belly and unveiled her secret.

"I had every opportunity to run. Weeks upon weeks while the baby grew, my expanding waistline like a slow, inevitable march to the gallows. He'd warned me before. I can't even claim ignorance. But I was just ... I ..." She swallowed a whimper.

"Not a day goes by I don't regret not fighting for my child. Or running away sooner. Or being brave enough to ask for help. I was terrified, but I could have saved him if I'd only done something. I thought about it a million times. I'd wait until AJ was good and toasted, passed out, and I would run. Find a shelter, whatever. I didn't dare involve my dad because he'd end up collateral damage like so many others. And I'd already lost my mother."

Taking a deep, shuddering breath, she forced the words from their safe little hiding spot. "I waited too long. AJ terminated the pregnancy with his fists, and then threw me down a flight of stairs and left me there, broken and bleeding for two full days, as punishment." Cold tears soaked down her cheeks remembering those long hours. The puddle of blood that soaked her head. The unnatural bend in her leg, the crushing pain in her pelvis. The sharp spears weaving through her ribcage. The blackouts. The delirious dreams.

But worse than all that, the birth and the blood. The echoing sound of her unanswered screams. The tattoo of unending pain marked over her very soul. And that precious tiny boy she couldn't even reach to hold just once. "I *killed* him with my cowardice. This is who I am. Who I've always been. I'm just like her, Dorian. Only worse."

He didn't speak, so she let her head fall back against the board, felt the icy tears slip into her ears. "I've never told anyone. There was no one to tell, and even if there had been, I was so ashamed. If I die today, I'm glad someone on this earth knew I had a son whom I loved for sixteen weeks and three days. And every day since. Even if I failed to prove it."

If everything about her was still weak, how could she ever produce a love strong enough to weather the aftershocks of the past, let alone the storms of the present? And furthermore, why would a man like Dorian Salivas want a heart as tarnished as hers?

Why am I still so weak? And if you're so strong, why don't you show up and rescue me?

With nothing but the silent promise of impending agony, she strained against the straps, feeling some sort of sheet scoot over her bare skin as every flimsy muscle shredded to nothing under her pathetic self-rescue attempt. Panic and frustration surged through her veins, the devil himself laughing in her ear, challenging the faith as fragile as she.

Did I not pray it right? Am I simply unworthy because of all I've done?

A still small solo wrapped around her, a wordless melody drugging her with something like … peace?

Here?

Now?

Her raging pulse hit a speed bump, the hiccup trapping a zing of heat in her chest. For as long as she could remember she'd been alone in her misery, with only her music to ease the ache of her circumstances.

All of her songs had died with her mother, the cassette tape she'd made still serenading Torrie Bristol's bloodied bones when Candi had found her remains.

But for the first time in sixteen years the music sprouting in her mind didn't turn her blood to ice. Instead, the breathtaking symphony of notes dancing through the darkness filled the emptiness inside with a feeling of hope.

Had the music been a gift of compassion, a gracious escape from her painful reality? Always before, but even after the miscarriage, the music had called to her so strongly. Especially that last night in Jersey. Luring her out of AJ's room almost against her will, bolstering her decision to run right then. No looking back.

A new identity. A fresh start.

All this time she'd been hiding from her past, fearful AJ might still be out to reclaim his property. All this time, she'd held on to her disqualifiers, certain she was broken beyond repair.

And yet, she'd never fully embraced the possibility that she could truly find forgiveness. As much as she tried to take a leap of faith out into the great unknown, she'd let herself remain shackled to that phantom noise. Merely grasping at faith in an attempt to reinstate her old bodyguard instead of finding the source of her true strength. One leap at a time.

Her heart surrendered. Freeing the music from the vault in her chest, the vibrant melody awakened her oppressive world. In the natural nothing had changed. She was still strapped down in the dank, drippy darkness. There was no light, no silver lining, no backup. No audible music, not yet at least.

But instead of the old haunting masterpiece, relentlessly ringing in her ears since that fateful day, this song was new.

And without lyrics or instruments or even a single curl of sound, it was singing over her, and nothing had ever sounded sweeter.

Even when the crash of a metal door announced her finale.

Chapter 40

Dorian Salivas

Footsteps drew near in darkness, a faint light tracing the path of the killer's cowboy boots to where Sal estimated Candice to be. A click brought a burst of brightness, then another.

The light reached him but wasn't directed his way. Once his eyes acclimated, the terror of what was laid out before him snatched his breath and buckled both knees to the point of collapse.

Hitting the cold concrete floor, he swallowed a cry. Not for the pain spearing through his knee, but for the agony of what he was about to witness.

The killer's back was to him, his form a black cutout against the spotlight. In the halo of light was Candice, draped with a pristine white sheet, strapped on some kind of surgical table. A decade of blonde blood like layers of paint on the floor beneath her.

Her eyes were open and eerily calm for the tray of knives and a mechanic's blow torch set up in her line of sight. As well as a collection of syringes Sal guessed would be filled with something to keep her awake and screaming long enough to satisfy Vivaldi's perversion.

Sal's heart couldn't decide which course to run. One second it was hitting a wall, draining into a lifeless weight in his chest, the next it was jumping to light speed, fighting to find some hulking strength that would bust off the chains keeping him from her.

The silence was ripe with tension. The rise and fall of Candice's chest beneath the sheet the only movement he could detect until she spoke.

"Will I be your first brunette, Director Jensen?"

What!

"Jensen?" Sal called from his cage-less prison. Scatters of information downloading all at once.

An inside job. Limitless resources. Vanishing evidence. Could it really be?

The figure did not move, his eyes presumably feasting on his next conquest.

How much time had passed since they'd been taken? Was Archer out of court yet? Had anyone noticed they'd failed to show up with the evidence? Was there even the slimmest possibility they would leave here alive if no one came?

"Yes." The word slithered out with sickening delight. "Though I'm still not sure how you connected me and my daughter." The voice, rusted with grit and heavily accented, didn't sound like Director Jensen's.

Him and his daughter?

Either Sal's brain had been damaged from the zap of the cattle prod or his ears were distorting echoes. *Vivaldi* was the director of the FBI. The analyst he'd brought in to help catch the serial killer had really been his daughter covering his tracks?

Sal saw what Candice had seen sketch out in his mind. How could he not have noticed the first moment Jill barreled out of Jensen's office?

The distinctive eye color, the square jaw, the dimple. Yes, Jill Chrissick/Maura Masterson was Carl Jensen's daughter. Both obviously adept at playing a part.

Vivaldi turned and walked to where Sal crouched on his knees. Raising quickly to stand, he met Carl Jensen's cold-blooded blues.

"Great job uncovering the mole, Salivas." His lip

twitched, bunching the aged acne scars like hash tags on his cheeks. "Unfortunately, if you'd returned with those prints I'm guessing Jilly left on the Maserati, well, things could get sticky for me. But don't worry. She's learned her lesson. She won't be making any careless mistakes ever again."

The twinkle of arrogance in his eyes was almost playful. He stood close enough to exhale in Sal's face, as if he were no more threatening than a bunny in a cage.

Fury bubbled beneath the surface, Sal's arms straining against the chains with so much rage he was sure the links would shatter.

Jensen's amusement stretched his thin lips in a grin so inherently wicked Sal wondered how he could've missed it. Then again, he'd always known Jensen was hard to read. Sociopaths always were. But he'd been duped by the authority of Jensen's position and his drive to catch Vivaldi and the mole. It was a well-played bluff, and unfortunately, Sal didn't have any tricks up his sleeves.

"I saved you a prime seat, Sally-boy. Hope you enjoy the show." His sinister laugh hit Sal square in the face, then echoed back on another round ricocheting off the walls.

On instinct, Sal leaned back into the slack chains and thrust his head forward. Contact sent a spark of white and a ripple of pain thundering through his skull.

Jensen, no Vivaldi, fell back with a curse. Then jolted to his feet and wrapped his fingers around Sal's neck.

Sharp cracks of air fed fiberglass down his throat. Vivaldi's hand tightened until he'd wrung moisture from Sal's eyes, but he remained silent, knowing Vivaldi wouldn't finish the job this way and not wanting to give him the satisfaction of his panic as the air deflated in his lungs. It dwindled further until dark splotches bled through his vision.

"I'm gonna make you regret that." Vivaldi shoved him back and released him. Sal couldn't help but gasp to restock his air supply. Without a moment's pause, the killer gripped Sal's shoulder for leverage and stomped his knee with such violence he felt the artificial joint hyperextend, felt the screws writhe in his bones as if they were being torn through his skin.

A grunt smothered in his burning throat, the shakes barreling through his nervous system as all his nerves pulled their pins and started exploding.

"Mmmph." Sal ground his teeth against the agony, something he'd done all his life. "You lay a finger on her, I'll stuff one of those knifes straight down your throat." If he could keep Vivaldi's focus on him and buy some time perhaps he'd come up with a plan. Or maybe someone would find them.

But those thoughts were futile, the threat as empty as his pockets.

Vivaldi let loose a patronizing roar of laughter. "I always did like you, Salivas. It's a shame things turned out this way." He sniffed, wiped his bloody nose on his hand before using Sal's shirt as his own personal dish towel.

Who is this madman?

The man Dorian knew had always been so stoic, detached, and professional. This man, the monster, was a strange and unstable mix of chemical imbalances. Wild eyes, deranged smile, cliché villain laugh, and country-boy twang.

Before Sal could muster up another act of retaliation to keep the hits flying his way like he always had, Jensen about-faced and strode his cowboy strut back toward Candice's carving board.

"All right, *Candi-love*." He tossed his hat aside. "You ready for your final song?" Candice gasped when Jensen gripped the edge of the sheet. "Without further ado, your entertainment this evening: Miss Candice Stevens."

"—It's Rodriquez. Candice *Rodriguez*." She looked him square in the eyes, her face suddenly as white as the sheet covering her.

Sal saw a tremor shoot to Jensen's fingertips. Then, balling the sheet in his fist, he tweaked his wrist as if controlling his rage.

Her name rattled him. Why?

Candice stared a long moment at the sheet in his hand before glaring boldly into the eyes of a killer. "That's right, *Texan*. Candi from New Jersey. Daughter of Steven Rodriguez and Victoria Bristol." Candice was rambling, the effects of her words a virtual stun gun to the serial killer.

"I was a musical prodigy. You may be familiar with some of my recordings. Like, for example, the audition tape I made for my mother. You remember *Torrie-love*, don't you? The woman you cut to pieces on her bed while my song dragged her to her grave."

Her words were as sharp as a blade, though the tears glistening on her cheeks gave away the emotional torrent of this great revelation. "You uttered those same final words into the phone before you killed her."

Vivaldi had murdered her mother?

"Torrie." The name grumbled out on a sob as the psychopath continued on his way to displaying a full spectrum of emotions in ten minutes. "Oh, I loved her. She was my first. Every woman I've killed has been in her honor, to extend her song in death as the music lives on and on. Forever mine."

How sweet.

"I wanted to give her everything, but she threw it back in my face. She *made* me love her with that voice and then used it as a weapon to slash my heart out. Like my mother did to my father. Left him, a renowned surgeon, a dignified man for her trash of a co-star." His fingers lifted to absently touch the scars on his face. "He took his vengeance elsewhere. But I vowed," bone-chilling menace shook his baritone, "vowed the beauty of the music would be mine and mine alone. That there would be no escape. No encore. No shadows of betrayal left behind to darken another dawn."

His heaving breaths cleaved the haunted pause. "But Torrie, she was the only one, the last one I gave a choice.

Like scraping the flesh from my bones, she said she would never leave your father. Sick little mixed blood that he was. And you! *Trash.*" Another visible shiver worked over him. "White, black, Hispanic." He spit. "Your muddied race is the only reason I'm not going to have my way with you before I make you scream to death."

He ripped the sheet away.

Sal squeezed his eyes for her sake, horrified she was laid bare before the carver ready to wield his knife.

"Not bad." Sal heard the clack of Jensen's boots like he was circling his prey. "In fact, I can finally see the resemblance."

New fury erupted in Sal's veins. He couldn't let this happen. This couldn't be it for them. Yes, he'd been momentarily paralyzed by her confession about her child. Swept away by the monsoon of memories tossing him back to that old place of agony. But didn't she see she'd only been a kid? Abused and controlled. Fighting her trappings the only way she knew how?

How could she have blamed herself all these years for something she didn't do? She didn't kill her child. A monster did.

The truth in that thought swung back around to wallop him upside the head. Yet another blade of truth cut away the blame he'd bound to his heart. What she felt, those chains that kept her in torment … were the very same shackles of guilt he carried on his shoulders for Gabe's legs.

Loretta Mae used to say, *"Trust is earned. Forgiveness is granted."* Candice's shame wasn't for him to absolve. But just maybe, they could learn to lean on each other and attempt perhaps the most difficult feat of all. Forgiving oneself.

He opened his eyes, hating every second she was exposed and vulnerable, but knowing he needed his sight to scrounge up a plan.

Vivaldi reached out to the surgical tray to collect his first instrument of pain. Spastic breaths heaved silently from Candice's chest in wait of the first slice.

Sal heard something then. An invisible masterpiece sifting through the air on a melodious sigh from above.

Candice tucked her head to the side where her eyes aligned with his, almost as if she could hear it too.

Sal's gut twisted, the knife in Jensen's grip might as well have flung across the room and pinned him to the wall.

Wait. *Pinned*! That's it! "No soundtrack this time, Carl?"

The serial killer couldn't seem to hear the chorus of angels singing here in this dungeonous hell on earth.

With the knife mere millimeters from Candice's flesh, Vivaldi stopped and craned his head. "You're right, must've slipped my mind. Time to see if this girl has pipes like her mama."

She was shaking all over, her voice now quivering with the rest of her. "I'll do my best to disappoint."

Without replacing his weapon, Jensen walked to each surgical light and returned the room to perfect darkness, broken only by the faint light he used to trace his way out through the heavy door.

"You are so brave, honey. Just hang in there. I'm gonna get us out of here."

She said nothing, only a slight whimper cutting the eerie silence.

Sal slunk back against the wall, letting the chains gather as much slack as possible to afford more dexterity. His arm reached its maximum leash at the opening of his jeans pocket.

It had to still be there. Had to be. Jensen might have taken Sal's gun and emptied his pockets but could have easily missed the miniscule bobby pin.

The one Sal had plucked from Candice's hair in lieu of a key to release Blaine from his arrest. The one Sal had slipped into his pocket since he liked the way her long loose bangs kissed her face.

It was a tight fit, the blunt metal edge digging a painful crescent indentation in his soon-to-be-dislocated wrist.

His heart was surging so fast he didn't have time to think about the restless jab in his knee, nor the tearing effect of the crude metal cuff splicing his hand in two. Only that no matter how he lifted, twisted, and strained, he couldn't get his hand the last two inches into his pocket.

Please. Please *help me save her.*

Right then, with the final straining pressure, his wrist slipped from its socket. *No!* A fresh lash of pain whipped up his arm, his fingers rendered numb and lax and useless.

Abandoning his post, he lifted his arm, used his jaw to pop the joint back in until a carbonated tingle pumped feeling through his fingers. He had to try again.

Except—there, resting between his first two digits, was Candice's hair pin.

"God, I know you aren't keeping score, but I owe you one. *Another* one."

Candice had grown real quiet. He wanted to assure her of his plan, but he also didn't want to tip his hand in case Vivaldi could hear. Slipping the pin between his teeth he craned his throbbing wrist and made quick work of picking the lock.

The moment the second chain hit the floor, Sal took off in a full sprint, nearly crashing into the table in the dark. He anticipated Candice's scream, gently covering her lips with his palm and whispering close. "It's me, honey. Just hold still so I can release these straps."

Her head nodded beneath his touch, wetness from her tears soaking his hand. With no time for propriety, he swept his hands over her, finding each strap and jerking it loose. "I'm sorry, sweetie. Hang in there." Her arms and chest were free, his fingers fumbling over the bind at her stomach. Icy sweat broke out over his face, his racing breaths inadequate against the greedy demand of his faulty lungs.

"Here." He placed her hand on the buckle at her hip so she

could work it loose while he finished at her ankles.

One foot was free, her body surrendering to gravity from her release, when the sound reached him.

"Oh, no." His fingers strained on the last buckle, so tight it wouldn't wedge free. The door moaned and quickly slammed, the chime of a key locking them in this giant cell with the swelling echo of Vivaldi's "Four Seasons—Spring."

"I was growing tired of '*Winter*.'" Jensen mused as his boots sang in canon with the orchestra. Another of the same cheap untraceable MP3 players he left with the remains of each victim setting the mood as he strolled through the darkness without his trusty little light.

With no time left Sal abandoned the last strap, carefully lifted a knife off the tray, and pressed the handle into Candice's quaking palm.

Sal scooped up two more with his old sleight-of-hand agility and stowed one, blade down, in his back pocket.

It took him a second to realize the music was no longer approaching them. The sound of Candice's strained breaths seemed as loud as the furious strings in the classic composition. And then the last strap zipped past the buckle, announcing their escape. The element of surprise was lost. The darkness—their shield and their weakness. Each brush of movement a homing device for the killer's senses.

Sal prayed Vivaldi's skills of observation were not as highly evolved as his. Otherwise, they were in for one heck of a stand-off.

Candice groped for the sheet at their feet. But even the faint rustle of cotton was as potent as each instrument's distinctive melody holding its own in the grand symphony.

Stilling her hand, he urged her to release her cover, hating how vulnerable she must feel but needing to keep the upper hand. Her skin pebbled as he skimmed a touch down her other arm to be sure she still possessed the knife. Then reclaiming her free hand, he led her silently to the center of the back wall away from the slaughter table, rationalizing

Vivaldi would check there and the corners first. He tucked her behind the protection of his back.

His other senses heightening with the blind obscurity.

Candice's satin skin grainy like sandpaper.

The remnant scent of scorched flesh from Sarah Hoyt who'd breathed her last cutting breath in this tomb.

The distracting harmonies peeling out full swells of sound from the center of the room where their stalker had abandoned his tell. Each strand of lyric ping-ponging off the acoustic cell, bending Sal's placement of breath sounds, carefully planted boot soles, and the phantom sense of Vivaldi's heartless pulse.

Each piece of sensory input downloaded to be quickly calculated in Sal's mind.

Then something scraped near the side wall.

Sal excelled with knifes, but he wouldn't be able to inflict a deadly or even a stalling wound if he threw from where he was. And they couldn't make a break for the door without that key. He had to get closer to the target.

Reaching back, he lifted her trembling hand, curled her fingers into his shirt and eased them away from the wall on a route he estimated varied from that of their serial killer but still brought them together.

For a single moment all the notes held and hung in the air, dissolving to nothing and raising a warning. Vivaldi would know every curve of this piece, would know which parts would leave them more susceptible to detection.

That knowledge, and pure intuition, lifted the hair on his neck.

Not even a breath later Candice screamed just as her hand ripped from his shirt. Dorian lunged toward her, grasping at nothing by musty air.

Panic doused him with sweat as he groped the darkness, his knee barely keeping his weight. The pain, so intensely deep, had simply become a part of who he was.

"Mmm!" Candice's muffled scream whipped him in

another direction, the frantic puff of her breath straining against a smothering hand, her feet kicking Vivaldi's legs with near silent thuds.

Good girl. She was fighting, helping him find her.

"I'm impressed, Salivas. That was some Houdini magic you worked there." Jensen's voice placed him back near the operating table. Sal was there in an instant, trapping his breath to remain invisible and pin-point their exact positioning in his mind.

He tightened his grip on the knife.

"Ah, ah, ahhh." Vivaldi tsked. "There is a very sharp blade against your girlfriend's throat. One flick of my wrist and her song ends."

If Sal was standing where he thought he was, the blow torch was about two inches from his right foot. The nearest surgical lamp still five paces to his left. Just one second of light would be enough.

Even without it he might be able to lock in. He'd done it before during target practice. But no one would have gotten hurt if he'd miscalculated.

He could sense they were standing still, but what if Jensen moved at the last second?

What if he missed his mark and killed Candice?

He might just barely be able to live with himself after essentially killing his mother and paralyzing his brother, but if his own hand delivered Candice's fatal blow he'd let Vivaldi have him.

The outcomes weighed in his mind. Each second increasing the odds Vivaldi would tire of his stand-off and slit her throat out of sheer boredom.

A silent premonition to let the knife fly whispered through his subconscious.

No. He couldn't. It was too risky.

But in truth, it was risky either way the cards landed.

Throw it. The voice seemed to say.

Are you sure?

The last note of "Spring" began its descent to nothing. He had one, maybe two seconds before the song ended. Game over.

Guide me. His prayer shot up in the first moment of silence.

Cocking his arm at the ready, he kicked at where he estimated was the lever on the blow torch. Butane blue spit out like a jet stream, the slim cast of light giving him just a glimpse of assurance before he let the bladed bullet leave his grip.

Time slowed. His heart refusing to beat as the knife suspended between them with the uncertainty of their future. Vivaldi's mouth parted, his eyes afire as the knife in his fist drew first blood. Candice's wide gleaming eyes somehow found Sal's in the tiny swatch of fate, a bittersweet love song written in her gaze as a dark trickle stained her neck.

He wanted to plead with God for her life before the spear met its target, but the second the blade left his grip, he could only hold his breath and pray.

Knowing he could do nothing but catch her, Sal was sailing forward, the clumsy leap of his feet catching on the torch and snuffing the flame against the site of the relentless drip, plunging them back into darkness.

The knife struck, the sound like a hiccup in the pulsing silence before Vivaldi's "Spring" score would start up again.

Time snapped back on its axis. Sal's arms closed around Candice's waist as the three of them slammed back onto the ground.

Pain shredded through his chest, and the first slice of heat puddled into his shirt.

And Vivaldi's swan song began anew.

Chapter 41

Candice Stevens

"Dorian?" She wrapped her arms tight, smothering his face to her neck, a sticky warmth pooling against her sternum.

He was bleeding.

Her stomach dropped out, and a fresh batch of panic drugged her senses into a frenzy. Tugging her arm from the crush of their bodies, she shoved her fingers to his neck.

"Brat." He mumbled into her skin as the assurance of his pulse thumped against her touch. Sucking in a sharp breath, he propped up on his elbows and smoothed his hands over her hair, the tip of his nose touching hers. "Looks like you caught me this time."

She smiled, immediate relief making her heart float. "You can land on me *anytime*."

Vivaldi's arm was still lumped behind her back. Liquid heat crawled beneath her shoulder blades. "Except right now, maybe it would be best if we got up."

He chuckled; the sound lifting away another piece of the heaviness.

They needed light. Needed to confirm Jensen was down for the count and wouldn't be rousing to finish in time for the second "Spring" finale. She needed to check Dorian's wound.

And she really needed clothes. Preferably first, though that probably wasn't realistic. Dorian lifted off, his blunt intake of air doing little to assure her the blood painting her backside wasn't also his.

"You're bleeding. Are you okay?"

"Ahh ..." He grunted as if unburying a knife from his flesh, confirming it when the metal sheaf dropped to her left. "Yeah, just a scratch on my shoulder. A slice. A hole really. But I'll be fine."

Jensen's knife must have snagged him during the fall.

"And hey," his laugh was tight. "At least the knife in my pocket didn't damage anything vital." That one clattered to the floor next.

He must be in agony. She couldn't help but remember the sound of his knee snapping under Vivaldi's kick. She rolled to her side and stood, feeling the cold, wet blood she's lain in skate in gruesome lines down her back. After helping him to his feet, she crept on her bare, frozen toes to where she remembered the lamp stands.

With a few gropes of the air, the light came on with a deafening click that echoed over the din of forever tarnished beauty playing on repeat. Dorian kept his back to her while she wrapped her blood-smeared body in the sheet. But after she was covered, she could only stand and stare at the horrifying fate she'd just escaped.

Though clean on the surface, dried splatters and violent slashes of red marred the floor. The artists tools dormant and harmless on the tray and yet still terrifying since those blades had ended over forty lives and destroyed so many more.

She closed her eyes and shook her head as Vivaldi's music played on, still shaken by the connection to her past and only now bludgeoned by all the similarities that should have tipped her off long before now.

Her mother's cop, the Texan, initiated his killing spree in her childhood home. That defining act of violence had shaped Candice's future, driven her to pursue forensic science, and ultimately led her here to St. Louis, right back to the source of it all. No matter how far she'd run, the past kept finding her. Would it ever end?

She'd come clean to Dorian and he'd responded with silence. Their quest for Vivaldi was over, but were they?

"I don't think we'll have to worry about him hurting anyone else."

Crossing to Vivaldi's body, she scanned upward from his cowboy boots to the yawning crimson grave adding his final contribution to the floor. Atonement. Though not near enough.

Then she saw his face and gasped. "Whoa. I guess you made good on your threat."

He nodded. "Loretta Mae used to quote a scripture about the mouth being an open grave. I think that about sums it up."

Indeed. Because right there, marinating in his own blood and his favorite finale, was Vivaldi. Mouth open, his weapon of choice piercing through the back of his throat to his brain stem.

A perfect fatal blow.

How on earth had he done that? In the dark, with only one second to aim? The margin for error so slim one tremor could have ended her instead.

"How about we get the heck outta here?" He waggled the keys he'd plucked from Jensen's pocket, tipped his head toward the patched steel door, and extended his hand.

Lacing her fingers with Dorian's, she turned her face into his sleeve, drinking in the sense of rightness and relief in his scent. The sweet taste of peace melted over her tongue, sipping down like an orb of sunshine to reawaken her heart. "Where do you suppose we are?"

This place was a thousand times more nauseating than any of Vivaldi's dump sites. Her tummy squirmed in agreement.

"If I were a bettin' man, I'd say Jensen buddied up to Preston Bradley for more than the free food and drink. This could be the old Bradley Steel plant in Troy that relocated to downtown ten years ago. Been abandoned ever since. It's really remote but with easy access to the city."

Dorian released her to unlock the door and then grabbed on again, this time lifting the back of her hand to his lips.

She didn't dare hope it was about more than comfort after all they'd endured. But the warmth of his touch and the soft stroke of his thumb over her wrist were enough to unravel her on the spot. And since she was only wearing a sheet she really needed to focus on keeping all her threads in place.

He was nearly dragging his leg behind him, so she pulled her hand away, stretched his arm across her shoulder, and proceeded to act as his crutch to help him up five flights of stairs in search of an exit. Which would have worked a whole lot better if she wasn't so short.

The second they breathed their first breath of freedom a procession of cop cars and a SWAT van whipped into sight. The chopper lowering to the parking lot played a dangerous game with her bloodstained sheet, and the random strokes of light played like a laser-light show against the onyx, country sky.

Dorian's hand tightened on her shoulder, his body angling in to shield her from the cold and the whipping winds of the helicopter.

She clung tight while a swarm of people rushed at them, trying to pry them apart and offer medical attention. He held on for a long time despite their prodding, then leaned back and cupped her face, swiping at the tears she hadn't realized were leaking. Surprising her further by raising his shoulder to dry his own cheek.

Since they were finally safe, all the pent-up emotions tumbled out—the fear she'd managed to keep in check even when Vivaldi's knife cut a superficial stripe across her neck. The agonizing anticipation of knowing from the last autopsy exactly what she was about to endure.

And then the emotional torture of laying her heart bare for Dorian to scrutinize, seeing a future she'd never let herself imagine slip away before she had the chance to dream of a better life. All of it culminating when she realized she was staring into the eyes of her mother's killer.

"Sal!" Archer pushed through the crowd they'd been ignoring.

Dorian smirked at his partner. "A little late, aren't you?"

Archer barreled in to their little huddle, trapping them in a group hug. When he pulled back he glared at the gawkers, barking orders for special teams to sweep the building.

"*Oh, sure.* Now that we've taken down Vivaldi you can just ride in and play the hero, huh pal?"

Archer laughed. "I'm just glad you two are okay. Free pass to dish out as much crap as you want."

Dorian clapped Archer's shoulder. "Don't I anyways?"

"Good point."

"How'd you find us?" He voiced the question she wanted to ask but couldn't get her tongue to cooperate. Her legs wobbled. The lack of food, caffeine, and sleep threatening an all-systems shut down.

"Apparently you were riding the tail of some old guy in a Cadillac. He called you in and reported your plates for reckless driving. Probably just as reckless for a senior citizen to be operating a phone while driving, but in this case, I'll take it. When he caught up with you a while later your car was abandoned on the side of the road and an unmarked cop car was pulling away with no visible passengers in the back. Guy called that in too. Took us a bit to track you down from there, but here we are."

"Citizens in action. Gotta love it." With a warm smile, Dorian shifted his weight, drawing away from their half-remaining embrace to swap more shop talk about the other suspicions that led Archer here.

Without Dorian's steadying arm her body swayed, and before she could so much as stagger, a rush of asphalt rose up to meet her.

When she came to she was in an ambulance. Alone. It was as it had always been.

Only now, it wasn't what she wanted. She accepted it with a heavy heart, seeing all that might have been slip like sand between her fingers because she was finally trying to grab on.

It's okay, Jersey consoled her as tears streamed back to wet her hair.

And it was. Or rather, it would be. It didn't feel like it. It felt like Vivaldi's blade was stuck to the hilt, piercing her heart.

But she'd proven something to herself down there. She hadn't tapped out. She'd fought to the very end when she'd been sure there was nothing left. But even more, she'd stood on the edge of hopelessness, looked death and defeat in the eye, and had found the strength she'd had all along.

So as much as it hurt to wake up here alone, as much as she wished things could have been different, she could hear that song, feel the melody stir within her as if it had never left.

She closed her eyes and, for the first time in sixteen years, allowed the notes to carry her heart to the dream of something more. Something beautiful.

A sweet something that sounded like …

Hope.

One week later …

"Sorry, Sadie. I'm really not up for it." Candice swapped ears, wedged the phone against her shoulder, and turned onto her street.

"But, umm … it's been a couple days since we've seen each other and, uh, I have some big news." Something in Sadie's voice was off. But after almost twenty-four hours in the morgue the last thing Candice wanted to do was go back out. Especially feeling the way she had in the week since the showdown with Vivaldi.

And the suspicious absence of a certain FBI agent. Though Gabe had brought over take-out every night, he'd cleverly evaded each of her questions about Dorian's disappearing act.

"Just tell me your news then." *And maybe tell me why you really want me to go out with you tonight.*

Sadie huffed her impatience. "I wish you'd change your mind, but I guess I can tell you later. On another note, did you hear about Jill Chrissick? I mean umm, I guess her real name was Jillian Calhoun."

Candice noted how Sadie didn't ask if Dorian had mentioned it.

Nope. She'd heard through the grapevine at work. From Blaine actually. *Their* relationship had somehow survived her butt-whoopin' and emerged stronger.

But her and Dorian's …

The heaviness re-settled on her chest like a corpse. The blood had all been washed away, but the wound was still fresh. She told herself the ache would go away eventually. But right now it felt like she'd slipped with her scalpel and severed an artery in her heart.

It was different this time. Perhaps because her heart was finally ready. Like all the old hurts had been grafted over and new life beat within something she was sure had long since died. Or perhaps it was because she'd gotten a taste of what real love felt like, and her ever-voracious appetite just couldn't help but crave something so irresistibly sweet.

Would spring ever come for her? Could love bloom after a lifetime of winter? Or was she destined to walk through each season of life shadowed in solitude?

Candice shook her head, wishing some new thoughts would hop on the carousel and give her heart a break. "Yeah, Jill, I heard they found her this morning caged up in a secret room below Jensen's garage. Horrible. If there hadn't been enough water in there she'd never have survived." And they wouldn't have known to look for the secret sanctuary of keepsakes and accidentally discovered her if Dorian hadn't pegged Jensen, or rather Carlton Calhoun II, to be the sentimental type. Or so the story had been reported on the news.

Cramming an already nubby thumbnail between her teeth, she nibbled away a stress-relieving sliver and forced her thoughts back on point. "Heard she's in pretty bad shape though. Who could blame her after twenty-plus years of brain-washing and abuse. They found scars all over her body." Jensen's too, she silently added, cringing in memory of the man stroking what she'd assumed were acne scars. "Uh, about the only thing she'd admitted so far is that he used to practice on her." And his father had practiced on him. Lord, what a sick legacy.

"It's crazy, because I know she gunned down all those people in the lab and who knows how many others, but I actually feel sorry for her." Candice mumbled against her finger and then spit the shard of nail.

"Me too."

"All right, well, I'm pulling into my driveway now. I'm really beat." And thinking any more about Vivaldi and his accomplice was making her queasy.

"You're home already? Shoot." Sadie cleared her throat. "I mean, yeah get some rest. Gotta go. Bye."

"Sadie?" Candice held the phone away, frowned at the screen showing the call had ended. And rather abruptly. Hmm.

Turning off the engine, she let her head tilt back against the headrest and considered sleeping in her car since she wasn't sure she possessed the energy to even walk inside.

But then she saw it. Dorian's Challenger. The sight alone was enough to dissolve her to tears.

He's home?

His car hadn't been there all week. If it wasn't for Gabe checking up on her she'd have thought he'd moved away without a word.

She missed him so much it hurt. Even if they could only be friends, she missed his easy smile. The way he knew exactly how to draw her out of herself. How to make her laugh.

By sharing her past with him she'd known she was jeopardizing the hope of a future together. She just hadn't expected it to cost her best friend too.

Managing to drag her weary bones out of the car, she trudged toward the front door. She tugged at the gaping waistline of her pants, reminding herself not to let her appetite sulk from the heartache any more unless she wanted to lose all her hard-earned curves. In the meantime she should probably invest in a belt and double up on the Ben and Jerry's therapy.

She heard a phone ring and stopped on her porch to dig it back out of her purse. Elbow deep in her bag, she couldn't find it but deduced it wasn't her cell phone that was ringing.

Though it was nearby. In fact, it sounded like it was coming from inside her house.

"Hey." Whatever followed was muffled behind the door.

She froze, heart thudding in her ears.

Someone broke into her house? Again?

This cannot be happening. She dug back down into her giant purse for her phone, ransacking the contents without success. *Come on!*

She shot a desperate glance to Dorian's house. Should she? Wasn't he still recovering?

No. No way. She shook her head to banish the thought and continued the fruitless quest for her phone.

The old cowardice rose up and told her to run. But was it cowardice, or was it common sense?

She told her feet to inch back off the creaky old porch to put distance between her and the intruder. And probably put this house on the market as it was proving to be anything but the haven she'd imagined. But for some reason she stepped forward.

What are you doing? Jersey panicked. *Do what you're good at and run away!*

Candice took a bracing breath and felt her pulse click down a notch, feeling the panic recede and strength fill in its place. After all, she'd just faced down one of the most violent criminals of all time. A common criminal should be child's play in comparison, right?

She took another step forward, resolved in her decision. Closing her hand over the doorknob, it gave without effort and eased open. Just inside she grabbed the umbrella propped in the corner by the door, set her purse on the floor and crept into the living room, feeling stronger than she'd ever felt in her life.

Here she was, little Candi, facing her fears head on. *Take that, Jersey.*

"*Now*? For Pete's sake, I told you to stall! I'm almost done."

Closer now, she could make out his voice more clearly. Tingles tiptoed down her spine, but she was no longer afraid.

"Dorian?" She called out just before she stepped into the back room.

He froze, only his eyes darting to the red umbrella she had casually poised over her shoulder like a baseball bat. "Gotta go, Sadie. Thanks a lot." Without looking away, he set down the phone. "Hiyya, Brat." His lips tugged in a timid grin. "I wanted to surprise you, but you're a little bit early. Hang on." He turned away.

It was then she noticed the red-tipped paint brush in his hand. The palette of colors on the board by his phone. Something painted on the canvas hidden behind his broad shoulders.

And just beyond that a beautifully broken baby grand piano in the corner of the room. Its keys stained, its finish dull, but its silent song full of promise.

She was compelled forward until she was close enough to

peek around him.

A piano and a painting? Did Dorian paint?

He whirled back around, hiding what he could of the large canvas and wiping paint-smudged hands on a cloth.

"It might still need some fine tuning. Well, both this and the piano—just in case you ever decide you want to play again—but I guess it's good enough." He stepped to the side, and her heart burst out into song. Her breathless gasp trapped the notes in her throat until they swallowed back down and poured through her veins like the most rapturous ballad on earth.

Before her was a poster-sized landscape. The bottom half showed a meadow lush with pink and orange and yellow blooms. Sweeping up and to the right a hillside with budding trees of springtime. She moved closer as if to step into the scene and saw she was already there.

At the crest of the hill, silhouetted by a blast of sunshine, were two figures. One tall and one very short. Both mere shadows except for the one with freshly painted red shoes. Streams of light burst with the most radiance from the couple's joined hands.

Tears swelled in her eyes until the whole breathtaking sight became a blur.

"The artist calls it *Finding Home*."

She turned to look at him. The artist. So unexpected and yet somehow she'd known. She'd felt the deep sadness and pain in that first painting in his living room. Bound to it in much the same way she felt connected to him.

He reached out and stroked away the tear rolling down her cheek. "It's incredible." She whispered, unable to speak any more for the sheer, awe-struck beauty of the gift he'd made for her. And what it might mean.

"You know, I used to think I'd just wander alone, never finding this place everyone seemed to know by heart. But what if I'd been looking for home in places it could never be found? What if instead of being here?" He nodded to the room. "Home is here." Gathering her hand, he pressed her palm to his chest. "With you." Then he curled his fingers through hers and held tighter to his heart. "Wherever you are."

"That ... that sounds about right." She eked the words out on a whimper, desperate to keep her fragile emotions at bay in case this speech didn't end the way she was imagining it would.

"Candice, we've all done things we regret. But sometimes we have to walk a broken path before we can realize what it means to be whole. And this past week while I've been helping with the manhunt for Jill and living at an intensive rehabilitation facility, I felt lost again. The rift like a giant hunk of my heart had wandered off in search of you."

"Then why'd you stay away?" She sniffled, hating the way her lips wobbled on her words. More tears careened down her face, each one swept away with his gentle touch.

"I needed to rehab my knee as fast as possible. I knew I wouldn't be able to wait if I saw you or heard your voice, and there are certain things a man needs to be able to do when he does this."

Without stepping back, he lowered to one knee, looking up with those rich chocolate eyes, with a sweet and spicy twist on his lips she wanted so desperately to claim before she started blubbering and ruined the magic.

"Kitten, our pasts might not be perfect, and I can't predict the future, but I know I'd still be looking for a place to belong without you. I want to be the one who fights right alongside you, the one who kisses your scars and tells you how beautiful they make you. I want to be the one who gets to keep you safe. Who gets to be your refuge whether evil seems like it's winning or if justice rules the day. I love you, Candice Rodriguez-Stevens-Gutiérrez ... will you be my wife? And make a home with me?" With a small tilt of his head he added, "And Gabe?"

Her smile stretched so wide her cheeks burned. "Aren't

you forgetting something?"

His eyes crinkled with uncertainty. "I wanted to do this right. I tried to track down your dad for permission, but the records I found said he had a heart attack some years back." He smoothed his thumb over her hand and turned to press her wrist to his lips.

"Yeah, two weeks after he passed I knew I had no reason to stay anymore. AJ lost the last of his leverage so I finally found the courage to escape. But that's not what I was referring to. I was thinking of something round and metal." A ring might seem inconsequential, but she wanted to be his. Marked. Taken. What had once terrified her now felt like the safest, most enviable place in the world. A small circle of silver would do just fine so long as she could be Dorian's forever.

Dorian twisted Mrs. Gutiérrez's fake ring where it remained on her finger—the stunner she just couldn't seem to part with. Maybe because it had been a symbol of all she'd wanted and all she thought she'd lost. A tangible hope still dormant in the ground waiting for the healing stroke of time to bring back the sun and rain.

"This is the real deal, babe." He winked, and there was that dopey smile again. The one that turned her insides to mush. The one she loved more than she ever imagined was possible.

"But you bought this ... before ... I mean, how did you—"

With a hapless shrug he turned up the wattage on his grin. Her stomach grumbled in response.

"When you know, you know. I think I knew the first moment I laid eyes on you. Don't forget, I'm very perceptive." He flicked his gaze at her tummy and raised a playful eyebrow.

Perhaps the way to a Jersey-girl's heart was through her stomach.

"But don't be a brat." He tugged at her ring finger. "This

isn't exactly comfortable down here, and you've yet to answer my question."

She gave her best vixen grin, knowing it likely wasn't very good but would probably work for him just fine. "Maybe I'm still thinking."

"Oh, I'll give you something to think about." Vaulting to his feet, he erased her smile with his lips. Though there was no doubt she was still grinning from ear to ear.

Rising up as far as she could stretch, she twined her arms around his neck and unleashed her love. The heady intoxication of his scent infused the kiss until she could taste every savory promise of a life with Dorian Salivas.

She buzzed with anticipation, burned with desire, got swept away with the power of her affection and the truth she'd never uttered. "I love you." She smothered the words against his mouth and let the depth of the emotion spill with renewed fervor from her lips. Passion sizzled through the room even as the winds of spring played against the windows in its own sort of love song. The music was everywhere. In his painting. In this room. In his kiss. And forever playing in her heart.

"Yes, Dorian. Yes, yes, yes." She kissed him until she couldn't breathe, and then kissed him some more. One kiss melting into the next. She clung to him, heart full, praying she would never forget this moment. He lifted her off her feet, and she drove all of her love and desperation into the tango of their mouths. The thought of joining their lives together, of becoming his, finding home, and even the possibility of playing again, made the notes dancing silently in their midst brighten and pour through her soul like lyrical sunshine.

He eased her down, her toes dusting the floor as his kiss searched and slowed to a hesitant stop.

"You're gonna kill me, woman." He growled through a breathless pant. "Perhaps we should talk. Yes. Talking would be safer." He nodded as if to convince himself. "Let's see.

Hmm. How about a practical question of home? As in which one, mine or yours?" He lifted a dark, delicious eyebrow. His expression ridiculously suave and his lips so darned enticing she and Jersey were getting some of the same ideas for a change.

"Yours. It's already more home to me than any place I've ever known. And besides, that couch is heavenly."

"Oh, Kitten, there's no way you'll be sleeping on the couch." His arms held tight around her low back, his fingers tracing the spot where her tattoo bared another man's name. And Dorian was right, it did sort of look like "AL." Maybe she'd add an S and make it official.

"But it smells like you. I slept so good on that couch." She tickled the skin of his neck until the heat in his eyes warned she was playing with fire. But as it turned out, Candice was more of a troublemaker than Jersey had ever been.

And when he looked at her and smiled like that she amended her theory. It was Dorian who was trouble. The very best kind.

"You know what else smells like me?"

She raised an eyebrow in question.

"Me."

"Mmm, mmm. I see your point." The tigress in her tummy let out a purr of wanting. She could do nothing but laugh. "And it seems I'm suddenly starving for dessert." And she was.

Even though it had never been sweet or brought her anything but pain and loneliness, for the first time in her life the thought of intimacy was undeniably enticing. That, in and of itself, was the most beautiful gift for her mended heart. "Wanna fly to Vegas?"

He closed his eyes, tilted his head back, and groaned. "Don't tempt me. I'd drag you to the courthouse right now, but we're talking about forever here. We don't need to rush this."

Leaning down, he nudged her eyes shut by feathering a

kiss over each eyelid. "I want to fill up on every course." His lips caressed each cheek. "I want to enjoy every minute of wooing your socks off ..." each corner of her lips branded, "while you plan the wedding of your dreams." He planted the most delectable kiss on her mouth. His skilled lips like the twist of a fork making every tender strand of her being come completely undone.

It took her a long moment to compose her senses. So enrapt with him she could hardly breathe and couldn't see the allure of oxygen if she could live on this instead.

Lifting her hand, she swept her fingertips through his plush hair, then held the strong edge of his jaw in her palm and sank down deep into his unraveling eyes. "What if I don't like wearing socks?" Playing his game, she sipped gently at his top lip. "What if the only thing I want is right here in my arms?" Then nipped the bottom. "The teaser, the main course, and the sweetness, all in one." Soothing next with a soft brush of her mouth. "And what if I would rather not wait six months to become Mrs. Candice Rodriquez-Stevens-Gutiérrez-Salivas?"

"Well then, Brat," he boosted her up in his arms, her legs wreathed around his waist as his smiling lips whispered against hers. "Perhaps we'll get to dessert sooner than we thought."

The End

Dear Reader,

The original title of this book came to me before I wrote a single word of the story—this was before the other books acquired seasonal themed names. The phrase "Sing Over Me" sang like a chorus in my head when I was thinking of Sal and Candice and how they might come together on the page. I knew from the first two books there would be quite the clash. Because, well, Candice is rather prickly, and Sal is anything but. Yet there was something so sweet in the sound Sal created in my heart with each story in this series. And I knew he had the potential to become my favorite hero thus far. (I hate to play favorites, but I mean. Sal! SWOON!) Yes, he comes across as the comedic relief and made the perfect sidekick in both *When Fall Fades* and *From Winter's Ashes*, but there was something so profound hidden in his depths. A generosity that I couldn't wait to tap in to. The boundless and sacrificial way Sal loves was inspired by the greatest love of my life. A love that defines the word.

And yet, despite the allegorical shades of Dorian Salivas, he became flesh and blood to me. I started to feel his scars. And I often stopped myself when I was writing his backstory or considering his motivation to think... who would *I* be if I hadn't been raised by the kind of father I am lucky enough to have? The father's love is perhaps the most powerful center in a person's life. Mother's give us something else unique and special. There's no way to compare the two. But a father's love tends to instill a sense of identity. Without it, life goes on. I've seen it. But the hole for that need will always be there, waiting to be filled by the love only the father can give. In the same way, Candice's troubled childhood shaped her into warrior of sorts. Her value in her ability to atone for her past, and her armor as hard earned as it was for Sal to breech. And yet, despite the years they put in the rearview, they both remained marked by the sins of their pasts. Most of it was the sin or consequence of another, as it often is in life. I could feel those shackles of guilt hanging on their every word. Who of us can say that we don't feel like our mistakes are weights we drag through life with us? Whether we like it or not, those are the things that shape us the most. They inform our choices and our convictions. They push you forward or hold you back. They are the reason you are where you stand today. Sometimes they inspire. Sometimes they haunt. The villain in this story was that deceptive voice of defeat that keeps us enslaved to fear. It strips us of our strength until it's all we hear.

We all live with very real fear. It feels inescapable. And perhaps it is when we try to fight it on our own. But I want to encourage you that there is another voice that sings louder. It sings hope and grace and beauty over your life. No matter how broken or low.

Music might be something of a metaphor in this book but it has always held me in thrall. It was my first dream. According to my mama, who to this day swears she thought the radio came on when I started singing "Once Upon a Dream" from my carseat, music has always been my escape and my joy. From Disney to show tunes, to worship teams and albums of my own, it ministered to my soul when I was bullied or heartbroken. It restored my faith when I was weary. And it still speaks a universal language of its own to me when I'm twirling my kids around the kitchen. Make sure you are tuned in to the right station. It makes all the difference.

Dream big, love bigger, and let the Father's love sing over you all your days!

Amy

Acknowledgments

Oh, goodness… where to begin? While this is my third book baby, and perhaps I should have my sea legs by now, I'd be lying if I said it wasn't uniquely special to me. And most of that comes from the people who have become a part of my writing journey and who have championed these words with more gusto than I can believe or adequately express my appreciation for. But I'll sure try. Here goes …

To my crit partners and writing buddies, whose keen insight, endless cheerleading, and unwavering support helped me love this story and believe in myself more than I ever imagined was possible. Pepper Basham, Amber Lynn Perry, Jill Lynn Buteyn, girls … let me know where you want me to send the truck load of gratitude chocolate. I'll keep it coming.

My Alley Cats: Pep (again), Ashley Clark, Angie Dicken, Casey Herringshaw (almost Apodaca!!! YAY!), Sherrinda Ketchersid, Krista Phillips, Cara Putman, Julia Reffner, Karen Schravemade, Laurie Tomlinson, and Mary Vee. Thank you for always praying me through. You're friendship and our time together is perhaps the greatest reward of my writing career.

Ami McConnell-Abston, for swooping in like a fairy-godsister, lifting my weary head, and being the voice of encouragement I needed to press on through a very long, difficult valley. Perhaps things didn't exactly go as we'd hoped, but the journey is far from over, and I'm so blessed to have gained a friend in you.

My early readers and cherished friends (and family), Karen Denson, Colleen Phillips, Alyssa Schweich, Renee Murphy, Patty and Britt Buersmeyer, Beth Erin, and Amanda Belcher. For real, your enthusiasm for this story was a remarkable gift. Good reviews or bad, your texts and emails about this book will remain the loudest in my ever-grateful heart. And Schweich, your artistry on the page is a thing of beauty. Thank you for blessing me with your gift and your friendship. Someday your Sal will come. Only the best for you, beautiful friend.

To my razor-sharp editor, Andrea Ferak, for being the unsung hero behind my stories and for challenging me to dig deeper into the mind of my villains. Muahahaha! ;)

To my family. My mom and dad, who simply couldn't be more spectacular. I don't know what I did to deserve you both, but my life is so blessed because of all you've done and continued to do for me. Thank you for all the dark roads I never had to walk, for all the valleys I didn't walk alone, and for the confidence you've given me to keep running the race to win.

To my awesome big brother, Jeremy, for being (mostly) patient with me in designing these covers. For not complaining (too much) about my artistic temperament. For, forever and always, having my back. Praying and listening and battling unseen enemies alongside me on every front and in every season. And for being the kind of man I'm proud to call brother and friend.

My home crew, my greatest adventure. To my husband, for being the most devoted, loving daddy. We're so lucky to have you. Thank you for making home the only place I ever want to be. And to Kael, Rafe, and Eisley, you are the very best of me and so much more than I ever could have dreamed. Be strong and courageous all your days. I couldn't be more proud to call you mine.

To law enforcement officers and agents from every branch. You're heroism inspires great stories. Hopefully my fictional accounts do you justice. Endless thank yous for serving and protecting.

To every reader, your messages, posts, reviews, and emails are some of my favorite words on earth. I started writing to have something for me. I'll keep writing for us. I pray you keep loving this as much as I do. Thank you, from the bottom of my heart, for being a part of my dream.

And to the Author and Finisher…my words alone have no light. But I pray they reflect yours; that hope would ignite and linger long after the end. Once again, every word is for you. Always.

Made in the USA
Middletown, DE
26 May 2018